RAZZLE
DAZZLE

RAZZLE
DAZZLE

Stella Stevens

& William Hegner

A TOM DOHERTY ASSOCIATES BOOK

NEW YORK

RAZZLE DAZZLE

Copyright © 1999 by Stella Stevens and William Hegner

This book is printed on acid-free paper.

A Forge Book
Published by Tom Doherty Associates, LLC
175 Fifth Avenue
New York, NY 10010

Forge® is a registered trademark of Tom Doherty Associates, LLC

Designed by Lisa Pifher

Library of Congress Cataloging-in-Publication Data

Stevens, Stella
    Razzle dazzle / Stella Stevens & William Hegner. — 1st ed.
        p.   cm.
    "A Tom Doherty Associates book."
    ISBN 0-312-85379-3
    I. Hegner, William.   II. Title.
PS3569.T45315R39   1999
813'.54—dc21   99-22071
                                                                            CIP

First Edition: July 1999

Printed in the United States of America

0 9 8 7 6 5 4 3 2 1

to ELVIS

with love and gratitude

PROLOGUE

Some said she was so pretty it made them cry. Rita Tyson was like a lovely weed, the kind that decorates the fragrant mountains in springtime, wild and shallow rooted but beautiful to look at. She had only made it to the seventh grade, but by then she had been made in many other ways.

Clifford Gault was crazy for her. He even recklessly abandoned his moonshine stills at times just to chase her down. They were married when she was thirteen and he was a burly thirty-two. Those statistics were of no real surprise to the folks in and around Memphis. What amazed those who knew the taciturn Cliff was that he was capable of the passion it had taken to claim her and the endurance it would take to tame her.

The baby had come just as naturally as the seasons with no doctor within miles, only the presence of a midwife named Agnes. Cliff was proud and happy. He had prayed hard for it to be a boy.

"He'll be John," his father declared, "after my daddy."

It was a marriage doomed from the start. Rita had learned early on that most men's central artery swelled at the sight of her. She took to wearing short, seemingly formless shifts that assumed tantalizing curves when she chose to twist her body. Writhing had become something of her style, her compensation for a basic insecurity. Then Cliff decided to settle in the city and commute to his crude laboratory in the woods.

It was a decision he would live to regret.

*   *   *

Rita Gault was like a wild animal set loose in the city. Temptation was every-where, and she succumbed readily, hungrily, as though she had been starved in the country. To her credit, she did not neglect her son. The bond between them was so passionate it bordered on the erotic. She never really weaned him, and he came to her for love and sustenance well beyond what baby doctor Spock might recommend in such a relationship.

"Those lips wasn't meant to be wasted," she declared with maternal affection each time they kissed. Her fingers reveled in the curly mop of his hair as they shared their very special relationship.

Johnny did possess an unusually ripe and sensual mouth from birth. She nurtured it first with lengthy embraces and prolonged suckling of her breasts, then gradually encouraged her "dolly-boy" to test his tender masculinity with her.

They were always close, and after Cliff was sent away to prison they became inseparable. Cliff had killed a local ne'er-do-well raiding his still, an act a good lawyer might have gotten reduced to justifiable homicide. But in a drunken rage, fueled in part by his marital frustrations, he had tracked down the man's com-mon-law wife and shot her as well. Even though she survived, it ruined his chances for any leniency. The consensus was he would remain in prison for life.

Rita showed him little compassion. She was now not only desirable but available. If she was not the talk of the town she was at least the talk of the riverfront.

Hard by the river at the edge of Memphis, in a run-down backwater of rotting piers and abandoned barges, stood a nondescript building marked by peeling paint and broken windows, most likely a former warehouse. But unlike the other build-ings hunched around it, it was neither empty nor lifeless.

Inside the decaying shell of this structure, like some mammoth mollusk or turtle harboring life, a Quonset-like shelter had been jerry-built. This was home to Leo Hatfield's Warehouse Arcade & Pool Hall, destination one for most of the wilder Harleys and souped-up Mustangs inhabiting the state of Tennessee. Bikers and hot-rodders flocked to the place as though it offered nirvana—and to some degree it did.

Everything went at the Warehouse without regard for the law. The law and Leo, while familiar to each other, were quite incompatible.

"The sons of bitches," he frequently complained, "won't let an honest man make an honest buck."

The place was seedy. Revenue came from the bar, the pinball machines, the jukeboxes, and the worn fuzzed green of the pool tables and upstairs beds—not from the atmosphere. Lights were kept low for a variety of reasons, in part to hide the omnipresent dust but even more to disguise the ongoing shenanigans. One could deal at the Warehouse just about any way one chose to—so long as the dealing was kept low and Leo was cut in.

"River rats" was the police aphorism for the Warehouse crowd. These social renegades, kept under a loose surveillance, were indifferent to their trademark. They lived in their own world of isolation, one that was cool and ultimately reassuring. Even pariahs appreciated acceptance, and Leo Hatfield made no secret of his affection for their soiled dollars, which were readily transformed into the crisp, fresh bank originals he always carried.

"Fuck the cops," he admonished them. "You can't get hurt at Leo's place."

They believed in him. He cashed their hot checks without hesitation or cross-examination. He loaned them money when they were broke. He even showed up at some of their invariably raucous and ill-conceived weddings. Leo was A-OK with these tattooed hard cases and their tough-talking, leather-jacketed girlfriends.

His come-on was as compelling and contagious as that of a sideshow barker. He was a natural promoter, and when he started adding country rock entertainment on weekends, "the joint"—as he himself liked to call it—even attracted a few suits and ties.

Rita Gault had started working the upstairs cribs. Young Johnny had loved the place from the first time she brought him there. As little more than a toddler, he looked upon Leo Hatfield as a god. After all, the man wore a glistening diamond pinkie ring, smoke-tinted glasses and lizard-skin boots, and tooled around Memphis in a shark-finned, blood-red Coupe DeVille.

Leo could barely disguise his passion for Rita. "I knew her old man when he didn't have a pot to piss in," he confided to several of his regulars. They sat together watching her dance between tricks in front of the huge main jukebox. "I sold a lotta his 'shine over the years."

"Looks like she's got some o' his white lightin' in her ass," the fellow next to Leo commented.

They sat transfixed, watching her gyrations with keen appreciation. Not many of the women in their lives had what she had. Poverty had a way of wearing women down.

"Who's gonna take care o' her now?" one of the group asked.

Leo stared at him but said nothing.

It was midday. What sunlight crept through the cracks gave a tawdry, surreal patina to the place. It seemed as though it was all underground, even in daylight.

As if in response to the unanswered question, Leo called out abruptly, "Rita!"

She turned slowly, tantalizingly, as though she had been expecting to be summoned.

"Come here!" he said.

She smiled in an odd but telling way. It was happening just the way she had been planning it. Her now practiced slither, executed in deliberate slow motion, was calculated to drive men to passion beyond reason. No one had taught her this and she had not really learned it. It was genetic, instinctive, and as destructive to her as it was to her victims.

Leo was a slicker in a town where only a select few knew the angles. His thin lips curled at the corners when he smiled, but his eyes never changed no matter what they were observing. There was the quality of a statue about him, perfectly smooth and neatly contoured, yet cold and unyielding to the touch. He was known as a man not to be messed with, and few did.

When Leo took Johnny and his mother to a diner and it came time to pay the check, he riffled through a roll of bills as thick and hard-packed as brake lining. Small wonder, then, that little Johnny never flinched or pulled away when Leo patted him on the head and ran his fingers through his thick dark hair. Johnny liked Leo right away.

Johnny Gault had been the result of a misalliance, but he now became the victim of a misalignment. Leo Hatfield knew nothing about children, nothing about tenderness or compassion. He had ignored Johnny and pounced upon Rita with his fly open and his ears closed.

Outwardly, Rita seemed to thrive in the Warehouse atmosphere, always the smiling center of attention when Leo chose to use her as a lure.

"Ain't no sharks in the river," one regular observed, "but they got a mess of them here in this aquarium."

"That bitch's got an ass and a half," one of the sharks confirmed.

"If you cain't get it here," Leo responded, "you cain't get it nowhere."

If that sounded like he was pimping, he was. Cash was king in Leo's kingdom.

Somebody had given the Kid, as juvenile Johnny was known to the habitués, an old guitar to pluck on during those long interludes when his mother was in the back office with Leo, plucking in her own fashion. There was a phallic symbiosis between boy and instrument from the first moment.

"The kid takes to it like jerkin' off," Leo observed in passing. It represented his most profound interest in the boy to date.

The relationship between Leo and Rita inevitably went downhill. Their only real means of communication was sexual, and as she began to drink even more heavily, even Leo's lively libido began to falter.

"Fuck a drunk and you're fuckin' a balloon," he said ruefully, alluding to the blown-up, life-size dolls that decorated one end of the Warehouse.

"You know, Warehouse and whorehouse ain't that far apart," his manager had observed, guffawing at his own feeble humor.

It had amused Leo at the time, but the remembrance of it did not amuse him. After the state moved in and took Johnny away, to be placed in a series of foster homes, Rita began disintegrating with frightening rapidity.

Leo usually remained outwardly stoic and in control, wandering among his jukeboxes, pool tables, and pinball machines with the gritty aplomb of a natural-born con man. This time he could fool no one, least of all himself. Rita was spending most of her time in the upstairs cribs and drinking heavily day and night.

"There ain't a thing Leo kin do about it," the regulars agreed. "And he don't give a shit anyway. Hell, he's gettin' a cut. He's gittin' what he wants."

There was a measure of truth to that. It was for him—and for her as well—a selfish, carnivorous relationship. He had been deeply aware from the start that Rita and him was all just doomed delight.

Life for Rita Gault was destined to be short and not really sweet at all. She sat up in bed one morning, fell back into her pillows, and never woke up again. They said at the hospital that she was killed by a pulmonary embolism. Her liver was shrunken and discolored like a rotten orange.

"Her own lungs suffocated her" was the way Leo translated the autopsy information.

"The Lord took her last sweet breath away," Johnny would later sing. "She only lived as long as a lilac blossom."

BOOK ONE

THE SIXTIES

I t was as a teenage reporter for the liberal afternoon newspaper, the *Memphis Press Scimitar*, that Sidney Bastion first honed his communications skills. He might have been a small-town boy, but he thought like a big-city man, and that city was not Memphis but the Big Apple.

It was a Bastion theory that a hundred-percent Manhattan native could not know what he knew, do what he did. Understanding the small-town mind was every bit as important as understanding the complexities and aspirations of urban intellectuals and social sophisticates. First he would conquer Memphis, then New York City, then the world.

What he knew was that true success required the invaluable, God-given gift of cunning, and this Sidney had in abundance—instinctively, inexhaustibly, infinitely. Except for this crucial ingredient there was little else left of the boy who had been born and grown up in a suburb of Memphis called Germantown.

Attitude and ability made him a natural ally of a local character named Doc Diamond, who was not really a doctor of anything except perhaps obfuscation. Joseph Diamond had acquired his nickname early in life as a result of his curiosity about the anatomy and physiology of young ladies, particularly their subnavel regions. He often referred to himself with a sly grin as an "amateur gynecologist."

The nickname—as well as his interest—had stayed with him throughout a varied career as carnival hustler, used car salesman, and striptease promoter. Sandwiched in between these career endeavors had been a stint in federal prison for mail fraud. Sidney learned this long after he had come to know Doc, and by then it hardly surprised him.

The assignment had been routine: check out a young local singing guitarist who was working a nearby roadhouse. He was rumored headed for bigger things, but Sidney knew how little that probably meant. He sighed at the prospect. At least it meant an afternoon out of the newsroom.

Could there be anything more devoid of glamour than a nightclub in the sunlight? Sidney squinted as he entered the low-ceilinged room, its tables stacked with chairs, a small wooden stage with a worn upright piano at the far end. A sallow-faced young man cradling a guitar sat perched on a tall stool next to the piano. He listened halfheartedly to a dark-haired man who was riding the back of his chair as if it were a mount.

"Gotta git that catch in y'r voice right there," the man was saying. "Gotta gulp it like you was fit t'cry."

The young guitarist lifted his eyes at Sidney's approach. Sidney was struck immediately by their incredible mixture of softness and sensuality.

"Somebody's here, Doc," the young man said.

The dark-haired man turned slowly. "You're from the paper," he said matter-of-factly. "Name's Doc Diamond, and this here's Johnny Gault, the star."

"Doc?" the young man pleaded.

"Grab a chair f'r y'self," Doc instructed, ignoring the entreaty.

"I'm Sidney Bastion, *Memphis Press Scimitar.*"

"Don't apologize," Doc said with a thin smile. "We all gotta start someplace."

"I been picked up on the wires," Sidney replied defensively.

Doc eyed him with what appeared to be amusement. "I like that," he said. "Think big. Maybe we kin dream up a real shitkicker between us."

He was arrogant for a small-time promoter, and yet there was a strange vitality to his attitude. It was as though he knew things no one else did.

"Want to start from the beginning?" Sidney asked.

"The beginning is now. Forgit about the past."

"He had to come from somewhere."

"Make it Memphis."

Sidney glanced at Johnny, who was idly plucking his guitar and seemed disinterested in their biographical collaboration.

"Handsome, all-American boy type? Looking for the all-American girl?" Sidney asked.

"He'd fuck a ferret."

"Erotic intensity onstage, sweet innocence off it. Look, Doc, even I caught those eyes when I walked in."

"He's got a cock to match."

"Keep the sensuality subtle. It's there, and it's unmistakable. Merchandise the look and the sound and let the rest speak for itself."

Doc leaned back and studied Sidney.

"Y'know," he said, "I think I'm jist gonna take the dogs and let you hunt the coon y'rself. You think jist like I do 'bout Johnny."

"I heard the record. I didn't expect him to look as good as he sounds."

"Write 'im up good."

"I'll get a photographer out here. We'll shoot for a major feature."

Sidney had managed to get himself excited for the first time in months. The raw material was there and he had the opportunity to shape it his own way. Doc had given him carte blanche with both facts and fiction. He had stayed up all night laboring over the details, revising the plot, toying with statistics, selecting and distributing the ample supply of adjectives. It had been akin to an orgasmic experience. The Johnny Gault he created even Gault's own mother wouldn't recognize.

"You got a real flair for bullshit, Sid," Doc complimented him.

"Image making," Sidney corrected him.

Doc looked up and smiled. "Bullshit," he repeated.

The story was picked up by one of the Memphis paper's syndicates. National exposure. Sidney was encouraged by what it would do for his credibility with Doc in helping to create the myth he himself had become enchanted by.

On the strength of their own record—and Sidney's feature—Doc and Johnny were invited to New York to audition for a major recording company. Days, then weeks, passed with no word from them. Sidney considered a move on his own. He had been to New York City once to attend a newspaper convention and had liked it. Things seemed larger, more lucrative, more significant up there.

It was ironic that Johnny Gault and Doc Diamond should kick start his career. Sidney, who despised the South for its provincialism, was now milking its very backwardness for all it was worth.

The Mississippi River looked uglier than usual as he drove home. He saw rust and decay everywhere, especially in the faces of the people.

"Stay tuned for more hits on WMIS," the friendly voice of Jimmy Jay declared over the car radio. Sidney preferred modern jazz to pop, but as a local reporter it was requisite to listen to Jimmy Jay for any local news bulletins. It had been Jimmy who first gave Johnny Gault the airtime he needed to be noticed. Hour after hour, day after day, he had played Johnny's "Do or Die" until eventually several Little Rock, Springfield, and Saint Louis stations picked up on it.

"Just got the call, y'all," Jimmy Jay interrupted as he spun yet again the only Gault disk in existence. "Ole Doc Diamond on the horn from the Big Apple— that's New York Citeeee, folks—to tell all you maniacs the good news about our own J. G., Johnny Gault himself. The Memphis duo has just signed a contract to record for Solar Records—ain't that sunny news?—and Johnny'll be in the studios there within a week to put that aural sex of his down on some mighty big-time vinyl . . ."

Sidney heard no more. His head was flooded with a rush of thoughts and sounds. If it was now or never, then he would do it now. The suitcase was out on his bed the moment he got home. Tomorrow would be a busy day. He had to quit his job, clean out his bank account, sell his car, and catch a plane to New York.

His time had come.

_2_

J ohnny Gault, phenomenon.

In the best tradition of American excess he had become overnight both a Christ and an Antichrist, a hero and a devil, an idol to be worshiped and an object of derision. He proved the fulfillment of Doc's vision, a combination of saint and satyr, his baby-faced good looks intriguingly in contrast to his sultry voice and animal grace.

Young girls had not gone so utterly berserk over a performer since Guy Sonata, whose appeal was far less carnal than Johnny's. Rumors of masturbation at Johnny's concerts were prevalent, and movements to curb his sexually explicit gyrations and provocative lyrics found quick support among church and parental organizations.

Johnny Gault was a maverick of his day. There were still distant echoes of shock among the older generation at Clark Gable's daring _Gone With the Wind_ declaration: "Frankly, Scarlett, I don't give a damn!" Comedian Lenny Bruce had been arrested and all but banished for using four-letter words in his nightclub material. A French actress named Simone Silva had been railroaded out of Hollywood by columnist Louella Parsons for daring to bare her breasts on the beach at Cannes. A postwar bestseller by James Jones entitled _From Here to Eternity_ dared to go only so far as to spell it "fuggin' " when referring to that most popular four-letter verb for copulation. So the sight of Johnny making erotic love to his guitar—syncopating his movements to accentuate the size of the penis within his trousers and grunting and growling like a sleek jungle animal in heat—was a compelling and controversial factor that contributed to his sudden fame.

And then there was Sidney, magnifying, refining, coloring, and dramatizing everything about Johnny Gault. Sidney had found his métier. Handling the onslaught of media seeking to probe and pummel this newest box office sensation was precisely his forte. Doc, on the other hand, chose to remain in the shadows, out of the limelight, allowing Johnny to proceed with his own unique blend of pseudo-innocence and primitive passion. With a shyness that bordered on sullenness, he dealt almost exclusively with Sidney. But Doc was no ordinary manager toiling for a niggardly percentage. He had quickly and cleverly established himself as Johnny's full partner.

"Sidney tells people some really crazy shit about me," Johnny told Doc on more than one occasion. "Sometimes I don't even know what they're talkin' about."

"You just sing, Johnny," Doc advised. "Don't you worry about anythin' but singing."

Johnny was not to concern himself with anything but performing. That coddling extended even to his sex life. A continuous, ever-changing succession of hookers was kept on hand to satisfy his youthful libido and keep the dangerous amateurs, the groupies, at bay. Bodyguards had become a necessity. The crowds were simply too large and enthusiastic. Sidney fretted over most of the choices, cronies of Johnny's whom Doc had hired to keep him company as much as guarantee his safety.

"There're some bad apples in there, Doc," Sidney complained. "They could get Johnny into trouble."

"They're too dumb to git int'a trouble," Doc disagreed. "All they kin do is play pool 'n fuck."

"I'm talking drugs."

"Then you're talkin' horseshit. Let 'em alone. They keep the kid happy."

Sidney was unconvinced. But he had increasingly less time to observe the hijinks of the close-knit group surrounding Johnny in his idle moments. Demand for material, for interviews, for pictures and special benefit appearances had soared even more since Johnny's appearance on a major network television show. Once again, he had shocked America's heartland with his graphic eroticism.

Johnny Gault is corrupting our youth!" the evangelists screamed. But it seemed that the more they sermonized against him, the higher his ticket and record sales climbed.

"He's a fine young man who neither smokes nor swears," Sidney declared in a press statement. "One would have to go a long way to discover a better example of a physically and spiritually healthy, wholesome, humble young person. Granted he's athletic, sure he's ambitious, and yes he's tremendously talented. But what is wrong with any one of those qualities? The youth of America have someone to admire and emulate in Johnny Gault. May God bless him! Let's hope he goes on forever."

Hokum, corny hokum, but already Sidney knew how to gauge a market and tailor his style accordingly.

Doc Diamond coped with the cash flow. What had begun as a trickle was now at constant high tide. The sheer abundance of the concert and record returns might have overwhelmed another manager, but not Doc.

"You're gettin' a helluva sal'ry," Doc told Sidney.

"Fee, Doc. I'm not on the payroll per se. I'm performing a service."

"You're performin' a raid on the bank," Doc grumbled as he went through Sidney's expense vouchers.

"Campaigning is costly," Sidney explained.

Sidney had been educating Doc all along about his present role and eventual goals. He had no intention of being a permanent advance man or road manager. But when Sidney finally made his big move, Doc had been wary.

"New York, eh? That's where all the slickers set up camp."

"With an office there, Doc, I could do twice what I'm doing now. I can't keep going out on the road and expect to do Johnny justice. New York's where it's all at: the networks, the syndicates, the magazines."

"Seems you been doin' all right hoppin' back 'n forth."

"Most of it's just local stuff. Johnny Gault is national now, Doc. He needs national representation. The local flimflam pretty much takes care of itself at this stage."

Doc eyed him coolly. " 'Spose so," he said. "Kinda like throwin' up a smoke screen. Then when y'got ev'rybody coughin' and rubbin' their eyes y'tell 'em what it was they just seen—except'n' they never did really see nothin'. They jist thought they did."

"Something like that," Sidney agreed with a faint smile.

"You're a smart bastard, Sid."

"You're no dummy yourself, Doctor."

They left it at that. And Sidney took off for the last time a few days later. His permanent address from now on would be midtown Manhattan. He resisted shouting out "Hallelujah!" But it echoed throughout his body all the same.

3

I t was a relief to have Johnny and Doc off on the road without him. Twenty-seven cities in almost as many days. It provided Sidney with his first chance to evaluate his New York operation without distraction.

Sidney was not a hick, and he was determined to prove it. He moved through Manhattan with positive assurance; savoring the cuisines and studying the clientele of famed restaurants; taking in Broadway hits; attending art galleries, clubs, and concerts; even squirming through several productions of the Metropolitan Opera as part of his crash course in social and artistic awareness. His companions on these forays were mostly members of the media, insurance that his evenings would be as visible, talked about, and as productive as possible.

The name Sidney Bastion began early on to have a familiar ring within the inner circles of power and prestige. His ability to present himself exquisitely and then be admirably remembered was remarkable. Of course, all of it had been accelerated by the meteoric success of Johnny Gault. That was undeniable, but Sidney had sought from the beginning to establish a separate identity. The suggestion that he was destined to be permanently linked only to Johnny and Doc was anathema to him. More and more he found himself denying his origins. Given the way he had adapted to the city, his denials were plausible.

One of his first business associates was Claudia Rogers. She was precisely what he had sought as a cohort, a beautiful, aggressive, articulate young lady who coped intuitively with difficult situations. Her previous experience with several influential public relations firms, if only in secondary positions, was an added plus.

"The opportunity of a lifetime," he assured her over dinner.

"Cliché," she said.

"There are times when clichés say it best."

"You could have said 'An opportunity like this knocks only once.' "

"I wouldn't insult you with putrid platitudes."

"I don't like the term Girl Friday, either. It's full of sexism and subservience."

He lifted a glass of pale golden Chardonnay and offered a toast: "To Claudia Rogers, Associate, Sidney Bastion Associates."

She raised her glass in response. "To Sidney Bastion Unlimited. May the truth never interfere with the strategy."

He sipped with a puzzled frown.

"Only kidding," she assured him. "You can't take this business too seriously."

But he did, and her comment vaguely troubled him.

"And that's a yes, Mr. Bastion. I'd be proud to be your associate."

"You've made my day." He smiled, but deep inside he had the feeling this new associate's warm brown eyes could see right through him.

She beamed a dazzling smile at him. Their epic alliance had begun.

4

They called it the Gaulter—a magnificent machine custom-designed to please Johnny and keep him happy on the road. True to his upbringing, he was suspicious and even fearful of flying.

"If God wanted me t'fly," Johnny argued, "he'd a put wings on these shoulder blades."

The bus was a beautiful compromise. He liked the hum of the wheels on the highway, the cradlelike rocking motion, the kaleidoscopic scenery beyond the windows. When he got bored with all of it, the bus would pull off somewhere spacious and isolated and Johnny would roar off on his dirt bike or ATV, stored in the rear. The abandon of these interludes energized and revitalized his spirit.

It was true that traveling by bus complicated scheduling and eliminated certain lucrative appearances, but it had the considerable virtue of pacifying the main man, the star. He could lose himself within the vehicles' surprisingly spacious interior as the miles slipped by.

There were almost always interim guests aboard, one-two-three, XYZ. They were unfailingly female, and he rarely knew any of them by name, using the British nickname "Love" to cover his lapses in identification. Johnny, after all, was Johnny. He could turn a one-night stand into a religious experience.

"I fucked her through Ohio all the way into Indiana," he would report to Doc at intervals. "Couldn't make it into Illinois, but I was hot as hell in Iowa. I must be violatin' all kinda state laws. Cross-country fuckin' ain't on the books nowhere, is it?"

There were such laws, especially involving minors, but Johnny was erotically oblivious. Pleasure was his primary motivation, and nobody seriously questioned or interfered with its pursuit. It was that tendency to concede everything to him on the basis of his stardom that had most damaged him.

The geographics amused Johnny, but they were wayside waste to Doc.

Box office was the banter that intrigued him.

"He's a spoiled son of a bitch," Doc admitted. "If he was mine—I mean really flesh-and-blood mine—I'd kick his cocky ass."

Among the cognizant that feeling was more or less universal.

That he kept an altar to his momma in the locked cabinet by his mobile bedside was known only to him. He played his role as a single-minded playboy— it kept people from prying into the well of his loneliness and discovering the depth of his longing for his doomed mother.

He worshiped her in a way no one else would understand. In private moments, when no one else but his driver was on board, he cradled his guitar and softly sang words from his soul.

Momma built me from a seed,
Grew me like a weed,
Ain't nothin' more I need
Thanks to Momma . . .

Pure Johnny Gault was difficult to come by. He shared that only with Rita. Everybody else got a diluted version.

C laudia did not learn of Sidney's past until months after she had joined him. The revelation came during a telephone conversation with Doc Diamond.

"Where's Sid?" Doc always asked before divulging anything to her.

Among all those with whom they did business, including Johnny Gault, Doc was the only one who abbreviated Sidney's given name.

"Sidney's out," she informed him.

"Tell 'im Johnny's gittin' a big place in Memphis. Kinda like a mansion."

"Memphis?" It took her a moment to recall the connection from his press biography.

"Not too far from where Sid hisself was born."

She laughed at what she thought was a rare Diamond jest. "Sidney?"

"You didn't know he's from Memphis? Hell, we're all three shitkickers— Johnny, Sid, 'n me."

Claudia could not fully contain her surprise. "Sidney from Memphis?" she asked incredulously.

"Ain't where you're from that matters," Doc reminded her. "It's where you're at."

He subjected her to a litany of complaints about their latest press coverage, then ended the conversation on an upbeat note.

"We're cuttin' a new one in Nashville next week. We're gonna ring up a billion sales."

"Only a thousand million? Are you going to tell me the name or is it a state secret?"

" 'Homeless Heart.' "

Claudia scribbled the name on a memo pad. Nothing was impossible for Johnny Gault, not even a billion sales.

Later that night as they watched the final network newscasts of the day, Claudia ran her fingers along the naked track of Sidney's spine.

"Memphis," she said out of the blue.

Sidney twisted about and stared at her. "What's that supposed to mean?"

She shrugged. "I don't know. Doc said to tell you Johnny's buying a palace or something there."

"Fuckhead," he muttered, burying half his face in a pillow.

He volunteered nothing further and asked no other questions. Abruptly, he turned off the television, his back to her, and assumed the posture of sleep.

"Sidney?"

"What?"

"I love you no matter what."

He grunted and then lapsed into slow, shallow breathing. She allowed him his silence. The big mystery was why he should be so mysterious about something so elemental. It kept her awake long after he was asleep.

6

I n the wake of Johnny Gault's success, others sought out those responsible for it. Doc Diamond spurned them. With his percentage of the take he had no need to assume added responsibilities.

Sidney Bastion, however, welcomed new clients. He openly took credit for Johnny's "instant immortality."

Claudia Rogers proved to be a godsend. Her ability to manage and inspire a fresh staff enabled Sidney to devote the larger share of his time to account solicitation and major client pacification.

His only regret was that he could not immediately extricate himself from the mire of show business. His most difficult clients were show biz personalities, and his most fervent wish was to fire them and concentrate on more lucrative possibilities like international companies and foreign countries. It took the full measure of Claudia's persuasiveness and threats of resignation to keep him from getting ahead of himself.

"Sure you like board chairmen," she said, "and presidents of nations and influencing public opinion through them. That's big stuff, Sidney, and you're right in going after it. But, damn it, not at the expense of the Johnny Gaults."

"They're nothing but headaches," he responded. "Drinking problems, marriage problems, drug problems. Deal corporately and you deal out of that shit. Hand-holding these immature, oversexed, shining narcissists just eats up the clock and your stomach."

She sighed in frustration.

"Not too long ago you were drooling over the prospect of signing Reverend

Billy Sunshine and his Cathedral of Divine Destiny. Now you duck his phone calls, and I'll bet you haven't watched his TV broadcasts in months."

"He's bullshit."

"He's the biggest thing in this business, that's all. You knew what he was when you took him."

"A charlatan."

"You're trying to move too fast, Sidney. This is a very fragile business. You came into it from out of nowhere, and you could land right back there if you're not careful."

"You don't think I'm good enough to survive?"

"That's the problem, you're too damned good, but you're getting over-confident."

He moved to embrace her. "Not oversexed?" He smiled faintly. "I'm restless, Claudia. I know what's out there, and I want it . . . for us. All of it, for us."

He covered her warm lips with his own and gently teased her with his tongue. Slowly he caressed her breasts until she uttered low moans of pleasure. He loved the sexual power he had over Claudia. His passion burst into burning lust. He pulled up her skirt and ripped open her blouse. Her perfect breasts with their rose-colored nipples sent his hormones into a frenzy.

She was equally excited as she unbuckled his crocodile belt, unzipped his trousers, and pulled his eager penis through the opening of his shorts.

They sank to the floor. He slipped her panties off and entered her quickly. She gasped, then sighed as he controlled his performance until they reached a perfect moment of mutual release.

They were as one in such moments of intimacy, and Claudia was reluctant to let them go.

C laudia was enthusiastic over Sidney's decision to move Sidney Bastion Associates, Ltd., to elegant new midtown offices more in keeping with the image he sought. Done by an eminent decorator, photographed from design to completion by *Elegance* magazine, they pleased Sidney's appetite for the trappings of solid success. His own office was resplendent with important modern art and designer furniture all set off by a magnificent skyline.

Claudia did not completely share Sidney's enthusiasm, however, for what he liked to call "significant" business and government accounts, particularly not to the exclusion of the entertainment personalities contributing so generously to SBA's cash flow.

One of their chief competitors, Adrienne Gale, was quite content to represent top show business names exclusively. Sidney had steadfastly refused to recognize her as a threat until the illustrious playwright Pierce Agee, complaining of gross neglect, left the Bastion roster for Adrienne's agency.

"Keep looking over your shoulder, Sidney," Claudia warned him. "That shadow you see bears the initials A. G."

"She's only a press agent," he said disparagingly. "Names in gossip columns, pictures in centerfolds, paragraphs in news roundups. She can't handle a full-scale PR campaign."

"She keeps her people happy."

"Who? A bunch of limelight lamebrains like Mick Logo and Cynthia Wharton? Come on, Claudia."

"Pierce Agee is a lamebrain? Come on, Sidney."

He paused in reflection. "He must be back on the stuff," he decided.

"Cop-out," she retaliated. "How about the fact you all but ignored him for the last six months? Six months, I might add, during which he was being hailed all over as the most promising dramatist in America since Eugene O'Neill."

"He was covered."

"By whom? One of your gagwriters, one of your lackeys? A man of his stature has a right to expect your personal attention, particularly when he's paying damned good money for the privilege."

"I listened to plenty of his drunken bullshit. All that maudlin, self-destructive introspection. There's only so much of it a guy can take."

"Pierce is an excellent writer, maybe even a great one. You can't lose sight of that. And he can do what he does with or without you. It doesn't quite work that way in reverse."

"Let Gale take him and his horseshit. She's welcome to it."

"Very generous of you. Only problem is she took the gift before you offered it, so don't expect a thank-you card."

"I'm sick of egotistical crybabies."

"Better keep your eye on Johnny Gault. He's right up Adrienne's alley—and you pay him even less attention than you did Pierce."

Sidney stared at her, but she did not flinch or look away.

"Doc and Johnny would never leave me. We go way back together."

"I know. To Memphis."

"I never thought you'd play cat-and-mouse with me," Sidney said. His annoyance was obvious.

"Why is it such a secret?"

"It's not a secret. It's a nonessential statistic."

"It's such a petty thing to be so private about. Who the hell cares, really? I just don't understand why you never told me."

"There are lots of things I never tell anybody."

"For a change, I actually believe you. One hundred percent." There was a moment of silence, then Claudia changed the subject. "Gray Matthison called. He said you were supposed to get in touch with him."

"Just what I need—another actor."

"He's not *just another* actor. He's got the hottest series on television."

"All right, I give in. Have someone get him on the line."

"See? You can be reasonable when you want to be."

He looked out of the window at the silent skyline for a long time without speaking. Without further comment, Claudia walked out of the office.

*   *   *

It was too easy landing Gray.

Claudia recognized that, even if Sidney did not. A reluctant phone call, a lunch date, and bingo.

"Do you know who Gray was talking about when he said he wanted to get in out of the Gale?" she questioned him in bed that night.

"I have an inkling."

"Adrienne Gale is a tiger. She won't take kindly to losing Gray."

"The feminine is tigress."

"She's a tiger."

He rolled over in the king-size bed and pulled the black satin sheet over his body.

"You're not thinking right, Claudia. You keep pulling in the horizons. For Christ's sake, what happened to Sidney Bastion Unlimited?"

Her hand felt cold on his back.

"You're too new in this business to be so blasé. It's a very competitive business, Sidney. There are a lot of smart, slick people who can see exactly what you saw in it. Look at what it offers. You don't need a degree, you don't need a franchise, you don't need a damned thing but an address and a telephone. There's hardly any investment involved. All anybody needs are guts and ingenuity. Believe me, lots and lots of people have those ingredients."

"You downgrading me?" he asked wearily.

"Anything but. You're unbelievable at times. It scares me what you can do when you want to."

"Right now I want to go to sleep."

"And you'll do it, too." She sighed. "I won't, but you will, you beautiful son of a bitch."

The invitation to the Gotham Castle party arrived the next day. It was to be an exclusive preview party celebrating the grand opening of Manhattan's newest and most ambitious hotel.

When Claudia learned of the invitation, her reaction was decidedly mixed. Whether Sidney recognized it or not, he did have his limitations. Reese Roberts and Paula Castle, the owners of the hotel, represented a whole new plateau of society, a level of wealth and holdings far beyond anything he had encountered before. They were real estate Gargantuans in a city of realty giants. The Gotham

Castle would be their eighteenth major hostelry in the city, the largest and most lavish of them all.

"Congratulations," she said without enthusiasm.

"I'm going with Zoe Greene," Sidney said.

Surprise number two: Zoe Greene, syndicated columnist for Federal Features. She was considered the most influential of her ilk. Her inclusion on the guest list was decidedly more understandable than Sidney's.

"Congratulations again," she said. "You're really getting up in the world."

"Zoe was surprised I got an invitation."

"Weren't you?"

"No. Not really."

She smiled faintly.

"No," she said. "I guess not."

Moments after Claudia had left his office, Sidney turned to the telephone and dialed hooker-cum-actress Christina March. Her time was almost as expensive as his, but even an hour was infinitely more rewarding under the circumstances, not to mention under the sheets.

Y ou look ready for a tongue-lashing," Christina greeted him as he crossed the threshold of her penthouse.

She was a tall, pale-skinned angel, a natural redhead.

"Don't attack me, Chris. You know I'm in an oral business."

"So am I," she responded, her practiced hands rendering him almost instantly naked.

She wore a red silk teddy with very high scarlet heels.

He did not quite go around the world in eighty days; his globe-girdling journey took less than eighty minutes. It was, however, a rapturous trip all the same. Her educated mouth with its pink and potent trigger explored the entirety of his body, toes to ear canals, not missing an orifice en route.

Like an erotic snail, her gifted tongue left a moist silvery track along the length of his anatomy, eventually curling under the elevated contour of his derriere.

"Suck me!" he gasped, already in ecstasy well before she settled her mouth on his monument to the moment.

If what resulted was an anticlimax, few of his prior conquests would have believed its abundance. Least of all dear Claudia. His passion for her had cooled quickly.

"Are you trying to drown me?" Christina laughed.

"No questions while I'm in the throes."

She rearranged their dampened bodies so that Sidney now knelt in front of her, his head at the delta of her thighs.

"Eat me!" she cried as his tongue found the key to her passion. "Ravish me, Sidney. Make me come and come!"

"My pleasure, my dear," he said, and set to the task.

He pulled back, deciding to take it slow. He slipped down the straps of her teddy, then eased it down to her feet. She deftly stepped out of it, as he removed her shoes. He toured her supple body just as she had traveled his, stopping to nibble and suck her milk-white breasts and their pale pink nipples, finally returning to linger where she wanted him most, at the deepest and most delicious crevices. There were ever so many succulent nooks and crannies to explore.

It all proved to be one of the better deals he had negotiated in months.

8

P ublic relations was not a clearly defined area of operation. No accredited colleges or universities offered it as a major or even a minor. It hovered in the shadows between journalism and business management. What it amounted to in reality was putting the best face possible on a person, a company, a country, or a situation by any means possible.

Sidney described it as "crisis management in a crisis" and "media masturbation," and he practiced it with Merlinesque wizardry. From his point of view his clients were forever faultless, possessed of Bastion-embellished pedigrees.

Sidney Bastion and Adrienne Gale were in the same business in the way that artists are in the same business. Their tools were basically similar, yet their styles were markedly different.

Adrienne Gale's modus operandi was much more intimate, familial, and personal than that of Sidney Bastion. She took an often intrusive interest in all aspects of her clients' lives. Sidney, on the other hand, avoided venturing beyond pure business as much as possible.

"She wet-nurses her accounts," he complained.

"She has the equipment," Claudia observed, alluding to Adrienne's ample bosom.

"Take away her tits and what've you got?"

"A Sidney Bastion with long, black hair."

"Come on. She couldn't carry my typewriter in a real media campaign."

"She's attractive and she's smart, Sidney. Paul Sebastian worked with her before he came with us. He counted twenty-two clients while he was there."

"Quantity but no quality."

"She just got Space."

"Nightclubs! What can they be paying?"

"Five, maybe seven-fifty, a week."

"Max. Probably half that. I wouldn't touch it for double—or even triple."

"Clubs generate a lot of their own copy."

"A lot of their own headaches, too. Club owners are the cheapest, most demanding ingrates who ever got their names in print. They're always crying."

"You should know."

"I haven't accepted a club in years, not since I first got started. That was Doc's fault for shortchanging me."

"You keep knocking Adrienne because she does so much with the gossip columns. They're important. Repetition, Sidney. Whether it's a gag or a romance or whatever, it fills in those big voids between mag covers and headline features."

"She plants items in lieu of the latter. Her mind only functions in one-liners."

"I hardly think Pierce would've gone to someone limited to single-sentence gags."

"Pierce Agee's a traitor."

"Because he atrophied from gross neglect?"

"Four pages in the Sunday Times Magazine is gross neglect?"

"That was a year before he left."

"Quality, Miss Rogers, over quantity. That's the credo here."

It came as a surprise to Sidney, perhaps even a mild shock, when Zoe Greene navigated him through clusters of early arrivals at the Gotham Castle party and confronted him with a stunning, stylishly groomed young woman displaying a striking yet tasteful décolletage.

"Sidney," Zoe said in her brusque say, "this is Adrienne Gale. Can't believe you two never've met, but anyway . . . Adrienne, this is Sidney Bastion."

Adrienne's graciousness was as unsettling to him as it was unexpected. "I've heard a great many good things about you, Sidney," she said sweetly. "I understand we're more or less jumping through some of the same circus hoops."

"I consider it more of a carnival," Zoe commented.

"Oh no, Zoe," Adrienne disagreed. "Carnivals don't have wild animals—or clowns."

"You have a point, dear. I'll have to remember that." And remember it she did, in a column quote the following day.

Sidney noted how skillfully Adrienne had challenged Zoe Greene. One more assumption would have to be revised. This was not the obsequious, pandering creature he had envisioned, or perhaps hoped for.

"I'm really surprised, Sidney, to find us both here," Adrienne confessed candidly. "These affairs are usually all PR or no PR."

"Reese Roberts has a reputation for being antimedia," he responded, "so I figured that included us, too."

"But Paula loves publicity," Adrienne said.

"Adores it," Zoe agreed.

"I've learned something," Sidney said.

The hotel's lobby expanse was filled now with a penguinlike mass of animated dignitaries. Eminence was everywhere. Sidney found himself in the unfamiliar role of tagalong as Zoe maneuvered familiarly through the throng.

"This is my friend Sidney Bastion," she introduced him, first to a senator, then to an ambassador. She proved unfailingly generous in sharing her associations.

"Pay attention," she advised him. "There's a lot of heavy voltage in the room."

"You're very kind, Zoe."

She lifted her face to him, and he dutifully kissed her lips.

"You're a devil," she said, "but also a dear boy."

None of this escaped Adrienne Gale, who was mingling on her own across the room. She was as curious about Sidney as he was about her. Neither enjoyed the current ambience in the same way Zoe did. Zoe did not have to study and scheme; her position of power was secured by her popularity with her readers.

Zoe had the power to trigger avalanches of attention. Her daily column did not have the massive syndication of a Walter Winchell or a Louella Parsons, but she commanded a kind of grudging respect from the loftier tiers of publishing; that is, books and magazines. A mention in her column was considerably more likely to stimulate interest from this more esoteric area of the industry. With his increasingly mixed bag of clients, Sidney had good reason to cultivate her.

She was a small woman, slight really, with a sparrowlike tendency to dart about in an endless quest for information and attention. There was a kind of voracious hunger about her manner and features, however well-groomed they were.

Sidney had said she reminded him at times of a baby bird in a nest with its head tilted upward, ever waiting for nourishment. She was quite pretty in that quaint birdish way, and yet she had never married. Power had provided her with sufficient eroticism to sustain her libido between scattered affairs.

Zoe eventually led Sidney to the queen of the Castle herself. "Paula," she said, interrupting Paula Castle's ongoing conversations with a seemingly endless parade of guests, "I'd like you to meet one of our brightest new public relations people in New York, Sidney Bastion."

"Sidney Bastion," Paula acknowledged by repeating his name, "welcome to the Gotham Castle."

He was struck immediately by her hard sophistication. She was more an industrial diamond than the crown jewel he might have expected.

"My pleasure," he said smoothly. "Your Castle's magnificent."

She granted him a swift second glance and a small percentage of a smile before turning to the next person being ushered into her presence.

"Lovely woman," he said to Zoe in retreat.

"Bitch," she responded.

The hotel itself was a monument to excess. Zoe and Sidney agreed on that.

"Imagine a whole wall of Picassos!" she groaned. "One on top of the other yet! It's just incredible anyone would even think of it, much less do it!"

"Just an expensive way to make the Guinness book."

"Paula's taste is in her sphincter. How she ever landed Reese Roberts remains one of the great unsolved mysteries of modern matrimony."

They wandered about examining the hugely ornate lobby, dominated by a mammoth crystal chandelier that hung glacially above. It all but overwhelmed the expansive rotunda with its sweeping staircases and marble balconies, gold and silver divans, erotic statuary, and ornate fountains.

"What're you going to say about it all?" Sidney inquired impishly.

"I'll be kind," Zoe promised. "I'll list who was here, give the name and address of the place, and let it go at that."

"As her PR rep, I wouldn't be happy with that, Zoe."

She patted his arm reassuringly. "Thank God you're not that, Sidney."

Oddly, or perhaps not so oddly at that, he was even then thinking the very antithesis of what she had said.

As they prepared to leave—Zoe always had a deadline to meet—she stopped abruptly in mid-lobby.

"Norman Prescott!" she exclaimed.

Sidney's eyes followed hers to the main entrance. Sure enough, there he was, eminently recognizable despite his aversion to being photographed. Sidney had never seen him before in the flesh and was surprised at how cherubic he looked considering his sinister reputation. The man was not only Zoe's employer but the owner of so many newspapers, magazines, and television stations around the world that he constituted a huge media conglomerate unto himself.

"I thought he never attended these things," Sidney said.

If Zoe heard him she did not respond, electing instead to wend her way toward the new arrival.

"Sidney is a first-rate public relations man," he heard her say as he joined them after a reasonable delay. "And a good friend."

Sidney was surprised by the firmness of Prescott's grip as Zoe completed the introduction.

"A manipulator of the truth," Prescott said with some amusement. "Hello, Sidney Bastion, how are you?"

"I'm honored to meet you, Mr. Prescott. However, I prefer to call it *flexing* or *rearranging* the truth rather than manipulating it."

Prescott smiled and nodded appreciatively. "Bright fellow," he said to Zoe. His tone and manner indicated that the brief audience was over. "Our omniscient hostess has beckoned. Will you excuse me, please?"

A flick of his hand for Sidney, a peck on the cheek for Zoe, and he was gone.

"I'm impressed," Sidney said.

"You should be," she replied. "He's one of a kind." They left soon after that. Zoe Greene had gathered enough to feed her typewriter, Sidney enough to feed his ego and his dreams.

Claudia was interested but not impressed by his recounting. Being naked in bed together did something to diminish the impact.

"Paula Castle's a dynamic woman," he reported. "Almost like an empress."

"Any account potential?"

"How'd you guess?"

"Whenever you say anything nice about a woman, you either want her in bed or on your client roster."

"Low blow, Claudia."

"Who else did you meet?"

"Norman Prescott, like I told you before."

"That's it?"

"You're hard to impress. Lots of others, of course. Ambassadors by the yard, all my neighbors from the UN . . ."

"No showbizzers?"

"None. No wonder I had such a good time."

She had begun to move against him as they talked. Now she turned off the light and softly encircled the cluster of his crotch in her hand.

"Fuck me, Sidney," she whispered hoarsely.

Their discussion of the evening was over. But even in the throes of passion, Sidney remembered the one person he had met and deliberately failed to mention. It was to her that he silently dedicated the abundant climax Claudia only imagined she had inspired.

9

Sidney made certain to call Zoe Greene first thing the next day and thank her for everything. Maybe Claudia was right; maybe the old gal really was after his body. It seemed so improbable on the surface that at first he denied it as ridiculous. But why had she selected him to be her escort; why had she covertly arranged to have him invited in the first place? She knew virtually everybody who was anybody from one coast to the other, among them numbers of attractive playboys and handsome actors as well as appealing specimens from the social and political elites. Any one of them would have leaped at the opportunity to be at her side.

The question continued to vaguely disturb him even as he placed the call. He liked *creating* mysteries, not being the victim of them.

Zoe gave small credence to any such erotic speculation when he finally got through to her. She was even more brusque than usual, rejecting his offer of lunch and hanging up without a good-bye. Some hots, he thought. It was more like cold shoulder.

"Lunching with Zoe," he nevertheless told Claudia a short while later.

"Aha!" she reacted, smiling.

That was a strange thing about Claudia. She would actually condone, if not exactly encourage, his going to bed with the likes of Zoe Greene. It simply amounted to sound business practice to her. He mused over this in the cab taking him to his real mission for the day.

He got out at Fifth Avenue and Forty-second Street. Quickly he climbed the steps of the main public library.

Years before he had refused to fill out the required questionnaire to obtain a biographical listing in *Who's Who in Media, Publicity & Public Relations in New York City*, knowing full well that his unwillingness meant reduction to a simple alphabetical name-and-address inclusion. He had likewise ignored opportunities to purchase any of the volumes of the annually updated series. It was all a hype, he argued, a waste of ninety dollars a year for a superficial, incomplete, and frivolous compilation of information. For the same reasons he had never joined any of the professional organizations in the industry, preferring to be regarded as a maverick and a loner among his peers.

Now, however, curiosity compelled him to seek out the book he had so long shunned. It was the only ready source for background data on the new nemesis in his life: Adrienne Gale.

A guard in the main lobby directed him to the section where reference books were cataloged and kept. All twenty-six years of the volume's existence were there, all but the current one on microfilm. Inexplicably, he looked up his own name first. It was there in minimal form, surrounded by fat paragraphs celebrating the backgrounds and achievements of others of whom he had never heard.

Adrienne's listing proved easy to locate. "Gale, Adrienne," it began. "President, Adrienne Gale, Inc., 444 Madison Avenue, New York, N.Y. 10022."

He recognized the Newsweek Building address immediately. His eyes moved swiftly to the lines that followed.

"Born Riverside Drive, New York, N.Y., daughter of Blair and Sylvia Gale." The year of her birth was discreetly omitted. The capsule bio further revealed that her father was a Wall Street broker, her mother an administrative assistant at the Julliard School of Music. Under education it read: "Attended Dalton School; B.A., Finch College; M.A., Columbia University School of Journalism."

He refused to acknowledge his disappointment over the extent of her education. Diplomas were merely so much window dressing, he rationalized, not worth the parchment they were printed on in practical application. In reviewing her statistics again he noted with delight that everything in which she had been involved, along with her education from beginning to end, had taken place in Manhattan. She was insular, in violation of his contention that it took a broader background with wider geographical range and experience to be truly accomplished in urban PR.

Reassured now rather than intimidated, he descended the broad steps between the library's stone lions and headed up Fifth Avenue. In a mood of inner triumph he decided to lunch alone. Some satisfactions were meant to be savored in solitude. A solo sandwich in some cozy little pub, perhaps with a jukebox and maybe even a pool table, seemed particularly if oddly appealing to him.

Sidney was weary of gourmet wining and dining encounters. Even in Memphis, he had intermittently enjoyed escaping from routine. He would drive somewhere at random to find a temporary refuge where his identity and occupation were unknown. It was like being a soldier on a pass from a combat zone.

He headed west now, toward the Hudson, a somewhat unusual direction for him, unless he was going to the theater district or to a bon voyage party at one of the piers.

On this afternoon he found himself on the fringes of Hell's Kitchen. The place was called simply Buddy's, three steps down into the semibasement of a modest brownstone. Despite the neighborhood, the place was neat and clean, paneled in comfortable light oak and moderately lit with synthetic Tiffany lamps. There were only two other men at the bar separated by several stools.

"Serve lunch?" he asked the barmaid, a bleached blonde who looked to be in her middle forties.

"Soup and sandwiches," she replied. "Yankee bean t'day."

"Sounds good," he said, sliding onto a stool. "How about soup and a cheeseburger, medium."

"Fries?"

"Why not?"

She placed a paper coaster on the bar in front of him. "Drink?"

"A brew. Whatever's on tap."

"Bud."

He nodded acceptance. For the moment a delicious sense of abandon, maybe even of triumph, invaded him. He professed to hate nostalgia, yet here he was subconsciously indulging in it. For all his pretensions to success and the social graces, Sidney Bastion was not truly that comfortable in the environs of elegance, nor was he really that enamored of haute French or any other fashionable cuisine. Like it or not, he was basically an accomplished overachiever with indestructibly common roots.

His reverie was interrupted by the arrival of the cheeseburger. To hell with the past, let's dine on the present and save the future for dessert, he thought to himself.

"Ev'rything okay?" the barmaid inquired.

"Another beer," he said.

He pounded the bottom of the ketchup bottle with the heel of his hand unsuccessfully.

The barmaid returned with his mug, smiling at his dilemma. "Havin' trou-ble?"

"Watch it come out all at once and splatter all over the place."

Of course it happened. His french fries lay bathed in a sea of scarlet. The barmaid laughed and he joined her.

"Everything in life should be so predictable," he said.

"How come all them scientists don't come up with somethin' to fix that?"

Sidney pondered her proposition with amusement. "You know, I never thought of that. H. J. Heinz should put a research team on it right away, if he hasn't already."

After finishing his food, he went to the jukebox. It offered a hundred selec-tions of which he recognized only a few. Even the lone Johnny Gault choice was unfamiliar to him, something titled "Pretty Please." It must not be an A side or he would have known it. Or so he assured himself.

The bar emptied as his selections droned on. He switched to Scotch and water after reaching his capacity on beer.

"You get busy later I suppose," he said idly, not really caring.

"Sometimes."

A trio of young men in T-shirts sauntered in, and the barmaid turned her attention to them. Again his mind drifted, but forward this time rather than back. There was no denying Adrienne Gale had gotten to him. What he had difficulty determining was exactly how, why, and to what extent. There was something in her attitude, a kind of subtle insolence, that for some reason he found challenging and provocative. Erotically so, which made it all the more difficult to ignore or deny.

He stayed at the bar longer than he had anticipated, drinking considerably more than was usual for him. Perhaps that accounted for his deepening deter-mination to find out more about this woman, this Manhattan Mata Hari, whom he now suspected of using seductive tactics to lure the unsuspecting into her fold.

10

Sidney had always pushed the premise of Johnny Gault's basic purity. He chose to ignore the persistent negatives.

"He's overcome so many personal liabilities, we should worship his tenacity as well as his talent instead of questioning his morality. He is without question the Jesus of rock and roll."

"We're going with the pilgrims to retrace the path of Jesus," he told Johnny early enough for him to clear his schedule during the Easter-Passover period.

"You're crazy, Sid."

"You'll come off like a saint."

Johnny was amused. "You're pounding sand up my ass, Slick."

"The coverage will be worth it."

"I like my holies surrounded by pubic hair."

"Exactly why we're going to Bethlehem," Sidney said.

It worked out even better than Sidney had anticipated. There was massive media coverage of Johnny in ashes and loincloth, shouldering the cross, on his knees in the holiest sepulcher, riding camels in the desert, bestowing blessings and baskets of food on small impoverished children.

His concert of religious anthems drew hundreds of thousands of fans.

"Smooth, smooth shit," he declared after examining the results of the trip.

"Johnny Jesus," Claudia sighed.

"Just destroy the negatives of him fucking a camel," Doc grumbled.

Claudia wasn't at all sure if he was kidding or not.

idney Bastion never really had a childhood, at least nothing approaching a Tom Sawyer/Huck Finn version. He had always been a success-oriented individual, driven by the desire not to repeat the failures of his mother and father.

"They tried," he reluctantly dismissed their memory. "They just didn't have anything to try with."

He refused to be drawn into any in-depth discussion of his early experiences.

"My life began on my sixteenth birthday," he declared when pressed. "Those are all the stats you get from me."

"What happened then?" he was asked.

"My eyes finally opened."

For a man considered a master of the information business it was a remarkably spare and unrevealing one-paragraph autobiography.

"I live for my clients, not for myself," he once said in a rare, terse interview.

There was cold truth in his words. He could be vehement and verbose on behalf of others but was generally silent about himself.

Johnny, on the other hand, seemed to be enjoying his postponed childhood. Had he not been a star of such magnitude, his juvenile behavior might have been more seriously questioned and analyzed. There were times when he seemed barely out of the playpen.

Doc allowed him to be indulged. He would allow the devil into heaven if he could turn a profit on the deal. Keeping Johnny pacified was his primary concern. On tour, the Doctor was usually curled into the stage curtains, sunglasses hiding his steely eyes. He listened to the applause, his body revealing no response to the intense sound waves surrounding it.

Doc became more visibly energized in the back rooms where the cash count-downs took place. He moved smooth as a snake and quick as a fish among the auditors. There was a lot of loose cash in the promotion business, and not all of it by a long shot found its way into the financial documentation. Especially into the Doc-umentation he provided Johnny.

"Ah'll take a string o' one-nighters out in the boondocks to Carnegie Hall any day," Doc declared.

He loved the hand-to-hand cash count with fly-by-night promoters best of all. They were his kind of people, ever ready to cut a deal.

One hand washes the other, even when it leaves a stain.

12

J ohnny Gault harbored a strange mix of ego and humility.

"When they tell me I'm larger than life," he said, "they must be lookin' at my crotch."

"You're bigger than your cock, Johnny," Sidney assured him. "There are lots of guys with big pricks pumping gas and flipping hamburgers."

"How come that's what they always bring up? How come they keep writin' about my joint?"

"You're a star, John. Your anatomy has star value. Who cares if Sam the sewer man has a great build and a ten-inch cock?"

Sidney's response amused Johnny.

"His wife and his bitches," he said.

A brief smile surfaced on Sidney's usually intense and serious face.

"Nobody ever got anywhere major on the basis of his cock and balls. Everybody's in the race on that level. You're way beyond that, Johnny. You don't seem to realize you're not in the same league as your gofers."

"I got them all beat anyhow," he said.

Johnny was clearly enjoying this little confrontation. Occasional verbal exchanges with Sidney were one of the by-products of his success.

Johnny's overall playfulness, especially its juvenility, worried Sidney considerably more than it did Doc.

"He's a poor kid gone rich," Doc said, dismissing his antics. "Don't expect no choirboy."

Sidney understood the environment and the rationale. But they were all investing their time, their careers, and their credibility in this boy-man with the haunting voice and the sexual magnetism to promote it.

"Doc is no guardian angel," Sidney had confided to Claudia from the beginning. "He's a total mercenary. He'd bottle Johnny's sperm if he thought there was a market for it."

"There probably is. Imagine what he could get for it."

Sidney shook his head.

"Sometimes I wonder about you."

Claudia laughed. She enjoyed tantalizing her mentor.

"Think about it," she said.

On the road Johnny was often a wild animal, alternately predatory, quiescent, creative, and self-destructive. He spun like a top at times, was strung out like a yo-yo at others. The pressure of success was there, but he was strangely oblivious to it. He never regarded himself as anything but what he was—and that was a musician from Memphis who now functioned as a national hero.

"The kid has no ego," Doc had once told Sidney. "He thinks he's just another soldier in the army of assholes."

"Don't knock it. It's part of his charm."

They both recognized Johnny's value, even if Johnny did not.

"Ain't no way I'm important," Johnny was fond of saying. "I'm just another rock rollin' in an avalanche."

Johnny's home on wheels was repainted at intervals to insure its anonymity. Music magazines and gossip columnists took a perverse delight in reporting its chameleon colorations. These led inevitably to highway ambushes by the rabid across the country.

"Hide," Sidney advised, "and never confide. Truth is a lot harder to deal with than fiction."

Johnny found amusement in a variety of disguises—wigs, mustaches, beards, and an assortment of outlandish costumes. However, his singular mouth with its petulantly provocative lips were all but impossible to hide.

"Anybody ever tell you you got a mouth like Johnny Gault?" he was asked even in the remotest locations.

"Can't sing a note," he usually responded.

"Too bad," he was told. "You'd git rich impersonating him."

laudia left the news on his bedside answering machine. Reverend Billy Sunshine had decided on a three-day rally and crusade at Yankee Stadium the last weekend in July.

Christ, Sidney thought with no religion whatever in mind. Why couldn't he stay on the West Coast, where he belonged? He would surely expect mass media worship in the East for weeks in advance. Plus he would expect Sidney to become a full-time disciple at his beck and call for his entire stay. It might have made Sidney nauseous had he not already been feeling ill from the night before.

Claudia had apparently slept elsewhere. There were no signs of her presence other than the message, which could have been called in from elsewhere. She had probably come home, found him in disarray, and decided to go to a hotel or stay with a friend.

The other information included in her brief update was considerably more pleasing. Gray Matthison was being considered for the host spot on the *Now* show, with its nationwide morning audience. What an entree that could be for Sidney's whole roster of clients, current and future. He made a note to call Gray later and set a lunch date. It had been too long since he had sat down with him anyhow, as Claudia repeatedly reminded him.

The usual early call from her did not come. Pam Garson responded on her private line.

"She's not in yet, Sidney," her assistant reported. "She called but didn't say when she'd be in."

"Did she say where she was?"

"No. I just assumed she was with you."

Sidney frowned. One afternoon off the beaten track and his whole operation was out of sync.

"I'll be in before lunch. If she comes in before me, tell her to wait until I get there."

"Will do."

The letter to Paula Castle thanking her for the invitation, flattering her and her hotel, and making as subtle a pitch for the account as possible should have gone out the day before. It would positively have to be mailed this day. He called his secretary and reminded her to remind him later.

"Has Claudia called?"

"No, Mr. Bastion."

He slammed down the phone, vexed. She was his sounding board and it was like operating in a vacuum without her. No one was quite like her in her ability to weigh all the diverse factors in a given situation and come to the most sensible and logical conclusion. That he did not always follow the most sensible and logical course was another matter entirely.

The morning rundown of calls included a mysterious inquiry from a writer for *Camouflage*, a controversial new weekly only recently founded by none other than Norman Prescott. Would he consent to an interview? Sidney had never before been approached by any Prescott publication except for confirmation of something scandalous. The call, coming as it did only a day and a half after his introduction to Prescott, caused him to wonder. He decided to check with Zoe Greene.

"Beats me," she responded. "I have no idea if he had a hand in it. I just happen to be free for dinner. Want to bat it back and forth over some calories?"

"Excellent suggestion."

"Pick me up at the office. I'll be in costume—as an ink-stained wretch."

"Gucci work boots and Saint Laurent overalls."

"Six-thirty or seven?"

"Perfect."

Claudia had still not arrived when he finally got to his own office. She had not called in again, either.

"Where the hell do you suppose she is?" he asked her assistant.

"I'm as baffled as you are, Sidney. She had a lunch date on her calendar with a *Newsday* editor, but I checked with him and he said she called yesterday and postponed it."

"Could she be sick?"

"Anything's possible."

His anger began to turn to concern.

The letter to Paula Castle went off without benefit of Claudia's input.

"A copy to Miss Rogers," he instructed his secretary.

Perhaps she had orchestrated her absence to win greater appreciation, Sidney speculated. Everyone, Claudia included, was suspect on his list when things did not go his way.

Dinner with Zoe proved more ordeal than pleasure. In the interim since he had spoken to her she had become touchy and bitchy. He found it all but impossible to carry on a conversation, let alone bring up the Prescott matter.

"Sidney," she said after another long lapse of silence, "you're far too engrossed in yourself lately. Where's that old sparkle and spontaneity that always made you special?"

"I guess this is just one of my dull days," he replied. "Even diamonds don't always sparkle."

"The copy from your office is just not the same lately. I don't think I've used an item from you in a month or more."

He forced a smile.

"I'll have to check into that," he said.

He did not tell her that he had long since relegated gossip items to lesser members of his staff. His only interest in most of the columns now was getting full pillars devoted solely to his clients. But he never pressured Zoe on this. She was much more valuable to him on the personal basis they had established.

"That girl you have working for you—what's her name again?"

"Claudia?"

"That's it. Just what is it between you two?"

Sidney forced another smile.

"Man works from sun to sun, but woman columnist's work is never done."

Her eyes flashed. "You're not important enough to make the column, Sidney. I thought we were talking personally."

"We are, Zoe, of course. Claudia's simply my number-one, all-but-irreplaceable assistant."

"She lives with you, doesn't she?"

"That's incidental to her importance to me."

She laughed hollowly.

"Do you tell her that—in bed?"

"I might."

"You're full of it, Sidney."

"What is this—Bash Bastion Day?"

"Norman was right the other night. You like to manipulate the truth."

"He's pretty good at that himself."

"Should I tell him you said that?"

"The name is spelled B-a-s-t-i-o-n," he responded boldly.

Zoe studied him across the table. The lines in her face slowly converged to form the semblance of a smile.

"Do the piece for Norman, Sidney," she said without elaboration.

She was there in bed when he got home, breathing softly. The sudden flood of light awakened her.

"Claudia!" he exclaimed, dropping fully clothed beside her.

"You're not mad at me?"

"I'll decide that later. Right now I'm just happy you're here and okay."

He pulled her to his chest.

"I'm sorry, Sidney."

"I'm going to have to get one of those little transmitters for you—the kind they attach to wild animals so they can keep track of them."

"But I'm not wild, Sidney. Sometimes I wish I were."

"You just stay the way you are."

"I hope you mean that."

She felt his lips against her cheek as he kissed her.

"Don't we in PR always say what we mean?"

"I'm serious, Sidney."

He pushed her away far enough so he could see her face fully.

"What is it, Claudia?"

"Sidney," she said softly. "I'm pregnant."

14

Johnny's mother, Rita, was a phantom figure by the time her son achieved most of his success. Her absence from the limelight was a sadness for Johnny but a boon to Sidney. It enabled him to ennoble her beyond all plausibility. He pursued this aspect of his campaign with exceptional diligence and relish.

"I never had a mother I knew," Sidney said, his voice ringing with sincerity. "All the women in my life were loaned to me. Johnny was lucky enough to know his mom for a while, and he loved her. That's pure gold. Whatever happens to him—good, bad, or indifferent—no one can ever take the memory of her away from him."

Sidney was seldom sentimental. It interfered with business and suggested uncertain control of a situation. Yet he softened perceptibly whenever he entered the area of mother and son relating to his most prominent client.

"Johnny's life and his songs are a lament over the loss of his mother," he told one interviewer. "His sadness colors his music and his words project his grief."

Whether deliberately or inadvertently, Sidney had hit upon a theme that sold solidly to the public. Any man could be forgiven his animalism if he worshiped his mom.

"This one's for momma," Johnny would whisper softly at calculated moments in his always-sold-out concerts.

"Mom!" his audiences would scream in response. "Mom! Mom! Mom!"

"Mama madonna," he answered the acclamations. "God knows her goodness."

Sidney savored the smoothness of the sale. Johnny Gault full-blown and into his act entered all the emotions. He was the boy next door turned porn performer, momma's boy as moral marauder, abandoned child coveting love and adulation, seducing millions en masse.

He was indeed what the critics said he was. Phenomenal. Magical. Unique.

"He's got the heart of a hunter and the soul of a bandit," Sidney summarized him. "If he can keep his act together he'll be bigger than Jesus."

The deterioration had already set in. Sidney saw Johnny only superficially. He had neither the time nor the inclination to go deeper.

"I varnish," Sidney said. "I don't scrape."

Johnny was a troubled individual who found it difficult to cope with his lionization.

"I'm shit," he sometimes said.

His humility only intensified the adulation. Few artists had ever achieved his degree of intimacy with the masses.

"He's one of us," a fan told a TV interviewer. "It's like having God sit with you in the bleachers."

"He's my love and my friend," said another.

Fantasies fed the myth, and Sidney was always there to add another paragraph.

"Johnny Gault has sold more records and set more records individually than anyone in the Guinness book, the Bible, or the *World Book of Weights and Measures*."

The latter publication was an impromptu, nonexistent contrivance. But that mattered little, if at all.

Sidney was merely blowing wind on a fire that was already raging.

One of the music world's key critics had called Johnny Gault's style "singing with a hard-on" and the tag stuck. His fans were accustomed to eyeing his crotch as he sang, encouraged by the undulations of his hips and groin. It was a revolutionary blending of body and beat, a kind of bawdy ballet accompanied by the phallic stroking of his guitar.

"Musical masturbation," that same critic summarized it. "This is autoeroticism in the fast lane."

Johnny himself was as oblivious to criticism as he was to praise. But just to keep things on the up side, Sidney's staff filtered out the fulminations and fed him only the sweet ones.

"Johnny gets the bonbons," the Bastion staff contended. "Sidney gets the bombshells."

It was the function of public relations to cushion the client.

"Pile up the pillows," Sidney instructed his aides. "Make it all as soft as you can for the buckeroos."

The bucks came from those buckeroos, and nobody knew that better than El Sid.

He called frequent meetings to reemphasize his direction. The New York staff was sometimes California loose and then abruptly East Coast tight. Sidney liked it that way. It kept them all on their toes despite his celebration of at-ease postures. There were definitely some drill sergeant qualities lurking beneath the surface of his charm and smoothness.

Although he was neither saint nor serpent, he had been portrayed and projected as both. It was the nature of his nefarious business to be both subject and suspect in all matters involving his famous clients.

"I can't help it that my people are the people other people want to know about," he complained to Claudia.

"You've used up all your peoples," she retorted. "Ten yards back to the goal line."

"Facetiousness is your forte. You sometimes seem to have no concept of what Sisyphean labor we're involved in."

She laughed.

"They don't wheel that word around Memphis too often, Sidney. I think you're losing your roots."

"I'm a weed. I take root anywhere and grow."

"You've got that right, mister."

"Capital M?"

"Lowercase."

Banter was one of the strengths of their relationship. They both loved dialogue, and the more brittle the better. Coping with the monosyllabism of the likes of Johnny Gault could otherwise wreak havoc on any decent vocabulary.

15

From the outset the reporter from *Camouflage* seemed inordinately interested in Sidney's client list, the mechanics of his operation, and his equipment and physical plant, as opposed to his philosophies, methods, and techniques.

He did peruse several of the scrapbooks maintained on major accounts, occasionally questioning the reasoning behind certain stories, but Sidney had the distinct impression that he and his organization were being professionally evaluated—sized-up, so to speak—rather than profiled for a *Camouflage* article.

"Mr. Bastion," the reporter asked late in the interview, "would you consider yourself fully capable and qualified to represent, say, the Queen of England or perhaps some ruler of less popularity and palatability like Muammar Qaddafi or Fidel Castro?"

"Unquestionably," he replied. "The techniques, the methodology, all the various communications strategies are similar to those employed in handling any person of prominence and power."

"Would you be opposed to representing a negatively perceived individual such as, say, the head of the Mafia?"

Sidney smiled before responding.

"I'm not an attorney, sir, I'm a public relations adviser."

"If you'll permit me, sir, I find that an evasion of my question."

"You are being serious, so I would have to reply affirmatively. Yes, I would represent such a person. Not condone his activities, mind you, but offer him professional assistance in sprucing up his image, most definitely yes."

Their dialogue lasted several hours. Sidney felt emotionally drained by its conclusion.

"I'd appreciate an advance copy or tearsheet," he told the interviewer at the door.

"I'll see to that."

"My regards to your boss, Mr. Prescott."

The reporter smiled feebly.

After he was gone, Sidney activated the secret tape he had made of the entire interview. Grading himself as impartially as he could, he gave himself a B+. Not bad, but he could have been better.

Now it was up to Norman Prescott to evaluate him.

Prescott was a massive man with a penchant for privacy and elusiveness. It was difficult to ignore a big man who traveled about in stretch limousines, frequently wearing a cape and carrying a cane. The contradiction of image and attitude was either part of his problem or part of his modus operandi. Sidney had not determined which it was, but the conflict intrigued him. The man had public relations substance.

As a Canadian, Norman Prescott not infrequently came under attack for the size and scope of his American media acquisitions. They called him a carpetbagger and an alien, two of the milder references to him and his marauding style of grabbing foundering enterprises and injecting them with liberal doses of sex and violence to rebuild their popularity and sales.

He metaphorically thumbed his nose at this sniping by using a maple leaf as his logo and flying the flags of both the United States and Canada from all his buildings. No one shamed or intimidated Norman Prescott.

With practiced eye Sidney spotted the maple leaf logo one morning on an envelope in his own mail. His silver dagger sliced eagerly into the vellum.

"Dear Mr. Bastion," the letter read. "Would you kindly arrange an appointment with my secretary so that we might discuss a matter of interest to us both at a mutually convenient time? Thank you. Very truly yours, Norman Prescott."

He buzzed Claudia immediately to share the news.

"I'm impressed," she said.

"It's like an audience with the Pope."

"Better," she said. "At least you have a shot at this account."

"I could do him big," he told Claudia.

"He's no Saint Francis of Assisi."

"No, but he's not Attila the Hun, either."

"Closer to the latter than the former."

Any celebration was premature, but this was a business built on just such flimsy foundations and on dreams manufactured and magnified on the premises.

"You must have said something right, Sidney."

"I just said, 'Look, Norm, you're a bastard and I can make you a pussycat,' that's all."

He insisted she join him in champagne.

"Sorry, Sidney. I just can't."

The reminder of the pregnancy brought Sidney back to reality just moments before they were interrupted by a phone call from Billy Sunshine.

"You sure he won't talk to somebody else?" Sidney asked his secretary.

"Take it, Sidney," Claudia advised. "You're on a roll."

He picked up the phone with some reluctance.

"Reverend Billy," he said cheerfully. "How's the Jesus business?" He switched on the amplifier so Claudia could hear both ends of the conversation.

"I'm going bigger than big, Sidney," Billy began in his nonstop, cascading style. "After the Yankee Stadium rally we're goin' for a super Jamboree for Jesus in a 'round-the-clock nationwide telethon. I'm gonna get druggies and drunks, hookers 'n pimps, swindlers and killers up there confessin' their sins and gettin' down on their knees beggin' the Almighty for forgiveness and salvation. It's gonna be blockbuster television 'cause you're gonna help me get the best writers goin' to script the whole damned thing . . ."

"Emmy Award winners only," Sidney promised, winking at Claudia.

"Know what we're gonna do with the fortune that'll come in? Get this, Sidney. We're gonna build one helluva university, that's what, and it's gonna have the best football team, the best basketball team, the best baseball team, the best everything in the world, all in celebration of the glory of Jesus our Savior—"

"I can only say amen to that, Billy . . ."

"I want a resort to come outta all this, too—a fantastic resort for God-fearin' people to enjoy, a place where they can have fun solidifyin' their faith. They'll salivate for church, I guarantee ya, and we'll broadcast our services all over the world to show mankind the joys of goodness 'n worship . . ."

"Where do I sign up?"

"God bless ya, Sidney, you're one of the copilots in gettin' it all off the ground. I thank the Lord ev'ry day for leading me to ya."

"We'll get on all of this immediately, Billy. I'm calling a meeting of my department heads this very afternoon to get them revved up. It'll be one helluva campaign, I promise you."

"I know it will. God be with ya, Sidney."

Claudia joined in the sigh that followed the click of the phone.

"The surprises never cease, do they?" she said.

"Never."

His eyes fell back on the letter from Prescott.

"Tomorrow we respond," he said.

"Tomorrow," she repeated after him as though that day were light-years away.

He looked at her abstractly.

There was often a faraway quality, a present-but-absent aspect, to Sidney. For a change he managed to return to reality while she was still present.

"I don't know what I'd do without you, Claudia," he confessed softly.

The unexpected purity of his statement moved her to embrace him more warmly than she had in weeks.

"You're something else," she said. "Sometimes I wonder how you explain yourself to yourself."

He seemed fleetingly amused.

"Whatever I am, I'm less without you."

They hugged again, then fell to the carpet together, two seekers nearing a crossroads but still passionately on the same highway. They did have a lot in common. It was just a matter of how much each was willing to sacrifice to finish the marathon together.

t was not so much feast or famine as it was epicurean or everyday. Account prospects came and went with almost cyclical regularity, but seldom was an agency blessed with back-to-back blockbusters.

Only days after the Prescott overture a letter arrived at Sidney Bastion Associates, Ltd., bearing the engraved signature of Paula Castle in the corner of its envelope. Receiving such a rapid response from the likes of Paula Castle would ordinarily have engendered much more excitement than it did. But the invitation from Prescott had definitely lessened its impact. Sidney had a way of rising to the highest level of his associations, relegating everyone else to the lower plateaus.

"A year ago, maybe even a month ago, you would've drunk blood for a shot at the Castle account," Claudia reminded Sidney. "Now it's treated like an opportunity the firm deserves on its own merits."

"Maybe it's a sign of professional maturity."

"Maybe also it's a sign of cockiness, which can be fatal in this field. A woman like Paula Castle is never going to take a back seat to anybody, Norman Prescott included."

"By the same token, a man like Sidney Bastion is never going to relegate her to such a position. Come on, Claudia, you're like a mother hen at times."

He recognized immediately his unfortunate choice of words. Her eyes flashed and then faded, their vulnerability visible for just an instant.

"I'll set up that meeting on the Sunshine project," she said in a quick switch of subjects.

"Good. Keep me posted."

He stared at the city skyline for a long time after she was gone. It was amazing how still and mute it was in view of all the frenetic activity beneath it. In many respects, he was the same way, particularly at this moment.

17

They compared him to Jesus and his mother to Mary. It made his erotic
gyrations and suggestive lyrics religiously licensed rather than licentious.

Sidney fed the myth. If Johnny had not been a totally immaculate
conception, he was now an immaculate perception.

It was like the way he approached the words of "Highway to Heaven,"
another immediate hit, with his unique blend of innocence and sexual insinua-
tion. The leer and the lick of his tongue over his sensuous lips enhanced the
words he sang and fed the fountain of his image.

Highway to heaven,
Dangerous curves,
Watch for the signals,
Damage your nerves;
Stop at the red light,
Go at the green
Yellow spells caution,
It's hell in between.

His breathless chanting and voluptuous beat mesmerized his audiences coast
to coast. It was not easy looking shy and vulnerable while having a visible erection.

The boy-man who responded to what he called his "scrotum-totem" and claimed he heard from the tower had difficulty living within the restraints of a saintly image.

"I ain't no saint," he repeated often to Sidney.

His personal paparazzi could testify to the veracity of that statement. All of them by now had enough file film to indict him on multiple morals charges. Fortunately for Johnny, there was no money in that.

He was magic and tragic in the same breath.

You got a sweetness 'bout you boy," his momma had told him often enough for him to recall it with depth and clarity. He remembered those special words well enough to inspire yet another hit song. It quickly came to symbolize him and became a sort of theme song.

"You got a sweetness 'bout you, boy," he sang with stage glitter in his eyes, as though his real tears were not enough.

Doc believed in laying it on. More was better than less. Magnify the effect. If that represented the extent of his show business wisdom, it did seem to be enough.

"The Kid," Doc said, "is as softhearted as he is hard-dicked."

He harbored many secrets for someone promoted as a simple country boy. There was his penchant for wearing sexy undergarments designed for women, dainty and lacy and always in black, under his macho stage costumes.

"It gits me hard," he claimed, dismissing intermittent objections.

Performing with an erection had become a trademark of his act. His female fans brought binoculars to his concerts to insure full visual appreciation of his artistry.

"Crooning from the crotch," said some critics.

"The guy has balls," others reported, "and he lets you know it."

All of it contrasted to Johnny's semishy, polite, and soft-spoken personality.

"Momma," he would whisper softly into the mike after bringing his audiences to a boil. It drove them into a frenzy. He knew they shared his sense of love and loss.

Nobody else in the business possessed that kind of alchemy with his fans. They were not just his admirers—they were his mothers and fathers, his grand-mothers and grandfathers, his sisters and brothers, his aunts and uncles, his cousins and in-laws. They shared life with him, they rejoiced with him, and they grieved with him.

"When he lost his momma," one of his fans declared on national television, "he lost his heart. But not his soul."

The mama myth kept growing. Big-time. Sidney fed it with gusto.

"There's nothing more vital or valid in our society than the mother-son relationship," he contended. "Johnny is a victim of a vacuum. His father was never there. His mother died young and left him the prey of others. You've got to admire this man for becoming what he is on his own. Johnny Gault qualifies for sainthood. His mother has already attained it."

He said it with all the authority vested in him by the likes of Sidney Falco and P. T. Barnum.

18

S idney was a professionally serious person, but there were streaks of mischief in his modus operandi.

"Even societal parasites need to have fun once in a while," he contended.

That statement belied his steadfast belief in his work. He believed in the virtues of image making, of making people of prominence appear as sacrosanct as possible.

Johnny Gault, star, presented him with an ongoing challenge. Johnny was part himself, part Doc Diamond, and largely a figment of Sidney's biographical imagination.

"You can make anybody somebody," Sidney was fond of saying, "but if you have a somebody to begin with, you can make him a god."

Johnny was a somebody. He had the magic. He had the looks, the voice, the body.

He also had habits that many people found distasteful.

The function of Sidney Bastion was to hide, deny, and distort the truth to make Johnny Gault appear to be what he was not—a flawless hero who said his prayers with regularity and always stepped out of the shower to take a piss.

He would never, ever, come in a call girl's face. Or take advantage of a thirteen-year-old fan by showering her with penile champagne, as one supermarket tabloid had alleged. Not Gentleman Johnny.

The Johnny Gault of Sidney's sorcery was a beautiful person who cared about everybody, worshiped the memory of his mother, and by and large led an exemplary life. The most recent incantation of that image was his involvement with the Kickapoo Indians.

Sidney loved the name of these Native Americans. Johnny at first could not believe Sidney hadn't invented it and their tribal existence.

"You're bullshittin' me," he said when his PR guru first proposed a tie-in.

"Valid," Sidney replied in the staccato style he affected in verbal battle.

Johnny shrugged.

"You call the shots," he said. "Just be around when the shit hits the fan."

Building images, maintaining images, was the business of the industry. Sidney liked to think of himself as innovative—and he was—but he basically followed standard procedure: Make your man look good. If the truth hurts, lie. Sugar-coat him; honey-dip him. Slather him in likable, lickable stuff.

Johnny was basically a barnyard bigot, but Sidney projected him as a civil rights crusader with a passion for righting wrongs. Johnny did truly identify artistically with the blues of the black man, and much of his singing and playing style was to some degree derivative. "The white nigger," many rednecks had branded him.

For all the comparisons and acknowledged indebtedness to black musical heritage, Johnny avoided any serious associations with contemporaries of any color but his own. No blacks in particular had ever been part of his professional retinue. That was as much Doc's doing as it was Johnny's preference. They had both seen and turned away at the sight of Johnny's momma in flagrante delicto with black field hands in the more desperate moments of her short life.

As for the Kickapoos, they were safely ensconced on reservations in Kansas and Oklahoma. He could dedicate his songs to them, donate royalties to their welfare and make eloquent tributes to their native Americanism—always with appropriate Bastion fanfare, of course—without the necessity of actual corporal involvement.

"The Kickapoo kick," Sidney reminded Johnny from time to time. "Keep on the Kickapoo kick."

"When you gonna git me some Kickapoontang?" he usually responded.

"You've got all the squaws and maidens you can handle now."

"Never had an Indian."

"Make a reservation."

Johnny groaned. "That's sad, Sid. You're losin' it."

Sidney laughed. It was seldom he was able to engage Johnny in even brief repartee.

"We're getting you a ceremonial headdress from one of the chiefs," he reported. "Should make for a good photo op."

"Poontang," Johnny repeated. "Git me some Kickapoontang."

"You've got a one-track mind."

"One after the other or half a dozen at once."

"Keep gargling, kid. I'll be in touch."

The Indian stuff made the wires—AP, UP, INS—and some important magazine covers. Johnny Gault as a man of compassion and concern for the underdog. The character building process was coming along very nicely. Johnny Gault was a satyr-turned-saint, narcissist-become-altruist, prodigal-turned-prodigy. It was slick selling, almost beyond the subject's ability to comprehend.

"You just move when you're told to move and stand still when you're told to stand still," Sidney instructed Johnny with Doc's tacit approval. "Keep a smile on the ready."

Little wonder that Johnny was more insecure when he succeeded than when he had been ignored.

"You're meat," one of the casuals working the cameras at a photo session told him. "Maybe filet mignon but you'll get burned just like hamburger."

Johnny filed such remarks in his head.

19

W ith his organization now numbering well over a hundred employees
Sidney often had difficulty remembering the names of all of his staff,
much less their backgrounds. But it did occur to him all at once that
someone who had worked for Adrienne Gale had come over to his agency with
the Gray Matthison account. That someone might very well prove very useful
to him now aside from any assigned duties.

"Claudia," he said over the intercom, "who came over here with the Matthison account?"

"Gray Matthison? You, Sidney Bastion, are actually asking a real, live question about the Gray Matthison account?"

"A reply would be appreciated."

"You're probably referring to Jason Welles."

"What's your opinion of him?"

"He's capable. Very quiet and thorough."

"Thanks."

Claudia had been unable to cure herself of trying to figure out what Sidney
was up to. In all the months Welles had been with the organization Sidney had
not uttered so much as his name, much less requested a character critique. She
was all but beside herself with curiosity when she learned later that Sidney had
gone to lunch with him.

"What did you think of our man?" she inquired that night as they lay together watching the late news.

"Our man who?"

"Jason."

"Welles? What makes you ask a question like that?"

"You had lunch with him today."

"I didn't realize my luncheon appointments were subject to general release."

"When the boss goes out with staff, a real rarity in the Bastion trenches, then staff has a tendency to inform other staff, etcetera."

"Gossip."

"It's a key part of our business, isn't it?"

He sighed in resignation.

"We discussed the account, what else? Gray's on the verge of big things."

"He is a big thing. You've just never acknowledged it."

"Let's watch the news. You've become a real pita."

"That must be from one of Gray's quiz shows. A noun meaning a fiber used in making paper. Right?"

"P-i-t-a. It stands for pain in the ass."

"How affectionate. It's the nicest thing anyone's called me since baptism."

"From now on you're Claudia Pita Rogers."

"You're unbelievably sweet."

They watched the remainder of the news in silence. The times were becoming more and more frequent when she felt she was lying in bed with a stranger.

Sidney was first and foremost a manipulator. That was the nature of his business, but even more importantly that was the nature of his nature. He looked at the public at large as his target area. They were not there to be befriended but rather to be seduced and then conned into believing his clients were premier people whether they were or not.

Polls and surveys were also pet tools of Sidney's in providing him desired statistics favoring his clients. He had surreptitiously set up a separate company in downtown Manhattan to guarantee not only the results but to make certain of their acceptance as the product of an independent and impartial organization.

Even Claudia did not know positively of his affiliation with this company, but she had come to suspect as much. The deception was possible because it did operate legitimately in all of its areas except those rigged for Sidney. Satellite Surveys was a young but respected member of the community of opinion pollsters and product survey researchers.

"The public goes with the flow," Sidney said. "You tell them so-and-so is king of the hill and goddamit they'll argue the case in the affirmative even if they once had doubts."

"They're suckers."

"There wouldn't be a PR business without suckers," he said.

20

Sidney continually linked Johnny romantically with the sexiest stars and the lushest models, none of whom Johnny had ever met, much less seduced. It was an ongoing part of the business to fictionalize romances between prominent personalities. His peers cooperated. It was good for both ends of a false liaison.

But the manufacturing went beyond simple pairings.

"Anybody can get involved with anybody," Sidney contended. "Anybody can fuck. You've got to be more distinctive than that. Males have balls and females have cunts. What separates them is how they utilize their weaponry."

Sidney wanted more for Johnny than the routine matings of the media-manufactured magnificent. Here was a talent beyond contrivances, a talent as pure as maple syrup fresh tapped from a tree.

"This is a man who symbolizes America," he declared. "This is the living monument of our country's roots."

He had hit upon yet another theme of promotion: Johnny Gault, the true American.

"We're going to wrap you in the flag," Sidney advised him. "You'll be the greatest patriot since Nathan Hale."

"Who's he with?" Johnny questioned, figuring Hale to be a talent agent.

Sidney showed rare patience in his response.

"He's with all of us," he said.

*   *   *

It was a Sidney Bastion theory that saturation beat subtlety every time out. When Johnny's long-anticipated and much-Bastion-ballyhooed solo instrumental album, *Finger Plucking*, died on the shelves, Sidney diverted the stats and criticism by focusing immediately on Johnny's follow-up collection, *Honeycomb Heart*.

"His versatility as an artist is legendary," he told the few trade reporters who responded to his call for a press conference. None of the major dailies sent anyone. "He's not so much a guitarist as an interpreter of contemporary culture. In this sensitive and soulful collection of songs we're privileged to hear Johnny Gault open himself to the heartaches and vicissitudes of life."

There were those who called Sidney "the Pirate of PR."

"He loots space and steals headlines," one journal report contended.

Whatever they said, selective cuts from the *Honeycomb* album quickly infested the bestseller charts. "Dilly-Dally," "Upside-Down," and "Absent Without Love" entered the top ten singles category in such a rush no one remembered the disastrous guitar-only album Johnny had prized.

"Forget it," Sidney advised. "You're too big now to think small."

When "Jump Start My Heart" surged to top billing in national popularity polls, Sidney finally demanded covers from the major newsweeklies.

"This young man is our nation's single most eloquent spokesperson," he argued. "Nobody, not even the President, reaches people as deeply."

The pitch was provocative and it did produce results. A quickie poll indicated that among young Americans, name recognition was higher for Johnny Gault than it was for the President of the United States.

21

S idney engineered the coup that made Gray Matthison the beneficiary of Johnny Gault's television debut. The competition had been fierce since his latest album, *Emergency Landing*, had swept into first place in a matter of hours after release and one of its cuts, "Crash," simultaneously attained the number-one spot among singles.

No one in America, perhaps in the world, was hotter than Johnny Gault. Every variety show, every talk show on the network, vied for the ratings honor of presenting him to the nation and the universe for the first time.

Gray's show was hardly the logical choice. He conducted a relatively conservative hour of vaudeville bits and banter, witty at times but hardly the gaudy burlesque atmosphere best suited to Johnny's volatile and erotic style. It confirmed once again a Doc Diamond theory that substance was secondary to suck.

Gray had been reluctant to introduce Johnny to the masses when Sidney first approached him months before Johnny's breakthrough albums.

"He's cheap shit," Gray protested. "You're trying to use me, you bastard."

"He's a guaranteed great guest," Sidney argued. "Your ratings'll go through the ozone layer."

"A year of free PR," Gray had bargained.

Now he was all gratitude and genuflection.

"Slick and silvery PR guru Sidney Bastion put together this masterpiece of mismatching," reported the influential trade journal *Telly Scope*. "In no way is this a valid or proper showcase for the premiere video presentation of such a dynamic new personality."

Gray brushed aside the negatives. He was understandably, if belatedly, ecstatic. His recent flagging ratings soared from the first revelation of Gault's pending appearance.

"I owe you, babe," he told Sidney.

"Just don't hit on him," Sidney responded. "You're going to have more eyes than Mississippi on you for this one."

"That's a vowel pun."

Sidney smiled fleetingly. He liked the gay son of a bitch. He could almost understand Gray's attraction to Johnny's feral grace. Even he once in a while recognized and momentarily succumbed to the androgynous attractiveness of his ultimate client.

It was crazy and chaotic from the beginning. The rehearsals were like something out of Kafka with the Marx Brothers and Three Stooges thrown in. Nobody showed up on time. Johnny's stagehands rearranged props and scenery, oblivious to the protests of the Matthison show's regular union crew.

"I'm not sure the honor's worth it," Gray confessed to Sidney.

"Three major covers already," Sidney reminded him. "You're getting more coverage than World War II."

"The kid's high all the time. I don't know if we can trust him."

"I guarantee he'll be cool and straight for the show."

Gray sighed deeply.

"Today he comes up wanting a chorus of Harley Davidsons revving up behind him while he sings 'Hit the Road.' "

"Give it to him. The bikes turn him on. You'll get him in tight jeans with a hard-on."

"This is dangerous shit, Sidney. We could get cut off the air."

"No problem there. The reaction'll be fantastic."

"You're as crazy as he is."

"He's beyond normal constraints. Everything about him is marketable. You could sell the sweat off his balls. Nobody knows that better than Doc."

"It could also mark the end of my career. Ever think of that?"

"End? This is a new beginning for you, Gray. You're going to be hotter than the equator after this."

*   *   *

Sidney was accustomed to alarms. Every time the phones rang he anticipated the worst. His function was to facilitate and then finesse. It was never easy to cope with disaster on any level.

"I try to put the best spin on the top," he explained. "If it wobbles, I take the string and try something else. One thing I never do is give up."

Tops, he liked to point out, had a lot in common with yo-yos.

Johnny Gault, mostly via Doc Diamond, had tested his ingenuity and endurance from the beginning of his career in public relations. The battle raged endlessly.

It continued with a call from Gray's producer.

"I don't believe this shit," he began without formalities, his voice rising as he spoke. "Your baby Gault is in the studio shooting out the lights and windows."

"He's a growing boy," Sidney said. "Where's Gray?"

"Probably under a desk somewhere. What the fuck is going on, Sidney?"

"I'm not there, so you'll have to tell me. But don't let any of this leak and deny all of it if necessary. I'll get there as soon as I can."

"This is High Noon at High Midnight."

"He won't hurt anybody. Just stay away from him. Don't try to reason with him now."

Sidney heard the high-pitched zing of a bullet as he hung up.

"Idiot," he mumbled.

His phones were already ringing as he headed out of his office, bound for the studio.

Johnny Gault's appearance on the Gray Matthison show was part miracle, part miasma. It relied heavily on the patriotic theme, with Johnny dressed in satiny, skintight red, white, and blue. With Old Glory as a backdrop, he sang "The Battle Hymn of the Republic" in a way America had never heard it sung before. His provocative posturing, enhanced by a suppressed but still obvious erection, delighted most of his fans and enraged most of his critics.

"His costume was so tight it could detail his pubic hairs," wrote one reviewer.

"He is a disgrace to decency," commented another. "Why must honest music suffer this sort of sexual harassment?"

The public for the most part loved it.

"They ate it up," Sidney proclaimed after studying the overnight ratings.

Johnny himself celebrated later by shooting out most of the lights in the network parking lot, then eluding the police chasing his limo by switching to a backup car. It gave him special pleasure to outfox the New York City cops.

"Mark one up for the country boys," he exulted.

22

Rather soon after his meeting with Sidney, Jason Welles submitted his resignation from Bastion Associates to become a codirector of Satellite Surveys. The sudden move did not escape Claudia's attention.

"Gray is not going to like that," she told him. "Especially since you got him
the job."

"I knew of the opening and I recommended him."

"You hardly know him. And what the hell does he know about opinion
research?"

"It's a closely related field. He's alert and adaptable."

"That qualifies him as codirector?"

"It's mostly routine."

"Then why would Jason be interested?"

"It's a boost in stature. Maybe he's tired of browning Gray Matthison."

She shook her head in disbelief.

"It doesn't add up," she said.

"We're not scientists. Mathematics are not required."

He was obviously anxious to change the subject.

"Look," he said. "I just got the results of a Satellite survey we commissioned
on Billy Sunshine. He's going to love this. By an overwhelming margin, the
public perceives him as the most popular, most respected, most influential evangelist on television. How's that, Pita *puella?*"

"Unbelievable."

He didn't even look up as she left. This was his forte: calling a client with good news. He put his feet up on his desk and leaned back. It had been an all-around good day, no matter what anybody else thought or said.

Adrienne Gale herself took the call from Jason Welles.

"Congratulations are in order," she greeted him. "You broke away from Sidney Bastion."

"Mr. Pressure," he said. "You had him pegged."

"It's a hot agency."

"A lot of hot air, too. I did hate leaving Gray."

"Gray's a big boy."

"Any residual bitterness about his leaving?"

"None. I'd rather have you back than him."

He laughed. "The old left hand can still dish out the compliments."

"What's really on your mind, Jason?"

She knew he hadn't called just to chitchat. Neither of them was the type.

"Could we have lunch? There's something I'd like to talk to you about."

"Let me take the pinch test. I guess I've got room for maybe a dozen more calories."

"You worry with that figure?"

"No worry, no figure."

"Any day this week is good for me."

"I'll bump Charlie Quade from Thursday to next week. How's that?"

"Good old portable Charlie. Thursday's fine."

She disliked squandering valuable lunch time. After all, Jason was on a new job and no doubt looking for business. But Adrienne and Sidney had had an impact upon each other in their first encounter—a rather belated one, in view of their years of coexistence. Now Adrienne's curiosity had been piqued. Besides, Adrienne liked Jason. A little trade-off of information in exchange for a survey assignment struck her as a potentially fair exchange.

It's absolutely absurd!" Adrienne shrieked when Jason told her of Sidney's plan to have him infiltrate her organization and report his findings to him. "If I didn't know you, I wouldn't believe you at all."

"He's a hundred percent serious."

"Is he demented or just suffering from espionage of the brain?"

"I've been with him a year, and I've never seen him so intense."

"Isn't it ridiculous? I mean, absolutely juvenile."

"I played it straight. I figured we could have some fun with it."

"Jason, it's delicious."

They spent lunch devising schemes to intrigue and ultimately frustrate Sidney Bastion.

"You'll be acting as a double agent," she told Jason, laughing.

"Does that carry a death penalty if caught?"

"That depends on the mastermind, Sidney Bastion."

"The unscrupulous one."

"Let's hope not also the unbalanced one."

"I thought that was a requisite in this business."

They parted in high spirits, committed to confounding Sidney. He had perfected duplicity to such a degree he had forgotten others could practice it, too—perhaps also to perverse perfection.

23

Sidney's meeting with Norman Prescott went famously. They seemed to share a certain pleasure in the gullibility of the masses. The Canadian mogul was amused by Sidney's disclosure that he created his own awards to accommodate and celebrate his clients. Best dressed, most desired, sexiest, most admired, handsomest, loveliest, what have you—they were all within his domain to dictate. He conceded the ploy but defended its usefulness in terms of the public's unfailing belief in the alleged results.

"I couldn't do it without media cooperation," he confessed.

"I assume my own publications have been guilty of aiding and abetting these frauds?" Prescott questioned slyly.

"On rare occasions."

Prescott smiled fleetingly at Sidney's diplomatic response. "You've gone beyond Marx in your opiates for the masses," he said.

"The masses are asses," Sidney boldly asserted.

His calculated risk paid off.

"I'm not interested in interviews of any kind," Prescott said in a seeming non sequitur.

"You're right. You shouldn't do them."

"What I'm looking for—in the subtlest, most subliminal way possible—is a gradual lessening of the ogre-hermit perception of me in the minds of too many people. I don't give a damn about the opinion of others regarding me except for its negative interference in negotiations and acquisitions."

"Are you currently involved in any philanthropies, Mr. Prescott?"

"Nothing significant. I prefer that my assets remain as liquid as possible."

"It won't be necessary to touch your assets to enhance your reputation as a generous contributor to worthy causes."

Prescott contemplated Sidney's pitch impassively.

"Discretion is absolutely essential in anything done with me," he said after a lengthy pause. "I needn't emerge as a deity, but I don't desire any further satanic implications, either."

"Should my organization become involved in anything pertaining to you, Mr. Prescott, everything personal will be handled solely by me. Nothing will be relegated to staff beyond routine releases and the mechanics of distribution."

"You alone will shoulder the blame?"

"I alone will capture the credit."

In his quietly imperious way, Prescott seemed amused by Sidney's self-assurance and conviction.

"I haven't done too badly without you," he said. "How would I benefit *with* you?"

"You would become beloved," Sidney responded without hesitation. "Become not just a monster mogul with millions but a respected, revered, idolized leader of the human race."

Prescott did not dismiss Sidney's bold suggestion.

"I'm not looking to finish first in the human race," he said.

"You could qualify for the Olympics."

Sidney had hit upon something special within the granite man.

They discussed other aspects of a possible campaign to soften the hard image of Norman Prescott and modify the overall perception of his publications as sensationalistic, often gross, and sometimes pornographic. After two hours nothing was finalized between them, but Sidney sensed it was only a matter of time.

"I'll make him a saint," he later declared to Claudia in a mood of jubilation. "They'll be hanging icons of him in hallowed places."

"Did you like him?"

"What has that got to do with anything?"

"I was just curious."

"Still searching for nobility among the nabobs. That's juvenile, Claudia."

"Pita."

"You're right. I forgot."

She refrained from saying just how much he had forgotten about her lately.

"Jason called while you were with Prescott."

"Oh, yeah?"

"Said he had an interesting lunch."

"Good for him. I like having former employees report to me on the caliber of their lunches."

"With his old boss."

"Refresh my memory."

"Adrienne Gale."

"I don't know why that should interest me, do you?"

Claudia spared him her suspicions. Let him savor his session with Prescott. Besides, she had little beyond intuition to rely on. That would never be enough to trap Sidney in anything.

No article ever appeared in *Camouflage*, of course. Sidney never really expected it, nor did he really want it. The same space devoted to one of his clients would be much more gratifying, especially now that he would be involved with the executive publisher himself. That association, even in its pending state, was heady and seductive to him.

He was hesitant to confide anything about their meeting to Zoe Greene. Prescott was difficult to figure out with any certainty. He had never mentioned Zoe once over the course of their long discussion despite the shared awareness that she had been most instrumental in getting them together.

It made him wonder whether he had exaggerated the extent of Zoe's influence. People in Sidney's profession had a tendency to deify media stalwarts, especially those who swung from the ankles. Zoe could be a dirty fighter, a sly-rapper, when she chose. She had street smarts. He was well aware she went for the balls when she kicked. In spite of it all he chose to be less than forthcoming with her about his session with Prescott.

Whom to tell what was a continuing dilemma in the game of masquerade, hide-and-seek, and liars' poker that constituted personal public relations. In Zoe's case there was the added element of her position plus her contractual commitment to Norman Prescott Aggregates. Never timid or retiring, she resolved Sidney's perplexity herself.

"You had an audience with God, I hear," she said as soon as he picked up her call.

"Your grapevine must be made of electronic cable."

"How did it go?"

"Amiably."

"Anything concrete come out of it?"

"More like Silly Putty."

"That's how Norman operates. But don't worry, he never wastes time speculating. If he called you in, you're in."

"If that happens I've got only you to thank, Zoe."

"Nonsense. Nobody influences Norman."

Her conversation were always terse, somewhat by necessity. The multiple lines to her office were always busy, overloading her with information from which to glean her daily columns:

"Later," she said abruptly, her stock cutoff phrase.

Sidney put down the receiver and peered vacantly at the skyline behind his desk. Zoe Greene could very well present a problem to him in his future relationship with her boss. It was her nature to meddle, part of the reason she had become so popular and successful as a journalist. In the Prescott situation, more than any other he had yet encountered, confidentiality seemed an absolute necessity. There could be no leaks other than those authorized by the man himself.

His meditation was interrupted by the insistent buzzing of his private line. Claudia came on with an air of detachment in her voice.

"Doc Diamond's had a brainstorm," she reported. "He wants Johnny to appear with Billy at Yankee Stadium."

"A prerequisite to a brainstorm is the presence of a brain."

"Do you want to deal with it now or later?"

"For crissake, Claudia, we're not booking agents."

"Tell that to Doc."

"God knows they deserve each other, but I don't know if it's a good idea for either of them."

"Line seven as in heaven, please? I've already done my time with the lecher."

Sidney sucked in his breath and exhaled slowly before picking up the phone. There was one thing about the business that was consistent: It never got any easier.

24

B illy Sunshine, shorn of his ecclesiastical garb, was really quite a mischief maker. His Puck factor was a prominent part of his personality, especially to those who knew him well. In private he did not regard himself with anything near the adulation his believers bestowed upon him.

"I'm a fastidious fuck-up," he confessed on occasion. "Given the opportunity I can and do mess up magnificently."

This askance, semiamused, self-deprecating appreciation of his prominence and influence is what initially attracted Johnny Gault to him. Billy was easily the least reverential reverend Johnny had yet encountered despite his enormous following and universal respect. The fact that Billy was also a closet roué with a pedophilic proclivity further endeared him to the increasingly isolated icon known as Johnny Gault.

They were both idolized by millions, if for quite different reasons. Their enormous popularities plied the mainstream of America. There was power in their very presences, and it seemed to have a bonding effect on their relationship. Somewhat surprisingly, Doc Diamond encouraged their friendship.

"Can't hurt," he reasoned with his sly simplicity, recognizing its reinforcement of the choirboy image Doc subscribed to and Sidney liked to peddle.

B illy regularly beleaguered the Devil in his sermons, but he was quite a devil in his own right. Lowercase, perhaps, but just as guilty of providing temptation and tantalization.

Johnny Gault was scheduled to be on yet another of his now-endless road tours when Billy's logistics secretary detected a coming collision of destinations with the gospel crusade. Conveniently, there were days off in between.

Reverend Billy reacted with visible pleasure to the disclosure.

"I've got to do something special for that boy," he declared. "He's like my son."

He truly did love and relate to Johnny. And Billy was nothing if not imaginative in all phases of life. His sermons were masterpieces of fantasy and muddled Christianity spiced with sexual allusions and innuendo, delivered with positive, self-righteous enthusiasm, and ending always with the most humble whispered "Amen" imaginable.

"He's the Orson Welles of the Jesus business," wrote one media critic. "He's devious and dangerous in a gently diabolical way."

Billy chortled at such evaluations of himself. He was more aware of his own prominence and presence than Johnny could ever hope to be.

"Johnny's a baby," Billy said often. "Innocent as a newborn. I love him like a child."

Billy's dangerous mix of love and lust for children was known to few. His own background of early molestation was obscured by his rosy childhood biography, another Sidney Bastion improvisation. Yet somehow this secret dalliance and disturbing desire in the orchard of forbidden fruit communicated to Johnny and his own concealed past and privately clouded present.

They had never verbally shared their experiences, yet somehow their hidden distress was apparent to both of them. It put a strong knot in the short rope between them.

In his ever-inventive manner, Billy Sunshine—Johnny called him B. S.—concocted a party to celebrate Johnny's new album, *Virgins in Love*.

"We're having a blessing of the virgins by the river the weekend after next," Billy told Johnny. "I checked with Doc and you're free as a bird. Come soar with the saints."

It tickled Johnny to have Billy—B. S. Billy, Big Bad Billy—going to all this trouble for him. They were both in their special ways superstars. It was good to find a kindred spirit.

"Baptism," Billy declared, "cleanses away all sin. All that has gone before is washed away in the beauty of deliverance into God's kingdom."

Girls in white cotton frocks, naked under their knee-length covers, stood about his pristine pool and stared mostly at Johnny Gault. He was there in flowing robes, as naked as they were underneath, serving as Billy's ceremonial assistant.

"You young and pure creatures are entering a covenant with the Lord," said Reverend Billy solemnly. "These rites of puberty are a holy passage into womanhood."

Johnny had selected a pair of prize prospects even before Billy's sermonette had begun.

"God is in the wings waiting to greet you," Billy continued, "waiting hungrily to absolve you, wanting you to commit a sin of sensuality so that he might bring you into his kingdom a rescued soul, forevermore committed to his glory, a newly born child of Jesus."

The saintly bullshit worked smoother than snake oil. Girls slid into the water of Billy's pool and shed their skimpy raiment with biblical dedication. They were greeted by the rods and the staffs of Billy's invited guests, Johnny Gault's prominent among them.

Before it was over the pool had turned cloudy with semen, the fish of love and lust.

A sated Billy finally held his arms aloft and announced: "You have all entered the kingdom of heaven and you are all now pure as God incarnate."

Johnny lay back and shook his head, smiling blissfully.

"You're a healthy boy," Billy said, stroking his matted hair. "God wants his favorite children to be healthy and happy."

25

None of the vanity, none of the pettiness, and certainly none of the ruthlessness of Norman Prescott survived the sanitation process administered by Sidney Bastion. Norman's junk bond takeovers and the subsequent union busting, and purges of loyal and longtime employees emerged through the Bastion filter as akin to acts of beneficence.

Reality was always secondary to preception in the mind of Sidney. He did not believe in subtle rebuttals. All-out counterattack was his favorite way of confronting negative situations. Immediate, categorical denials were his standard means of dealing with surprise changes. Attack the attackees and hold your breath. It gave one time to think. And to scheme.

Norman was a mystery to most people, even to many of those close to him. In a sense, this made Sidney's game a bit easier. He had fewer flaws to paint over in developing his own managed portrait of the man many called the most powerful unelected official in America.

They were millions apart in accumulated wealth, but they did have some characteristics in common. Neither of them ever looked up or down—just forward. The sky was out of their lives, to hell with the sun and the moon, it was the next corner that mattered. Who or what challenge was coming around it?

In his rare ebullient moods, Johnny Gault liked to call Sidney "Slick." Slick he was, or he would never have been in the employ of Norman Prescott.

Paula Castle saw Sidney as "the master of manipulation."

Whatever his designation, he was a nonpareil in public relations.

As he slowly and cautiously acclimated himself to the elusive and secretive

Prescott, Sidney began to discern some of the patterns and methods involved in the man's major dealings. He moved like a killer shark through the sea of sages and swindlers who populated the marketplace, ever alert to any sign of weakness in the fish about him. He had single-handedly made himself the Croesus of the media world, but he had no intention of emulating that king of Lydia's demise on a funeral pyre.

Sidney set up a foundation to further the education of disadvantaged children under the aegis of the Prescott empire, a move to soften Prescott's image as a cold-blooded, unfeeling takeover tycoon. Sidney sold the foundation hard even before requesting Norman's personal participation.

"The concept has merit as a PR ploy," Norman reacted, "but don't expect me to deal with their shit and snot on a personal basis."

Sidney was not so much surprised by his reaction as by his earthy language. Perhaps he was human after all.

Truth is malleable," Sidney insisted. "You can bend it to fit any situation without destroying its basic credibility."

He demonstrated his theory when handling accusations that Prescott had taken over large segments of his media empire in ways that were less than pristine.

Prescott was charged with consorting with the notorious arbitrager Elias Trotsky in gaining control of Epictures, a onetime giant but now only a moderately successful film production company, in an insider-leveraged buyout that had blatantly shortchanged the company's stockholders. Sidney played hardball with a softball.

"Norman Prescott is first and foremost a humanitarian," he began the takeover press conference. "His interests lie in perpetuating the quality of Epictures's product. The means of acquisition are of no consequence in the larger scope of the company's future under his experienced stewardship."

"What about Trotsky?" a correspondent questioned.

Sidney paused and let a smile form slowly on his face. "I thought he died in Mexico a long time ago," he said.

The question and the subject were lost in a chorus of chuckles.

Sidney was being Sidney on behalf of Norman being Norman. It was an arrangement increasingly beneficial to both of them.

26

Claudia Rogers found it more amusing than upsetting that Paula Castle was attracted to Sidney. Or so Zoe reported. Claudia was not the possessive type, particularly when it involved an older woman—and potential client.

Claudia and Sidney lived together, so inevitably he approached her in moments of desire.

"Why don't you check that into a Castle hotel?" she responded to his frontal firmness. "Maybe you could get a rate."

"Don't play bitch. It doesn't become you."

"Paula's pretty."

"She's a gargoyle."

"Be kind, Sidney. Beauty is in the eye of the image maker."

"Do we ever stop being in business and get down to the fundamentals?"

"I don't know. Do we?"

"Not much lately."

"You seem enchanted by her."

"Claud—!"

"I mean, you're at her beck and call lately, baby."

He began to wither under her verbal assault. A once-imposing erection was now only a percentage of its original self.

"Business is business."

"And orgasms are orgasms."

He sighed deeply.

"It'd be like fucking granite with her."

Claudia was enjoying the turn-off. He had been so preoccupied and indifferent lately that it gave her pleasure to occupy his mind so fully and resist his advances.

They both lay back on the bed and stared upward.

"We're in a sick business, Sidney."

"Wrong," he said. "We're in a noble business. We make something out of nothing, somebodies out of nobodies."

She rose on an elbow and looked into his eyes. They were pale blue and vacant.

"Sometimes we also make nothings out of somethings," she said.

P syching himself for his meeting with Paula Castle proved far less stressful for Sidney than facing Norman Prescott. This despite the fact that she was in many ways an even more formidable personality.

In the case of Prescott, it was the extent of his power that was unsettling; with her it was her reputed abuse of power. And, of course, there was the matter of her sex. Sidney did not relate readily to females, especially extravagant, domineering females.

His encounter with Prescott had strengthened his conviction that he was rapidly becoming preeminent among his peers. His confidence had been bolstered further recently by the increasing numbers of television and print journalists who sought him out for story angles and rewarded him with national time and space.

"The prince of PR," Claudia dubbed him in jest. But privately she brooded over the changes she witnessed. There were generous rewards for her materially— salary increases, bonuses, jewels, and furs. But he became increasingly obsessed by the game he was playing to the exclusion of almost everything else.

"The whole chain," he announced with smug satisfaction when he later returned from his confrontation at the Gotham Castle. "I landed the whole fucking chain."

"That's wonderful, Sidney. Congratulations."

"They'll all be storming the Bastion now."

"We can't really handle any more without expanding."

"You're looking at Sign-'em-up Sidney. They'll pay just to say we represent them."

She cleared her throat, an act he recognized as an expression of dissent. He chose to ignore it.

"Tell me about her," she said. "I thought it was her you were going after."

"It is her. She *is* the chain."

He opened the bar refrigerator and pulled out a bottle of champagne. Tearing the foil seal and then popping the cork, he poured the pale gold liquid into two glasses. Claudia took hers and waited for the inevitable toast."

"To success," he said.

"To Sidney, synonym for success." She raised her glass but didn't drink.

Their eyes met directly for the first time in days.

"Was she the bitch you anticipated?"

"Not to me."

"All culture and breeding?"

"No, a real mother-F. But I can handle her. I think her greatest ambition is to wind up a trivia question in the year 2000."

"You weren't expecting Mother Teresa."

"The whole emphasis will be on Paula Castle as the reigning empress of the luxury hotel business, not just in New York but all over."

"What about Reese Roberts?"

"Forget about him. He just forks out the money."

"Sounds like a lovely relationship."

"It's practical as hell."

"You're happy, aren't you?"

"I'm glad I got the account instead of some gossip factory."

"When Prescott comes aboard, too, we might get a little swamped. Especially since I won't be around as much."

He looked startled. "Why?"

"The baby," she said evenly.

"Baby? You still carrying that thing? Christ, I thought you got rid of that long ago."

Tears welled in her eyes. Sidney Bastion, master of all situations, stood by helpless and uncertain.

"I'm sorry," he muttered. "Pita, I'm sorry."

27

S IDNEY BASTION ASSOCIATES, LTD. That was what the gold logo stated on the lobby door. Inside, a labyrinth of elegant offices lined the path to his own opulent executive suite fifty-seven stories over Park Avenue. The "LTD." had been an afterthought really, an Anglican pretension based on Sidney's belief that the British were the class act of the human race. He loved their history, their manners, their nobility, their gardens, their diction, and their graceful ability to use it all whenever they needed to fuck someone over.

He looked out through his windows to lovingly peruse Manhattan's majestic skyline. New York was his favorite city in all the world, and this view usually nourished his ego. But today, for the first time, he had to question whether he could trust his own instincts.

Penetrating the Adrienne Gale organization had become something of an obsession with Sidney. Outwardly it seemed perhaps as difficult a task as sexually penetrating Adrienne Gale herself.

Claudia interpreted his preoccupation as stubborn unwillingness to cope with her condition. He had become distant and elusive, avoiding any further discussion of her pregnancy. She was left feeling disconcertingly empty even as she was beginning to become physically full.

Both were guilty of conveniently escaping into the almost incessant turmoil and turbulence of their profession. It afforded almost limitless opportunities to busy oneself and find detachment from ordinary life.

She was thirty-five, single, and was probably facing her last opportunity to have a child. That had never been of much real consequence to her until very recently. In fact, she had been quite surprised at herself for the maternal feelings that surfaced when she had discovered her pregnancy. She was preoccupied with the prospect of motherhood since it had become a viable possibility.

Sidney regarded children with indifference, if at all. He lived in an adult world that dealt with children only occasionally and then as commodities.

"What's your opinion on abortion?" she recalled someone's once asking him.

"No opinion," he had replied. "I don't feel any need to have one."

It was strange how an exchange like that, so inconsequential at the time, could be retrieved from one's memory on demand. Though it was of no comfort to her now, it did reveal something of his thinking then and most likely now as well. Sidney had never had any intention of fathering a child.

28

B oth contract and check were anticlimactic. Sidney had already counted
Norman Prescott in his fold. The wordage of the agreement was expectedly
obtuse, with sizable loopholes favoring the Canadian magnate. No matter.
Sidney was so enamored of the prestige involved that he was ready to accept on
almost any terms.

The check was drawn on a bank in the Cayman Islands. All the more mysterious as far as he was concerned. Sidney would never see a Norman Prescott
Aggregates check from any financial institutions other than ones in the Caymans,
the Bahamas, or Switzerland.

Zoe Greene had been right. The media overlord perhaps was eccentric, but
he was also swiftly decisive. There had been no follow-up meetings or inquiries.
It was Sidney Bastion from the outset, for better or for worse.

This finalization of their arrangement might have been more festive had it
not been clouded by Claudia's decision to move out of the apartment. She also
withdrew from all negotiations for a multimillion-dollar Beekman Place townhouse with him.

"Never call me Pita again," she warned as movers gathered up her personal
effects at the duplex. "My name is Claudia Rogers. Nothing more, nothing less."

She did not look back or say another word. As the last packing crate was
inched through the front door, Sidney, for the first time in his adult life, felt on
the verge of tears.

*   *   *

*Z*oe Greene could seem omniscient at times.

She was not, of course, but even Sidney was occasionally surprised—and sometimes annoyed—by how rapidly she learned of the most intimate details of other people's lives. Every now and then a negative disclosure involved one of his clients.

"No one is sacrosanct, Sidney," she reminded him when he protested.

"I thought friendship was sacred, above and beyond the call of duty."

"It is, but then so is a prayer from Billy Sunshine."

With that in mind he should not have been surprised by her call the very morning of Claudia's departure.

"Sidney, darling, how is everything?" she inquired with uncharacteristic sweetness.

"Thanks to you, everything's splendid, Zoe."

"You're such a fabricator, you dear boy."

"Why? Just two words sum it all up: Prescott and Castle."

"You add but you never subtract."

"I was never any good at arithmetic."

"Two minus one equals bachelor, I'm told."

"In some formulas maybe."

"Claudia's moved out."

"Temporarily."

"Is she staying with the firm?"

"Of course."

"There'll be an empty hollow in your bed tonight. I just might be able to recruit a very passionate volunteer."

"I have to be in L.A. by morning."

She paused, a rare occurrence.

"Let's talk about it all when you get back."

"In bed?" he jested.

"Where else?"

*C*laudia's departure left Sidney with little enthusiasm for anything but escape. He decided to make good on his spur-of-the-moment evasion. A trip to Los Angeles was not unreasonable—there were always client needs to be fulfilled on either coast—if he felt so inclined.

Four hours sans telephones. Blissful on one hand, frustrating on the other. It would take a quota of vodka to calm him after the past twenty-four hours.

He tried not to think of Claudia. Instead he mulled over the rumor that Jason Welles and Gray Matthison were lovers.

Gray was an attractive, athletic man with a columnar reputation as a contemporary Casanova, and that image had figured into his selection as a talk show host. The network had conducted its own survey and found that he had wide appeal among women of all ages while men also found him interesting and engaging. Any homosexual innuendos at this formative stage could jeopardize the show and certainly Gray's career.

Jason was tall and slender with wheat-colored hair and a bespectacled face that could best be described as average. He hardly fit the role of partner in a romantic liaison with someone as striking and accomplished as Gray. Sidney knew both men and had never detected anything amiss, but it bothered him to think that somebody else had.

He had his own problem with Zoe to brood over as well. In the absence of Claudia he felt more vulnerable to her. And Claudia had been right all along. Zoe was after his body.

There was no comfort to be found in his new collusion with Paula Castle, either. So far there had been nothing overt, but his animal instinct warned him of the potential. Her manner had been quite suggestive during their contractual conference, and he had come away with the account much more easily than he would normally have expected.

Of all the women who ran through his mind, though, the only one who aroused him was Adrienne Gale. Even now as he thought of her he could feel the response in his groin. It occurred to him that his curiosity about her professional operation might actually be the result of a desire to get further inside her.

Amid his contemplations he fell into a fitful sleep.

29

J ohnny Gault was always challenged by competitors who resented his domination of the industry's all-important hit listings. Hitting the charts was tantamount to being a home run leader in baseball. Everybody in the game wanted to be listed there.

Prominent among them was Kid Cody Cameron, a brash and eccentric pianist-vocalist who tended to terrorize his audiences with his violent antics both onstage and off.

"He stole my act!" Cameron claimed on numerous occasions. "I ain't really gonna live till he dies!"

His animosity provided nervous amusement for his fans, most of whom were dually devoted. They saw the wildness of Kid Cody tamed and considerably refined in Johnny without any real loss of intensity.

"He's a kiss-ass!" Cody screamed at the media. "He's a motha-sucka an' a faggot with cunt lips!"

The denigrations were strong and specific, full of blipped phrases, energized and enlarged by Johnny's total disregard of them.

"Kid Cody is a talented performer," Johnny responded to the onslaught. "I respect his abilities and I have no comment on his evaluation of me."

Sidney Bastion had trained his premier client well. He was improving steadily on the diet of words he was fed.

*   *   *

Guy Sonata was a hangover from another generation, a legend in his own right. But he fulminated over the Gault mystique nonetheless, issuing more elaborate but disappointing versions of Johnny's hit songs. It was embarrassing to Johnny, who had always been taught to respect his elders.

Sonata was reputed to have connections that could seriously damage Johnny Gault. An aura of shadowy power always lurked just behind the relentless glitz of his career.

Johnny played the situation with his natural, cool grace. He never demeaned his competition.

"What's your word on Guy Sonata?" he was asked.

"Immaculate," he replied.

"A master?"

"Without a doubt."

"He says you're shit."

"He's entitled to his opinion."

The media loved to parry the pair. Sonata with his awesome past and rather mediocre present facing the reverse in Johnny Gault.

"Treat him with respect," Sidney counseled his client. "Just because *he's* got a bad mouth doesn't mean you should emulate him. People admire people who suffer abuse gracefully, especially when it's obvious they could easily strike back and win."

"He shouldn't say some o' the things he says," Johnny complained.

"He's got a New Jersey mouth and a Mississippi mind," Sidney said. "If he didn't have talent he'd be sucking up fish in the Hudson River."

"I should shoot his balls off," Johnny said with a sly smile.

"He'd never make it as a soprano."

There were few if any crossover fans. Those who adored Guy Sonata almost invariably detested Johnny Gault, and vice versa. Teens tested their parents' tolerance by blasting Gault over their loudspeakers. To them the smooth crooning of Guy Sonata represented a form of social surrender. They liked Johnny kicking ass.

"Don't lick nothin' that sticks t'yer tongue," he sang over a beat that rattled bar glasses. "Don't eat the meat till y'know where it's been hung . . ."

The Sonata generation, mellowed out on their idol's delicate definitions of romance, looked upon Johnny with contempt.

"He's passé," Sidney said privately to Johnny, despite his own predisposition to Sonata. "Johnny Gault is America now."

"There's a whole new breed of fucking fakes in the music business," Sonata declared in a much-bleeped interview. "What's his name—Guilt or something—he doesn't know shit about music; can't play it, can't sing it, can't even hum it in tune, and he's got these asshole drumbeaters pounding out the myth this ragtag country boy can sing and play. It's a sad day in America when this kind of shit passes for modern music."

"Ignore the prick," Sidney advised.

"He might come back," Johnny replied.

"What—as an asshole with hemorrhoids?"

Doc agreed with Sidney. It was Sonata persona non grata in the Gault ménage from that day forward.

Johnny had quite a different relationship with another singer, a contemporary who was far less jealous and belligerent. He was closer to Sonata in style and song selection than to Johnny, but it was obvious he aspired more to be like the boy-man the fan magazines called *"Hunker."*

With his high-pitched falsetto and distinctive vibrato, Jesse Robinson had cut into the charts with plaintive renditions of originals Johnny Gault was unlikely to even consider covering. Sonata might have, to his regret, overlooked them but even then he could not have duplicated the special tonal touches Jesse added so naturally and originally. The game, after all, was one of gimmicks, wasn't it?

Guy Sonata sang straight. He bent a lyric or melodic line a bit now and then, but he was basically right on with the composer and conductor. Jesse, by contrast, had a plaintive quality that overcame his lack of power or purity. But neither he nor Sonata possessed the animal magnetism of Johnny Gault in full stride and full voice.

The imperiousness of Sonata, his mixture of indifference and condescension toward them both, bothered Jesse and Johnny.

"He's a god but he ain't the only god," Johnny said.

"He's gay," Jesse declared.

If it was wishful thinking on Jesse's part it nonetheless defined the debate. They were all stars, all part of the celebrity constellation, and yet the pettiness among them was every bit as plebian as that among fishmongers and street whores.

"He can suck my dick," Jesse reacted to the latest Sonata put-down.

"You want pleasure with your pair." Johnny laughed.

They were both high and naked on the king-size bed dominating the rear of Johnny's bus. Jesse was there incognito, of course. No one in the media suspected that a relationship had developed out of their joint appearances at a fundraising music festival in Nashville months earlier.

Fortunate timing of tours had made their current liaison possible, and they both delighted in the magic and mystery of their carnal collusion. It was like a secret masquerade, outfitting themselves in costumes of disguise and decorating their faces with spectacles and mustaches to achieve anonymity through commonality. At Johnny's discretion the bus pulled into stops frequented by truckers and the hookers who serviced them. These encounters delighted Johnny, his obscurity delicious to his psyche.

"It's a real treat t'git sucked off without havin' t'sign an autograph," he told Jesse.

"You're primitive, man," Jesse responded.

They got on well together, but there was seldom enough time to expand their relationship. The vultures of the tabloid press had already begun circling over them, alerted to the potential for a scarlet headline.

"Success means never taking a leak behind a tree," Sidney told Johnny, "because the branches are probably filled with paparazzi."

J ohnny Gault, Johnny Gault, wooeeeee. He was like a locomotive racing across silver tracks, the rhythm infectious and mesmerizing as a speeding train.

Sidney not only recognized the force and the speed but also his own inability to control it. That bothered his sense of personal dynamics. He preferred to mastermind situations, but Johnny was beyond him. Doc had surrendered easily. He operated on the no-clash-with-cash policy. And the cash was sizable and growing astronomically.

Johnny's trademark wink and the single dimple in his right cheek were extra touches of magic that enhanced the deception of a little boy grown erogenous. The public looked beyond the pubic. They adored his down-home country image done up in silks and satins like the prince they knew he really was. He inspired all sorts of devotion from women—he was their son and their husband and their secret lover—and men envied his fame and facility with females.

"He's no cunt," they agreed at the Warehouse.

Even Leo, jealous of his exclusion, joined in the evaluation.

"The kid's as straight as a corkscrew," he said.

Coming from his skewed perspective, that could be regarded as a compliment.

Johnny reacted to his mounting success like a schoolboy. He shot out streetlights and tossed firecrackers from his bus. He left smoke bombs in roadside delis and tossed horse condoms filled with purple paint at local monuments. Nobody ever told him no. When he giggled, everybody around him giggled. The game of his personal groupies was to keep him entertained.

"I don't want him to hear nothin' but good news," Doc charged the troops he had assigned to protect his protégé. And good news was all he heard from them. The news from others, like the media, was far less encouraging.

Life for Johnny changed momentarily, like the flash of a camera. He was caught in a snapshot, a fleeting picture of his real self that no one but a stranger recognized.

Johnny had a reputation as a winker. It was his way of communicating his humanity in the midst of the bedlam invariably surrounding his appearances. He had an uncanny ability to single out those in the crowds—males and females alike—who understood what a captive he was of the masses who adored him. It was this extra gift that enabled him to endure the relentless pressures of his prominence.

"They ain't all crazy," he often told his roadies, "jist ninety-five percent of 'em."

On this one night one girl in particular had caught his winking eye by winking back. She was almost as pretty as his momma, and that was about as pretty as a girl could be to Johnny. He got one of his stage crew to invite her to his bus after the concert.

When she arrived, he was still perspiring and stripped to the waist after the grueling ordeal of performing. Wet with animal magnetism, he was enough to overwhelm most young admirers.

"What's your name, honey?" he asked politely.

She reacted shyly, but it was obvious she was not overwhelmed.

"Peggy Sue," she said. "Peggy Sue Porter."

"Peggy Sue," he repeated after her. "That figures to be about the sweetest name I ever heard."

She blushed at the compliment.

"After my grandma," she explained.

She was honey-haired and willowy with mischievous blue eyes and an incandescent smile. There was an air of sunny wholesomeness about her that instantly intrigued Johnny. He was not used to this kind of easy grace and authenticity in girls who sought his attention.

"Peggy Sue," he repeated again, reaching for his guitar.

He cleared his throat and began improvising, focusing his sensually lidded eyes on her upturned face.

Peggy Sue, hear me through,
First sight love has just come true . . .

She blushed again.

"Thank you, Johnny," she said. "I feel like I've just won some kind of contest."

"Maybe you have." He smiled.

She had indeed. He seldom spent time with fans who were not obvious and declared volunteers to surrender virginity or some percentage of the myth.

It was strange. He had never before felt such tenderness and fascination all at once toward a girl without simultaneously wanting to seduce her.

Somehow it was the sum of her rather than the triangle of her torso that intrigued him.

"Are you here with anyone?" he asked.

"I'm on vacation," she replied.

That was all the response he required.

"You got yourself a free bus ride to Baltimore," he told her. "Room and board, too."

Nobody had seen Johnny so happy in months. Maybe years. Maybe ever.

Claudia was the first to chronicle it officially. She had joined the Gault entourage on one of the periodic service-the-client road trips Sidney insisted upon.

"I got the Peggy Sue hots, the Peggy Sue blues, and the Peggy Sue can't-live-without-you infatuation situation," he confessed to her somewhere along Interstate 95.

"Let me go back to journalism school. Who, what, where, when, why?"

She had never before witnessed Johnny so animated offstage. Or so eager to talk.

The story and the chain of events were clearer to her by the time they reached Washington, D.C.

"Johnny," she advised him, "do you realize what's at stake here? You're an icon. You can't just flip out over some passing fancy."

"Passing fancy," he repeated after her. "Now, there's a song title if I ever heard one."

She looked at him and knew all at once why Doc had insisted she make this trip. It was all just a part of Johnny control.

"Someday I'd like to meet this Peggy Sue," Claudia said.

Johnny winked, touched a button, and spoke into the intercom.

"Peggy Sue," he said. "Front and center."

Inadvertently, it was Claudia who wrote the ending to this happy chapter in Johnny's trouble life.

"She's 4-H wholesome and honeysuckle sweet," she reported to Sidney after her trip aboard the Gaulter. "He's honestly crazy about her."

The words were a red flag to him. He was on the phone to Doc immediately.

"Git her off the bus and outta his life yesterday," Doc reacted. "Nobody's riding our meteor with less than a Blue Book rating."

"Claudia's given her the Good Housekeeping seal of approval."

"Royalty doesn't mix with commoners. It ruins the image."

"You're a natural-born PR man, Doc. Any time you need a job give me a call."

The good Doctor never laughed when he was serious.

And so it came to pass that Johnny Gault, king of all he surveyed, was abruptly and totally cut off from all communication with this guileless intruder into his domain.

Peggy Sue Porter was removed like a cancer from the king, the operation performed without anesthesia by master surgeon Doctor Diamond and his gifted assistant, Sidney Bastion.

It might not have saved a life, but it had at least temporarily prolonged a career.

The Doc/Sid emergency team had moved in swiftly once it realized the seriousness of the Peggy Sue situation. She simply did not fit into their master plan. True, she was pretty enough, intelligent enough, and perhaps even adaptable enough, but she also threatened to be independent enough not to follow the scenario they had written to guarantee continued success.

"Johnny's a commodity more than a person," Sidney explained futilely to Claudia. "We can't let him make a fool of himself over some star-struck groupie."

"I think she loves him. And what's more, I think he loves her. It's like a miracle."

Sidney scoffed at the suggestion.

"Making a multimillionaire out of a Mississippi mudfish is a miracle. Come on, Claudia, get real."

Alone later she wondered once again how she could care so much about someone who cared so little about others. To Sidney, "Peggy Sue" was nothing more than a potential hit recording.

She wept quietly for the girl and for Johnny as well. And that same night she made passionate love with Sidney.

None of it made any sense. None. It was all razzle-dazzle, hootchy-kootchy, and whoop-de-doo.

Meanwhile, time was ticking.

A brief, healthy interlude in Johnny's wanton life was over.

It was brutal how swiftly and totally Doc and Sid combined to eliminate the girl from the god. All her letters to him were intercepted and destroyed, all her phone calls diverted to an empty number. The same formula was applied to his efforts to reach her. An electronic device installed on the bus relayed calls to her to a recording announcing that her number had been disconnected.

It would only be a matter of time until she was forgotten. They wanted Johnny to remain footloose, unattached, addicted to excess. He was only controllable when he was out of control, not when he was content.

As much as anything the realization of what was taking place inspired Claudia's escape to the other coast.

"There has to be some form of sanity somewhere," she reasoned. "If not, I'll just dive into the Pacific and swim for the Fiji Islands. Underwater."

The joker wasn't wild. She was serious.

31

Adrienne Gale loved the new intrigue and the private gossip it spawned. The gamesmanship involved was captivating. She could not have selected a more engrossing or entertaining opponent than Sidney Bastion had she devised the covert competition herself.

"You're somewhere between a madonna and a Mata Hari in his eyes," Jason informed her. "You have him buffaloed."

"People have always told me they have me pegged," she responded. "It's refreshing to find out I'm not an open book."

"Only fools would claim that."

"Then I've known a lot of fools."

He knew her better than most. She was quite an actress when she chose to be but open and honest with those she trusted.

"I don't understand this Satellite Surveys bit for you," she confessed. "You're a very capable account exec, you're tied in with a major client, and he farms you out to a bunch of pollsters."

"It's just his way of being devious. A spy from his own ranks was just too obvious."

Neither of them suspected any Bastion affiliation with Satellite other than the usual producer-consumer relationship. Sidney was known as a heavy user of the firm's survey services.

"What exactly do you do there, Jason?"

"Beats me. There's more title than substance to the job, from what I've seen so far."

"He does play it cute. I'm surprised Paula Castle bought his bullshit."

"He's a very manipulative fellow."

"Malevolent, too?"

"I'm not sure. He's good-looking—and he can turn on the charm."

"He's a pro, in other words?"

"Definitely."

Adrienne knew for certain what others only suspected about Jason. It made for an unusually personal bond between them.

"How does Gray relate to him?"

Jason smiled. "I think he'd like to make it."

"Maybe I should specialize in dykes."

"After letting Paula Castle get away?"

"She's not?" She said it with half conviction, half reasonable doubt. She was well aware of some homosexuals' tendency to attribute gay qualities to others.

"She shows me a lot of butch."

"I think more bitch than butch."

Jason backed off. On second thought, it was unlikely Paula would have passed up such a ripe prospect as Adrienne if her appetites ran in that direction.

"He's going to have his hands full with her, that's for sure."

"I'll just stay under the basket and wait for the rebound."

Her reference to basketball terminology was no casual allusion. Among her recent account acquisitions were the New York Skyscrapers, known more familiarly as the Skies, a major pro basketball team renowned also for being owned by a striking and tempestuous redhead, Vicki Summers.

Sidney Bastion was not the only player in the field despite his recent self-imagined dominance of the industry. She had also signed Evan Braxton in the past month. Though he might not be the equal of Norman Prescott in terms of power and holdings, he was younger and his potential was enormous. His cable news network was already a threat to the majors, and it was only in its beginning stages.

There had been other additions to her roster as well, but these two represented her prize coups. It was a pleasure to give Jason permission to break the news to Sidney in the guise of privileged information.

"He'll shit," Jason said. "He wants everything himself."

Adrienne studied him over coffee.

"Why don't you come back to work for me?" she questioned. "You're just spinning your wheels with Satellite."

"I really just started there, Ade."

"I could use your expertise now more than ever."

"Let me think about it."

"Take all the time you want—provided I have your decision by nine to-morrow night."

"Women," he muttered, smiling.

"It won't interfere with our little game, either, I promise you."

"I think it's probably what he wanted in the first place."

"You're probably right. That makes it perfect."

"I demand my hours of contemplation as promised."

"Take them," she said. "We need the time to get your office ready anyhow."

The operating director of Satellite Surveys was a man named Adam Wiest, a wispy little fellow with a narrow gray mustache and neatly trimmed goatee. His public air of professorial solemnity was contrasted privately by an elfin manner and a pixie sense of humor.

For his own amusement Wiest had set up among the numerous dummy organizations under the Satellite umbrella one known as the Zweistein Institute ("Einstein times two" was his poker-faced explanation of the name). ZI regularly released such gems of alleged research as: (1) at any given moment of the day 491,873 people are engaged in sexual intercourse in New York City; (2) four out of every ten straight women and six out of ten gay men proficient in oral sex attribute their superior embouchures to the high potassium levels resulting from daily mastication of bananas; and (3) ambidexterity in masturbation is practiced by seven out of ten men and only two out of ten women. The latter statistic he attributed to "the prevalent belief among females that it is best never to let the right hand know what the left hand is doing and vice versa."

Sidney was not always amused by Wiest's skittish humor and its erotic emphasis, but he tolerated it because of its distractive benefits. No one would likely suspect this scholarly eccentric of entering into a pact with him to distort certain findings by his generally respected organization to enhance the stature of Sidney's clients.

The secret was shared only by the two of them. In true conspiratorial fashion, they never discussed any of it except in clandestine meetings on park benches or abandoned river piers. The success of the deception was a source of special pride to Sidney, and he regretted being unable to boast about it.

Jason was much more open in his communications with him, frequently resorting to the telephone to file his reports. But he did go to Sidney personally after his last meeting with Adrienne.

"She just got the Skyscrapers and Evan Braxton," he reported.

"Shit! She can't do a job for either one of them. She's nothing but an item planter."

"She's got 'em all the same."

That it riled Sidney was obvious. Jason enjoyed observing his displeasure. If only he were wired so he could play it back later for Adrienne—inflections, nuances, and all.

"They need broad, all-encompassing campaigns like Castle and Prescott."

"Another victory for cleavage over clout."

Sidney pointed his finger emphatically in his direction. "You've got that right!"

"She offered me my old job back."

"Hey!"

"I told her I had to think about it."

"Abandon all thought. That'll be perfect for us."

"It's kind of short shrift with Satellite."

"No problem. Adam Wiest's a good friend."

"Tell her yes, then?"

"The sooner the better. It's like planting a tooth in the horse's mouth."

Jason smiled wanly.

"A mole in a molar."

"I like that," Sidney said.

32

Whether Sidney believed in inevitability or not did not prevent him from being a victim of it. Zoe Greene had targeted him for eventual conquest from the first time he approached her, an unknown upstart with a press release in hand.

She had been through many men in a long lifetime. Now she was more patient and selective but no less passionate or determined. Sidney was an attractive specimen whose wiliness only made him more appealing to her. She enjoyed entrapping men who thought they could elude her.

Power had corrupted Zoe in some ways. She was so accustomed to it she accepted its side benefits as her righteous legacy. After all, most people sought her, she did not seek them.

Sidney was aware of his special status with her. No one else in his field had more ready access to her valuable column. Had it not been for the presence of Claudia in his life, the showdown undoubtedly would have occurred much sooner. Now his protective barrier—that "bastion for Bastion," as Claudia had once dubbed herself—was no longer in place.

"I'm dining in tonight, Sidney," the familiar voice had announced earlier. "I'd like you to join me."

"Zoe, I . . ."

"No excuses are being accepted. Monsieur Henri Leroux is preparing a special dinner for us and is sending it over at seven. I'll expect you before that for cocktails."

He knew he was cornered. Surrender was the only choice.

"I'm delighted, Zoe. Imagine having you all to myself for a change."

After making the commitment he summoned Pam Garson. She had been Claudia's trusted assistant, and now she handled much of the liaison activity between them. The days of Claudia's casual and constant roaming in and out of his office were over. Pam roamed there now.

"Tell Claudia she wins. I'm having dinner tonight at Zoe's place."

"Just the two of you?"

His nod resembled a wince.

"So Claudia was right all along."

"Maybe she can derive some sadistic delight from her witchery. It's more than I'll get out of it."

"I don't know about that. She's been banking a fire in that furnace for a long time."

"Why me, God?"

Pam laughed at his look of futility. She had assumed Claudia's former function as his sounding board and rather enjoyed the increasing confidence he showed in her, particularly the more intimate insights.

"Order flowers," he said as she was leaving.

"Any preference?"

"Yeah, ragweed."

She lived in a Fifth Avenue duplex overlooking Central Park. It was a lovely apartment, filled with pictures and other mementos of her long career among the rich and famous. She lived alone there except for a live-in maid. By coincidence, this proved to be the maid's day off.

Zoe was small and birdlike, in contrast to her power and influence. She sometimes moved with fluttery gestures, but more often her manner was that of a predator waiting for her prey to make a big mistake. She had the patience of a vulture with the small hovering delicacy of a hummingbird. She was large bird and small bird in one feathery presence, darting and deliberate at times, silent and elusive at others.

She was pretty the way that seashells are pretty—hard and ribbed with delicate colorations, the sound of power like the sea in her very presence. It was this quality of tidal relentlessness that enabled Sidney to respond to her sexual voracity.

In his fantasies Sidney imagined her face buried in the thighs of Paula Castle and himself fulfilling two obligations by fucking her from the rear.

It could never be that erotically simple. Both women were too narcissistic to subscribe to any roles but dominance pure and simple.

"You'll have to pop your own cork," Zoe informed him even before taking his coat.

"I think I can handle that. My, don't we look fetching?"

"Thank you, but what an odd word choice. Sounds more rural than urban."

"It's the Central Park influence. I look across the resplendent beauty of the woods and it makes me think in agrarian terms." He handed her the dozen long-stemmed red and yellow roses provided by his cohort, Pam.

"You surprise me all the time. Yellow for friendship, red for love. I didn't know you could think that way."

"I think in all kinds of ways. That gown of yours—silver lamé, isn't it?"

"By Pauline Trigere. She designed it for me as a gift."

"Fetching." He smiled. "Very fetching."

She laughed as she placed the roses into a crystal vase behind the bar. They framed her smiling face as she turned to him. "Any preference in cocktails?"

He shrugged.

"There's a pitcher of martinis already made."

"Fine with me."

"Olive or twist?"

"A Dickens of a choice."

"For compatability's sake we'll both have lemon."

She poured from the pitcher into each one of a pair of elegant, slender-stemmed glasses, then expertly twisted lemon peel slices over the liquid, rubbed them along the rims of the glasses, then dropped them into the drinks.

"These are gin," she said as she handed one to him. "Vodka is for pretenders."

"I'll have to remember that."

She touched her glass to his. "To your continued and complete success," she toasted.

"Thank you. And to Zoe Greene, a friend for all seasons."

They stood by the windows overlooking the sequined carpet that was the park at dusk.

"Our next toast should be to Frederick Olmsted," Sidney proposed. "I thank him often for this beautiful park."

"Did you play in it as a boy, Sidney?" The question was quite unexpected.

"Rarely," he finally managed to respond. "We lived too far away to make it regularly."

She slipped her arm around his waist. "I loved it as a child, but no more than I do now."

"Would you like another drink?" he asked.

"Of course. It would be a sacrilege to have only one martini."

Dinner arrived as they sipped their second cocktails. They decided to have it served by the windows.

"The city at night is terribly erotic," Zoe said.

She squeezed his hand as they watched the table being set up by Henri's personal sommelier. Henri, whose four-star restaurant bore his surname, had surpassed himself with the special feast that had arrived only moments before. It included an appetizer of lobster, crabmeat, and caviar, followed by an exquisitely tender entree of unborn baby lamb.

"Superb," Sidney declared as he sampled the fifth wine of the evening.

"Henri's a dear," Zoe beamed.

Henri's assistants served them espresso accompanied by a rare Napoleon brandy before Zoe dismissed them. Zoe stood up and rounded the table with her hand outstretched. Sidney rose, took her hand, and followed her to the plush velvet couch in the dimly lit adjoining room. "Dessert will be served in here by me personally, Zoe Flambé," she whispered in his ear.

Sidney was hardly surprised when her hand slipped under his belt to ford through several layers of fabric to the juncture of his thighs. More perfunctorily than passionately, he responded in kind, peeling away the wrappings of lamé and lace packaging her feminine credentials. She writhed as his fingers made contact with the damp petals of her pubes.

"The key to success, Sidney," she informed him in a throaty voice, "lies in the first syllable of the word."

He bent to the task without hesitation, though the semidarkness was a welcome cosmetic. He imagined her in her youth as he darted his tongue randomly over her naked silhouette, settling finally into the nest of her quivering thighs.

"Suck!" she gasped. Her familiar rasp was more pronounced than ever. He buried his face in her, lost to the power of her petite shape and floral scent. With his tongue as a fulcrum he swung his body around until the measure of his manhood hung poised over her open mouth. Only the sound of their heavy breathing intruded on the ensuing stillness.

They lay there in damp silence long after passion was spent. It was Zoe who spoke first.

"You're a bastard, Sidney. I love bastards."

It was not yet over by any means. She fondled him with seeming casualness until he had been coaxed to new solidity. Then she mounted his supine body, hovering over him with fresh enthusiasm.

"This is for all the times you've wanted to tell Zoe Greene to go fuck herself," she jested. "Well, fuck you, too, darling."

Her hard humor in the guise of passion aroused him anew. This sharing of secrets, the freedom of communication, was oddly rewarding for him. She was a woman of importance, and now he knew her as intimately as anyone could. It was an act of ultimate professionalism in his mind.

"I am a bastard," he confessed. "We're both fucking bastards, Zoe."

"Come with me," she demanded.

And he did. And somehow he felt complete, if only for a moment.

BOOK TWO

THE SEVENTIES

33

I n the hurly-burly of it all Sidney Bastion rarely had time to reflect on what had been. The present and future demanded his full attention. Much had changed in the years since he had migrated to Manhattan. He very definitely had changed.

The Bastion organization was thriving, with offices in Beverly Hills as well as Manhattan. Claudia Rogers was now in charge of the California branch. The honored position had been awarded her by Sidney during a dark, tense period folowing a late miscarriage that had deprived Claudia forever of having what had become the most important thing in her life.

She felt unproductive, unnecessary, unloved. She contemplated suicide during a prolonged depression and developed a dependency on tranquilizers. Sidney had concurrently decided to establish a West Coast branch and cajoled her into heading the office there.

At first Claudia had been reluctant to leave the urgency and velocity of New York City life, but she knew a change could help heal her pain. She agreed finally to give L.A. a six-month trial.

U nder the suave coolness Sidney was a carefully engineered by-product of his turbulent youth. Both of his parents had used him as a pawn in their own struggles to succeed individually and as a show business pair. Their alcohol-fueled quest to become country music somebodies had left him with little but his own resourcefulness to depend upon.

"I was weaned on Dr Pepper instead of milk, and I got my nutrition from Cracker Jacks," he recalled to Claudia in a rare moment of candor. "Mom and Dad were always out hustling, always drinking, trying to get the Big Dream Machine going."

"They didn't abuse you, did they?"

Sidney hesitated momentarily.

"Abuse is a broad term. They *neglected* me, which I think is worse. Abuse is something you can react to. How do you cope with being kissed on the cheek and patted on the head, then left alone or with a parade of baby-sitters, never really getting to know your own mother and father?"

"I guess I was luckier than you, Sidney. My mom and dad were always there for me, and they still are."

He turned away for a moment.

"You know what happened to mine. They died together in a car crash, trying to make it to some two-bit gig in a Tennessee roadhouse."

"They were pursuing their dream, Sidney."

"They left me a nightmare."

It had become increasingly clear to Claudia that her latent maternal instincts were clouding her perception of the man she once had thought she loved. Sentiment was sediment to Sidney. It only impeded his progress.

Now as never before Claudia realized she was caught up in his semischizophrenic world of flapdoodle, manufactured biographies, altered statistics, and puddle-deep loyalties. Unlike him, she could not bring herself to continue just skimming surfaces like a flat rock on a stagnant pond.

There was more to life than this. Yet the lure was addictive. She had tried more than once to quit cold turkey, but Sidney, ever the enabler, had always before moved to prevent her withdrawal.

It was now more than a year since she had left. The sun and subdued lifestyle had indeed proved therapeutic. She was off the pills and seemed healed and happy. Those who knew her best now doubted she could ever be lured back permanently to Manhattan.

Pam Garson had worked out well. Claudia had recruited and trained Pam in her own image to assume the role as Sidney's alter ego. In this capacity she had Claudia's blessing—and sympathy. Whatever Pam's relationship with Sidney became, Claudia did not care anymore.

One avenue over from the Manhattan Bastion headquarters, Adrienne Gale,

Inc., had grown and prospered. Sidney and Adrienne continued to compete for accounts, yet both maintained key associations. She still represented Evan Braxton, whose Braxton News Network was now a giant, making Evan more powerful and influential than ever. She also still had the New York Skies with their volatile redheaded owner, Vicki Summers.

By the same token, Sidney continued to create a mythic aura of modesty and generosity around Norman Prescott, and kept Paula Castle looking regal on her imaginary throne. He and Adrienne had even begun a kind of tentative friendship, the outgrowth of her confession that Jason Welles was not his informant but hers.

Sidney's embarrassment was considerable, but Adrienne attributed it all to mischievousness rather than malice. Jason further smoothed things over by claiming it had all been done in fun as a kind of grown-up game. It mattered little that none of them really believed the others. They were all skilled in deception and enjoyed practicing it. Jason, not entirely by coincidence, now headed his own PR firm, benefiting from the overflow of the Basation and Gale agencies.

A major professional loss to Sidney had been the retirement of Zoe Greene. She had moved to Santa Fe, New Mexico, to write her memoirs. Her withdrawal had, however, come as a personal relief. He had grown weary of trying to elude her, though she did continue to haunt him by telephone, complaining lately how much more difficult it was to write books than columns.

"Like agents and producers, Sidney," she lectured him in her increasingly irascible and preachy manner. "You'll never really understand the pain of talent. You know how to use it, how to manipulate it, how to publicize it and further it, perhaps even occasionally how to stimulate it, but you'll never know the abject agony of it."

"Or the ecstasy?"

"Touché. A perfect example of exploiting the talent of someone else." She laughed.

"I love being touched by your wit and wisdom."

"Sidney, you're a dear." She sighed, believing his words of flattery to her were solid truth.

He was hesitant even yet to engage in conversational combat with her. He could get much more out of her by being sweet to her, and thank God she was in New Mexico. Still uncertain of the nature and extent of her relationship with Prescott, he continued to allow her to harass him via long distance. But only a little bit.

"Got to go, Zoe." He smiled. "I'll speak to you soon."

"Take care, Sidney, ta-ta."

There were problems coping with female clients as well, one in particular. Despite his chauvinism, he managed to relate quite well to female employees and could handle himself with considerable facility in most romantic and erotic situations. But being subservient was extremely difficult. This made Paula Castle his most exasperating and ultimately most frustrating and unsatisfying account.

His campaign for the hotels had been centered almost entirely on her. Her wealthy husband, Reese Roberts, was a mere name in the background. It was Paula Castle here, there, and everywhere—uttering bons mots, celebrating the famous, delivering eulogies to departed luminaries, presiding at groundbreakings, cutting opening day ribbons, attending major events with the illustrious, ever and always in the forefront of both local and national social events. There was hardly a person in New York or elsewhere who had not heard of her, verified by any number of polls emanating from Satellite Surveys. Not only was she never satisfied, she was never less than impossible. And to make matters worse, she had lately taken up where Zoe had left off in the carnal energy department.

"I have thousands of beds," she boasted, "and I intend to be fucked in each and every one of them."

Sidney had never intended this stud aspect of life to become intertwined with business, but it had.

"I get calls every day from people wanting to represent me," she sometimes threatened when he faltered or sought escape.

There was a kind of brutal beauty to her, this woman who had outwitted, outfoxed, and outlasted her competition to become not only the wife of Reese Roberts but the reigning monarch of the entire hotel industry. He could relate to her ambition and even be aroused by her achievements.

But the pressure from her was relentless, forcing him at times to neglect less demanding accounts. Making every client seem to be the only one was the essence—the art—of the business. She made certain she was never for a moment ignored or forgotten.

They should all be like Reverend Billy Sunshine. From Sidney's standpoint, he had become positively angelic since the construction of his own university. There was also in his name a resort facility so luxurious it bordered on being sinful.

Billy had become obsessed with the notion that God intended him to enjoy only the finest things in life as a reward for his ministry. Accordingly, he had become an elegantly bejeweled fashion plate surrounded by beautiful young

women he called his "Haloettes." All together they kept the Reverend so occupied he rarely had time to bother Sidney.

Since doing Yankee Stadium revival meetings together, Reverend Billy and
Johnny Gault had become fast friends. It was Billy who first alerted Sidney to
the singer's increasing drug dependence.

"The boy is headed for disaster," Billy warned. "God gave him talent and
success, but he's a jealous God and he can take it all away, too."

"Doc doesn't see things our way, Billy," Sidney responded. "He lines up the
hookers and the peddlers as though they had no bearing on Johnny's career."

"He's evil. He's satanic."

"He owns half of Johnny no matter what."

"Half a corpse won't be worth much."

"Johnny's already a legend, Billy. Legends never die."

"I'm going to pray for him."

Sidney knew when he could be playful with Billy.

"God," he said, "now he's doomed for sure."

34

There were those who said nobody really understood Johnny—that nobody had ever taken the time to understand him, that Johnny had been left to fend for himself and had assembled his own aura via fantasy and imagination through a troubled childhood and adolescence.

It was the kind of creative reconstruction of background in which Sidney Bastion specialized. "Poor, abused kid struggles to success" would be the file category.

In reality, Johnny Gault was more simple than he was complex. It was amazing to Sidney how shyness and taciturnity were so often mistaken for depth and self-contemplation.

"Johnny's deep," some reviewers insisted. "His songs come from an all but unfathomable depth of emotions."

To his credit, Johnny laughed at such analyses.

"I'm as deep as piss on a hard road," he said.

It amused him in his clear-thinking moments that so many people associated success with intelligence.

"Y'don't have t'be smart t'git rich," he declared. "Y'just gotta be lucky and have your ass in the right place at the right time."

The Johnny Gault menagerie was an insular crew. The demands of success forced them into a moated life, cut off from normal human intercourse. Whether they liked one another or not, they were limited to each other in their selection of buddies.

The boredom of the road was manifest. None of the chemistry and excite-ment of concert nights permeated the long miles between engagements. There was pressure to maintain schedules, yes, but otherwise they were just one of the endless mobile caravans crisscrossing America. The potential for being different, for being special, was eliminated by Doc's insistence that, for security reasons, none of their rolling stock be identified. Their very blandness was a form of protection from fans as well as hijackers.

"Think o'all the cunt we're missin' by not advertisin'."

"You got that right, buddy."

They laughed ruefully. The abundance of erotic entertainment was a decided perk in their profession. But it required publicity, not slipping through the coun-try in silent and anonymous caravans.

"Them diner Donnas would spread like eagles if Johnny's name was splashed across the trucks."

"You know it. But they been bullshitted by so many horny truckers they hardly believe anythin' anymore."

"I gotta take this up with Doc," the driver said facetiously. "The man don't realize all the cunt he's costin' us with these blank-sided rigs."

They chuckled at the absurdity of such a request. Doc was somebody none of them messed with. He could be a mean son of a bitch when he chose to be.

Johnny Gault was both a paradigm and paradox. He'd never intended to be either. He was basically a country boy born with the curse of talent.

"I'd rather pump gas sometimes," he said.

The whole climate of adulation had frightened him at first. He'd never really gotten used to it, but it was there and it had to be dealt with.

Doc and Sidney both liked this quality of vulnerability in their main man. It made him pliable so they could both exert their separate and distinct influences upon him.

Johnny could be stubborn in his seemingly passive way, but he was no match for the pressure tactics of his premier professional advisers.

"Shit!" he would scream in rebellion at times. "Shit! Shit! Shit!"

"It! It! It!" Doc would echo, dropping the lead consonants. "You're gittin' richer ev'ry minute."

"I don't wanna git richer," Johnny insisted. "I wanna git happier."

They both tended to hide from him when he was in a mood of disenchant-ment. The very inkling of any serious unrest or introspection was a potential threat to their own existences. Johnny was someone who had to be sold over and over on the wonders of success. What he truly felt, without being able to precisely articulate it, was the enormous loneliness of fame.

"It jist ain't what it seems t'be," he confessed to one interviewer. "Nothin' I have is really mine. I don't even have my privacy like other people."

If he found the aura of acclaim oppressive at times, he also enjoyed its benefits along the way. Most importantly, there was the ready availability of female companionship—two or three per pit stop was the usual count—and when he particularly enjoyed one of the ever-changing cast he took her aboard his bus and "honeymooned her," as he called it, until his passion cooled. Doc referred to these women as "cross-country cunts," and occasionally when one of them lasted too long on board he moved surreptitiously to have her extricated before matters got too serious.

"Put what's between your hips 'tween her lips," he advised Johnny repeatedly. "Don't let any o'these bitches trick yuh into pregnancy."

Potential paternity suits were a constant concern to Doc.

"Make 'em sign releases," Doc instructed the road manager.

That amused the boss of the roadies. "Fuck forms." He laughed.

Doc was not being facetious. Johnny's promiscuity and recklessness were constant concerns to him. True, somebody was almost always with him, but bodyguards had bodies, too, and Johnny could be seductively persuasive when he "heard from the tower"—his pet term for a full-blown hard-on.

Accordingly, the road crew developed a modus operandi to cope with the threat, limiting opportunities of this sort. Johnny was kept busy and sexually sated by paid companions in compliance with Doc's original formula.

When he tired of any one of them there were always fresh substitutions.

It was not all sex and gluttony on the road, either, not all fun and games. There were days and nights when Johnny chose to be alone with his thoughts. It was then that he toyed with the fragments of lyrics and melodies that sprang so spontaneously from his musical mind. His compositions ranged from primitive to surprisingly sophisticated. He was nothing if not versatile; the scope of his creativity was the hallmark of his success.

As his bus roamed the Southwest he entered a writing frenzy, completing an entire album of original songs in a matter of days. No one rode with him then, nor did he emerge from the confines of his home on wheels. Doc called him "the hermit of the highways" during these infrequent but highly productive sieges of activity.

Johnny's manager-partner was kept well-informed by his carefully recruited drivers. They were a full cut above most of the entourage, the stage crew in particular.

"Let him alone" were Doc's emphatic instructions when Johnny needed creative freedom. Doc's core sensitivity might have been decidedly limited, but he was shrewd enough to recognize that genius needed space to function. He knew these erratic binges transformed the bus into a gold mine on wheels.

The desert album—as it came to be known among the clique around him—proved to be a masterpiece. Under the title of *Johnny-Come-Lately*, it soared to number one on the charts in a matter of weeks. It was this album that included only Gault originals orchestrated to his own simple but compelling dimensions.

Its titles alone indicated the versatility of its contents. They veered from ballads to rock to playful punning: "Random Love"; "Put on the Brakes"; "A Blessing in Disguise"; "Riddle-Rattle"; "Mission Accomplished"; "Ragtag Romance"; "Lickety-Split"; "Cross-Country Cowboy"; "So Long Sunshine, Hello Heartache"; "In the Junkyard of My Dreams."

Sexual innuendo was always present, obvious in his words and implicit in the beat of his music. The movement of his body was mesmerizingly metronomic. He was always involved in some form of intercourse as he sang.

"You're an animal," somebody of note had categorized him. He was, in his own way, graceful and erotic like a huge jungle cat, evoking a threat of danger and destruction with the flare of his nostrils and the snarl of his lips.

"This is one helluva complex creature," Sidney once summarized him, his seminal account. "He's a sexual chemist. In no way is he just a media creation. He's a brilliantly creative original, an enormously valid talent, a star of heroic proportions."

He made those comments the same night Johnny was found in a Biloxi, Mississippi, motel in the company of a big-titted fifteen-year-old runaway. Johnny was so stoned he thought he was in Atlanta visiting relatives who didn't exist.

Days later, when he had tentatively regained his balance, Johnny displayed his sly humor by sending Sidney a taped reaction to a recording of his remarks.

In song, with guitar backing, he crooned softly and earnestly: "Have you heard the news? Sidney Bastion's got the Bullshit Blues."

The personalized message went on to declare:

He tells lies from blue skies,
Lost the truth in his youth;
He's slick as a dick
Smooth as gin and vermouth . . .

Sidney loved it and leaked it. What greater tribute to his own public relations prowess than to have the ace of America compose a ditty just for him?

Johnny Gault was not just sugar in the morning and sugar in the evening. He was money in the bank all day long.

Sometimes he sat on the bus in his favorite swivel chair for hours, drinking in the panoramic views of the countryside, sipping Sambuca, turning like a sunflower to catch the solar rays. No one but him knew the depth of his exhaustion, mental and physical.

The hum of the tires on the highway, the shifting drone of his bus as it coped with stops and starts, had become the reassuring sounds of his private, inner life. Like much of the America he excited, he was a mobile creature. The very rootlessness of it all created a hunger and longing for some form of solidity. Johnny translated this quiet anguish into words and music that touched the souls of his believers.

"Smooth times," he sang softly to himself, "storm clouds gather like heaven'ly lather, smooth times . . ."

He liked going nude through the landscape, donning only a jockstrap when it was necessary to be a bit discreet. That was the way he greeted the occasional media people who were successful in arranging en route interviews.

"Hard as a hammer," he sometimes sang to them, especially the females.

This aura of quiet abandon was more than most of the mini-media—as Sidney called the small-town, small-time press—could readily digest and describe. It quite readily overwhelmed them. As a result Johnny's mythic image grew. They tended to describe him as some sort of portable Proteus, a god who could at will be anything he wanted to be.

His frequent, sullen silences intrigued all of them, major as well as minor, only serving to magnify his periods of magnanimity. Johnny could be as warm as his hometown river in July or as cold as the marble in a mausoleum when his mood darkened.

"Great people grate people at times," Sidney had once observed.

By that criterion alone, Johnny Gault had achieved greatness.

*   *   *

If Johnny was a mobile hermit at times, he never lost his playfulness. There was always something mischievous about him, the bottled-up little boy finally exorcising his elementary emotions. Nobody had ever taken the time to understand him. They used him and abused him but never really understood him.

"I'm a loner with a boner," he liked to jest. His boast only betrayed a loneliness that trailed his life.

"Wasted Woman," he sang, and it was immediately interpreted as a lament for his mother, Rita.

The myth of her sometimes threatened to suffocate his own.

"Momma's gonna be the major in the big book in the sky," he sometimes said. "Her John-John's gonna be the minor."

Everything involving her with him had a magical Midas quality to it. The very idea of a son's dedicating his life and career to a mother who was a memory brought tears to the eyes of his fans.

"Good shit," Sidney Bastion called it. "It plays everywhere."

There were always new hits. Johnny was on a roll.

"Cock o'the Walk" was out only five days before hitting the charts.

"Seeds of Surrender" took a day longer to be recognized as a winner.

There was the aura of invincibility about him, and Doc pushed it to the limit.

"Keep producin' while you're hot," he urged Johnny. Stockpiling was part and parcel of his managerial master plan.

"You'll be ninety and still puttin' out winners," Doc assured him. "That'll be fifty years after you're rich and retired."

Security was something unfamiliar to Johnny. He wasn't even sure he liked the idea.

"I jist wanna rock," he said, "and let the bus roll."

35

Sidney's role in Johnny's career was now more functional than creative. With sold-out concerts throughout the world and an imposing collection of gold and platinum hits, Johnny Gault was hardly in need of anyone to beat the drums for him or trumpet his name. The media was there—needed or not—ever ready to add to his deification. Would that all accounts suffered from such a ready abundance of attention.

He had worked wonders as well for Norman Prescott, turning about his so-called sinister image through subtle repetitive recognition of real and imaginary good deeds. The humanitarian emphasis had gradually softened the public's perception of him as a granite ogre. Recent polls, even a few beyond Sidney's control, indicated that despite Prescott's continuing purchases of long-established publications and subsequent large-scale staff dismissals, he was no longer regarded as a ruthless tycoon.

Most effective of all had been an autobiography Sidney had engineered and promoted with every offensive weapon at his command. Titled *I, Etcetera*, it had been carefully constructed, page by page, to glorify the image of Norman Prescott as an independent, forthright, dedicated entrepreneur with a passion for truth and a distaste for corruption and immorality in the world at large. It was skillfully laced with anecdotes and one-liners to keep it light and readable.

Prescott complained of being unable to identify personally with most of it, but his instinctive sense of product marketability induced him to permit its publication. An America hungry for guidelines to wealth and power bought it with gusto. It remained on the respected *New York Times* bestseller list for thirty-seven weeks. That it was a wishful, fanciful portrait of a man who did not truly exist was a private matter between a tycoon, his public relations counselor, and a talented ghostwriter named Sloan Bannister.

Sidney had proved his adaptability and resourcefulness over his first decade as an image maker. As the numbers of newspapers shrank and magazines shifted titles and formats, he had found new outlets in radio and television to offset any losses in contacts, time, or space. Cunning and ingenuity were still the key concepts. And cunning and ingenuity were the hallmarks of Sidney Bastion.

36

S ome people change, others adjust. When Claudia called Sidney and sang an impromptu ditty—"the West Coast is the best coast, the East Coast is the least coast"—he was not absolutely sure which transformation applied to her. She had indeed discovered fresh approaches to business problems in her new locale that had proved difficult if not insurmountable in New York. But he clung to the notion that people became geographically committed somewhere in late adolescence and never lost that dedication.

Whatever, it worked. She seemed to enjoy her break from the relentless stimulation of New York. And also her new autonomy. Sidney's interference was negligible. She spoke to him frequently via the company's WATS line, communication's predecessor to toll-free talk, but he rarely overrode her judgment. Putting the breadth of a nation between them had made it possible for them to cope with each other in a professional rather than personal manner.

"I advised Gray that the only way to put a halt to the innuendos is to get involved in a major romance and wind up getting married," she declared in one of her late-in-the-east, not-so-late-in-the-west night calls. Gray's show was now broadcasting from Los Angeles permanently at his own request, so Claudia had assumed most of the account responsibilities.

"Do you think matchmaking should be one of our subsidiary services?"

"I don't propose to pick his partner."

"But if the sponsors aren't concerned, why should we be?"

"They are. Very. It's come up for discussion at production meetings any number of times."

"With Gray?"

"No."

"He's bright and he's been around. I trust him to know what can and can't be done."

"He hasn't got the most sophisticated audiences in the world. They don't catch on fast, but when they do—forget it. They don't like being deceived."

"Marriage sounds like the ultimate deception to me."

"It would work for his kind of following. It's what the housewives and little old ladies would accept as proof Gray's really the handsome, witty, regular guy he projects."

He had not challenged her in some time.

"He's thirty-seven, Claudia, and never been involved in a serious heterosexual relationship in his life. We've had to manufacture all the romantic interludes in his press biography."

"So why not manufacture the real thing?"

Sidney laughed. "I don't propose to pick his partner," he said, repeating her earlier line.

"By coincidence I've got just the girl for him."

"Is she inflatable and puncture-proof?"

"She's alive and well and living in Los Angeles."

"Jackie Brell?"

"Eastern humor."

"Do I know this mysterious creature willing to sacrifice her sexuality to the gods of fame if not fecundation?"

"Sidney, no number of dictionaries will save you from being from Memphis."

"He's an important client. I'm not trying to be flippant."

"I'm thinking of Eden Langford."

"Eden? Why would she possibly be interested in such an arrangement?"

"She's got her own image problem. She could use the trappings of marriage to help her own career."

"She could get any number of prominent guys."

"Not of Gray's stature."

He paused to think it over.

"It would be a sacrifice in many respects," he said.

"Don't underestimate Gray. I think he can handle both sides of the fence even if he does prefer to graze with the stallions."

"You must have done some homework to come on so positively."

"I ran a few subtle tests. Nobody lunged to dial 911."

"Should we plant some seeds in the columns?"

"I've already done that, boss. I called so you wouldn't be taken by surprise."

"If I had a quarter for every fake romance published in the papers I'd buy out Prescott. I don't believe any of them."

"Believe this one."

"If you say so."

"I say so."

He hung up with a strange feeling of satisfaction. Claudia was going like a guru with a gun permit. It pleased him immensely.

Eden Langford was, to put it mildly, unique. And unorthodox. And uninhibited.

She had managed through dedicated, single-minded concentration on her career to surpass others who might possess more talent or natural beauty. She had succeeded in landing a series of motion picture roles that had gained her recognition as a ferocious femme fatale. It was her ability to lightly mock her own image that had further enhanced her popularity and made her a regular guest on top-ranked talk shows like that hosted by Gray Matthison.

It was during one of her appearances with Gray that the idea of a matchup between them had first occurred to Claudia. They seemed to share a sense of the ridiculous along with a mutual desire for celebrity. Claudia had arranged to meet Eden through Gray, ostensibly to discuss bringing her into the Bastion fold. They had since developed an open friendship, so strong a friendship, in fact, that she had no qualms about suggesting an alliance between Eden and Gray.

Eden's initial reaction was hilarity, but Claudia quickly convinced her that she was serious.

"Claudia, this is Eden Langford you're talking to," she declared with dramatic inflection. "The name Gray is only one consonant away from his sexual orientation. I, on the other hand, am bilingual, bicoastal, and bisexual."

"It'd make great copy and add a new dimension to both your images."

"Gray's sweet—but marry him?"

"Think about it. The more you do the more you'll see it's not really a far-out proposition."

"If I didn't know you better I'd think you were on something."

"I am. I'm on to a great idea."

Claudia persisted in the days that followed, arguing the validity of her proposal in terms of publicity rewards. Gradually, Eden's outright opposition turned to amused skepticism. At Claudia's urging she went out with Gray a few times, hardly a sacrifice since he was an attractive, famous, and witty raconteur. The columns picked up on the twosome immediately, celebrating a new duet with all the usual speculations.

"I may be coming down with acute voyeurism," Eden confessed to Claudia after one of her dates. "I'm actually beginning to dig the idea of watching two guys make it."

"Progress! Lasting marriages have been built on less."

Gray had a history of submitting to any proposition that promised to further his career. Emotion was a commodity he used as needed. He would never permit himself to become its victim.

Public response to their pairing had been strongly positive. On one night when Eden was scheduled to be a guest, the Gray Matthison show achieved its highest viewer share in three seasons. Even she had to be impressed by that.

"If this ever comes off," Eden confided to Claudia after the show, "it won't be a marriage made in heaven but one manufactured in the West Coast offices of Sidney Bastion Associates, Ltd."

"Anybody can have one made in heaven."

Sidney himself flew out at Claudia's request to discuss the situation with Gray.

"She's ideal," he told Gray. "Very marketable." Sidney had met Eden only once.

"We've never really talked about it. Everybody else has, but it's never been broached between us."

"It's not necessary. Not until you're ready with the key question."

"Cue me."

"I've talked to Reverend Billy Sunshine about conducting the ceremony from his cathedral during his weekly TV broadcast. It'd be a first for him and that super audience of his."

An astute student of television ratings, Gray responded with enthusiasm.

"I like it. I like it a lot."

"Billy does, too."

"He's a shrewd programmer."

"He thinks it'd provide him with a novel opportunity to sermonize on marriage."

"I'm not sure I could make it through one of his sermons from start to finish."

"O ye of little faith."

They laughed together, sharing the special luxury of an inside joke.

37

S he's good venison," Johnny liked to say. It was his pet term for a vagina, a throwback to his upbringing. "Ain't nothin' like good dear meat—spell it with an A."

His acolytes caught the wordplay and appreciated it.

"Johnny's goin' for dear meat," they whispered among themselves. They could afford to be generous as well as smug. There was always plenty of that venison left over for the disciples.

For all of them, Johnny in particular, it was an out-of-focus, kaleidoscopic life. Johnny had become unbelievably, insanely reckless at times. His newest gambit with girls was inserting long tapers between their legs and then lighting them.

"When the flame gits to your pussy," he assured them, "I'll put out the fire with my tongue 'n spit."

His willing but wary victims watched with mixed emotions as he masturbated them, crooning "Happy Birthday" all the while, watching and waiting for the flame to threaten their pubic hairs.

At the crucial moment he would go down on them. "Bite the fire!" he would cry out to trigger his passion. Then he would lick out the sputtering flame.

"Him and his random fucks," Doc complained. "He thinks every time he gets a hard-on it's a God-given to have it reduced by sex. His cock almost never dies a natural death."

Johnny's recklessness with his body was matched by his disregard for his reputation. Doc only knew the half of it, and even that was enough to alarm him. It was not enough, however, to inspire his intervention. Doc cared—but only about box office receipts. He left it to Sidney to make it all look good.

Neither Doc nor Sidney really gave a damn about Johnny the human. They were solely concerned with Johnny the star.

In the Gaulter, Johnny's rolling harem, the music was turned low. The ride was so luxurious there was no sense of wheels.

"What's your name?" he asked in the semidarkness.

She was like all the others: beautiful, voluptuous, and intellectually vacant. For now they were the most intimate of acquaintances.

"Vicki."

"I like V names," he said.

"Autograph my belly."

"Come is invisible."

"With a pen and ink." She laughed nervously.

Johnny got up from the bed fully hard and reached into a side cabinet.

"You're special to me," he said. "I want us to make it like we'll both re-member."

"Oh, Johnny, so do I."

She writhed on the bed, her eyes closed tightly in expectation. Quickly and expertly, he injected her with a dose of his favorite cocaine-heroin recipe.

"You're beautiful," he whispered as he repeated the vaccination on himself.

She did not see the gun, the .357 magnum he held against his right buttock.

"I'm going to fuck you," he promised, "but first we're goin' to play a little game."

"Fuck me," she repeated.

"It's called Pussy Roulette."

"Fuck me, Johnny!"

"The odds are all with you, babe. There's only one bullet in the chambers."

"You're crazy, Johnny."

He had already begun masturbating her with the barrel of the gun. Her haunches rose to meet it even as she groaned in protest.

"Tell me when you're going to come," he whispered softly in her ear.

She moved violently against the challenge, her body arcing, momentarily oblivious to the danger.

"Now!" she screamed.

He pulled the trigger, and they both heard the empty click. Johnny was surprised by his own coming at that dramatic moment. It pleased him more than he had anticipated. Getting off was getting more and more difficult.

"Ain't nothin' like a good gun-fuck," he later declared.

If Johnny was an enigma, he was also a quiet rogue. Within his inner circle he could be mischievous and outgoing at times. His road companions did everything they could to amuse him. There were farting contests. There were masturbation competitions in trajectory and accuracy. They counted pubic hairs on selected groupies and allowed quantity winners to kiss the phallic crown of their idol. There were volume pissings as well. Anything and everything to please and amuse Johnny.

"Ev'rybody moon," Johnny would say from time to time.

He was spoiled beyond all imagining, and he was not happy.

The guns that had become so much a part of his life were like toys to him. He liked the firecracker pop of a release and the whine of a bullet. He seemed oblivious to their danger.

"Ain't a dressin' room coast t' coast that ain't got a Gault bullet hole or six ventilatin' it," his road manager attested.

"He's gonna kill somebody one o'these days," a roadie predicted.

"More'n likely himself."

"There goes our pensions."

They laughed at the absurdity of the remark. Their jobs—their very futures—were day-to-day tenuous, subject to the whims of their boss and his manager. The pay was good, but there were no contracts and no guarantees. A dirty look from Johnny was tantamount to termination. He treated them as family but only as long as they did what he wanted.

38

Leo Hatfield's Memphis arcade had for years satisfied Leo's need to be relatively free while making money in the process. But now, after months of frustration trying to set himself up in Nashville as a rock and roll entrepreneur, music publisher, and talent agent, he decided to return to his original role. Nashville seemed ripe for a reincarnation of the Warehouse. He envisioned a hip gathering place for all the renegade rockers and country crooner wanna-bees testing their luck in the city. Above all, Leo loved the riffraff, petty crooks, poachers, strippers, pimps, and con men, the flotsam and jetsam of show business.

Abby Ashley had never been part of the original Memphis Warehouse, so Leo did not include her in his planning for the new one. Instead, for reasons of vanity as much as anything, he decided to keep his office on Music Row and let Abby operate it. That way she would continue to be available to him without getting in his hair. As luck would have it, Leo found a site on the Cumberland River that bore many similarities to his former Memphis locale. It was seedy, it was isolated, it was empty.

"Perfect!" he rejoiced, and he began conducting his usual circumspect negotiations to acquire the property.

"Storage space," he told the realtor, a tall, smiling, blond woman in a beige pantsuit.

The property had been vacant for years, guaranteeing that no interested party would be unduly questioned.

"Perfect." She echoed Leo's assessment from a different perspective and smiled even more broadly.

The deal was struck in a matter of days. When Leo wanted something, he could camouflage his intentions like a chameleon and move as swiftly as a lizard. He mentioned nothing whatsoever about any of it to Abby

With money in hand he was able to quickly find contractors who would do his bidding. Purple hard hat on his head and steel-toed work boots on his feet, he intended to supervise every detail of the reincarnation.

Abby suspected he was up to something, but then so was she. One fox does not question the activities of another fox.

Adaptability had been a key quality in the brief, crowded life of Abby Ashley. She had lit like a butterfly on the tenuous terrain surrounding Leo Hatfield, and she had intended from the start to use it as a runway for a takeoff into some more promising place beyond.

If he was all too often Leo the Letcher, that did not really distract or disturb her. She had dealt with sex almost as long as she could remember. There had always been males, men of all ages as well as boys, seeking to fondle and penetrate her. Her own father, Arlan, had been one of the first.

What mattered most to Abby was forward movement. A powerful thrust toward the future drove her toward some unknown reward by her stubborn pure will alone, and she had never looked back. Leo was the most important person she had ever seduced and sublimated. She had utilized her young flesh like a postadolescent Lolita and enticed the portly, graying Hatfield. The conquest was made.

"You really knew Johnny Gault?" she responded to Leo's casual claim.

"Honey Bunch, I could have cut the umbilical cord."

"He sings so sexy. I just love his music."

"I kin tell ya some juicy stories 'bout him."

Thoughts stirred instantly in her head. She lay back and accepted his hand between her thighs, a forerunner to another firmer and even more resolute appendage.

All through the construction of the new Warehouse she persisted in her questioning of Leo regarding Johnny Gault. There were times he resented it, and other times he was flattered by it. Had he not been preoccupied with building matters he likely would have been more suspicious of her motives. As it was, he attributed her curiosity to youthful idolatry of the boy who was mesmerizing America and much of the Western world.

She knew by now what he was up to but had little interest in his renovation plans. He had inadvertently kindled a creative fire within her that burned more fiercely with each new nugget of information about Johnny.

"You writin' a book or somethin'?" he asked in exasperation one day.

She was momentarily taken aback. Had he somehow surmised her intentions?

"If I get enough good stuff together I might try to sell an article to the *National Inquest* or someplace."

Leo scoffed at the suggestion.

"You never wrote nothin' bigger'n them song poems, have ya?"

"I got a diary big as a dictionary."

"Nobody reads diaries but the fools who write 'em, sugar. You got to be a pro to sell shit big-time. You better stick to what you know best, and plenty of it."

He grabbed her in a sweaty bear hug and planted a wet kiss on her mouth. Then he held her at arm's length and looked into her eyes.

"You know I tell it like it is, Abby. You ain't got the goods to write newspaper articles. Don't go breakin' your heart wishin' for somethin' that ain't never gonna be."

"I appreciate your caring." She smiled at him, but her eyes were blank. "You're right, Leo."

She permitted him to put her down, and even agreed with what he said. It was better than having him suspicious of her real intent. Now, even more resolute, she was on to something bigger than the Warehouse even if Leo could not see beyond it.

39

T here were those who contended that while doctors took the Hippocratic oath upon entering the medical profession, public relations counselors took the oath of hypocrisy. Sidney resented that implication, while Adrienne Gale found it amusing.

"It's a bullshit business," she freely admitted to Vicki Summers. "We are engaged in the manufacture of idols. Therein lies a sacred trust, a noble responsibility to uphold and bolster mankind's belief in those whom fate has chosen to lead and inspire them."

"You're too intelligent for this game, Adrienne. Why don't you do something more constructive with your life?"

"Like buy a basketball team?"

"Bitch. Always getting personal when you're cornered."

They were lying next to one another on the huge expanse of down and white silk that covered Adrienne's bed, nakedly philosophizing, their passions temporarily stilled. It had not taken long in their business relationship to discover an added dimension of compatibility between them.

"The titian titan," Adrienne teased, repeating the sports media's favorite alliteration for Vicki.

"Suck on these," she responded, cupping her breasts. "The titian titan's tits."

They wrestled briefly, playfully. Their passions had been spent earlier. This was simply an interlude in a busy day for both.

"Tell me, T. T.," Adrienne said, resuming her kidding, "are all the organs on those seven-foot protégés of yours proportionate to their height?"

"Why don't you drop into the locker room sometime and check that out for yourself."

"May I?"

"I don't see why not. There are at least three girls covering the Skies, and they go in after every game."

"And you?"

"On occasion. But I don't think it's good policy to interfere with my coaches."

"Vicki! I spend half my time defending you against fan and media charges that you do nothing *but* interfere. You've even been thrown out of games by the officials."

"Just protecting my investment."

An investment inherited through the sudden death of her fifth husband, Adrienne might have elaborated. Vicki Summers was very sensitive about the fact that her spouse had died soon after willing her his favorite possession, the New York Skyscrapers.

"Would you be interested in doing a *Playboy* layout?" Adrienne asked suddenly.

"All the way?"

"I wouldn't let them shoot you, all the way down into your own centerfold, if that's what you mean. It wouldn't be dignified."

Vicki laughed.

"I'll explore it further, then?"

"Why not? But I've got to hurry now. The coaches'll think something's wrong if I'm not there."

"They might get the idea they're actually in charge."

"Bitch."

She slapped Adrienne's derriere. Business and pleasure really could mix, intimately and rewardingly.

Adrienne initiated the contact with Sidney Bastion. An idea had come to her as she sat semisubmerged in the black marble floor tub of her penthouse. The spontaneity of her call was certified by the cocoon of soap bubbles still surrounding her as she spoke.

"Sidney, I don't know if it's your policy to accept telephone calls from naked females but this simply couldn't wait."

"It's an honor and a pleasure to receive a communication from such a lovely lady under any circumstances."

He was taken aback, but his voice remained smooth.

"I won't waste time beating around the bush since we're both in the same racket."

"Profession is the preferred term."

She laughed lightly.

"Delete *racket*, substitute *profession*. At any rate, I was just sitting here in my bath when I got this great idea involving both of us."

"Given the same circumstances I'm sure I could come up with some great ideas involving both of us, too."

"Now, Sidney, let's be professional."

"Always."

"Here's what I have in mind. You represent Norman Prescott, I represent Evan Braxton. They're both prominent media hotshots, though my man is admittedly something of an upstart compared to yours. However, that's neither here nor there in this case. What matters is they're both good copy. In fact, Evan's expanding his cable network to Europe and Asia very shortly . . ."

"Are you still naked?"

"Constant professionalism, remember?"

"Of course. I simply like to keep an extremely accurate log of all business discussions."

"Now, where was I before being so lewdly interrupted?"

"You were plugging your boy Braxton."

"I'm very serious about this. I propose we engage Evan and Norman in a kind of running war with one trying to take over the other. By controlling both ends of the wheeling and dealing we could get front-page play at first and continuing heavy coverage on the financial pages for months. Plus some likely in-depth profiles of our clients."

"I like it but with two reservations. Norman would have to be the takeover target, because he wouldn't abide being the loser in any such setup. Number two, nothing derogatory could be said at any time about him or his operations."

"We'll be in complete control, Sidney, so nothing like that could happen. That's what's so beautiful about it."

"I think we need to discuss it in more intimate detail."

"Your tub or mine?"

The tease worked its magic on Sidney. Adrienne herself was as enticing as her business proposal.

40

T he wedding of Eden Langford and Gray Matthison was going so beautifully that even Sidney couldn't resist pondering who else in his stable might in some way benefit from the joys of matrimony.

"Nice touch," Claudia whispered in his ear toward the end of the ceremony as the Haloettes, all three hundred of them, sang a final blessing. As bell ringers chimed out the last notes of the service, the bride, the groom, and the Reverend Billy Sunshine slowly rose into the air as the entire altar was elevated two full body-lengths.

"I present now, for the first time, to you here in this beautiful chapel, and to the outside world joining us in this celebration, Mr. and Mrs. Gray Matthison."

The organ music swelled as stairs rose out of the floor to meet the front of the altar where Gray and Eden, holding hands and smiling, waited to make their descent.

"I checked the wedding cake earlier," Claudia said quietly, less afraid of being overheard now that the formal part of the ceremony was over. "Only one bride and groom on top. Looked kind of lonely up there."

"You see," Sidney replied, "they're really just another traditional couple interested in traditional values."

"Any regrets over not accepting as best man?"

Sidney shook his head. "It would have given away the whole scheme, especially with you as maid of honor."

"Nice of them to ask, though," Claudia smiled as she watched Gray and Eden take the first step down.

"Sure was," Sidney agreed, playing along with her. "They make a beautiful believable couple."

Believability was most important to a man on his mission.

It had been a television drama, really. A piece of visual fiction about as real and substantial as a mirage.

A dozen bubble machines were strategically placed about the Sunshine Cathedral auditorium. The floating bubbles they produced added to the soap-opera effect of this illusory extravaganza. It was as transparent as the bursting bubbles, and glowing and enduring as a rainbow.

"There's no such thing as true bisexuality," Eden had confided to one of her bridesmaids shortly before the ceremony. "The homosexual side prevails in those situations always. It's the overwhelmingly dominant factor"

"Then, what is there in this for you?"

"Prestige and publicity," the bride to be smiled ruefully, "It's a career move— a starring role on the big stage."

Her bridesmaid took her hand and gently kissed her on the cheek. "Break a leg, then," she said.

"Thanks. No cherries will be broken, I guarantee you."

They giggled like schoolgirls at that.

Claudia called Sidney the next morning.

"Sidney," she said ominously, "I've just gotten an advance copy of *Revelation* It features a real rip on Gray and Eden."

"Shit! You mean the honeymoon's over already?"

"I knew you'd be happy. Want me to read it to you?"

"Highlights only." He sighed.

"Here's the over-the-masthead streamer: MARRIAGE AS MIRAGE: THE UNLIKELY UNION OF GRAY MATTHISON AND EDEN LANGFORD."

"Bad enough. What about the story?"

"Ugly, awful, very detailed. Can you get Prescott to pull it?"

Another sigh came out more like a groan.

"You're asking a load, Claudia. He's always claiming no interference with his editors."

"You know that's bullshit."

"I know it, you know it, but he's a weird guy. I could blow the account going to him with this and then wind up with the story still in my lap."

"Damn it! It was going so beautifully."

"Look, I'll take a two-martini brain rinse and get back to you."

If Norman Prescott was formidable to deal with as a client, he was foreboding to approach as a good Samaritan. It was not his nature to be helpful or compassionate. Sidney decided the lone alternative was to appeal to his bargaining instincts.

"I need to have that story killed, Norman," he explained urgently after briefly outlining his case. "I'll make sure Gray makes it up to you."

"You never read my book, did you? I don't meddle in editorial affairs, Sidney."

"You also said you don't abide by rules. That means you could break one of your own."

Prescott looked at him with cold amusement.

"What can Matthison do for me?"

"He hosts the top-rated talk show in the country. I'll get him to do back-to-back exclusives on you. Not even the President has ever had that."

"Do you have any idea of the production costs involved in recalling that issue? Millions, Sidney, millions."

"You couldn't buy a hundred and eighty minutes of the Matthison show for twenty million, Norman."

"I'll see what I can do," Prescott said finally.

41

S idney had agreed, reluctantly at first and then with a mounting sense of self-importance, to address a seminar on public relations at Billy Sunshine University. The school of journalism there had been among the first in the nation to offer a bachelor's degree in the subject. That neither the school nor the major were yet accredited by any of the reputable college-evaluating associations did not deter Reverend Billy from hailing it as "the premier prototype for all PR education in America."

Billy Sunshine University had grown and prospered almost magically in its brief existence due mainly to Billy's recruiting zeal and his constant hyping of its campus and curriculum on his weekly television show. He had paid particular attention to luring top athletes, giving the school a kind of instant credibility through sports achievements.

Rumors of payoffs and illegal subsidies were rampant, but he and Sidney countered these by hiring renowned researchers and learned academics for the faculty and citing a variety of scholastic achievements.

Satellite Surveys had, in fact, determined that BSU was "among the ten most respected universities" in the United States. Quite an achievement for a school not yet half a decade old, Sidney slyly noted in his congratulatory message.

In such an atmosphere of artifice it was no wonder Sidney felt right at home.

"Careful, cohesive character construction," he alliterated before the student group. "That is at the heart of personal public relations. For it is a business not only of ideas but also of illusions, not only of facts but also of fancies. The blending of these is the essence of the art . . ."

Mumbo jumbo, then back to other favorite themes.

"The essential function of PR is to manipulate the public perception of the truth . . . All words, even obscenities, can be reduced to liquid and made to flow evenly . . . Deal in quick, arresting, impressive flashes. Depth is no longer necessary—no one has time for it anymore . . ."

The students present were impressed by the suave, self-assured man who addressed them so earnestly. Sidney was in his glory masquerading as an educator and philosopher.

". . . The vast majority of people lead vicarious lives. It is up to you as public relations professionals to provide them with role models with whom they can imaginatively share their existences . . ."

In the question-and-answer period that followed his talk, Sidney demonstrated the art of elusiveness.

"There is no law that says all questions must have answers," he declared. "Dare to ask and be asked, but don't feel obligated to provide a substantive response in every case."

He might have remained on the speaker's platform indefinitely had there not been a university-imposed time limit to such seminars. Even after it was over he still felt a rush from the realization of his own professional stature.

Only recently the disc jockey Jimmy Jay, who had been among the first to promote Johnny Gault, had approached him familiarly and recalled: "You were just a cub reporter with a wad o'newsprint and a stubby pencil in your hands back then and now, gawdamit, look at ya—a counselor to kings!"

I am indeed, Sidney thought to himself.

As he made his way across the campus to his waiting limo he felt all at once inordinately good about it all.

42

J ohnny was giddy and naked as a jaybird. High as a buzz bomb as well. It was playtime, but not in his bus or the presidential suite of some metropolitan hotel. He was in the midst of recording. The place was a studio.

"Mood." Johnny laughed, explaining to no one in particular, "Nude mood."

He ran about in antic fashion, his guitar strung from his neck, his balls bouncing gaily under the instrument, his cock hidden momentarily by the anatomy of the box.

The juvenile abandon that struck him periodically was there again. Most of his band was into it; the few who were not faked enthusiasm and participated. Johnny appreciated a communal spirit.

"Ev'rybody balls naked!" he directed. "We're gonna do this like babies. Jist shit 'n piss when y'want."

He was energized by the silliness of it all, the defiance of convention, and encouraged by the relative privacy. Nobody outside the organization knew they had gathered in such a remote studio midway between nowhere and Pittsburgh— far from Nashville or New York. Money induced even the best talent to comply. The label credit was still a factor in the Scene. Being part of a Gault album had its own special cachet, its own currency in the business.

"Bare-ass them engineers," Johnny demanded early in the session.

There were some protests and some reluctance, but eventually everybody complied. Not a stitch of clothing hung from anyone as they did *Raw Love*, the album that inspired a rare personal denunciation from the Pope himself.

"My ass is fried now," Johnny said, reacting to the news with a trademark wink. "I been god-damned by the god-blesser. Whoooie!"

His words had begun to reflect his mounting loss of control. He had agreed to having his naked derriere the featured attraction on the album's cover.

"Now that's real nice moonshine," he said of the controversial photo, alluding to his father's old occupation.

The whole mix of sweet boy image, bad momma, old hierarchy condemnation, and a resounding and relentless beat sent sales soaring.

"He's one helluva sly promoter," Sidney had to admit. "He does it all wrong and makes it turn out right."

"He's a master masturbator of the public," Pam Garson agreed. "I don't even think he does it consciously."

Sidney smirked at that.

"How could he? He's unconscious seventy-five percent of the time."

Raw Love, with its implications of sexual abandon and revenge, took the charts and ate them to the top.

"Naked theft," declared a leading trade magazine. "Rabelaisian raunch pumped up by big-time PR. Where's the quality control?"

Sidney had surreptitiously planted the rumors of wild nudity and ribaldry surrounding the sessions, then denied loftily that any such activities had occurred. It was what he liked to call his Ping-Pong theory of publicity.

Within the steel cocoon of his bus only hours later, inside the sanctuary of his mobile bedroom, Johnny Gault lay stoned and praying to God and the memory of his mother, mumbling into his stew of vomit and tears.

"Peggy Sue, where are you?" he muttered.

No one answered that question anymore.

43

Claudia was not in her office. She might be at her Malibu beach house, her secretary thought, but she could not be sure. And there was no simple way of checking. She had disconnected her beach telephone months before to insure privacy and serenity, the girl reported.

"Privacy and serenity?" Sidney echoed aloud. "Since when are they part of the PR business?"

He took down the directions just in case she was not at her hotel apartment. As it turned out, she was not.

"She's at her beach house in Malibu," the concierge confirmed.

This was hardly the Claudia he had known in New York or even in the early stages of her California conversion. She had always been more job obsessed than anyone he had ever encountered in the business. Taking time off in the middle of a work week seemed out of character.

"Let's go," he instructed his chauffeur.

They had some difficulty locating the place. Very few houses were clearly identified. It was a necessary precaution with so many celebrity residents. When the driver finally did find it, he waited in the car while Sidney proceeded.

There was no bell, only a brass door knocker, which Sidney clacked several times. A lithe blond youth with a butterscotch tan responded. His bikini trunks were so abbreviated Sidney caught himself staring.

"Yeah?"

"Is there a Claudia Rogers here?"

"Who're you?"

"Sidney Bastion."

There was a sudden flash of a smile.

"Hey, man, the boss. Come on in."

Sidney followed him down a short stretch of corridor that abruptly opened into an expanse of casual furniture and floor-to-ceiling windows overlooking the ocean.

"Hey, Claude!" the boy called out. "Surprise! The boss is here!"

Her unmistakable blond mop rose over the horizon of a sofa, followed by another blond head remarkably similar to that of the young man next to Sidney.

"Sidney!" she exclaimed. "I should've known you'd track me down."

"I was surprised not to find you at the office."

She threw her head back and laughed.

"I've been Californianized, haven't you noticed? These are two friends of mine, Keith Laser and Drake Evans. Fellas, this is the big, bad boss from the East, Sidney Bastion."

They both nodded—rather shyly, Sidney thought, in light of their minimal wardrobes.

"You guys could pass for twins," Sidney said.

"They say all surfers look alike," Keith replied.

After a few more awkward moments Claudia's companions excused themselves and left. She slid down onto one of the many lounges and postured seductively in her white bikini.

"Let's hear what you don't like about the new me," she said.

"I didn't know there was a new you—just the old you acting ridiculous."

"You always called me a consummate professional. Why can't I be a consummate Californian, too?"

"Those two kids are twenty years younger than you."

"I know. Isn't it marvelous?"

He stared vacantly at the breaking surf.

"You know that Gray and Eden are due back tomorrow?"

"I haven't taken leave of my senses, Sidney. Only my clothes."

His eyes roamed.

"How long've you had this place?"

"Three, maybe four months. I'm leasing it."

"A playpen for you and your beach boys?"

She laughed as she poured a drink from a plastic pitcher.

"Consider it my alternative way of having children," she replied. "Care for a drink? It's pure vodka disguised as martinis."

"I have a car waiting."

She shrugged.

"You should relax more. It does wonders for your libido."

"My libido doesn't need any therapy."

She stretched out like a cat in the sun. In New York she'd been like a rattlesnake coiled and set to strike. It was difficult for Sidney to comprehend the change.

"As they say on the Strip, when it comes to lovemaking two heads are definitely better than one."

He bit his lip.

"I'll call you tomorrow before my flight."

"How did the lecture go?"

"I survived."

She smiled faintly.

"One thing you are for sure is a survivor."

As he picked a path over the wooden walkways moments later, he did not look back. This was a side of Claudia he wished he'd never seen.

44

eo's heavy cash investment in his new club called for an equally sizable investment of his time to oversee the operation. There was a new array of fresh bodies to seduce, and the music of the cash registers once again intrigued him more than the hits in the jukeboxes.

The change in his attitude—or rather the return to the original—played perfectly into Abby's evolving scheme of things. His lessening attention to her enabled her to more freely pursue a growing obsession. He had instantly agreed to her request for an assistant; he had even cosigned her loan to purchase a used Mercedes coupe. She knew when and how to approach him.

Abby chose a girl who was as awestruck as she had once been. Her name was Brie Davis—"Like the cheese," she said, "but you can call me Breezy."

She seemed to be a noncompetitive type who had reached her goal of being on Music Row and did not seek to go further. She fit perfectly into Abby's developing deception.

Leo, as expected, took an intimate interest in her.

"I don't know, honey," Brie said to him one day, "but it sure is lonely 'round here."

Abby was forgotten for the time being, as she deepened her forays into the past of Johnny Gault.

Although Leo Hatfield's new clientele was more diverse and eclectic than the clientele in Memphis had been, this reincarnation of the Warehouse in a different city on a different river bore enough resemblance to the original to make Leo feel he had never left home.

There was still the dim atmosphere with puddles of light illuminating the pool tables and kaleidoscopic flashes emanating from banks of game machines and jukeboxes, all juxtaposed with endless mirrors. Enough sound emerged from this potpourri to fill a canyon, and shouting was required to conduct conversation.

The new Warehouse, like the old, attracted bikers—the bearded and tattooed stereotypes in their boots and leather jackets. But studded among them now were more and more fashionably costumed denizens of Music Row along with collegians from Fisk and Vanderbilt Universities. Leo slithered among them in his reptilian fashion, wheeling and dealing Memphis-style in the heart of Nashville. He gave his patrons what they wanted, and if he didn't have it on hand he got it for them.

"The Warehouse is where it's at," he said, continuing his old pitch. "If you can't git it here, you can't git it nowhere."

That applied to just about anything. Drugs. Booze. Sex. Guns. Gambling. You name it. The back rooms could get very busy at times handling all the action. Discreetly, of course. Leo's momma had not raised a fool, he liked to say.

All this made dealing with Abby Ashley all the more exasperating. It had become all but impossible to keep track of her. Performers had itineraries, but Abby was all over the place, moving to her own mysterious rhythms. She no longer contacted him with any regularity and was prone to hanging up on him when he questioned her.

"You've turned into a slipp'ry son of a bitch," he accused her, "talkin' in goddamn riddles."

"I'm on a search for truth. You have to have faith."

"My faith is in my cash register. You understand that?"

"Have to run. 'Bye."

She hung up before he could react.

"Cunt!" he spat into the dead receiver.

More than ever he was beginning to think Abby was short for Abracadabra and that he was the one she intended to make vanish.

45

J ohnny Gault's celebration of the memory of his mother was as complex as it was cathartic. It had been a brief and troubled relationship between them, loving in a sick and tortured way, quietly desperate for both of them. With his own success, he sought now to somehow rectify the wrongs and establish in retrospect what had not existed in reality: the myth of saintly motherhood. Whether he realized it or not, he did it as much for himself as for her.

"My momma was Madonna," he said often without elaboration.

His emphasis upon her evoked cultish reactions among his already mesmerized fans. She was the mother of a god, and his obvious devotion to her crystallized her image and sanctified her life.

They loved him as Johnny-good-boy, especially his female following, and they adored his bad boy side as well. Here was a momma's boy they could take to bed and rape without guilt and without momma. It was all too sweet and unlikely to believe, but believe it they did.

Rita Gault might very well be in the river feeding the fish, as the locals contended, but Johnny had his own vision, his own high beams searching down a darkened highway. He wanted a mom, even if he had to manufacture her from the fragments of a troubled childhood. Otherwise there was nothing for him but the glare of the strobes on an empty existence. He had learned early on that adulation did not compensate for interior isolation.

"People don't realize that after y'reach the top you go all the way 'round and you're back on the bottom. Only diff'rence is your cash balance."

*   *   *

It was on one of his tour dates in the Midwest that Johnny saw a sculpture in a shopping mall that arrested his attention. The alabaster symmetry of it appealed to his plebian artistic tastes. Squatting there in the midst of a shallow pool, surrounded by coins, it projected a cheap elegance attractive to his country eyes.

"I want whoever did that t'do Mom," he said with a fervor that made his roadies relay the message.

Sidney heard the cry. He had his sources within the organization.

"Johnny, babe," he said when he called him in Saint Louis a few days later, "I've got Milo Staretti working on a statue of Momma."

"He did that mall?"

"This is a major artist, Johnny. He doesn't do malls."

Johnny was his usual fuzzy self.

"Mamma's gotta be done nice—the best."

"Your momma's gonna look like the mother of God," Sidney promised.

Sidney had not lost the capacity to become excited, and he saw in all this a fresh and unique challenge. Johnny would establish shrines to motherhood built around the idealized image of his own mother.

Doc Diamond loved the concept. He saw profit in every aspect.

Staretti did a job worthy of Michelangelo. The statue was Venus-like, enhanced by lovely arms and extraordinarily expressive hands.

"She's a beaut," Doc acknowledged. "The copies'll sell like hell."

Johnny was overcome by this idealization of his mother.

"My momma was the best and prettiest woman who ever lived," he declared through his tears.

They decided on gazebos as housing for the Rita Gault memorials. They were friendly, open-air structures, accessible and yet respectful.

It was amazing how quickly the public responded. The pilot project was naturally in the Memphis area not far from the site of Gaultland.

Sidney arranged for a coalition of rabbis, priests, and ministers to participate in the dedication. Billy Sunshine flew in from California to lead the quasi-canonization of this woman who had given birth to an immortal messiah of music.

Johnny sang a song he himself had written for the occasion. In a hushed and haunting voice that brought tears to the eyes of many, he delivered his "Prelude to a Prayer."

The son Rita Gault had both cherished and molested had washed her clean and in so doing ennobled her beyond her capacity to dream.

Gault gazebo franchises began at two hundred thousand dollars without the land. The design, by renowned architect Gabor Kosinski, was stark white like the centerpiece statue. Purity of person was the message no matter what else was conveyed by the carnivalistic huckster activity surrounding most of the shrines. Imitation ivory cameos of Rita, so soft and gentle in silhouette, were among the sales items available to franchisees.

Johnny was uncommonly moved by the response to the memory of his mother. His own myth had begun to merge with hers, and Sidney, his tireless advocate, blended them with consummate skill. Mother-and-son ideology sold well in America.

The franchises moved like Gault records. At the dedication of a new gazebo shrine in Ames, Iowa, Johnny put it all in perspective.

"Without her," he said solemnly, "I wouldn't even be here. I never would've sung a song or plucked one string of a guitar. My momma was a very special lady, and I don't want nobody ever t'fergit it."

They wept as he sang, and later the cameos sold like hell.

Wounded eyes, seein' the lies, laughin' on empty, losin' the prize . . ."

Johnny was relentless in his output, and his fans were voracious. Doc kept him studiobound for days at a time. He knew how to milk a cash cow and store the milk.

During these intense periods of production, Johnny welcomed the close-knit camaraderie of musicians and engineers. They were not only the nucleus of his success, they were his only, however tentative, friends.

"The shit is solid here," Razor Blade declared, licking the reed of his sax with lascivious delight. "Let's go for the gonads."

"Balls, baby," Johnny responded.

Razor blew such a lyrical, unbelievably original accompaniment that Johnny turned around and gave him a military-style salute in appreciation. To his credit, Johnny was one of the few stars to recognize the legion of overlooked talent involved in his success.

Doc was there, as always.

"He's one slippr'y son of a bitch," Razor observed during the session. "But the cat cuts the dough and bakes the cookies."

"Ask me no questions," Johnny sang, his sensually lidded eyes all but closed. "I'll tell you no lies, I got no answers why love flames and dies . . . "

It hardly mattered that Doc read no books and skipped the editorial pages of the few papers he scanned. He knew instinctively when Johnny was on the mark.

"Money in the bank" was his pet comment of congratulation after a productive session.

No one knew or likely would ever know if Doc felt anything but cash flow in his veins. He never showed any discernible response, positive or negative, to the power or poignancy of Johnny's words and music.

"He's a stagnant successpool," Sidney had once commented.

The brief, transcendent memory of Peggy Sue, with her promise of something approaching cottage-and-picket-fence normalcy in Johnny's life, was eroding steadily under the incessant glare of strobe lights and the relentless demands of fame.

Doc and Sidney had won another one. Ironically, they were convinced they had done it for Johnny.

Inevitably, Hollywood pursued Johnny Gault. After all, he met all the criteria for success in films. He was uniquely handsome, a popular icon, a viril presence, and an established marquee name.

"Get the Kid" was the message among the Beverly Hills movers and shakers.

Somehow, Johnny's compelling stage presence refused to translate to the screen. He was as wooden as a marionette in a string of contrived cinematic romances, embarrassing as a leading man and a disaster as an actor.

Johnny was too simple of heart to be frustrated easily, but Hollywood haunted him.

"I don't like this shit," he complained to Doc. "I'm better at playin' Johnny Gault than playin' the lame fuckin' parts they write for me. Besides, the broads are great, but they don't put out that easy."

His groupies had spoiled him forever. He'd never had to face the fact that he did not know how to talk to a woman who was not a whore.

The critical reviews of his films were devastating, but neither Johnny nor Doc ever read them, and Sidney never told them.

The movies more than cleared seven times their cost domestically and made millions overseas on the strength of Johnny's name alone. It did not matter that they were bad.

Even Doc Diamond thought, however, it was obvious that Johnny was better off performing live.

"They gotta feel ya and smell ya," Doc said.

Nobody knew the formula better than Doc. After all, he'd invented it.

46

The honeymoon was over in more ways than one. Gray and Eden would be allowed no peace. They were like royalty, forever damned to scrutiny.

What Sidney had managed to suppress in one publication by making a bargain with the devil inevitably found its way into another. Yet the obligation to Norman Prescott remained. It might even have been increased by a rival newsweekly's scooping the story.

"You've got to emphasize to Gray that the *Inquest* piece would've been out weeks earlier if Norman hadn't pulled the story from *Revelation*," he told Claudia over the phone. "I want his gratitude to Prescott guaranteed."

"Man from East talk big bamboozle," she jested. "California Claudia not sure can do."

Juvenile prattle invariably annoyed him, but he had no desire to antagonize her under the circumstances.

"After the job you did on their return from Tahiti, he should be ready to kiss your kazoo in Giorgio's window."

"No thanks. Just because Eden survived doesn't mean there won't be a casualty next time."

"Get Jason on it, too. He has a lot of influence over Gray."

"That he does. I'll fill you in when Eden gets through with her confessions."

"I don't think the *Inquest* story will have the impact the *Revelation* one would have had earlier. The public's had it with weddings and funerals for the time being. We got the saturation, the rest is just mop-up stuff."

"Excellent rationalizing, Sir Boss."

"Where does that shit come from?"

"That's what my boys call you."

He chose not to acknowledge that.

Adrienne made no effort to hide her anger.

"That son of a bitch of yours really *is* trying to take over Braxton. It took a little time to track the stock shifts, but they're definitely Prescott maneuvers. What a cheap double cross, Sidney!"

"Adrienne, it's without my knowledge, believe me. Norman doesn't consult me on his business manipulations."

"You had to know he was up to something. Why else has he stayed so passive during all the media byplay?"

"May I remind you this little game was initiated at your request?"

"As a game, remember that. But he's playing for keeps."

"Braxton's a big boy. I'm sure he can handle himself."

"Prescott's an even bigger boy and a bully besides."

"This is really outside our function, don't you think? We're not business advisers."

"I don't want to get into any pompous philosophies on what constitutes functions. Evan went along with this for its publicity value and potential stock stimulation, not to wind up fighting for his life."

"It may still be all hearsay. So far I only have you verifying it."

"And I only have you to tell that it's yet another example of what a cold, calculating bastard Prescott really is."

Sidney laughed hollowly.

"May I be the first to inform you that I've just received verification that Billy Sunshine University will imminently bestow its first honorary degree— Doctor of Divine Benevolence—on that very same Norman Ford Prescott?"

There was a moment of telling silence.

"I've got to get out of this business," she said finally, "before I suffocate in the sleaze."

"Adrienne," he began, but she had hung up on him.

Paula called him from the tower suite of her Castle-on-the-Hudson. She always sought maximum height when she was indignant. She imagined drawing herself up to the maximum height had a deifying effect, and in truth she only seemed slightly taller. She prowled with great pomp as she spat out the latest cause of her discontent.

"I'm incensed over the changes in Pierce Agee's play," she declared to Sidney. "What right has he got to tamper with words after I put my money on a different version?"

"Poetic license," he replied.

"I'll have his goddamned poetic license revoked! Nobody goes around playing with my life."

"He's trying to sharpen your image, I imagine."

"My image is sharp enough now to cut his throat."

"Paula, my dear, this is a coup! People die to be dramatized by someone of Pierce's stature. Trust me, you'll be the talk of America."

"Or the laughingstock."

"Is that what you're scared of?"

"Yes."

Her honesty surprised him. The word had come out in a plaintive cry. She took a few deep breaths and continued.

"I couldn't stand to be laughed at, Sidney!"

"Oh, darling, don't be silly," he quickly responded. "Nobody laughs at Paula Castle. They'll laugh with you, you beautiful goddess, all the way to glory."

"Thanks," she cooed softly. "I needed that."

"Anytime." He smiled, feeling as if flattery could get him anywhere. "Calm down and enjoy!"

"I'll try."

"Do it! That's an order from someone who cares. Now, I've got to attend to some real business We'll speak soon."

"Don't toy with me, Sidney."

"You're magnifying it all out of proportion."

"Like I do your penis?"

His laugh was perfunctory.

"Paula Castle and Pierce Agee are on the same wavelength. Believe me."

Despite her seeming hostility, Sidney sensed that Paula Castle was secretly flattered by all the indirect attention that talk of the play had generated for her. Although she had not been actually mentioned by name, all the allusions to her were so graphic her identity could hardly be mistaken.

"I'd wait to see and hear for myself before getting too excited, Paula. Pierce is not a cheap-shot artist."

"He's not William Shakespeare, either. He's in the business to make a buck."

"So was Willie."

It was hardly surprising she had learned of alterations in the play. Paula was not one to leave matters to chance, particularly when her money and reputation were involved.

Sidney learned later that she had enlisted one of the minor actors in the play as a confidential informant on the promise of employing him as a maître d' whenever he was between thespian assignments. He had called her about the changes during a tryout run in New Haven.

"They strengthen the play, but they might hurt your public image," the actor had told her.

"Words can't wound me."

"Maybe not ordinary words, Paula, but these are Pierce Agee words. They slash deep."

Her call to Sidney had come later, after a purloined, photostatted copy of the still-evolving script was smuggled to her. It had proved to be so marked up and technically confusing that she could not grasp it fully, nor did she possess the theatrical imagination to envision it in performance.

"Listen to this," she said dramatically, waving pages of the script. "One of the characters says 'They don't make tires that could handle the mileage on her uterus,' and somebody responds with 'it'd be a good year for Goodyear if they could get her formula.'"

"It's a work in progress, Paula. Writers play with lines. It doesn't mean they're in for good."

"I think they play with themselves."

Sidney sighed wearily.

"I'm sure there's an element of mental masturbation involved. It's part of the creative process."

"I don't intend to be some faggot's fantasy of a female ogre."

"I'll talk to Pierce."

"Get right on it, Sidney. Get it all straightened out."

A glance at the clock revealed it was after three A.M. It was not the first time he had felt like an emergency room surgeon called upon to operate at an ungodly hour. The difference was a surgeon could look forward to the final suture. For Sidney, there was no closing the case.

bby had surreptitiously tape-recorded her early conversations with Leo regarding Johnny Gault. Leo was, of course, unaware of it, just as he was
unaware of her real goal. It had been an ego trip for him and a gold mine
for her. Unaccustomed as he was to such tenacity and aggressiveness from what
he called "a slip of a girl," she cleverly balanced her inquisitions with a discreet
mix of sex and flattery.

"I can't believe I know somebody who knew Johnny Gault when he was just
a little boy," she had told him with just the proper touch of awe. She could be
marvelously deceptive when she chose to be. Now, with Breezy to cover for her
and Leo absorbed by his new business, she set out in earnest to construct the
foundation of a book. The seduction and sapping of Leo had been easy compared
to the task ahead.

In the same manner that she had learned the basic techniques of songwrit-
ing—by going to a library and studying a how-to manual—she had gone to a
bookstore and brought a volume titled *The Art of Biography*. It was much more
serious-minded than her intent, but it did spell out certain elements of the process
unfamiliar to her. She had never been a particularly good student in high school,
but given her motivation now she had become positively possessed.

It had been Leo's revelation that Johnny's father was alive and in prison—
contrary to the generally accepted Bastion biography—that had really jump-
started Abby's zealotry. All at once she realized more primary sources existed,

that living people could supply her with inside information that went far beyond Leo's somewhat limited recollections and jealous prejudices.

The guidebook, the bible of her new adventure as a biographer, emphasized the importance of original sources. She ran up Leo's phone bills shamelessly in scattered attempts to make contact with as many of them as she could.

"You really work the walkie-talkie," Brie observed good-naturedly early on in her role as Abby's assistant.

"All business, Breezy," Abby assured her.

The girl smiled. "Buzz me if y'need me."

"Will do."

It was not easy to restrain her excitement over locating Clifford Gault in a Tennessee state penitentiary. A call there had gained her permission to talk as a journalist to the senior Gault, provided he was willing.

For a man who'd had only two visits before, Clifford Gault was remarkably restrained about the arrival one Saturday of a woman listed on the clearance roster as Abby Ashley. He had received some correspondence from her but had left it all unanswered.

"I'm a friend of Leo Hatfield," she had written.

"Somethin's fishy if Leo Hatfield's involved," he said to himself. "Where's that sombitch been since I got railroaded?"

She had only used Leo's name to gain entree. It was her intention to use him sparingly and cautiously, since she was not sure of his real relationship to Johnny's father.

Gault's taciturn nature had grown stronger by his long confinement. He stared at his visitor evenly.

"Hello, Cliff," she said quietly, peering through the tinted glasses that hid her anxiety. "I'm Abby Ashley."

Gault nodded. "What's the gimmick?" he asked.

She glanced nervously around the small room with its bare furnishings and steel-grilled walls separating them. Two uniformed guards were standing nearby.

"Do they listen?" she asked.

"Do ya shit after ya eat?"

A thin smile played briefly on his lined but still handsome face. He was obviously amused by her naïveté.

Abby's face tightened. It was an ordeal just being there. "I'm doing a book on Johnny," she confided.

There was a long pause.

"Don't know no Johnny."

"Your son, Cliff."

"Don't got no son."

Clifford Gault stared back through her tinted lenses directly into the eyes of the tense young woman confronting him.

"I've got a copy of a birth certificate with your name on it," she said.

"Leo Hatfield'll git cha anything ya want printed on any kinda certificate ya want."

She waved the document in front of him.

"It's authentic, Cliff."

He got up slowly and motioned to one of the guards. The interview that never was, was over. But Abby was not entirely discouraged. She had established eye contact with the father of Johnny Gault. There would be another, more fruitful opportunity soon.

She would see to that.

Optimism was her new aphrodisiac.

Like most incarcerated humans, Cliff was both resigned and desperate. The prison grapevine flourished in a hothouse atmosphere. Things ripened and rotted in a hurry despite the slow passage of time.

Abby's foxy looks and come-on manner had definitely not gone unnoticed. A river of subsequent orgasms could readily be attributed to the sparkle of her eyes and the wiggle of her ass down the cell block corridors. She had left a most definite long-lasting impression on those inmates who had been lucky enough to encounter her.

In prison parlance, Cliff Gault was known as a pussy. No matter that he was in for murder one. He was a handsome man who kept to himself and wiled away his limited free time playing a harmonica some church group had donated to the institution's recreation program. He had shown some talent at it, too.

When the prison's director of recreation cooked up the idea of an in-house band, Cliff was invited to join. He was hesitant at first, but since it afforded some escape from the drudgery of his steam bath assignment in the laundry, he decided to accept. One hour a day jamming in the relatively loose-goose atmosphere of the gym. It was almost as good as being an outside trustee. Or so it seemed to him at the beginning.

Nothing ever went harmoniously within the walls. There were too many volatile personalities laboring under too many restrictions and frustrations. Some of the inmates were talented musicians—most of them working off serious drug convictions—and they resented the amateurish, untutored efforts of the likes of Cliff Gault.

"Fuckin' hick," they called him. "Blowin' barefoot bullshit through rotten teeth."

Cliff never responded verbally, preferring to express himself with surprisingly pretty little codas and brief solos and riffs from time to time. The director appreciated these staccato contributions and the man's reticence to strike back at the dominant brass and reeds.

"Nice touch," he complimented Cliff every now and then. "It offsets the trumpets and saxophones."

"You mean Murderer's Row," Cliff jested. "They got all the firepower in here."

Trumpets and trombones represented just one more battle in his life. His voice had never really risen above the clamor, inside or out.

"People on the outside don't give a shit about anything on the inside," he philosophized to his cellmate, a muscular black man with large hands and eyes soft as ripe olives.

"You got some bad cats in that band," he warned Cliff.

"Boppers or doo-woppers?"

"I ain't shittin', babe."

They talked softly while stroking one another. It increased the intimacy of their nightly ritual.

"Baritone sax did in a dozen boys. Rape and the reaper."

"Horny man."

"Y'all better watch his horn."

"I play with both eyes open."

"And all holes closed?"

Cliff chuckled quietly. "You're beginning to sound like m'wife."

"Don't git yourself hurt, that's all I'm sayin'."

They came almost simultaneously, silent in their submission to necessity.

After the lights went out, Cliff lay in his bunk and stared into the darkness. It had been a long time since he allowed himself to think about anything of consequence. He mostly dwelled on his prison routine and ran over the melodies of songs he liked in his head. Now he wondered for the first time if perhaps he had made some minuscule genetic contribution to his son's success. There was truly some music in his soul.

The mere thought of it gave him a moment of great pleasure, and he fell steeply into the warmth of sleep.

The next day there was an ambush in the gym. Cliff the pussy never had a chance. The baritone man was on him like a cur on a bitch.

"You wanna play mouth organ?" he hissed. "I got a sweet one for yuh."

There were two others, one from brass, the other from reeds. They pinned his ankles and his arms, spread-eagling him over the edge of the stage.

"Mr. Harmonica's got himself a pritty ass," the baritone said.

His accomplices chortled.

"Fuckin' dirty bastards," Cliff muttered in resignation. Then he screamed in pain.

The trio took turns assaulting him orally and anally for almost half an hour before the band director reappeared. He was an outsider and was clearly taken aback by the disheveled state of his harmonica soloist. But as a civilian on special assignment his credo was clearly "See no, hear no, speak no."

"Tonight's session is over," he declared nervously.

"How 'bout riffin' one chorus of 'You Go to My Head'?" the baritone man suggested.

There was sporadic laughter from the three. Cliff Gault knew for the first time how much he was a prisoner and just how little anything else mattered.

Leo Hatfield's place in Nashville was actually slicker and gaudier than the one that had burned down in Memphis. He knew what people—his kind of people—wanted, and he gave it to them. But mixed with his sense of achievement in conquering new territory with an old formula was an inner restlessness that told him he was missing out on something, the really big time of Johnny Gault and Doc Diamond, for example. Adding to his internal agitation was the vague sense that Abby Ashley was somehow on to it, whatever the hell "it" was. She had picked up fast on the Nashville scene, tested it, and now seemed to be moving on.

"She knows what turns people on," he grudgingly admitted.

The truth was that she had written perhaps two dozen fair-to-middling song lyrics, none of which had been published or recorded. Aside from keeping her diaries she had never written anything of any consequence.

"Bitches don't know no boundaries," was Leo's chauvinistic, philosophic assessment of how someone like Abby could have emerged from such an unlikely, unsophisticated background and had the gumption to try to better herself. "There ain't no limits to what ya can do with one o'them things between your legs."

"Fuck men," was Abby's philosophy. "Figuratively and literally."

She had practiced that principle with mixed results until chancing upon Leo and his tenuous connection to Johnny Gault. As a result, it was all going to be different from here on.

48

Some callers could not be ignored or even put on hold. A covert communication from Adam Wiest, the wily director of Satellite Surveys, always received an instant response from Sidney. Wiest was not one to cry wolf.

They met, always, in a downtown bar called the Fifth Amendment. It was generally uncrowded at night, deserted by the financial district patrons who jammed it at lunchtime and during cocktail hours.

The location was offbeat for both of them, perfect for the privacy they sought.

Sidney arrived first and requested the most remote booth in the lounge dining area. No one else was seated within ten tables. Despite his location, Adam found him immediately.

"Where there's no one, there you are," he explained in his fey manner.

"Adam," Sidney greeted him warmly. "Good to see you. It's so seldom I get to enjoy your company."

"I just hope you enjoy the results from our company."

"Satellite's been doing fine by us, thanks to you."

They were not out for an evening of conviviality, so they ordered immediately and got down to business.

"A new organization's been quietly challenging us," Adam reported. "You're probably not aware of it yet, but they've been making inroads and gaining some media credibility. They're called Contemporary Consensuses."

"That's a nine-syllable mouthful. It does ring a bell, though, but not too loud or clear."

"No matter. What counts is they've established a definite pattern of attempting to discredit or refute our findings, then substituting differing results of their own."

"Across the board, or selectively?"

"Very selectively. In fact, almost exclusively with regard to your accounts."

Sidney's brow furrowed.

"That's not the kind of information I hoped to hear."

"It could be destructive. They seem willing to play dirty. For example, they're out polling now, asking 'Should America's number-one talk show host consider changing his name from Gray to Gay?' They go for the bizarre and sensational. Their market seems to be *Inquest* or *Revelation* rather than the institutional press."

"I'm surprised I haven't heard more of them."

"None of us is omniscient, Sidney."

Sidney smiled faintly. "I guess I could only think I am."

Adam went on to reveal that Contemporary Consensuses was also engaging in a smear campaign against Norman Prescott Aggregates and Billy Sunshine University.

Sidney gazed across the table. "It's not very subtle, is it? You never know where the next punch is coming from in this business."

They spent the remainder of their time together plotting retaliatory moves. Adam was a respected pollster who won plenty of press and air time for his surveys. It was essential that he retain his credibility to insure continued general acceptance of his findings.

"Whatever it takes in funding and added personnel, count me in," Sidney pledged. "Just try to find out who or what's behind this."

Adam nodded. "Now for the good news."

"In a poll to be released Friday, eighty-six percent of a cross section favor Norman Prescott's taking over Braxton Broadcasting."

Sidney slapped him on the back as they parted in separate cabs. It was good to have an upbeat note to ride home on.

Gray Matthison was being obstinate about having Norman Prescott as a solo guest, not just once but two or three times.

"That's not my format, Sidney," he objected. "That's not what made my show."

"It's necessary, Gray," Sidney insisted. "You owe it to him."

"*You* owe it to him. I made no such commitment."

"All right, forget about who owes what to whom. This is a spectacular opportunity for you. Everyone's intrigued by Norman, yet he's largely a mystery. A series of exclusive interviews with him could only enhance your stature and ratings."

"We're already number one."

"It adds a whole new dimension to your programming. You can't go on forever with come-and-go comedians, Top Forty singers, and sitcom actors."

"If it ain't broke—"

"Gray, I've gone overboard to protect your reputation and polish your image. Okay, that's my job, you say. But I've gone way beyond that. I've put my own rep on the line to save yours."

"Sidney, this is the latter part of the twentieth century. I'm not on trial like Oscar Fingal O'Flahertie Wills Wilde. I haven't committed any crime beyond being human."

"Is that Wilde's full name? You'd make a great quiz show contestant."

"I admire the man. I don't want to forget how he suffered so unjustly."

"We're not dealing with justice or what's right and what's wrong, Gray. We're dealing with public sentiment and how it translates into ratings. Hell, we've gone over this a thousand times."

Gray sighed resignedly.

"I can think of a hundred other world figures I'd rather have on ahead of Norman Prescott if I ever did a single interview show. He even looks cold and humorless, and I'm sure he's not going to tell me anything he hasn't already said in his book—which, incidentally, was boring as hell."

"It sold."

"Trash sells. We all know that."

"What if I guaranteed you he would reveal something major on your show? Something that would get picked up by the wire services the way they quote the Sunday news specials."

There he was, going out on a limb again, ad-libbing promises and guarantees. It was all part of risk taking in pursuit of results.

Gray was silent a long time.

"I won't do more than one show with him," he said finally.

Sidney was ready for compromise.

"It'll be a blockbuster."

"Sure it will."

"Just one more thing before I go, Gray. You and Eden could do yourselves a big favor."

"I'm listening."

"Have a baby."

*   *   *

Gray, Eden, and Jason Welles had become quite a harmonious threesome. Captions under photos depicting them together invariably described Jason as "a close family friend."

" 'Intimate' would be more like it." Eden laughed.

She frankly confided to Claudia that she had come to enjoy the voyeurism and variety afforded by a three-way relationship.

"Millions of Gray's fans would bleed for a chance at my role," she told her, "and not just a few stars would, too."

There was the key—it was a role to her, and she played it accordingly, occasionally overacting.

"My husband at his best would put Valentino to shame," she was quoted in a joint interview with Gray. "Perhaps even Casanova."

Later in the same piece Gray inadvertently diluted the strength of her statement—to the consternation of Sidney.

"Haven't you noticed how close the beauty of men and women is? The eyes, the noses, the lips, the entire profiles of attractive people are often so similar it's necessary to look elsewhere for certification of gender," he was quoted as saying.

"Can't you just let it ride like a jock?" Sidney questioned him later. "Eden pins a macho badge on you and you rip it off."

Nonetheless, the seeming success of the marriage proved effective in blunting the rapiers of rumor and innuendo. Eden continued to appear as a guest on his show now and then, and they performed charmingly and convincingly as man and wife.

It was hardly surprising when an organization called the Congress on Conjugality listed them among the three most admired couples in the country a few months later. That the Congress was a subsidiary of Satellite Surveys was even less surprising to those in the know.

"There's such a thing as overkill, Sidney," Claudia complained. "You could wind up negating all the positive publicity by laying it on too thick."

"You know my philosophy. Nothing succeeds like excess."

"It's too bad it only applies to business with you."

"I'll attribute that to California cynicism."

"I think 'eastern experience' would be more accurate."

"Anon, Claudia."

He hung up, but her words lingered. She could still get to him when she chose. That disturbed him now as much as it ever had.

49

C laudia was adamant even from a distance. She had always been independent and outspoken, especially with Sidney. Now she could not contain herself.

"Something's sick about a society that celebrates a muddle-brained drug addict without any clear social conscience or moral direction, and elevates him into fucking sainthood!" she railed.

"You never did like him," Sidney said.

"I appreciate his talent and what he's accomplished," she responded, "but everything about him, thanks to you, is blown completely out of all proportion."

"Claudia," Sidney said in his stroke voice, "that's the business we're in."

"That's the business *you're* in. I deny being part of it."

"Whores can't become virgins no matter how many recantations they make."

"Recantations? Big word for a boy from the 'burbs of Memphis."

"I thought you'd lose some of that Broadway sarcasm in the California sun."

"It just ripens here. Like a banana."

There was an odd but insistent and continuing relationship between them despite their bicoastal separation. She was both an irritant and a stimulant to Sidney. Her goading annoyed and sometimes angered him, but it invariably motivated him. Whether she did it out of concern for his career or merely to hector him mattered little. It always jump-started him on a drive to prove her wrong.

The Gault cult disturbed her more and more as it expanded and enveloped so many young sensibilities. She considered it the worship of a wastrel, and it colored her memory of Johnny himself. Individual and career were always separated in her evaluations.

"He has been a victim in many ways, Sidney," she argued, "but he is also the beneficiary of a lot of immature and irrational adulation."

"Not entirely of his own making."

"The sound you hear is the patting of Sidney Bastion's back by his own right hand. You're hopeless, Sidney."

"I could use a feisty girl like you in my New York office."

Claudia sighed resignedly.

"I left New York just in time to avoid terminal disenchantment and disillusionment. You've got a chronic case of both and don't even realize it. You can't imagine how crass and cynical you sound to someone who has just spent the day walking by the ocean, peeing in the surf, and mining the gold of the sun."

"So you think I'm a sick son of a bitch?"

"I think your malady is incurable and terminal."

"A pretty grrr—l is like a malady," he sang.

"Ever the primitive press agent with a pocketful of puns."

"We did seven figures last year."

"Good night, Sidney, even though it's just sunset out here in heaven."

She was still the only stalwart in his life, the sole individual with whom he was in any way involved who sought nothing from him.

He actually needed her in many ways. Although it was difficult for him to admit it, he was incapable of sustaining a more intimate relationship with anyone.

50

Sidney Bastion in his Armani silks did not take kindly to redneck identifications. He resented that aspect of his association with Doc and Johnny most.

"Blue jeans are a brand of failure," he said privately. "Nobody with any class dresses in denim and sneakers."

He could hardly afford to espouse that attitude around his prime account. Jeans and sneakers were germane to the Gault entourage, principals included.

"I dress up when they make me," Johnny declared, "but I'd rather be buck naked."

"Buck naked you're just another hung honcho," Sidney told him. "Name me one porn star who ever made any real money."

"They git paid off in orgasms," Johnny replied with a wink.

"Ever take one of those to the bank and try to cash it?"

"How 'bout the sperm bank?"

"Your tongue's hanging loose lately, John. Maybe you're doing too many talk shows."

They shared a rare chuckle together. Sidney was too intense to laugh often or spontaneously. He first had to think about everything being said. When he did laugh there was a nervous quality to it belying the positive timbre of his normal voice.

"Billy Sunshine says I'm in line t'be a saint."

"You're in line for Saint James Infirmary."

Johnny giggled in his boyish way. "Whose side are you on?"

"The sidelines. I'm only the coach. You're the star."

They had an oddly impersonal relationship, all things considered. Sidney would never be on Johnny's invitation list for a personal party, and vice versa.

Sidney had learned early on that talent bore little or no relationship to intelligence. The public at large seldom perceived that, and perhaps that was a contributing factor to the growth of his industry. Manufacturing icons was easier when talent was the only motivating factor.

"Nobody dumb could be so good" was the public consensus about most stars. Sidney knew it to be a lie.

"Assholes and idiots only have to hit the right chord at the right time," he contended, "and they take the lottery."

He never said that specifically about Johnny Gault, of course, but the implication was there.

So was the money.

There were always problems with Johnny, but a definitive one was his hobby of pegging target shots from his bus. Out in the Mojave Desert was one thing— shooting at rocks and prairie dogs. But picking out streetlights and traffic signals in downtown Los Angeles was quite another.

Others had taken the rap for him so far, covering up Johnny's involvement. But recently one of the national tabloids had picked up the trail and sent a reporter to bird-dog the bus. A forewarned Sidney held one of his rare Daddy-knows-best conferences with his key client before he embarked on the next tour.

"You've got to keep all your guns under control," Sidney warned him. "Including the one behind your fly."

Johnny's smile was tilted.

"Is PR really the first two letters of *prick?*"

"Maybe."

"I know how far t'go, Sidney. I know when t'stop."

"I wonder about that."

"All my wheels are there, and so are the spokes."

"I'm on your side."

Johnny was toying with a .357 magnum as they talked. He had assured Sidney it was empty.

"Who's spyin' on me?" he asked.

"I think it's the *Inquest,* but I'm not sure."

"Faggots."

"Why?"

He put the gun to Sidney's head.

"Hey, Johnny," he protested, "don't mess with the head of a genius."

Johnny was as delighted as a baby by the reaction. It was so seldom he had any real, one-on-one interplay with people outside his entourage.

"Wanna play Russian Roulette?"

Sidney sighed. "Put the gun down, John, even if it is empty. You've got to start behaving like the star you are. These shooting escapades make you look like a silly ass with a cocked-gun mentality. I'm projecting your good-boy image and I need you to cooperate."

Sidney had finally, reluctantly, decided Johnny was high again. The gun, thankfully, had fallen into his lap.

"You gonna git those dogs off my trail?" Johnny asked.

"They're gone."

"You're one slick son of a bitch, Sid."

"I try."

From the begining, Doc Diamond had looked upon Johnny's film ventures with a cynical eye. The big buck was in getting him out on the boards doing his thing, certainly not in mouthing out-of-sync, inane dialogue to some centerfold of the month.

He liked the dollars at the concert gates, where he could apply his own creative accounting to the records and hear the music of his favorite instrument, the cash register.

To Johnny it was all one and the same. He got up each afternoon in a daze and went to bed in the early morning hours the same way. His voice and body simply took him along on a joy ride through his life.

"You like makin' movies?" a reporter asked him.

"I like makin' love better," Johnny replied.

For him, casting calls were really mating calls. His chief interest in movies was trying to seduce his leading ladies. No one cared about silly scripts or inept acting.

"Got me a good piece o'her," he'd brag to his roadies as they watched advance screenings of his sorry cinematics. This always got a good laugh out of them.

Johnny was Johnny. Nothing else mattered.

Peggy Sue who?

51

There were many competitors in the Manhattan marketplace, but Sidney chose to ignore them most of the time. Adrienne Gale alone had managed not only to intrigue him but to baffle him as well.

He was in many ways a victim of his own myth making. His poor opinion of her early on was buried and forgotten. It was as if she had submitted herself to him as a client, gone through the Bastion processing, and emerged with a new, nearly flawless facade. The gilding was thin and fragile, but Sidney did not strive for lasting effects. He cared for the luster of the moment.

Adrienne was aware of her effect upon him and in many ways quite amused by it. She did not allow it to deter her in her own quests, nor did it influence her judgment. His attempt to infiltrate her organization and sabotage projects and potential clients remained unforgotten and unforgiven. He was most definitely not someone to turn one's back upon. But with her impressive frontage she was seldom required to do so.

His repeated condemnation of show business was almost farcical in view of his continued involvement in it. Even when he seemed to be breaking free of it—in signing people like Norman Prescott and Paula Castle, for example—he still found himself operating in an essentially theatrical style. They, too, had to be idealized before they could become idolized.

Adrienne, on the other hand, had no more difficulty dealing with sequins than with diamonds. While Sidney particularly despised restaurant and nightclub accounts, she welcomed them along with all the rest. She had, in fact, become the premier representative of the most popular clubs, places such as Space and

Purgatory. Recently she had added Illusions, a warehouse building on the Hudson River that by day carried no identification and was as nondescript as the surrounding structures. But by night, transformed by lights and hidden panels, it was an escapist's fantasy. Through it she had acquired an entire new stable of entertainers as clients. Sidney dismissed their cumulative value as negligible.

"Give me one corporate account," he told Pam Garson, "and I'll concede a dozen of those petty, fly-by-night flashes in the pan to her or anyone else who wants them."

His cavalier attitude was conveniently set aside when he found himself one of two finalists in the Mimi Aurora account sweepstakes. Mimi had emerged from the nightclub circuit but had one enormous advantage over her peers. Her husband was the fabulously wealthy but little known Swedish shipping tycoon Lars Schwinn, who was ready, at any cost, to make his wife an international star. The other finalist eager to win the Aurora account was none other than Adrienne Gale.

There had been defections back and forth between Sidney and Adrienne in the past—Pierce Agee and Gray Matthison, to cite two. But this marked the first time they were going head-to-head over an open account. Sidney wondered if she was aware that the competition was down to the two of them. He decided on an exploratory phone call.

"That was a bad rap on Norman in the *Journal* today," he began.

Everyone who was anyone knew his reference was to the powerful *Wall Street Journal*.

"Haven't had time to read it," she lied.

"Braxton was quoted pretty liberally in it."

"They have some gung ho investigative reporters."

"Your man was really eloquent for someone taken by surprise."

"Are you accusing me of planting the story, Sidney?"

"Maybe just the seeds."

"I prefer not to discuss my clients or their comments."

"I haven't heard from Norman yet, but I'm sure I will," Sidney said.

"You're paid to listen to his complaints."

"All business today. How's everything else?"

"Aggravating as ever. Check with your spies, Sidney."

"You won't let me live that down, will you? There is no cure for curiosity."

"A brilliant line, Sidney. I'll send it in to *Reader's Digest* and split the fifty bucks with you."

"How'd you like to split an account with me?"

Adrienne laughed exaggeratedly. "For an allegedly complex conniver, Sidney, you're such an easy read. You're talking about Mimi Aurora, aren't you?"

He was momentarily taken aback. "Why not?"

"Because I intend to sign her up on my own."

Lars Schwinn listened quietly, a relaxed man considering he had an empire under his control. He was tall and craggy with the soft, watery eyes of a sheepdog. It was obvious he was enthralled by his much younger wife as he watched her animatedly discuss her ambitions and aspirations. To Sidney she seemed synthetic.

"I want films, I want stage, I want clubs, I want records, I want television, I want concerts, I want to be number one in everything in the world," she proclaimed, her small jaw set and her hands clenched in determination.

Sidney wore a mask of benign understanding and belief as she recited her litany from the center of their main drawing room, a space high-ceilinged and expansive enough to contain the New York Philharmonic.

No one had ever heard of her until she burst from nowhere onto international society pages as the new wife of one of the richest men in the world. This was no street urchin pleading for a break. This was a woman of substance dictating her expectations, and any cost involved was incidental.

"Do you understand me, Mr. Bastion?" she interrupted herself to inquire.

"Completely."

She was somewhere in the neighborhood of thirty but with the diminutive stature of someone in her teens. To Sidney her baby face seemed exhausted by the quest for celebrity and a man of means. Makeup appeared imbedded in her pores, and her eyes refused to dance to her smiles. All of her was spotlight oriented; it was difficult to imagine her in the sun.

"Lars and I acknowledge what you've done for Johnny Gault," she said in conclusion.

"He's one of a kind."

"Like my Mimi," Lars said.

"Like your Mimi," Sidney confirmed.

She's a no-talent little bitch with a dumb asshole for a husband," Sidney ranted into the phone.

"Dumb maybe, but rich, rich, rich," Claudia responded. "Aren't you glad the burden's been lifted from you and awarded to poor Adrienne Gale? I guess it's tits over talent again. But then it'd be terrible if you had to compromise your integrity by representing such a despicable creature as Mimi Aurora."

"They don't know the first thing about what they're doing. They figure money'll cover everything."

"It almost bought you. Now poor Adrienne has to suffer a fortune."

"You must have majored in sarcasm."

"Be happy you're not getting the headaches. There's nothing tougher than dealing with somebody who's got nothing."

"Except money."

"In the immortal word of Billy Sunshine, amen."

It was hours before he calmed down enough to compose a congratulatory wire. Once that was done to his satisfaction he turned out the lights and slipped finally into a deep and dream-laden sleep.

The vivid nightmare sucked him down the dark tunnel of time. He fell and fell fast through the darkness, feeling the wind against his skin, hearing it whistle past his ears. Down and down he fell, gasping for breath, trying to scream, but no sound would come out. Suddenly, with a thump that was echoed by the thumping of his own heart, his dream self landed in his tenth year of life on a soft grassy mound at the base of an old tree. He looked above him and saw his old treehouse perched solidly on the perfect base that had been left standing when the hickory tree had been cut in half by a lightning bolt. He was in Germantown, Tennessee, just outside Memphis, in the country by his favorite place, his secret hideout.

He heard voices approaching, then looming over him was a gang of dirty, preteen boys. One of them pulled a snake out of his pocket and poked it in Sidney's face. They all jeered at him when he recoiled. He dug deep into his pockets and came up with fifty-two cents in change and a small pocketknife.

They took the booty. The boy threw the snake on him anyway. Then the gang ran away laughing. The snake slithered off into the grass, and young Sidney began to cry as he started to climb the ladder up to his treehouse.

The ladder changed into the staircase in his childhood home. He walked past his father's room on the way to his own bedroom. There lurking in the shadows stood his father, naked and fondling himself. Sidney ran to him in his distress. Somehow in this strange convoluted drama, his father then hovered over him, fondling him instead.

It was all vague and hazy, dim and out of focus, like a bad home movie, but he heard himself crying "No, Daddy!"

He awoke in a sweat, repeating "No, Daddy!" aloud. Then when he realized it was a dream he cried for real.

It was a troubling, recurrent drama that invariably left him restless and inwardly unsettled.

Was it only a dream, or some deeply submerged, ugly and unfaceable memory?

Sidney had chosen never to truly confront the question. He lived well now, and to hell with the past.

he name of the game is fame. Fame is power. Fame is money. Fame is immortality."

They were his own words, delivered once in a seminar. They hung framed now before his eyes along with other original adages.

What the wall didn't acknowledge was that fame also often meant doing what one would rather not do. Such as accompany Paula Castle and Reese Roberts to the Sarah Bernhardt Theatre for the Broadway premiere of *The Bitch in Penthouse A*. There was no way for Sidney to avoid it short of resigning from the account. Paula's insistence was tantamount to a command.

Her moods generally ranged from imperious to tyrannical. This night, however, she was surprisingly sophisticated, trying hard not to resemble the play's central character, who spewed "Kiss my asperity" and "Lick my lap" at anyone who displeased her.

"You look handsome as Hades," she had greeted Sidney earlier. But that was before she entered the gilded coach—their silver stretch limo—and transformed herself into Cinderella, or some facsimile thereof, for her debut as a theatrical celebrity.

The opening night crowd was the usual glitzy mix of stars, critics, and socialites, most of them more interested in being seen than in seeing anything—other than each other. It was all playwrights' destinies to be damned on their most important night with the least theatrically minded audiences conceivable.

Adrienne was there in her role as Pierce Agee's advocate. She had carefully chosen an aisle seat half a dozen rows removed from that of Paula Castle. She had not spoken to Sidney since landing the Aurora account, figuring correctly that his loss to her had been a bitter personal defeat. It was hardly the occasion for salting any wounds, new or old. Instead of her usual precurtain flitting about the auditorium she stayed seated, cool and chic, her celebrated décolletage discreetly harnessed in a new Pauline Trigere gown. Sidney saw her—in fact, their eyes had met—but he did not acknowledge her.

Numbers of people gingerly approached Paula for her autograph on their *Playbills*, keeping her flattered and occupied until the curtain. Had he thought of it, Sidney reminded himself, he would have arranged for even more to distract her. It struck him as ironic that the man most responsible for her public notoriety sat silently beside her, undisturbed by anyone.

Finally the house lights flickered, then dimmed, and then all but the stage was lost in darkness.

Mesmerizing!" one critic raved. "Intensely incisive," stated another. "Is that you, Samantha Glick?" "Powerful and penetrating," "A Hit for Babe Ruthless!" commented still others.

Overall, the reviews were ecstatic.

Paula Castle uncharacteristically withheld her opinion. Sidney had waited for her in vain at the postpremiere party at Vivano's. Without knowing her reaction he found it difficult to proffer one of his own. It was not good business to disagree with one's clients.

In the course of the celebration, Adrienne brushed past him several times. It was a heady night for Pierce and therefore for her as well. As was customary, she had obtained capsule critiques from the key critics in advance of publication and broadcast. Their upbeat quality motivated her to break the ice with Sidney.

"We have a hit on our hands," she whispered to him at the next opportunity.

"Congratulations."

"Paula should be purring."

"Or clawing."

"Why should she be? This'll make her the talk of the nation."

"Notoriety's not the same as celebrity. Put yourself in her shoes. How would you feel?"

"Like a bitch goddess."

"You look the part tonight."

He slipped away before she could respond.

What about Paula? Where's Paula? What did Paula have to say? These were the questions that drove Sidney from the party early. He disliked being at a loss for words, especially when the loss was imposed rather than real.

It was well after one in the morning before he was able to locate her at one of the several penthouse apartments she kept, this one at the Gotham Castle.

She sounded surprisingly fresh and alert.

"The nature of the beast and the nature of the best are separated by only a vowel," she recited in response to his greeting.

"That's from the play!"

"There's a piece of land near the Battery that's so damned seductive I could lay on it and make love to it," she said quoting another line.

"You've committed the whole thing to memory!"

"Hardly."

"Seen or heard any of the reviews? The word is they're sensational."

"They're about a sensational subject."

"You're right about that. I'll get a messenger over there right away with tearsheets so you can see for yourself."

"Don't bother. I've got most of them already."

"I should've known."

"You should've," she agreed. "Let's get to work now and capitalize on it all."

"The goddess has spoken."

"No," she corrected, "the bitch goddess."

"You're in Penthouse A?"

"Where else?"

It was seldom, if ever, that Paula Castle contributed to a good night's rest for Sidney Bastion. But that night she did. She did indeed.

53

There were many mornings when Sidney preferred to work from his den overlooking the East River rather than in the spare elegance of his Park Avenue offices. On this chilly Friday in early April, a hard rain pelted the windows of his townhouse as he took the call from Norman Prescott.

"I blame Braxton," Norman said about a recent spate of negative references to him on radio and television as well as in print.

"Let's go after him, then."

"And this outfit called Contemporary Consensuses—who are they and where do they get off branding me 'one of the three major robber barons of big business'?"

"Contemporary Contemptibles would be a more fitting name. I'm still trying to get a fix on them."

"How do they manage to exist?"

"By being sensational. Even some of your own publications pick up their trash."

There was a pause. "They may have in the past. They no longer will."

"We're counteracting them effectively, Norman, with your recent awards and degrees, and the philanthropic associations."

"Braxton," Prescott repeated.

Sidney stared at the rain after the call was completed. Going after Braxton would be like going after Adrienne Gale herself. He felt energized.

54

A bby Ashley was quite amenable to working with another writer once she was persuaded that she alone would receive the cover credit and publicity as author. It was patently obvious she needed assistance in sorting out and organizing her hodgepodge of fact and fiction, assorted innuendos, and half-truths. Structuring sentences and then packaging them into paragraphs that fit seamlessly into chapters was anything but her forte.

"I like digging for the dirt," she told Gwen, her editor and encourager, "not making it pretty."

With terrier ferocity she did just that, pursuing every lead, gleaning bits and pieces of information about Johnny Gault from anywhere she could. She suffered none of the restraints of serious biographers, none of the impedimenta of intellectual integrity and source verifications. If somebody said something was so, and the individual wasn't a Skid Row drunk or in a mental asylum, then damn-it-to-hell it was so.

The break with Leo was swift and savage. She did not return to Nashville to declare her independence from him, recognizing the potential for violence. She called him instead from New York, a city he professed to hate.

"Leo," she began uneasily, "I called to thank you for all you've done for me."

The background noise of the Warehouse made her words difficult to hear.

"Hold on," he said. "I'll take this in my office."

There was a brief, unwelcome pause.

"Peace," he said in the quiet of his soundproofed office. "Now, what was 'at you were sayin' and where the hell are ya?"

"I said thank you for all you've done for me but I won't be back. I'm staying in New York."

There was a pause.

"You damned well better git back here and straighten things out with me," he said, his voice rising. "You lied to me about your momma. She ain't nowhere near as sick as you are."

"Breezy can handle everything for you. I'm sending you a check to cover whatever I owe you."

"Just a minute here, bimbo. I been gittin' all kinds a funny reports 'bout you and some goddamned book on Johnny Gault. You been sneakin' 'round on my time cookin' up somethin' for yourself. No bitch does that to Leo."

"Good-bye, Leo. Good luck."

"Cunt!" he managed to inject before she could cut him off.

Abby felt relieved that the break was final, yet her sense of triumph had totally vanished. Perhaps there were no victories in dealing with lives and emotions. Or perhaps she would feel more like herself again tomorrow.

Without a doubt the dark side of Johnny worried Sidney. Johnny was out of control, and the prospect of having his vices exposed in Abby's book was a major threat to his own financial well-being. The Gault account was his firm's premier account and a major source of revenue.

"She's got no line of credit whatever anywhere in the business," he said, trying to reassure Doc as well as himself.

"She's nothing."

But the creator of Johnny's holy all-American image knew that it could not hold up under any kind of thorough investigation. The ugly truth was bound to come out. This Ashley version of Johnny's story threatened to have real clout.

"People ask me about this goddamned book wherever we go," said Doc. "They bug Johnny about it, too."

"Johnny's bigger than Jesus," Sidney replied. "She'd have to write a new Bible to do him any damage."

"Jesus got crucified, didn't he?"

"Yes, but he rose again, remember?"

The whole situation had become a monumental pain in the ass. Sidney kept hoping it would somehow go away. There had been at least half a dozen books done on Johnny since his ascendancy. But those were mostly superficial, adulatory tomes with about as much depth and insight as a fan club newsletter.

Abby Ashley, whoever she was, was proving to be not just another passing headache to Sidney. She posed all the symptoms of an acute migraine.

Johnny Gault was basically a shy boy grown older without any particular agenda.

"Fun is what life's all about," he insisted.

His kind of fun was loose and immature, wild without malice, dumb yet understandable to anyone compassionate.

Early on Claudia Rogers had observed, "He's really so sweet for someone who's so successful."

"Cut off his cock and he'd be a saint," Sidney had responded at that time.

Little did he know then that Johnny's penis would become his main star feature, followed by his lips and tongue, then his eyes.

There was a gentle tenderness about him, mingled with a quiet hauntedness. He was a man and boy combined, strung as taut as the guitar he cradled and strummed.

"Ev'rybody stares 'n nobody cares," Johnny sang.

It was not true; they cared. People ached for him. He reached into their souls and massaged their hearts.

"I didn't ask t'be special," Johnny would say. "I jist am what I am."

They called him John-John, the Chief, Numero Uno, and Lover Boy or Rocker. They almost never called him Johnny Gault. He had become bigger than his name.

"You're nickin' my name," he would respond to chanting crowds, teasing them with puckish pelvic thrusts.

"Lover Boy, Lover Boy, John-John, John-John," one crowd countered.

"Call me anything," Johnny replied, "but don't call me late for the orgy."

Any and all sexual allusions drove his audiences into a frenzy. Auditoriums shook, and stadiums trembled, as his fans reacted to his vocal and visual stimulations.

"He's actually dangerous," a concert official complained to Sidney Bastion as he watched the mass reaction.

"Only to himself," Sidney replied.

In the underground world of celebrity, where moral debits magically became credits, Johnny Gault was a harvest and a feast. He had a tangible amount of consistency as a major player despite his sideline antics. Everything he did, positive or negative, enhanced his value in the media marketplace. People were intrigued by him, and everything he chose to do was observed, analyzed, and weighed.

"Nobody should be lookin' t'me for answers," he said. "I'm all questions myself." Stardom did not faze him but slowly, irreversibly eroded him. He derived little joy from being idolized.

Johnny had a remarkable capacity for remaining what he had always been despite all the attention and adulation. There was a loner quality to him that had been there from the time he was a toddler. It was more than likely self-protective, born of abuse and the missing pieces of his childhood.

"The muzzle's on the puzzle," he liked to tell interviewers who probed too deep.

It was surprising how few of them detected the sly humor, the native intelligence, of his retorts.

"I was born like ev'rybody else," he would say with a laugh on his good days. "Hangin' in a diaper from the beak of this Mother Goose of a stork . . ."

He always paused for effect at this point.

"That big bird dropped me like a turd on my momma's lap. She shrieked and I screamed, and that's where my musical heritage began."

It was the closest he ever came to describing his mother in anything less than saintly terms.

Always mischievous behind his clean-cut choirboy image, Johnny drove his road crew increasingly crazy with his antics. Success energized his playfulness, and he had become accustomed to being accommodated no matter what his desires.

Johnny got high as a kite and scared the hell out of a pair of young hookers hired to entertain him one night.

"This is Pussy Roulette night," he informed them after introductions. "You know bingo night at church? Well, this here's Pussy Roulette night at the crotch. You two gals've been picked t'have your pussies put up as prizes."

Jaded as their profession had made them, they were still young and vulnerable enough to appreciate their good fortune in having this John as their john. Having to fuck for a living was decidedly enhanced by fucking a star—and no star shone in the galaxy any brighter than the heavenly body of Gault.

"What do you mean, Johnny?" the girl named Vicki asked.

She was petite and big-titted, the combination he liked best.

"Tall girl, small cunt," he responded, "small girl, all cunt."

Johnny was fond of raunchy clichés. They were a release from writing original lyrics.

"Momma didn't give me no tit as a baby," he told Vicki. "I gotta make up for lost time."

"You want some tit?" Vicki asked, fondling her own, projecting them toward his face.

Her cohort, Nicole, had begun an oral massage of his cock, waddling about the room in a squat to follow his movements.

Johnny was hard, but his concentration was on finding the attaché case with his weapons. Moving all the time, switching luggage and packing items in different gear, made it difficult to locate specific objects when desired. Particularly with the distraction of a full erection and a pair of willing vixens.

He found the case finally and opened it with glee.

"Guns!" Vicki gasped.

Johnny laughed. He enjoyed inspiring terror.

"You got more to be 'fraid of from a dick than a magnum," he declared. "Y'can't git VD or pregnant from a pistol."

"You can get dead," Vicki said.

Nicole had taken a break from fellatio. Viewing her provocatively wet lips upturned toward him, he slid the barrel of the gun into her mouth.

"Suck it off," he instructed.

"You're acting crazy, Johnny," Vicki said.

"You ever been fucked by a genuine Glock?"

He reached behind himself and took out another gun. The barrel was hard and cool against her vagina.

"You're starting to scare me, Johnny."

"There's jist one bullet in each gun," he told her. "Wanna take a chance and bet your pussy?"

He had begun masturbating her with the gun as they talked.

"You okay, John?"

His eyes had become heavy-lidded, and before long his grip relaxed enough for the gun to slip harmlessly between her thighs.

The girls escaped with their fees—and perhaps their lives—as he slumped steeply into sleep.

Johnny-good-boy was veering out of control, and everybody around him hid in the box office and helped count the cash instead of helping the one who counted.

"He's sick," Vicki declared as they left.

She had performed as his erotic wet nurse, but she was hardly all wet as an amateur psychologist.

Johnny had always considered his entourage family. No one else had any deeply personal involvement in his life except his roadies, thanks to Doc and Sidney.

One of his crew described the job: "You ever work a circus as a kid—show up before daylight and wait in line to have some greasy, tattooed motherfucker pass judgment on your ass so's you could carry water for the elephants or shovel horseshit in the name of show biz and a free pass to the main tent? Well, that's the heritage of roadies. Those are the fuckin' forefathers of us highway refugees."

Being on the road with Johnny was a circus without elephants.

Entertaining him often required a kindergarten mentality. He could spend hours contending with the dings and flashes, the dits and dashes of pinball machines. Each new offering in the marketplace was a fresh challenge, and he met each with demonic determination. The games gave his life meaning and excitement. Their electronic trickery teased his competitiveness. His infantile Warehouse orientation was never more apparent.

"Better he plays with a machine," Doc said more than once, "than some bimbo who'll sue him for makin' her pregnant."

No one involved in the Gault entourage ever probed deeper than the veneer of their varnished lives. It was all gloss and no depth. There was money and booze and drugs and bitches galore. Why waste time thinking about anything like tomorrow and the possible end of it all?

They ran a glass truck by him, one of those odd-looking triangular jobs with huge storefront panes locked in by industrial latticework. It was a setup arranged by his road manager with the expense account blessing of Doc.

It cruised by slowly enough, enticingly enough, for Johnny to take notice.

"Look at them suckers," he exulted from his swivel seat. "Big mothers, baby. Must be settin' up a mall somewheres."

His driver laughed over the intercom.

"Why don'tcha drill the mothafuckahs?" he goaded him. It was all in the script Johnny hadn't seen.

"Shit!" Johnny cried out. "I jist might!"

"Blast those bastards!" his driver encouraged him.

"I'm gonna blow 'em away," he declared excitedly.

"Geronimo!"

Johnny reacted like a child at his first Christmas. He shattered the panels of glass with maniacal glee. Everything on the passing truck was reduced to shards and powder.

"Git us outta here," he gasped to his driver. "We're in deep shit now."

The joy was gone, and the guilt had set in. But there was something orgasmic to him in the combination of the act and the desperation of flight.

He was wet and drained as the bus slipped onto yet another strange road feeding into the helix of highways that had become his home.

Johnny could and would giggle when he was high. He giggled as he had when tickled by his momma as a baby. There was so much of the deprived infant in him.

"The aura of Aurora," Sidney liked to label it.

His was most definitely a unique piece of work. His charm permeated his music, his open lust defined its beat. It was a recipe whose ingredients were the secret of the chef.

"Listen t'me," he shouted at the crowds. "I'm cookin' and I want y'all t'eat. How's the taste?"

"Deeeeeelicious!" they screamed back.

Revered as he was by so many, Johnny was not god to everyone by a long shot. Certainly not in parts of Memphis, where he had been born. For the most part the locals resented his success.

"Don't do nothin' f'r me," one critic summed up the local attitude. "Don't make me a nickel ahead."

"Builds hisself a mansion and don't do shit for nobody else," said another local.

He had his personal paparazzi—photographers and journalists who trailed him relentlessly and made their living off his image and their destruction of it. The theory that there was no such thing as *bad* publicity was not shared by Sidney.

"A shot of Johnny jerkin' off to some dirty movie in his bus can't do anybody any good," he declared. "They've got the cameras to cornhole him."

It was a form of undeclared war, seeking attention on one hand while trying to block it on the other.

Johnny himself mostly took it all good-naturedly. He had been a lonely child, and having so many people around him, after him, and caring about him now subtly pleased him.

He had a special fondness for those who amused him. One of his concert warm-ups was a Kentucky comedian known as Skid Marx. Skid had sized up the star and chosen to put him down. It was a calculated risk, but it had paid off. He was now a permanent member of the entourage.

"Johnny Gault," he declared to an audience of devout fans, "is a myth. You know what a myth is? That's a miss with a lisp."

The laughter was invariably sporadic.

"I mean, this guy is a cunt. He plays with his guitar and wails out sad words and then eats gourmet room service superdeluxe. Come on, he's a pussy with a pretty face and no balls . . ."

Johnny's visible side-stage laughter made the put-downs acceptable to his fans and further endeared him to them.

The onstage fun and camaraderie were deceptive, to say the least. All the glamour of the shows with their spectacular lighting effects, their fireworks, their scenic majesty were diminished behind the scenes. Johnny's moodiness interfered with the relentless transitions, the pressures, and the movements. He had become less and less consistent in his relationships with his cohorts.

"Look at him and you know," observed one of his roadies. "If his lips don't curl up when he sees you, back off."

"Fuck 'im when he's in a mood."

"Duck 'im, dude. You're dead tryin' t'fuck 'im."

It was all part of the price of being so close to a star who was becoming increasingly mercurial.

None of them really knew about the haunting memory of Peggy Sue.

57

I n the course of her probing into the life of Johnny Gault, Abby Ashley had rediscovered a fundamental truth of human nature: Under the cloak of anonymity most people love to reveal their knowledge of the dark side of others, particular of the famous.

"The earth is made of dirt," philosophized her collaborator, Risa Bainbridge, "and everybody likes to play in it."

Abby readily admitted that her own life was as tainted as the life she was examining. The major difference, of course, was that Johnny lived in the limelight.

In her grab bag of miscellany were reports that Johnny had begun having orgasms at the age of eight—intriguing to her because it had taken her until eleven to really understand the oohing and aahing of intercourse—and that he had masturbated to climax six or seven times a day in childhood. The reliability of these reports were not of concern to Abby. If she heard it, she reported it.

"It almost can't be too erotic," her editor assured her. "Johnny's a walking phallic symbol with a voice."

Sex was the common denominator in life, something she was certain Johnny's fans could understand readily, relate to, and share with him.

"Don't hesitate to embellish and enhance wherever it seems logical or plausible," Gwen encouraged her.

"Regardless of the facts?"

"Creative reconstruction," she replied. "Remember that printing lends enchantment to words."

"And authority."

"You're a fast learner, Abby."

"It's a fast world."

"Keep digging. I'll turn you over now to Risa."

Abby had developed a tentative but amiable rapport with her "Ghost of Christmas Future," as she called her. The allusion was to the promise of riches ahead.

"Abby Ashley reporting from the land of tattoos and six-packs," she greeted Risa. "I'm in shitkickers' paradise."

"How's it going, silver sleuth?"

"It keeps getting better 'n better."

"You're smothering us in salaciousness. Your last batch was just unbelievable."

"I hope you can smooth it out; there's more coming."

"No problem on this end. Everybody here's excited about the book."

"Nobody could be more excited than me."

Those were indeed heady days for Abigail Rudner, aka Abby Ashley, formerly of West Memphis, Arkansas, and now laying claim to the world at large.

It was unlikely that Leo Hatfield or Doc Diamond had ever read a book, any book, cover to cover. Nor had either of them probably ever visited a bookstore or a library. Their only heavy reading involved legal contracts, and even those were turned over to lawyers.

Abby, on the other hand, had always been starstruck and loved to lose herself in the biographies and autobiographies of her idols. She had always found many unanswered questions in those self-serving portraits, and thus evolved her interest in literary espionage. She was determined now to provide answers to questions that had never even been asked about Johnny before she came along.

Was it really necessary to describe in detail his masturbatory habits and frequencies from infancy on? "Not necessary, but titillating," she would respond. "And if there's anything I love to do more than masturbate, it's titillate."

The Gorman Group appreciated her homespun lack of inhibition. She was definitely going to be promotable on the interview circuit. The copy she was providing was wildly episodic, but it was unfailingly commercial, and that kept interest high. Her ghost and her editor were there to give it form.

"The stuff from the hookers was pure chocolate," Gwen enthused, "and I'm a chocoholic."

"I'm tracking more of them. The guy goes through them like popcorn."

"One more thing before you hang up. We're a little leery of the Billy Sunshine material. He's a big man in the Jesus business."

"He oughtta be more careful, then."

"We'll talk about it next time you're in New York."

"That's liable to be very soon."

Gwen laughed. "Don't say 'libel' to an editor on edge," she kidded.

"See you in court," Abby said.

Gwen was as surprised as she was pleased by the quick pickup. A sophisticated Southern belle could be a fresh commodity on the book-boosting talk show circuit.

She began to feel more and more comfortable about her risky commitment to the neophyte author.

58

S loan Bannister had jumped at the opportunity to sign a contract with Sidney. That was before the success of his collaborative autobiography with Norman Prescott had made him a rich man. No one had expected *I, Etcetera* to do what it did in the marketplace. In the words of the industry, it was a sleeper and a phenomenon.

"You screwed me," Sloan accused Sidney.

"I own you," Sidney responded.

Sidney enjoyed having a writer of Sloan's caliber more or less in his employ. They were tied together for a minimum of five books, and the Prescott book had turned the deal into a bargain. It mattered little that none of the subsequent books had scored anywhere near the sales totals of Prescott's manufactured mythology. They had served as excellent promotional springboards.

Johnny Gault had lent his name to one of the books, which, despite its shallowness, had sold quite well.

Billy Sunshine had kept Sloan busy with his tracts on faith and optimism. Sloan compiled them patiently, and they were released under the titles *Jesus Can Take a Joke* and *God Is a Good Guy*. With Reverend Billy hawking them from his video pulpit they sold steadily with impressive cumulative totals.

The Gray Matthison book, a whimsical reminiscence called *First Person Plural*, had also briefly hit the bestseller charts.

All told, the Bastion-originated volumes had made Sloan Bannister quite wealthy and increasingly independent. Now, thanks to Sidney's considerable persuasiveness plus a higher-than-usual percentage guarantee on royalties, Paula Castle had consented to recount her life and career. The project had lagged along for more than a year, with Sloan sporadically swearing he was through with the entire undertaking, until the acclaim for *The Bitch in Penthouse A.*

"Wind it up," Sidney urged Sloan. "Bite the bullet and let her see what you've got."

"She's already seen what I've got more times than I'd like to admit."

Sidney laughed knowingly.

"The manuscript, Sloan. Let her see it so we can get her final approval."

"She won't like it."

"Pierce Agee thought the same thing."

"He wrote a play and it's metaphorical. This is supposed to be her version of her own life and philosophy."

"Knowing you, I'm sure you've captured her essence."

"She's really a caricature of herself. Beneath that callous exterior is nothing but a bunch of calluses."

"Would you let me read it?"

Sloan hesitated.

"Only on condition she never finds out," he agreed.

Sidney stayed up through an entire night to scan the lengthy manuscript with its patchwork of changes scribbled in the margins and between lines. He thought enough of it to forward it directly to Paula, despite his pledge to Sloan.

"You're a double-crossing son of a bitch, Sidney!" Sloan screamed at him over the phone. "I just got my manuscript back—from Paula Castle!"

"I'm an expediter, Sloan. I thought it was excellent and I just saved you the time and trouble of getting it to her."

"Remind me never to trust you again."

"Only if you tell me her reaction wasn't positive."

"She should be arrested for capital punishment. Imagine every other word in capital letters! And exclamation marks scattered like birdshit all over the place!"

"She loves the words you put in her mouth, son of Hemingway!"

"Don't butter me, you bastard."

The edge had gone out of his tone.

"Lunch tomorrow to celebrate. Okay?"

Sloan sighed softly.

"Afterwards, pistols at forty paces," he said.

aula Castle didn't view Sidney only as a paragon of public relations who could inflate her image by garnering coverage in major publications and on television. She saw him also as a handsome and successful younger man who aroused her libido and distracted her from the relentless maintenance of an empire and an image.

Her features seemed to soften in his presence. Sidney was quick to detect such things.

"You look wonderful," he said.

"I use a sperm bank for my cosmetics."

"Sure."

"All donors under twenty."

"Ease up, Paula. You don't have to be a pit bull all the time."

Paula had always met the masculine challenges in her life by practicing their sexist ways in reverse. Since men invariably dropped their gazes to women's bosoms when their meetings were frontal, or their buttocks when turned, she took to admiring males' crotches from the front, or their asses from the rear. It amused her to see how uncomfortable many of them became as victims.

"They can dish it out," she said, "but they can't take it."

She took a personal interest and found recreational pleasure in her male personnel, her standby army of studs. The doctor who had given them mandatory employment physicals also photographed their genitals under the guise of taking X rays, especially for Paula.

"Talented young man," she would say as she admired one with major endowments.

It was all a game to her. Her doormen and bellhops, her waiters and bartenders, all were her own private mass of masculinity to be alternately seduced and terrorized.

Sidney was the lone exception. She was unsure of her attraction to him. He had elevated her from being an unknown pariah with power to a colorful celebrity.

"You're sleek, Sidney," she said in a moment of passion. "You enter me without physical penetration." She eyed him evenly.

He leaned back in his Armani silks and smiled, a trace of smugness curving his lips.

"I understand you, Paula. That's what it's all about."

"No, Sidney," she disagreed. "What it's all about is that I'm wise to you and the way you play the game. And for some cockeyed reason that turns me on. Maybe bullshit, like water, seeks its own level."

His laugh was more like a cough.

"It's not bullshit, Paula. It's creative imagery."

It was her turn to laugh.

"It's bullshit," she repeated.

Her hand went to his lap.

"You're a pretty boy," she said. "I like pretty boys."

In a matter of moments he was back to securing the account.

60

atellite Surveys' Fashion Foundation released its annual list of the ten most stylishly garbed and groomed men in America, naming Gray Matthison, Reverend Billy Sunshine, Norman Prescott, and Reese Roberts. A week later a similar compilation was announced by Contemporary Consensuses containing the names of ten totally different men. Significant among them were Pierce Agee and Evan Braxton. There were also two men who owned the nightclubs Space and Area, and two stars of the New York Skyscrapers.

Sidney was simultaneously enlightened and infuriated. Adrienne Gale had caught on to his game.

He could not respond directly without confessing to collusion. At least in Adam Wiest he had a clever and knowledgeable front man who could withstand considerable interrogation and investigation. He wondered if Adrienne Gale had been as careful and astute in building a substantial foundation under her upstart organization.

He decided to chance that she had not.

Don Samuelson's nightly news program won awards for his intriguing and explicit exposes. He was always in the market for more shocking stories. Sidney considered Don a difficult and cynical commentator, but one with a tremendously broad audience.

Samuelson was characteristically skeptical and distrustful of a public relations source.

"Why should one polling outfit be suspect and the other not?" he questioned Sidney. "I think all of them could stand investigating."

"Exactly. I've dealt with Satellite Surveys for years, but I'd definitely want them included in any probe. I want them validated more than you do, Don, believe me."

Sidney's delivery was silky smooth, with a tinge of indignation in his voice. It was a nice touch.

"The guy to contact is Adam Wiest?" asked Don.

"He has an impeccable rep," said Sidney.

Adam had been calm and confident earlier when Sidney had suggested the plan.

"The computer's loaded with facts and figures," Adam told him. "It would take years of investigation to uncover any sizable disparities."

"Samuelson's a relentless bastard. He'll try to break you if he smells anything amiss."

"He has a better chance with the Sphinx."

"Right on, Adam."

Ironically, it had been Samuelson who initiated the nettlesome probe into rumors of sex and drug orgies on the campus of Billy Sunshine University. When he discovered that students and professors were jointly involved, he turned the investigation over to his colleagues.

"Too sordid for me," he declared.

Before withdrawing, however, he had denounced Sunshine's entire operation as "the church of self-aggrandizement and a disgrace to serious religions everywhere."

Reverend Billy pretended to be appalled by the revelations.

"God will punish the guilty," he declared from his video pulpit, "but He will also cut out the tongues of false accusers."

"These are not minors," Sidney rationalized to the media. "They're adult men and women exercising their rights of free choice."

As the tales grew increasingly bizarre, including reports of sexual sacrifices at the altar of the chapel where daily worship was an undergraduate requisite, Billy withdrew to his plush monastic retreat in the San Gabriel Mountains. From there he kept in touch with only God and a few mortals, Sidney among them.

"What hurts most," he confided to Sidney, "is that they had the audacity to do such things in the chapel. What hurts second most is that I was never once invited."

That was Billy Sunshine, as prurient as he was pragmatic. And he was all but unflappable even under siege. No sooner had these fires been banked than another damaging allegation was made. A *National Inquest* story accused the university of peddling phony degrees—bachelor's, master's, and doctorates.

Billy emerged to vigorously deny these charges, but the claims persisted. When the documented proof was finally undeniable, he purged part of his faculty, branding them "Philistines and panderers in the temple of God Almighty."

His rhetoric was riveting when he was aroused. Audiences responded with fervent pledges of continued support, underlined with donations in the hundreds of thousands of dollars.

"They want to break this great university," he preached with passion, "but it's built on the rock of Abraham, and what God has brought together here no mortal men shall ever put asunder!"

There were scholarship scandals in the athletic program as well, adding to all the other controversies. But Reverend Billy stood jut-jawed in his marble pulpit denoucing one and all who interfered with his mission as the agents of Satan himself.

"The Christly charlatan," as Don Samuelson had dubbed him, was nothing if not a survivor.

Eventually the media tired of the incidents of continuing abuses at and by the university. Sidney convinced Billy to back off from any further mention of past indiscretions at the university. They concentrated instead on a projected worldwide crusade scheduled to take Billy to forty nations. This "global gospel" would involve him with key world leaders in a quest for universal peace.

The tempest was over, at least temporarily.

BOOK THREE

THE EIGHTIES

61

Sidney Bastion moved to his own drumbeat, as he always had, but the tempo varied now. There were periods of adagio now, where once it had all been allegro.

In the world of professional humbug, time was measured by deadlines. Every day contained, in fractional doses, all the ingredients of a whole year. There were joy and sorrow, victory and defeat, pain and pleasure, love and hate. But there was never in all of it any abiding sense of contentment, or even of continuity.

It was no longer necessary for Sidney to cultivate the media as he once had. He had become something of a celebrity in his own right, which in itself guaranteed him a rather broad degree of access to major outlets.

Dependence was still there—it would always be—but now it was more of a two-way street. Modern media were lost without the input of the public relations industry. It had come a long way since his uncertain but determined entry into it a quarter of a century earlier.

Andy Warhol had pinpointed the era with his prediction that everyone would be famous for fifteen minutes. The world stage was cluttered with so many existing as well as would-be celebrities that it was difficult to gain attention for any one individual. Endless numbers nevertheless continued seeking to bask in the limelight and benefit from its haloing effect.

It was still a matter of seducing the public, and Sidney was more the master seducer than ever. Although he would never admit it, he had always been intimidated by the international aspects of the industry. But the worldwide crusade of Reverend Billy Sunshine had introduced him to many movers and shakers in all points of the globe, and now, after a long and exclusive love affair with Manhattan, his operation had finally gone international.

In less than a year he had established satellite offices in London and Monte Carlo. The techniques of his profession, like those of lovemaking, proved to be universal.

By computerization his offices had instantaneous transfer of photos and information. A storehouse of data lay banked in computer files, expediting the flow of stories as well as immediately authenticating facts for articles and speeches. Where rows of typewriters had once chattered in noisy competition or collaboration, silent word processors now commanded printers to do their bidding.

But in this business of creating, coddling, and often camouflaging idols and images, Sidney recognized that he was still the catalyst in command, essential to the energy and success of the overall organization.

His eastside town house had become a gathering place for all manner of rich and famous people—show world celebrities, diplomats from the nearby United Nations, sports heroes, top politicians, corporate moguls, and media luminaries. He now kept a permanent staff of twelve on duty there, ranging from doorman to chef to janitor.

Sidney took special pride in his growing modern art collection, which now included works by Andy Warhol, Frank Stella, and Robert Rauschenberg. There was a certain cachet to being an art collector that he enjoyed. But the truth was he almost never looked at any of the paintings unless he was showing them off to someone else. There was no private passion involved.

There was a yacht at the Seventy-ninth Street boat basin on the Hudson, a Lear jet at a Westchester airport, and a white stretch limousine complete with chauffeur in his garage. He had begun as well to harbor attractive, cultured young ladies to act as hostesses at his parties, the loveliest one of them invariably reserved for the right arm of the master of the house. Their dormitory, on the top floor of his stately urban mansion, had become an opulent playpen decorated with girls, celebrated by gossips.

Sidney, whom one disapproving journalist had labeled "that satanic sculptor of idols," was living quite well for an ogre. He had capitalized on his own insightfulness; he smiled knowing that he was at the hub of a powerful PR society in which celebrity was better than good, it was great, and image was everything worth living for. His own image as a giant was flourishing.

There were notable triumphs to savor. He had indirectly embarrassed Contemporary Consensuses into admitting improprieties in polling techniques and falsifications in the "best" lists, rendering the organization all but impotent for the future. An attempt by them to do the same thing to Satellite Surveys had backfired, strengthening rather than weakening Adam Wiest and company. Neither Sidney nor Adrienne had ever been implicated with either outfit, but they both knew the truth, and that was what really mattered.

Sidney had also been instrumental in choreographing Norman Prescott's takeover of Braxton Broadcasting. It was a sore subject between the principals of Sidney Bastion Associates, Ltd., and Adrienne Gale, Inc.

He continued to be obsessed by Adrienne herself, both physically and professionally. Though his fascination disturbed him, he could not shake her from his mind.

He imagined also that she was aware of his feelings, which made him act forever on the defensive with her, as if they were in some undeclared war of semantics and subterfuge. It was impossible for him to fully relax and savor the sweetness of his successes.

The Bastion company was indisputably the industry leader in one area. Sidney took justifiable pride in his technical inventory. It was duplicated in his offices on both coasts and in London. The range of media services it afforded clients was virtually unlimited, the firm's title notwithstanding.

Paramount among these services was a series of fully manned television production studios with standby video crews for location shooting. With their satellite hookup they gave his organization the same mobility and flexibility as network news units. The Sid/Bas Satellite Network transmitted video press releases, offered as "news" stories that appeared genuine enough to be used by local and network stations, and allowed clients the opportunity to answer any media charges instantly via taped statements. The spontaneity of it assured maximum pickup, which was what the business was all about.

Norman Prescott had also seen to it that Sidney was appointed to the boards of several influential companies under his control, one in publishing and another in the film industry.

It was all very impressive, except to Adrienne Gale.

"Hang all the titles you want on him," she said. "Pin all the medals you want on him, seat him on all the boards you can come up with, and surround him with beautiful women. He still emerges as nothing more than a glorified press agent just like all the rest of us."

It was enough to drive Sidney bonkers as he veered out of London into the sky heading for L.A. and the second quarter century of his curious mission among men.

"Damn you, bitch," he muttered to himself, seeing her smiling face in his mind.

62

Sidney disliked being reminded of his origins. There was always something forcing him to face the past, like Johnny's ridiculous idea of building a mansion in Memphis. Now it was Leo Hatfield and the damned book.

"Leo put that woman up to it, Sidney," Doc said.

"Leo always was a two-bit shithead. Don't worry about him. He's small-time slime."

"Johnny don't need no exposé book about him. No sir, not at all."

"What does Leo know about him anyway?"

"He knows some bad shit about the boy. Hell, Leo'd sell his momma quick and for a cheap price."

"Nothing can hurt Johnny now but himself."

"Yeah? You keep sayin' that, but I ain't so sure."

"We're not in Memphis anymore, Doc. Leo will fade out like one of those photos from his arcade. Remember them? You'd sit there, pull the curtain, drop in a quarter, and four flashes later, you'd get a strip of four small photos that faded like proofs in the light. Leo will quickly fade."

"I wanna believe ya, Sid."

"Believe me."

Sidney's confidence was short-lived. To their mutual dismay, they learned only a few days later that Leo had employed the woman, but not to write a book. Leo was due to become as much a victim as the rest of them.

*   *   *

Sidney was forever vague on the real details of Johnny Gault's background. He always preferred his own re-creations to his clients' past lives, embellishing even the most rudimentary facts with image-enhancing fictions of his own.

In the case of Johnny he had largely fashioned him out of blue sky. No papa. No momma, expect the vague memory of a sweet woman Johnny sometimes dedicated his songs to.

Abby Ashley was determined to change all that.

Like most mortals, Sidney did not want to hear what he did not want to hear. But the reports were mounting. People close to Johnny, Billy Sunshine in particular, were being approached by a woman asking too many questions.

"Bitch" was Sidney's staccato summation.

"What should I say to her?" Billy asked.

"Zero, Billy. Zilch."

"She knows I know him."

"You're a fan of his. You love his music. You admire his character."

"That's good but—"

"Don't tell her a fucking thing, Billy. You're his spiritual adviser, and so everything you know about him is confidential. She's out to do a hatchet job on Johnny."

"But why?"

There was a pause.

"Why? Because he's young and rich and famous, and she can't figure out any other way to get in on the gravy train. She's a fucking parasite, Billy."

If nothing else, Abby Ashley had succeeded in getting Sidney emotional about his star client once again.

It was not only Billy who was being pursued and bothered. Sidney's grapevine reported that "the bitch biographer," as he referred to her now, had even ventured into the call girl ranks to recruit witnesses to the naked truth about Johnny.

"She pays them to go down on her tape recorder," he jested grimly to his staff.

"If she's going to interview all the whores he's slept with," Pam said in the same vein, "this book won't be completed in our lifetimes."

"Let's not forget our roles in this," Sidney reminded them. "Johnny Gault is apple pie America."

A brief ripple of laughter greeted the boss's declaration. It was true that behind the scenes in this business of image engineering was a blunt and cynical world where fragile emotions were frequently bulldozed. "Stand your ground or become the ground," Sidney liked to say.

"Remember always that Johnny Gault is a legend. He's not to be judged by back alley standards."

"Too bad that catch in his voice isn't also a catch in his fly," Pam jested.

Sidney was suddenly not amused.

"You sound like you represent Abby Ashley," he said.

63

There was a semimagnificent arrogance about Paula Castle. Her very posture demanded attention. She stood foursquare at introductions, regal and resolute, as though every encounter was a challenge to her.

Somewhere in her history she had been a naturally attractive person. Now she was clearly the beneficiary of cosmetic science, smoothed and softened by the premier practitioners in the beauty business.

In the filtered light of evening, in the muted illumination of haut monde restaurants and supper clubs, she managed to maintain her myth of eternal youth and beauty. But the cruel scrutiny of sunlight and daylight revealed the valleys and furrows of age.

"The bitch is a witch," one of her newer sycophants observed privately after a sudden, unexpected morning encounter.

Yet there was no denying the underlying if blurred attractiveness, the not quite focused but still obvious allure. If there was something smudged about her image, it still demanded attention quite apart from her position in life.

Sidney had become able, mostly through will and wallet, to regard her with a guarded aplomb. She did possess a twilight sparkle that three martinis decidedly enhanced.

"You're all shadows and fireflies," he said as they looked at one another across a table on her terrace. He had returned from his trip only the day before.

The whole panoply of Manhattan was spread out before them. It was a perfect setting.

"You're all balls and bullshit," she replied.

Her primitive beauty shone through the curtain of cocktails. He lunged at her, and she spun out of his grasp, laughing.

"Never mix business and pleasure," she teased.

He tore at his pants and freed his cock. It stood at attention like a helmeted soldier.

"The beefeater!" she declared. "You belong outside the palace!"

"Suck me, you son of a bitch!"

Paula fell upon his penis as if it were a peninsula of choice real estate.

Client relations for Sidney were about as good as they could get.

64

P aula Castle had learned what Sidney already knew, that being hated was as good as being loved in terms of its publicity value. Perhaps it was even better. Her bestseller *Just Spell My Name Right* hit the truth in the title.

"In the cafeteria of success," Sidney told one of his university seminars, "sweet dishes are usually outnumbered by those that are spicy and pungent or downright sour."

Acidic, contentious Galen Jenkins was yet another example of the theory in practice. He had been unceremoniously deposed as chief executive officer of Allied Airlines in a family stock squabble—and left to die in ignominious anonymity—only to emerge as the swashbuckling savior of foundering, almost bankrupt Transcontinental Air. His brash, innovative style had won him as many enemies as friends over the years.

Sidney embraced the opportunity to putter with Jenkins's persona. He was determined to create an aura of invincibility beyond what Jenkins had already achieved on his own. It was yet another challenge outside the show business spectrum from which he continued to seek escape.

"I don't kiss anybody's ass," Jenkins warned him. "They kiss mine."

"We want them lining up to do it," Sidney assured him. "You deserve a helluva lot more credit than you've been getting for what you've accomplished."

"I want Allied up there sucking my wind."

Sidney smiled. He thrived on animosity.

"I've already talked about you with Sloan Bannister. He's as anxious as you and I to get out a book that smokes."

"You win by kicking the cocksuckers who compete with you right in the balls."

"That's meat. We'll have you running for president before we're through—and I mean president of the U.S.A."

"I don't want to be president of anything but Transcon."

"What about taking over Allied?"

"You're tapping into the futures file."

"You saw what we did with Norm Prescott in the Braxton Broadcasting takeover? That was eighty-five percent hype."

"A marriage of assholes."

Sidney chuckled. It was rare that a client amused him. He was perversely attracted to Jenkins's profane, pugnacious style.

"He's a pig," Claudia said, repulsed.

"He's raw power," Sidney replied.

He saw in Jenkins some of the flamboyant entrepreneurial style of earlier American industrial pioneers. It was refreshing, like a dash of cold water in the face, after decades of faceless, gray-flanneled executives all stamped from the same corporate mold. The rest of the country surely felt the same way.

"Galen Jenkins will be America's first superstar businessman," Sidney predicted. "We'll build him into a legend just like Johnny Gault, Billy Sunshine, and all the others. They'll be wanting his autograph on everything—not just payroll checks—and they'll pay to see him and listen to what he has to say."

It might have been just another optimistic, precampaign prediction from the inner sanctum of Sidney Bastion Associates, Ltd., except that this time Sidney meant it.

Sloan Bannister was a reserved individual who personally downplayed the sensational while spotlighting it in his literary collaborations. Like many writers, he was himself the antithesis of his work.

Thus, Sidney paid particular attention to a comment Sloan made after only a week with Galen Jenkins.

"This guy is unbelievable," he said. "He's got more original quotes in him than Bartlett's!"

"Maybe we should cut down your percentage," Sidney kiddingly suggested. "The book'll write itself."

"Sure," Bannister complained. "If it flops it's the writer's fault; if it sells it's because the subject's so fascinating."

"How's Galen to work with?" Sidney inquired.

"Impossible."

"More so than usual?"

"No, they're all impossible."

"The material's good, though?"

"Episodic—but commercial."

"Make him look heroic. We want him to be the first American business hero. It's about time we had some corporate stars out there contending with the rock and movie and sports idols. Galen's perfect for the part."

"Nobody believes that more than he does."

"Cocky and confident are good. Just don't let him come across as over-bearing."

Sloan smiled faintly.

"I handle the tape recorder. You handle him."

"It's got to be a winner, Sloan. The whole campaign's hanging on it."

"That has a familiar ring."

"More so this time. We're building this one from the inside out."

65

H e was riding the range, Johnny said, referring to his odysseys aboard the bus. For a Southern boy, he adapted well to the West. The expansiveness, the wide openness, appealed to him—along with the privacy that space provided.

"Born to ride the horses of hell," he wrote as he rode. His Harley was always hooked up and ready in the rear. "Smokin' the sweet weed with a fresh Jezebel . . ."

"Straddle the big bike," he said, trancelike, "like some quiverin' whore, ride on to t'morrow, yesterday ain't no more . . ."

"Born to Ride" was born that moment and ready to ride the charts. It was a hit from the moment of its introduction.

Johnny liked celebrating bikers. He identified with them in multiple ways. They were renegades and rogues, flaunting convention in lifestyle and raiment. He wore their sleek boots and studded leathers with a sense of camaraderie. Black was basic in his wardrobe.

"Rally in the alley," he wrote and sang, "to the Harleys not the hounds . . ."

He was making a social statement most of his fans likely missed. Johnny knew the pain of being an outsider. He identified with the surly blue-collar bikers who swarmed his concerts.

"There's rainbows in oil slicks," he sang to them. "It ain't all too bad t'be born in the country and love mom 'n dad . . ."

People wept when Johnny sang so plaintively of family ties. The celebrated adoration of his mother was part and parcel of his image.

"I'm a momma's boy," he repeated in all his interviews.

Whatever the chemistry, it was modern alchemy. He turned all the baser instincts into gold.

"Read between the lines," Johnny sang, "for telltale signs."

"Telltale Signs" was a designated future hit.

"Music's me," Johnny said of himself. "What else is there 'cept fuckin' 'n suckin'?"

He left out shooting up. The drugging aspect of his life, never a comfortable mantle, was ever more ominous. In his periodic bursts of creativity he was usually, amazingly, clear-minded and clear-eyed. These sieges of abstinence never lasted long but were spectacularly productive.

"All people of genius are beyond definition," Sidney said of him. "He's like a brilliant meteor, a shooting star."

There had always been an androgynous quality about Johnny. His features were so soft, his face and his mouth so provocatively feminine, they added an erotic urgency to his driving beat.

"Sweet as a cunt and tough as a cowboy," one underground press reviewer summarized him.

"You get the smell of a saddle and the piss of a horse in his upbeat tunes," wrote another avant-garde critic, "but his sweet stuff is as mellow as moonlight."

Johnny did not want to read his reviews, and Sidney obliged him by sending them to Doc and filing away the copies.

"What people say don't matter," Johnny said. "I jist do what I do."

He had a way about him that ranged from wicked to weird to wonderful. The ingredients of any elixir involved a touch of magic and a sprinkle of luck.

When the road crew talked about him they worried about him.

"Johnny's fucked up," an electrician declared during a concert break.

"Bull," retorted a coworker. "He's happy as a pig in shit."

As they debated in the darkness behind the main stage, Johnny was out there above and beyond them, sweating and singing in his all-out five-alarm-fire style.

"Wham bam, thank y'mam!" he shouted. "Y'all make a sandwich like nobody can!"

Sexual allusions were tantamount to his triumphs.

"Ah'm hotter'n hell and it sure feels swell."

When the crowds reached the zenith of frenzy he always calmed them with talk of and tribute to his mother.

"This one's for momma," he'd half whisper. A hush inevitably fell over the audience.

"Mary, mother of Jesus," he'd sing softly, "meet Rita my own, born in the valley, died all alone."

It was his special gift, his private magic, leading masses from delirium to melancholy, then rewarding them with a sense of hope and joy.

"He's a maximum mesmerizer," Sidney said in admiration. "It's just too bad that none of the joy goes back to him."

"He plays his crowds like he plays his guitar," Claudia had once observed. "He masturbates them, and they come when he wants them to."

Johnny himself was not unduly introspective. Why he did what he did and how he got where he was was of little or no concern to him.

"Twelve times twice," he chanted in the Tennessee–West Virginia–New Orleans musical mix he enjoyed most. "Double dozen, add a cousin . . ."

Flick, flack, scratch my back.

The bus rolled on.

If Johnny was bored and jaded and ready for a bit of sexual experimentation, no one could have chosen a better catalyst than Callen Ruark. He was classically handsome, smooth as marble, and gifted with a provocative persona.

"What is it that you do?" Johnny asked after their introduction following a concert in Atlanta.

"Whatever's required."

Johnny smiled.

"You're pretty," he said.

"So are you."

"We sound like a couple of cunts."

Cal winked.

"We are," he said.

Johnny succumbed to Cal Ruark rather readily, and he was not disappointed.

"Coming is coming," he said. "It doesn't really matter how you git to it."

Johnny had always been personally attractive to the gay community. His wanton exhibitionism, his flaunting of his cock, appealed to their own repressed desires to express themselves openly.

Cal stayed overnight on the bus and awakened him with a blue jay. That was a Gault euphemism for a blow job.

"You're somethin' else." Johnny sighed.

The body straddle that followed was positive and strong, knees paragraphing the rib cage. Cal's russet cock loomed large over Johnny's face.

"Suck," he said.

"I don't—"

"Suck!"

It was an erotic world he lived in, and he did nothing to curb its excesses. The lacquer on his face would be gone with a towel but the stain would remain.

"Your most famous fuckup," Sidney called it.

"Never happened," Johnny lied.

Callen Ruark made sure the 'loids knew about it. Their brief encounter made more supermarket headlines than a lobster giveaway.

In the cocoon of his bus—his rolling estate, as some tabloids referred to it—Johnny indulged some of his more bizarre passions. He liked dolling himself up with rouge and lipstick, accented with heavy eye makeup, and then donning the laciest of panties. He got hard putting on silken hose held up by garter belts. Sometimes he wore bras that teased the flat nipples of his chest.

It turned him on to march the length of the vehicle in this minuscule costume, elevated by high heels, and feeling himself as he strutted. No audience was required. He got off on his own.

"Here she comes," he would sing, mimicking the beauty pageant theme. He spent hours surrounded by the flattering lights of makeup mirrors, masturbating himself even as he altered his image, delighting in his binary deceptions.

His drivers were not surprised when he emerged at remote stops dressed in wigs and high heels, lipsticked and rouged, demanding the courtesies gentlemen extended to ladies. No one who knew only his semisavage stage presence would have recognized him and his moments of masquerade.

"I'm a woman at heart," he sometimes confessed. "You have to be entered to really understand the penetration of life and how much it hurts. That only happens to women. They're the only real people on earth."

"You gotta give a genius a lotta space," Doc contended.

Johnny was no genius; he was a satellite in an orbit all his own.

There was little happiness in his heart, particularly since the bypass of Peggy Sue. His music, though, could be remarkably joyous. He could wail and lament that he was "saddled in sorrow, dreading tomorrow," and then jump with abandon into the happy, wild, throbbing of "King of the World."

The range of his appeal was as broad as his musical scope. Honors, trophies, and laminated plaques from all manner of fans piled up to the size of a small mountain.

"I'll need a dentist to remove all these plaques," Johnny jested. "Look at this bunch of junk."

"You can never be too celebrated," Sidney contended.

The honors were stored in garbage bags in a barn in Gaultland in Memphis.

66

S idney was away for more than a week accompanying Billy Sunshine on his Caribbean expedition. The entire Cathedral of Divine Destiny troupe had come along as well, traveling with Billy and Sidney in the church's luxuriously appointed jet, the *Angel of Mercy*.

The trip enabled Sidney to confer as planned with a number of national leaders, including the notorious General Raul Tampa, who had risen to power in Vivado in a bloody coup six years earlier.

Tampa proved to be very much interested in the business of image making, not terribly surprising in view of the sordid international reputation he had managed to acquire on his own.

Raul Tampa was a kaleidoscopic personality. His manner and his moods ricocheted off the walls of situations, real and paranoid. He imagined himself a benevolent leader chosen by his followers to lead them to Utopia. In reality he had taken a lovely island filled with casual joy and constricted it into a tropical prison.

Death and dismemberment had become commonplace for opponents of the Tampa regime. Drugs flowed through his island like rivers of blood; guns and dangerous chemicals found the same smooth and open channels. The natives themselves lived in their accustomed poverty, struggling to exist, uncertain if the rumors were true, certain they could do nothing about them.

The official United States government attitude toward the small, lush island off its southeastern coast had been one of cool aloofness until recent intelligence reports began tracing the origin of terrorists and their acts of murder and disruption in South and Central America to Vivado and the regime of its dictator, Tampa.

Traveling under the guise of a religious pilgrim, Sidney felt free to talk openly with the alleged instigator of terrorism. Tampa was less wary and therefore more candid and less inhibited speaking to an American businessman than he might have been with a diplomat or a politician.

"We in Vivado are misunderstood by your countrymen," the General insisted. "As a consequence, development of trade between our nations has been hindered. I am particularly interested in promoting tourism in our land. Vivado has splendid beaches, perhaps the finest in the world. We are a peace-loving people who would welcome improved relations with you in America."

Sidney sensed the possibilities immediately. He was already envisioning a string of sparkling white hotels strung like a necklace along the virgin shoreline of the island's largely untouched eastern perimeter. What a network of Castles it could contain. But he knew American foreign policy discouraged—indeed, shunned—any relations with Tampa.

"It's a subject worth exploring, General. I'm certain my people have a misconception of both you and Vivado."

"Is there blood on my hands?" He held them up as he spoke. "Do I come at you with guns and knives? Am I sinister and foreboding?"

He laughed at his own description. In reality he was quite handsome, possessed of a face that offered many telegenic angles. He was an avid watcher of American television and a student of America's daily press. Sidney was more than a little impressed with Tampa's potential for PR sculpting.

"I suggest that a good opening ploy for you might be to establish some indirect contact outside of the political arena. Something like a Center for Christian Unity, perhaps—at a place like Billy Sunshine University, for example. It would demonstrate a real desire on your part for peaceful coexistence."

Tampa smiled.

"You are a shrewd thinker," he said. "There is much merit in what you propose."

"It's off the top of my head. I haven't mentioned it to Reverend Billy as yet. But I feel certain he'd be amenable."

"We must explore it rapidly, while all of you are still in Vivado."

There were distinct advantages to dictatorship, Sidney summarily learned. One definitely was the absence of red tape. He sat with Billy later the same day in private conference with General Tampa and several of his ministers, mulling over the very idea he had proposed earlier.

The visitors and the General got along famously.

"You are Billy and Sidney, therefore I am Raul henceforth," he declared with handshakes for both.

Sidney and Billy left the island a day later in a state of high anticipation, congratulating themselves for having set in motion a program that promised to eventually benefit all. Before they had parted, Sidney had managed not only to hint at some future involvement with the Castle hotel empire but also had suggested the prospect of persuading Galen Jenkins to restore regular air service between New York and Vivado. It all represented an act of unification surpassing anything the State Department had been able to accomplish in years of strained relations.

Sidney Bastion intended to make General Tampa a hero in the eyes of America—a hero sanctified by the Reverend Billy Sunshine.

67

I t was difficult to determine which idea Paula Castle liked most: meeting with Raul Tampa or building a resort complex on Vivado.

She had flown to the island kingdom on a chartered jet decorated on both sides with magnified images of her lush lip imprints.

"My lips and my mouth are what I'm all about," she explained to the quizzical local press.

Sidney had conceived the idea of expanding her empire into the tropics and flashing her image everywhere possible and he made sure there was mass media pickup. He had engineered the costume she wore as well—a provocative, bikinilike dress that took advantage of her ample breasts and subtly protruding buttocks.

For a woman her age she managed to project a mature sexuality that depended more on its motion than its material.

The photoflashes stormed. It was lightning everywhere.

Paula was in her glory.

"I adore dark, sinister men," Paula confessed. "Tampa is just about perfect."

"There are rumors he's heavily into sadomasochism," Sidney joked with her.

Paula smiled fleetingly.

"A little beating now and then never hurt anybody," she responded.

T he casualness with which Sidney and Paula pursued the possibilities inherent in dealing with the dictator gave pause to some members of the Bastion staff, Pam Garson among them.

"They're so cynical and venal, Claudia," she complained to her friend and ex-boss. "I'm no flag waver, but I don't think either one of them has a single stripe of red, white, or blue."

"Sidney's only tinge of patriotism involves worshiping the presidential por-traits on big bills."

"Between us, I'm sometimes embarrassed to be involved in the sugar coating we do on people."

Claudia sighed.

"Tampa is probably not that much worse than the Doc Diamonds, the Paula Castles, and the Galen Jenkinses of the world."

"Being obnoxious can't compare with murder."

"Nobody's proved any murders, Pam."

"That's a naive statement, Claudia, and you know it."

"We're in the PR business. It consists of putting the best face possible on a paying client."

"I'm beginning to wonder if I'd better get out before I become too cynical."

"Out to what, Pam? The rest of the world's exactly the same way. It's all tactics and technology. Tactics and technology will never replace feelings. If they do we're all doomed.

"Go to sleep, Pam. You Easterners get flaky after midnight."

Pam returned the phone to its cradle slowly and quietly. Sidney was asleep beside her, snoring peacefully, patently pleased by his fresh inroads in interna-tional influence.

She reached for a robe to cover her naked body. Maybe it really was the same way out there. Except there would be a major difference. It wouldn't be anywhere near as plush or meaningful. She slid under the covers. There really was something to be said for significance—however it was attained, however it was maintained.

68

A few days in the Caribbean had convinced Sidney he should spend more time away from New York. The lush tropical setting, fragrant balmy air, and laid-back lifestyle had refreshed him for the first time he could remember. Stimulated into elation, he returned to Manhattan brimming with ideas and effervescent with enthusiasm.

Pam Garson set up a meeting of his account executives as he had directed. They sat dutifully around a long conference table quite openly dreading the ordeal. Sidney had earned a reputation among his senior staff as a PR pedant, particularly since he'd received an honorary degree from Billy Sunshine University.

It was all glowing smiles and hearty cordiality, however, when he finally strode into the room—tanned, confident, and exuding goodwill.

"First of all," he began, "I want to thank all of you, collectively and individually, for the fine jobs you've been doing in maintaining the premier position of SBA Limited in the field of public relations. We are in that envied spot because of your separate contributions as well as your joint efforts. In the industry the byword has become Bastion, and in large measure I have all of you to thank for that . . ."

There was perceptible wincing among most of the long-term staff.

". . . The wonderful thing about imagination is its ability to make you anything and give you anything you want. So can public relations. It deals in facts and fantasies with equal adeptness. Then it blends them to achieve the ideal image . . ."

Pam joined the others who sought the ceiling with their eyes. Sidney's simplistic philosophies could be embarrassing. Employees endured rather than enjoyed them.

". . . You're undoubtedly wondering why I summoned you here this afternoon so soon after my visit to the Caribbean. I won't hold you for long from the various urgencies awaiting you. I'm here to announce to you privately, prior to public release, that from this day forward we're entering a new phase of international public relations, representing not just individuals but nations as well. This marks fulfillment of a personal dream for me, and I hope you share my excitement at the prospect of exporing a whole new realm of PR . . ."

There was animated applause despite the absence of any details. Their own leader was applying the tricks of the trade to his own employees, and he didn't even seem to realize it.

Claudia," Pam began her report on the meeting to her former boss, "I really think Sidney's been seduced by the very methods he uses on others. He thinks he can manipulate everybody, even his own manipulators."

"Relax," Claudia responded. "He's always been that way. He has to believe his own lies to be effective."

"He thinks he can bullshit bullshitters?"

"And con con men."

"I'm really beginning to worry about him. He takes himself so seriously at times."

"Don't. He's not worth it."

"I know."

There was an uncomfortable pause.

"I've been after him to transfer you out here," Claudia said.

"He told me."

"How do you feel about it?"

"Insecure, number one. Uncertain, number two."

Claudia laughed.

"That's why you're so good at this racket. You never take anything for granted."

"Nothing in life can be taken for granted, Claudia."

ess than a year after their marriage, Eden and Gray Matthison went beyond what could rightfully be expected of any client in terms of professional co-operation. Eden gave birth to a son.

A publicity harvest resulted, of course. But even more importantly, the event accomplished what no amount of story placing and story pulling, deception, and distraction had completely succeeded in doing before. It pushed all the annoying speculations about Gray Matthison's sexual preferences permanently into the background.

That it could hardly be documented that Gray was indeed the father was of little or no consequence. He played his role with easy, convincing charm, and baby Graham Matthison Jr. was adopted by his father's nationwide audience.

Would that all PR dilemmas could be resolved so profoundly.

"Eden's actually breast-feeding her baby," Claudia reported.

"Milk it for all it's worth," Sidney jested. "In this day and age that's good human interest crap."

"The baby's adorable,"

"I'm with W. C. Fields on kids."

"You should have been born sterile," she retorted. "Now the best the world can hope for is impotence."

"Ouch," he said, but she never heard it. She'd hung up on him as she often did when she was vexed. Sidney shrugged. Women were always impossible on the subjects of childbirth and children.

70

There were those in the media and the music world who speculated that Doc never tried to straighten Johnny out because Johnny might just be worth more dead than alive.

If there was any such master plan, Doc confided it to no one. But it would have been fairly easy to juggle the books and cook the stats to substantiate such a theory. There would be no split in the postmortem money, for example, and no partnership inclusion in the spin-off projects relating to Johnny's idolization.

Doc was unfazed by personal criticism from the press. It was what they said about Johnny that mattered. And even then his concern was metered only by the revenues.

Johnny Gault had no real friends; he had escorts and lackeys. True, they masqueraded as friends, as buddies, but they were all there to lick up his limelight and stuff their jeans with as much of the star lode as they could. Johnny was oblivious to their avarice. He enjoyed their company; he needed their company. Under the restrictions of success, his freedom was acutely limited. "The Guys," as he called them collectively, were ever present and ever willing to indulge his every whim from water pistol war to twenty-four hour orgies. They took the between-concerts heat off Doc, and so Doc tolerated them without really trying to supervise or direct them.

There were few if any opportunities for Johnny to establish lasting relationships of any significance. The roadblock on Peggy Sue was the most egregious example. Most were sexual and superficial. Doc wanted it that way and liked it that way. It made everything easier to control.

"Keep Johnny happy" was his simple admonition to the Guys.

Nobody responded to that directive more assiduously than Randall Wheeler, who was essentially road manager of the loosely floating entourage that surrounded Johnny. The paid hangers-on referred to him as "Randy the Roadie" and deferred to him since he was obviously first among equals.

Randy was superefficient, a skinny young man with long, dark hair and deep-socketed eyes who functioned like a nerve ending. He was everywhere at once yet always at Johnny's beck and call. It was Randy who always had the answers to operational questions when no one else did. His every waking hour was devoted to serving Johnny. Randy had no limitations. He would do absolutely anything for his hero boss.

Under the guise of logistics—arranging for transport of Johnny's most personal possessions beyond wardrobes—Randy had become the main source for Johnny's increasing dependency on all manner of drugs, from painkillers to life killers. He never questioned Johnny's choices or his appetites. He was the ultimate fan in the quintessential dream position, touching the flesh of his idol every day, nurturing him in both pain and joy.

Randy was the enabler.

Johnny passed days in a mellow blur, frequently unaware of time or place.

"He's a floating balloon," one of the Guys observed, "and one of these days somebody's going to puncture it."

"Most likely himself."

"You see those enlarged pupils, the runny nose lately? Johnny's gittin' t'be a mess up close."

It was one of the reasons so few got up close. Interviews had become severely restricted and subject to prepublication review. Otherwise getting any sort of an up-to-date story was a dead-end proposition.

Johnny had rapidly progressed—regressed, really—from the simple snorting of cocaine to freebasing and then speedballing. There was no heating and melting involved in the latter, and the one-two punch of a cocaine high followed quickly by a heroin downer delighted him.

Randy was like a chemist in achieving just the right balance of the two potent drugs. He mixed them in a teaspoon, added a bit of water, then made a small wad of cotton. He dropped it into the heated mixture and stuck the needle into its heart, sucking up the purified recipe. Tapping the syringe, he pushed out the air.

Johnny never watched the procedure, keeping his eyes closed in anticipation. With a tourniquet made from anything handy, usually his belt or a T-shirt, Randy forced Johnny's veins to the surface and, like a surgeon, he then deftly punctured the boy's arm and slowly released a stream of heroin into his bloodstream

"Sweeter than a blow job," Johnny would exhale.

So sweet he had begun to desire it almost constantly. More than fame, more than sex, maybe more than life itself.

Johnny Gault sometimes spent days cocooned in his bus, denying all of the world around him. In these times not even his driver could communicate with him. Suspicions that he was heavily drugged were sometimes valid. At rare other times he was lucid and reflective—and remarkably creative.

The road crew was close at hand but allowed him his space. Without warning he would summon them.

"Sucker alert!" he'd holler over the intercom.

"Yo, chief," would be the response.

"Mall ahead," he'd declare. "Arcade time."

"You got it."

Sometimes the stops involved only a few minutes, at other times he could spend hours. Johnny was a difficult child no matter his age.

The mall attacks were like raids. Johnny liked instigating action in remote places. Sometimes he drew his guns and fired, blowing the guts out of electronic games, then strewing the place with hundred-dollar bills to cover the damages. At other times he was reasonably calm, satisfied to ring up game scores like any other contender.

Difficult was not a large enough word to describe him.

In the insulated world surrounding Johnny, things began getting kinkier and kinkier. It was not just the gorging and the gunplay, the sex orgies and the drug blasts. It was the attitude.

Johnny had become increasingly paranoid, certain everyone around him was conspiring to control and confine him. He had become ever more furtive and reclusive. At the same time he'd also developed a more sadistic streak.

The roadies who traveled with him knew him better than Doc Diamond ever could or would.

"He's goin' t'hell in a hurry," one of the electricians said, observing Johnny sprawled naked, facedown in a pool of his own lime-green vomit.

"Goin'?" a coworker reacted. "He's already there. We better start readin' the help wanted ads."

"There ain't many openin's for star-puke cleaners."

"Ain't it amazin' how many folks want this kinda fuckin' job?"

"Show biz," laughed a cohort. "Moppin' up Johnny's slop's sheer glamour, man."

The most muscular among them took charge.

"Pass the bedpan, boys, and let's git this fat-ass mothafucka cleaned up and put away."

He was dead weight passed out. His technical crew were forced to function like circus roustabouts lifting a fallen baby elephant. They rolled him onto a makeshift stretcher of blankets. They knew he was a star with the potential to fulfill his own dreams of heaven, but now he was just a mass of jellied protoplasm with a wicked stench.

"The National Inquest would pay a fortune for a shot of this," noted one of the Guys.

The others glared at him. A day later he was no longer a member of the entourage. Bitching was one thing, but loyalty was quite another. If Johnny was a mess at times, he was also a musical messiah. They were his apostles, for better or for worse.

t was not yet dawn when Sidney was awakened by the insistent buzzing of
his private line. Only a handful of people knew the number, and none of
them would violate his rest without good reason. Still half asleep, he reluctantly reached for the phone.

"H'lo," he said without opening his eyes.

"Sidney, Claudia, Johnny Gault's dead."

His body jackknifed into a sitting position, his mind instantly alert.

"How? When?"

"OD, of course. About an hour ago."

"Son of a bitch."

"As soon as this gets out we're going to be avalanched."

"I'm dressing. Call me at the office in half an hour."

"Sidney?"

"What?"

"I'm really sorry."

He swallowed dryly.

"It was inevitable," he said.

Johnny Gault had become a permanent part of Americana, a symbol of its
native talent and dream potential. As the news spread, people wept openly on
the streets, in stadiums and malls, in all manner of public places. His songs cried
out to them from radios and loudspeakers, from cars and buildings, from the very
atmosphere itself. There was no shame in their sorrow, only the terrible, unified
sense of loss.

"He was like a son of God," one weeping woman told a TV interviewer, "and yet he was still like a child and a friend of mine."

Billy Sunshine called him "the brother of Jesus" in more than one of his many instant media eulogies. Sidney Bastion, with his addiction to fiction, compared him to Zeus, the mythological god of gods.

"He will live forever," he predicted. "His soul is in the company of saints, his mother among them. God bless their everlasting reunion."

"Eloquent," Claudia congratulated him by phone after seeing the wire service reports. "You do great necrophilia."

"I do what I have to do when it's due."

"Would you tell the world they're worshiping a graven image with grave shortcomings as a human being?"

"That California wine is more potent than ever."

"Potent and portentous."

"This is a difficult time for us, Claudia. A giant has fallen. Try to be understanding."

"You're consistent, babe. The beautiful bullshit keeps trickling out of your mouth even when you're half dead in the water."

"I don't know why I even talk to you, much less turn to you for consolation. *Dead* is such a drastic word."

"He was your cornerstone."

"He was a rock in it. But he wasn't the whole foundation. There's a structure now that will definitely survive."

"Like us?"

"The segue is less than clear, Claude."

"It doesn't matter, does it, Sidney?"

"Everything about you matters."

She laughed, briefly and emptily.

"Out here they call it 'Sid shit.' "

All of their conversations since their personal breakup were tinged with allusions to their past intimacy. He might have preferred that she no longer be a part of his organization—as he often angrily declared—except for the fact that she was the most accomplished and efficient employee he had ever had.

"Look," he reasoned, "you're going to be deluged. Just relay it all to us in New York. We'll handle it all from here."

"Sure you will."

"Your sarcasm's thick enough to stab."

"Go ahead," she said. "I don't bleed anymore."

*   *   *

Overnight a nondescript motel on a secondary road on the outskirts of Chicago achieved a kind of immoral immortality.

JOHNNY GAULT DIED HERE the pockmarked glass sign was quick to announce, lucky to have all the letters for a change.

Quicker than the sign, Doc Diamond acquired the property for the express purpose of turning it into a museum. Death sites of deities had historically shown dollar value. If others thought he had overpaid in haste, they would soon realize how much they had underestimated the power of the mounting myth surrounding Johnny Gault.

Doc Diamond moved with the velocity of light to maximize any and all potential rewards to be gained from his singer-composer's untimely but hardly unexpected death. His instructions to Sidney were succinct and decidedly lacking in sentimentality.

"Milk it for all it's worth," he said. "This'll be his last personal appearance."

The funeral would be the final concert in a brief, stormy, and undeniably spectacular career. Sidney was already engaged in planning a lavish media pageant by the time Claudia called back again with the sordid details.

"He was freebasing cocaine with a pair of hookers," she recounted. "Then they decided on speedballing. That's what did him in."

Sidney was no authority, but he knew that meant shooting a powerful mix of cocaine and heroin directly into the bloodstream.

"Asshole," he said.

"Do we go along with a natural causes obit?"

"The cops'll discount it. The whole story'll break eventually no matter what we say now."

"Let it come from them, not us."

"You're right. Exhaustion and heart seizure. You know the line. Overwork, poor diet, et cetera. Put it on the wire that way and let's wing it from there."

She did not have to be told to immortalize Johnny in the process of reporting his passing. All the adjectives relating to deification, all the superlatives referring to greatness, would automatically be brought into play in the death notice.

"Any funeral stats yet?" she asked.

"I'm on that right now. Just leave them as pending."

"Billy Sunshine'll want to be in on the services, don't you think?"

"He damned well better. This has got to be one helluva show."

"Count him in, then."

"Keep the line open."

"Right."

They were both like thoroughbreds in the paddock at the start of another grueling championship race. He hung up and was immediately immersed in a frenzy of organizational details. The funeral would be held at the still-uncompleted Gaultland. Doc Diamond had specified that immediately. Sidney dreaded such a highly visible return to Memphis, but there was no alternative.

Reverend Billy was easily recruited to conduct funeral services for "my dearly beloved Johnny," volunteering his own immensely popular television program as the showcase.

"It'll mark the first time we've ever gone outside the cathedral," he pointed out, "but for our glorious friend who sings now for Jesus and the heavenly multitude it will be a humble testimony to our everlasting love."

Sidney had to cut him short because of a serious backlog of calls. His secretary recited a list of callers holding and, at Sidney's request, put through Adrienne Gale first.

"Bastion Spectaculars," he announced into the mouthpiece. "Everything from joy to sorrow covered on a moment's notice."

She laughed lightly.

"I didn't expect you to be sobbing, but I did anticipate a small portion of solemn restraint."

"We're in ballyhoo, not boo hoo."

"Maybe you're a necrophiliac. You might get off on this kind of stuff."

"I love losing clients and then having to stage a celebration for my last payday."

"Ever faithful to the bottom line."

"I'd love to continue bullshitting, Adrienne, but I've got a million calls waiting and another million things to do."

"I know. I just wanted to extend my sympathy and let you know I'll gladly help in any way I can. I know the pressure."

"Sweet of you. I'll collect on the offer next time rigor mortis sets in between my thighs."

"Sidney," she said with a sigh, "you're sick."

The smile he wore briefly after her call would be his only one for days to come.

There was seldom any overlapping of client interests within any public relations organization. The tendency was to separate clientele to prevent any comparison and subsequent jealousies. A notable exception in the Bastion family had been the relationship between Gault and Billy Sunshine. Billy had always understood any preoccupation Sidney had with Johnny and forgiven it.

The policy of account isolation was put to a special test in the midst of the funeral preparations. All the "fellow clients" wanted their condolences to their "special friend" made very public. Sidney was already in Memphis, where he had established temporary headquarters until the wake was over. He had visited Gaultland earlier in the day and had been all but overwhelmed by the clamor and chaos.

Tents of concessionaires were pitched all over the estate. Multiple strings of lights illuminated the pathways with black balloons rising above them like lunar eclipses. The grounds were more carnival than funeral. Loudspeakers blasted one Johnny Gault hit after another. It was like the setting of yet another major rock concert. Unsettling to Sidney, though hardly surprising, were the ticket booths set up at the only two viable entrances to the property. Doc intended to charge admission to all but the invited guests.

"You'll be castigated by the media," Sidney warned him. "It's just too nakedly venal, Doc."

"Johnny and me don't put on a show nowhere for nobody for nothin'," Doc replied.

The park was on a pretty piece of land right up against the river. If the disarray created by construction crews could be overlooked, the setting was in many ways paradisiac. That was how his grieving fans regarded it.

"Johnny woulda liked this," even Doc was briefly moved to observe. Then he was gone to check the attendance count and, more importantly, the registers.

In many ways the whole park was still in a primitive stage of development, the construction plan having incorrectly assumed that Johnny would live out the decade. Symbolically, at the crest of an imposing staircase, there was a vacant throne resembling the Lincoln Memorial in Washington. Johnny had been expected to sit there at the launch of each new album.

The chair was empty now. They would fill it with a statue one day soon, but nothing made by man could ever recapture what God and Sidney Bastion had created.

"Pieces of My Heart" was played over the park's loudspeakers. It was the first of Johnny's posthumous releases. Now all that was left was to insure his image in immortality. Ironically, only a week earlier he had headed the list of the Ten Sexiest Men Alive, as reported by one of the research foundations under the umbrella of Satellite Surveys.

Questions came from everywhere about everything. The most persistent ones dealt with speculation on the true cause of Johnny's death. But there were others as well.

Why was he clad only in pink shorts when his body was found? Why was the predominant color of Gaultland and its surrounding stucco walls pink? Why did he always have pink roses at his performances?

"Pink was Johnny's favorite color," Sidney repeated many times. "To him it symbolized the beauty and innocence of little children—and he dearly loved children."

The truth was that Johnny privately despised kids. Their very presence annoyed him, and he sometimes refused to perform until the smaller of them were removed from audiences. "Anything under three feet is dead meat," he declared.

Sidney knew the real reason for his pastel preference. Johnny had told him that any number of times.

"Pink is the color of young pussy," Johnny would explain drolly, following the statement with one of his trademark winks. He had alluded quite explicitly to that explanation in one of his hit albums, *In the Pink*.

This had been one of the simplest deceptions necessary to maintain the image of Johnny Gault as a good-boy-gone-genius. Reverend Billy had been enormously helpful in this area. His praise of the troubled star from his influential pulpit had served as satisfactory response to many troubling questions.

Doc Diamond left the vital media arrangements to Sidney while he busied himself with the overall funeral production. It appeared at times likely to rival if not surpass the burial magnitude and magnificence accorded King Tut in 1352 B.C.

Hundreds of thousands of fans indicated their intention to attend the rites after news of Johnny's death was released. The threat of a mammoth invasion created immediate lodging and logistics problems. Thus, while Sidney occupied himself with celebrating the character and career of Johnny Gault, Doc was contracting for an army of portable johns to be scattered about Gaultland. Hasty deals with major concessionaires assured that a wide variety of souvenirs would be available. He also arranged for catering companies to handle the food for the crowds. Doc, of course, would win a substantial cut of the profits.

Sidney collaborated with Doc on a number of overlapping details. They agreed on a telegenic carpet of half a million pink roses resting inside a bright outline of pure white roses shaped like a guitar. Doc quickly made a deal to market the petals sealed in plastic medallions commemorating the event for the multimillion fans unable to personally attend the services.

"We'll never run out," he confided. "I've got a standin' order for ten thousand pink roses a week once the initial supply's gone."

Sidney smiled ruefully. "Who was it that said 'The universal mind pays attention to the smallest detail'?"

"I want you to stay on with me after the big show, Sid," said Doc. "Keep right on polishin' the image. No reason why we can't keep Johnny's name alive and cash-productive forever."

He briefly outlined his plans to make Gaultland a permanent tourist attraction with restaurants, nightclubs, a motel, and a theme amusement park for kids.

There was also a vault full of unreleased Gault recordings that he intended to place on the market at carefully-controlled intervals.

He kept quiet about the sexual videotapes of Johnny that were also stored away in the vault. Doc at last had the power he had sought in his partnership with the singer-satyr he had nurtured to stardom and then helped to destroy.

"This is only the begining, Sid," he declared with satisfaction.

It was the end only for poor Johnny Gault.

Sidney knew it was center stage time, the key lime pie of the PR industry. He arranged for the day of the funeral to be designated a state holiday in Tennessee. He tried to have it declared an American holiday as well, but was not successful.

He settled instead for the following declaration from the President: "Johnny Gault will live forever through the magic of his talent and the strength of his Americanism. He was a true patriot and a shining symbol of what a poor boy from the poorest provinces of our vast country can achieve through diligence and ability. God bless you, Johnny! A whole nation mourns you and loves you."

For once, Doc had spared no expense. He was banking on the almost certain returns he would see from his investment. The international publicity alone was beyond price—but that was something for Sidney Bastion to appreciate.

Professional grief counselors in somber tents had been strategically placed about the grounds. Their fee was fifty dollars for fifteen minutes. Half of that amount was marked for the pocket of the omnivorous Doc of Diamonds.

As expected, Reverend Billy Sunshine rose to the occasion. Doc had asked for "the Funeral to Outdo All Funerals, the Fuckin' Mother of All Funerals!" and Billy Sunshine met the challenge with his great ingenuity, the Haloettes, and the help of the sensational Billy Sunshine Tabernacle Choir. They rocked the holy rafters of the sky that day until the weeping mourners were smiling and cheering as Billy walked over to the lectern to speak.

"Destiny hangs in the air," he declared. "God is everywhere present. God is with us here, today, as we honor our dear departed friend, Johnny. Let us now observe one minute of silence for each of us to speak in our own hearts to God, and to Johnny."

Billy loved to work a crowd, loved the excess, the orgy effect. He was a master of mental masturbation, petting and stroking his audiences until they came in their minds. His orgasmic approach was not unlike Johnny's. Within the ministerial profession he was "Big Billy."

Billy had never felt holier or more inspired, more chosen by God and the angels, than he felt at the funeral of Johnny Gault.

In gowns of luminous pink, his Haloettes moved solemnly through the crowds. They each clutched a nosegay of pink roses and baby's breath, and carried pink balloons—in recognition of Johnny's celebrated fondness for that color—that they sold to the mourners. They also carried pink baskets for donations.

The masses of idolaters, waiting expectantly on the banks of the ageless Mississippi River, reminded the Reverend of the hordes who had gathered for the Sermon on the Mount.

"You and I are privileged to be present at a historic moment, the rites of passage of an American folk hero into the annals of modern mythology," Billy said solemnly.

With that, he took into his hands a single white dove from a cage beneath the lectern. He held it up high in both hands when he spoke, clearing his face for the cameras.

"May there be peace and everlasting salvation for the divine journey of our beloved and immortal friend, brother, and surely the second son of God Almighty, Johnny Gault, dear boy," he intoned, his voice choked with emotion.

He released the dove, and as it fluttered skyward the air was suddenly filled with the flapping wings of a thousand more doves climbing in rapid flight into the brilliantly blue clear sky overhead.

With that, he was joined onstage by the legendary crooner Guy Sonata, who had consented not only to come but also to sing at the event.

"Ladies and gentlemen, my good friend Guy Sonata," said Billy as he embraced Guy in a warm bear hug.

The screaming and cheering of the people went on for a full two minutes before Guy could calm them down enough to be heard when he spoke. He waved his arms for them to let up on the noise, then shook his head and told them, "I can't honestly say I'm glad to be here."

The crowd roared with pleasure, then hushed.

"The death of any artist is like the death of a forest," Sonata continued. "It is also like the demise of a beautiful tiny violet at the foot of a tree in that forest. Wherever you are, Johnny, God be with you. This one's for you."

The camera zoomed in for a close-up as Guy Sonata sang what was to become one of his all-time biggest hits, Johnny's own soulful ballad "Love Me Sweetly."

The Haloettes moved solemnly through the sad throngs overflowing the grounds of the already hallowed, if incomplete, Johnny Gault estate. Incense smoke curls wafted through the thick air, caressing the pink balloons dancing above the heads of the crowd as far as the eye could see. Guy Sonata had them mesmerized.

When the song ended the wailing began. Row after row of mourners cried out, weeping loudly and openly, wailing and hollering, howling in grief. Soon the whole crowd was baying like a pack of hounds. Thousands listened to the howling echoing over the loudspeakers throughout the grounds, causing an ungodly cacophony.

The Reverend spoke again, hoarsely and close to the mike: "There is no ending to one whom God has chosen to gild the magnificence of his universe, only beginings of new phases of glory and achievement. Our Johnny is not gone; he will never be gone. He is only on the road again, that beautiful glory road trod so many centuries ago by his brother, and our brother, Jesus."

"Hallelujah!" shouted thousands. "Hallelujah!"

"Glory to Jesus and Johnny," thousands more began to chant. "Glory to Jesus and Johnny."

"Amen!" cried Billy Sunshine.

"Amen!" a huge chorus roared. "Amen! Amen!"

Someone released a pink balloon, then hundreds more floated upward into the deepening sky as the Billy Sunshine Tabernacle Choir sang a harmonized version of "Amazing Grace." Everyone watched the departing flock of balloons until they disappeared into the cloudless horizon.

Observing it all from a choice seat near the stage was Abby Ashley. With tears in her eyes she had to admit this was a superb theatrical performance by a master showman paying dramatic loving tribute to a dear departed peer.

Disguised in a black wig and a demure black dress, Abby had the equivalent of a ringside seat at the greatest heavyweight fight of all time. It was her first real opportunity to see many of the key figures in the quasi biography she had so far constructed from a mountain of fragmented facts.

Her publisher, somewhat unnerved by this major development, wanted all the bizarre details obtainable surrounding the funeral extravaganza. He had made sure she was close enough to see right through the sham and hypocrisy of some of the principals yet not too blindsided to sense the genuine grief of the multitudes.

She saw Doc Diamond off to the side, his eyes as cold and furtive as a serpent's. He seemed to be counting the crowd and paying little or no heed to the solemn words uttered by Billy Sunshine. Every so often someone would walk up to him and shake his hand, transferring cash to his palm. Doc would always stick both his hands into his front pants pockets and dismiss the person without ever counting or even looking at the money. He went back to his assessment of this horde that was assembled before him and what its ultimate value could be.

The Reverend himself was pumped up like a peacock, spreading his arms out and flapping them from time to time as though he intended to take off. Abby thought it was a shame he did not have tail feathers to fan out behind himself. She also detected the narcissistic gleam in his eyes and the almost overbearing infatuation he had with his own bearing and eloquence.

"We're here to sing the praises of Johnny," he said. He seemed sincere, but Abby thought he meant "But look at me, am I not God's gift to you myself? Am I not magnificent?"

"Pompous ass," she scribbled on her notepad. "Gets off on his own rhetoric."

She had listened to Billy with a jaundiced ear. All of those sitting onstage behind him seemed more impressed by their roles as key participants than by the sorrow of the occasion. Many celebrities had come to share in the media attention, and the majority of them appeared uniformly remote to their surroundings. Lots of them wore dark glasses. Lots of them looked about blankly for the working cameras, flashing furtive smiles at intervals, appearing awkward and uncomfortable to the nation in mourning.

Nobody, least of all Abby, noticed the young woman attired in black who stood alone sobbing quietly by a tree whose trunk was carved with a heart surrounding the initials J. G. and P. S. Peggy Sue finally had eluded the barriers long enough to say good-bye to Johnny and the dream they had so briefly and intensely shared.

Abby, oblivious, scrawled on her pad, "A circus lacking only elephant turds and horse piss for flavor."

She was not about to let Johnny Gault rest in peace.

*   *   *

Cannons sounded in the near distance and a formation of black aircraft flew over and darkened the sky with tons of black confetti. Shortly after, a formation of white planes flew over and showered the estate with a purifying snow of twice as much white and pink confetti.

"Johnny is in the arms of the Lord and no harm shall ever again befall him," Billy Sunshine declared with arms outstretched, then clasped in prayer above his head. "Bless this divine being so briefly sent to walk among us. Take him to Your bosom and hold him close for us. We pray that we may someday be with You in heaven to look upon his beauty once more and hear again the magic of his voice."

A huge chorus of trumpets sounded taps, the final note of which was left to one soloist, who dramatically repeated the melody alone. The entire audience was hushed as the notes hung pure and crystalline in the summer air.

"Amen, and good-bye to you for now, our dear friend, our beloved Johnny boy," Billy said in a hoarse whisper that amplified through the hearts of the weeping masses.

He then collapsed in a swirl of pink raiment and had to be helped off the stage after the exhausting ordeal.

The thousand white doves released at the beginning of the ceremony magically returned to Gaultland. Doc said, "Like the swallows to Capistrano." They were caught and sold for a hundred dollars each as "living memorials to the legend of Johnny Gault." Doc said to Sidney that they were selling "like fried chicken in a famine."

The pockets in Doc's baggy pants were bulging. He made several trips to the men's room, in a cubicle of which he neatly formed the bills into small, tight rolls and bound them with rubber bands.

"I'll count it later," he whispered to himself. "Right now, I'm goin' back 'n git more while the gittin's good."

The air remained thick and fragrant with marijuana smoke. The ground was littered with all manner of drug paraphernalia mixed with food, trash, papers, and popcorn. Gaultland itself had been ravaged for authentic souvenirs despite Doc's hasty addition of hundreds of extra security guards. People had even pulled up sprigs of grass from the lawn and taken them home so they could press them in their Bibles.

The fireworks that followed the funeral replaced the solemnity with festivity. Gone was the theme of bereavement. It was replaced by the joy of Johnny's music and the mythical gladness of his life. A miniature Woodstock was in the making, celebrating the wonder of life in the wake of a profound death. Drug hustlers had managed to permeate the crowds.

"A send-off loaded with pot, coke, heroin, and acid," Abby reported to Gwen. "There were more people stoned at the funeral than in Babylon."

"Long Island?"

"No, silly, the one in the Bible."

Her editor laughed. "Just verifying the facts, Abby dear," she said. "Get all you can that's good, and then get it back here to us fast. We're on a real deadline now."

"Pun intended?"

"No pun intended, Abigail."

It was almost as if Johnny and Doc were cooperating with her in fashioning a bestseller, providing first the fable of his life and now its own spectacular coda. No one, least of all Abby Ashley, could have fabricated a more bizarre yet somehow strangely appropriate ending.

Sidney's strain and exhaustion were nearly overwhelming as he fled in his hired limousine hours later.

"Airport, please," he directed the driver. He was determined to return to New York rather than wake up another morning in Memphis.

74

D espite the cynicism and disenchantment of certain influential segments of the media, the happening known in cable code as "Gaulterminus" was by any gauge an enormous success. Only the reincarnation of Johnny could possibly exceed the ratings and range of coverage.

But Johnny Gault's death provoked havoc among all who had been immediately involved in his life as well as others who had only sought to be. Like an earthquake or a tidal wave, it had been anticipated yet not fully expected. Everybody in the inner circle knew it was coming and yet nobody was really prepared.

In the world of what could best be described as the business of Johnny Gault, the show was over.

His immediate entourage from Randy Wheeler on down was, of course devastated. They had been silent bystanders in his self-destruction, helpless witnesses hoping for an impossible miracle. Now, all the fringe positions had been eliminated. Mortality had succumbed, as it always did, to immortality.

For Doc Diamond, having his partner out of the way was in many ways an advantage. He no longer had to clear any of his moneymaking schemes with anyone. Clifford Gault was the lone family survivor, and he was still in prison with the prospect of many more years of residence there. That mattered little anyway. Doc had long ago legally cleaned the senior Gault's clock. In the estate of Johnny Gault, the sire was nonexistent. The Johnny Gault Foundation would handle all matters pertaining to the fifty percent of the empire that did not belong to Doc. It was the foundation that had paid double- and sometimes triple-time rates for twenty-four-hour-a-day crews to rush completion of the mansion in time for the funeral. And who might be the supervising trustee of that foundation? Say hello again to Doc Diamond.

Leo Hatfield had sent a blanket of roses to the funeral with a card containing a request for Doc to contact him regarding postfuneral business possibilities. "We share a mutual love for Johnny and Memphis and the potential of it all," it stated, with addresses and phone numbers included. Sidney had to smile when Doc asserted that the card was a gross affront to the memory of Johnny Gault.

At the Gorman Group, the book was being rushed to release. It was not as complete as at first anticipated, but all bets were off regarding its potential.

Abby was privately devastated by Johnny's death. Not only had she invaded the very core of his private life, but he had invaded her every waking moment. She realized to her own very core that her best efforts to delineate Johnny Gault's character and deeply probe his motivation had changed her life forever. He was her obsession and her reason to live. She thought of him all the time.

She hated most of all that she had not fucked him before he died. She deeply regretted not ever having fulfilled her many erotic dreams of one-on-one with Johnny.

Now, she faced strange frustrations. When she tried to masturbate, she'd think of Johnny, she couldn't help it, but then she'd think about him being dead and be put off and unable to come. Then she'd cry.

"The book will still do well," Gwen assured her. "Maybe even better."

"Death has a way of killing everything around it."

"He's not dead. He's a forever person. He's all over the bestseller charts and he'll stay that way."

He had attained the status of a folk hero. He might not have lived forever, but he would survive at least long enough for the currently living to buy Abby's book.

Sidney without Johnny was a whole new entity. There was a sense of loss combined with a sense of release. The specter of the doomed star—forever requiring fraudulent explanations for acts of indolence, immaturity, and much immorality— had vanished with his death.

Sidney loved the new feeling of freedom and security in his control of the release of stories of Johnny.

Meanwhile, the first mass mailing for Reverend Billy Sunshine went out shortly after Johnny's funeral. Reverend Sunshine was now available around the clock to give advice and consolation about Johnny on a 900 number, twenty dollars for three minutes and the same for each minute thereafter.

"Commercial religion," Sidney commented. "Does everything in life have to be a scam?"

oyalty to Johnny Gault proved to be anything but pervasive among his
entourage even in the immediate aftermath of the funeral. It was as if the
Guys had been released from the forced worship of a graven image. Unlikely
as it seemed, Abby found the most important of them all, Randy Wheeler, as
approachable as the others.

In the same disguise she had used at the funeral, and again flashing the same
false credentials of a Nashville journalist, she caught Randy's attention and set
forth her proposition about a story on Johnny.

"Git me some cash and we'll jaw," he said. "Hey, sugar, have mercy on the
unemployed."

Abby wrangled ten thousand dollars out of Gwen and the Gorman Group,
and Randy the roadie talked.

"He was a polite son of a bitch, but he was fucked up. I mean, really class-A
fucked up."

"Could you explain that, please?" She smiled.

"I'll try to give ya jist what cha want." He smiled right back. "He'd shoot
up anything t'git high, and when he was, he'd fuck anything that moved."

"Like who and what?"

"Men, women, children, animals. It didn't much matter to him as long as
he got off. He used to say that he was the only guy in the U.S. who'd fucked
and sucked his way through every state in the union. He did, too, and I drove
him through those states while he did it."

"Very patriotic," Abby responded.

They laughed. The former road manager assumed he was talking to a news-paperwoman and confided many secrets he was certain he would never see on the newsstands. The thought of a book was beyond him. These off-the-record intimate secrets, however, seemed to do the trick in bringing him closer to the pussy he desired. He figured he deserved a bonus.

Abby sensed the come-on and figured "Why pass up a good fuck?" She always carried condoms just in case.

They simply stopped talking. She set aside her notepad, and he dropped to his knees in front of her, slowly pushing up the hem of her black dress until it was around her waist. She wore black satin panties and a black garter belt with black stockings. Leaving on the stockings and garter belt, he gently slipped her panties down and noticed the blond patch of hair at her crotch.

"You know somethin', baby?" he whispered. "I've fucked a lot of blondes with brunette bases, but you're my first one goin' the opposite direction."

"I like to be different."

"You are, honey. Believe me, you are."

They were both starved for a good orgasm and used each other well, if only for a short time. Then Abby straightened out her dress and left without a wig hair out of place.

Despite the thoroughness of her research, Abby had failed to uncover any clues to Johnny's liaison with a girl named Peggy Sue Porter. It was likely because those few who had known about his involvement with her had forgotten the brief and outwardly ordinary interlude, including Randy Wheeler. Only Johnny knew she was more than a passing fancy. Except for the suspicions of Doc and Sidney.

The hurt of her disappearance and seeming rejection of him was the deepest he had experienced since the death of his mother, Rita.

It was ironic that his sometimes desperate efforts to contact her—deviously thwarted by the selfish self-interests of his *protectors*, Doc and Sidney—and her own futile attempts to communicate with him after their brief but incandescent relationship would surely have contributed at least a touching chapter. The Johnny of a thousand and one conquests pining for a lovely but hardly glamorous country girl would have added a bittersweet contrast to Abby's diligent cataloging of his carnal recklessness.

It was not meant to be.

Peggy Sue had suffered through her belief that she was simply a victim of out-of-sight, out-of-mind syndrome, quickly forgotten by the wayside of the magic carpet ride of a superstar.

It had taken her a long while, but eventually she had resigned herself to fate and slipped back into the anonymity of Johnny Gault fandom, sadly cherishing her sweet, brief intimacy with a legend.

76

I t was unsettling to Sidney to witness how indifferent Doc Diamond had become to the imminent publication of a major exposé about his late protégé. He was preoccupied to the exclusion of all else with completing construction of Gaultland. It was already an international shrine representing Johnny's birthplace, his home, his castle. Even in its incomplete state it was already overrun with visitors who failed to realize that Johnny had preferred to remain in his mobile home even when he visited the site.

"Doc's turning it into a goddamned theme park," Sidney complained to Pam. "The man's totally devoid of shame."

"We're still within budget, so I suppose we shouldn't care."

"That is called professional maturity," Sidney said.

Leaks from the book had begun appearing everywhere, even in respected news journals. The public was being tantalized. Sidney tried to put his finger in the dike, but the holes opened faster than he could hope to plug them.

"Doc is so busy playing P. T. Barnum, he's not worried," Sidney said. "I honestly thought he cared about Johnny."

She shook her head, smiling.

"Sometimes you astound me, Sidney. Here you are with all this power and influence and you're really just a little boy playing big games."

Her challenge aroused him. He felt his penis rise.

"Here's your little big boy, Pam," he said, clutching his expanded crotch. "Wanna play a game?"

It was the first time he had confronted Pam with a sexual proposition. And in the office at that!

"I was begining to get a complex," she said.

"Didn't Claudia ever tell you bitchiness turns me on?"

"She forgot that part."

"Well, don't you forget it, beauty. Come here."

She came to him as one spellbound. Her movements slipped into slow motion in his mind. Their brief but savage encounter was oddly empty of eroticism. Sidney's mind and his penis were in different places. It did finally establish a degree of intimacy between them, however, something Pam had been quietly seeking ever since she first laid eyes on her gorgeous boss.

s everyone at the Gorman Group had anticipated, Abby Ashley proved to be a natural on the talk show circuit. She knew how to be folksy, down-home, and girl-next-door. It was an appealing image to project to a wired-in America inundated with the sleek, self-indulgent, and money-oriented types who so far had dominated the decade.

The long-awaited book was released finally as *Johnny Gault: Savage Saint*. It was a title many of his fans rejected and resented from the outset. They approved of the second adjective but not the first. There were demonstrations outside several of the studios where Abby made live appearances.

ASHLEY TO ASHES! some of the signs read.

The threats did not bother her unduly. She was swept up on an emotional high. She defended her revelations with a perky charm and outward innocence that belied her often tawdry disclosures. "Sweetness with a little dash of spicy sophistication," wrote one critic.

"Johnny was a love," she would report in interviews, then reverse her position in more in-depth views into her knowledge of the star. "Johnny loved himself. He was really a narrow, self-centered bigot with mediocre intelligence and no morals whatsoever."

Call-in shows were bombarded with public opinions, many of which were ominous and derogatory. Abby had dared to challenge the concept of a deity, dared to humanize and demean a god. That this might be a reckless endeavor had never occurred to her. She had written of the threats to Johnny's life by deranged and obsessed individuals. Now she began to hear from members of that same segment of society.

"Lay off Johnny, bitch," they said in one form or another, "or you'll be layin' next to him."

"Another tattooed six-packer in a tank top," she would giggle in response. She never thought much of the threats.

Life for Abby had always been uphill and around the curve. She dismissed the hostility as jealousy and reveled in her newfound celebrity. She thoroughly enjoyed her role as interpreter of an idol and his times. Whether fame or infamy, it was all attention to Abigail, and she glowed.

"This book," she declared in a moment of elation, "is as important to the world as the Bible is to Christianity."

A book is a book is a book, Gertrude Stein likely would have written. The book on Johnny Gault went beyond any such declaration. Like one of his many hit records, it soared to number one on the industry's charts in the span of a week and stayed, and stayed.

Abby took it all with great joy. She became a household name almost overnight. Even the new breed of radio and TV celebrity abusers regularly included her in their routines. The most popular of the late-night talk show hosts annointed her "a nun, as in *anunymous,* who put the guilt on Gault and discovered her own Gault mine."

It was heady recognition for Abby. So what if Leo Hatfield had filed suit for participation rights? So what if Clifford Gault was suing her from behind bars for misrepresentation of intent? So what if an increasingly reclusive Doc Diamond issued repeated denials of her claims and allegations through his spokesman, Sidney Bastion? The book was a smash hit, and she was a star. Her only regret was that she'd never had a hands-on interlude with the sexy rock god before he died.

In an era of quick quotes and sound bites she was a rare and precious find. The media devoured her.

"He liked to wear pink lace panties under his macho leather costume," she revealed on one show.

Radio disc jockey Jimmy Jay celebrated her as a "prose photographer."

"She makes pictures with words," he said. "You read her book and you see in your mind the struggle Johnny went through and the true beauty of his being."

"Really, Jimmy Jay, Johnny never had no struggle at all, and he ended up a drug addict," said Abby. "Here's a word picture for you: Johnny was like an empty box, gift wrapped."

78

The media had become increasingly hostile to Raul Tampa. The reports of rapes and baby killings permeated the international press. Some of it was true; some of it was imaginary. But it was there to be combated, and that essentially was the job of Sidney Bastion Associates, limited or unlimited.

Sidney had gone to Vivado and been sickened by the rampant poverty, random violence, and punitive police. On this trip he watched in silence as a pregnant woman was shot in the belly, killing both her and her baby, merely for begging for food.

It was not an isolated incident. He had also witnessed a horde of protesters strafed by machine gun fire when they dared to defy Tampa's edicts against assemblage. Their bodies decorated the courtyard of Sidney's hotel, a surrealistic collage of flesh.

"No more than three persons are allowed to gather in one place at one time," the government-controlled newspaper casually explained.

Blood flowed freely in the streets of Vivado, the island Sidney had described as a model of modernism.

Even he choked at the imagery.

Combat fatigues were Tampa's basic uniform. He was almost never seen anymore in his full-dress, epauleted and medal-bedecked formal attire. In that sense he had become a carbon copy of his bearded friend and fellow agitator in the Caribbean. He adored Fidel openly and took every opportunity to develop military and economic ties between their countries.

"Negative," Sidney repeatedly advised him. "Stay away from Castro. He's Montezuma's Revenge transferred to the Carib."

Tampa believed in his own basic innocence and invincibility, while justifying his cruelty as necessary to the common good. He had learned early on in his life that money and power made people dance to their tunes and march to their drummers.

We are not apologists for Raul Tampa," the statement from the chancellor of Billy Sunshine University read. "But it behooves every American to understand and appreciate the goodwill and positive possibilities his financing of this Center for Christian Unity provides. There are no political implications, only the opportunity for better understanding between two diverse peoples and cultures . . ."

"Humdrum hokum," Don Samuelson termed it on his top-rated nightly telecast. "No amount of PR prattle can disguise the fact that this notorious dictator has succeeded in circumventing State Department restrictions against his government to set up his own little espionage camp smack-dab in the middle of our largest state."

"I wonder how much a hit man would charge to knock off Samuelson?" Sidney mused as he watched a replay later.

"He's not just a thorn in the side," Pam said, "but in the top, bottom, and middle, too."

"We have that footage on Tampa with the tears in his eyes and the break in his voice calling for friendship between us all. Let's give it a satellite release now."

"Is it all set?"

He nodded. "It was edited weeks ago. I was holding it for something more crucial, but we can't let Samuelson start a knocking trend."

"I'll relay the release okay to video."

"The sooner, the better. We're still in time to catch the morning shows."

The response was less than hoped for but in some respects better than expected. Samuelson's own network carried the full sixty seconds of Tampa's emotional plea for understanding and unity. That alone made the expensive release worthwhile to Sidney.

"The guy's not a bad actor," he observed. "I still think we can do something with him."

"Remember," Pam reminded him, "we don't represent Raul Tampa. We represent the sublime seashore resorts of Vivado."

"Of course. What kind of animal would ever represent anyone as vile and reprehensible as Raul Tampa?"

79

D amaging revelations about Galen Jenkins drew Sidney's attention away
from his new preoccupation with Vivado and General Raul Tampa.

It was always a delicate balancing act to keep all clients persuaded of
his concern for their welfare. Stress in one area, requiring more of his concentration, only complicated his performance.

It mattered little to Sidney that the information was essentially true. What
did matter was that it was harmful to Jenkins's image and credibility at a crucial
time. The publication date for his autobiography was only weeks away. Its entire
potential was based on belief in him as a self-made superman.

Sidney had rushed Galen into the firm's television studio at the first disclosure and directed him through the taping of a brief, earnest, and somewhat indignant denial. It had been charged that not only had he never graduated from
college as claimed, he had never even registered anywhere for any classes beyond
high school.

"I have all the documentation in my possession to prove that I am indeed
a bona fide graduate of a major university," he declared in front of the cameras.
"I find it despicable that someone unknown to me has seen fit to sully my reputation in this rank manner."

The statement had gone out by satellite and made a number of important
newscasts. It was backed up by hastily authenticated degrees from Billy Sunshine
University and Forsythe College in Canada, the latter a new affiliate of BSU.

Fortunately, there had been no follow-up to the initial charge and no investigation into the diplomas. A quick poll indicated it made little difference to the general public one way or the other.

The second accusation—that Jenkins not only was not a war hero but had never even been in the service—was considerably more difficult to repudiate.

Sidney again went to television to counteract the report. This time he advised Jenkins to generalize and stand strong on his image as a fierce individualist.

"My record speaks for itself," Galen declared forcefully. "The American people are not easily deceived by the forces of evil and innuendo. I'm proud of what I've achieved in this great land, and I refuse to be denigrated by the malicious falsehoods of others."

No questioning by the media or anyone else. No specifics, only dramatics. Don Samuelson made a point of this on his nightly newscast, but the majority let Galen's statement stand on its own. Sidney rated it ninety percent effective, extremely good under the circumstances.

"There'll be a poll out in a few days showing that an overwhelming majority of Americans believe in the integrity of Galen Jenkins," Sidney predicted.

Yet another negative report slipped out—this one from Nevada—stating that not only had Galen Jenkins never piloted commercial aircraft, as he often implied, but that he possessed no pilot's certification and had no crew flight experience at all.

Sidney went to the printed word to blunt this charge.

"As the chief executive officer of a major international airline employing more than one thousand pilots and many other highly trained flight personnel and ground crewmen," Galen was quoted, "I find it incredible that anyone would doubt the qualifications of the man in charge of the entire aeronautical apparatus . . ."

Weasel wording, Sidney called it. Sidestepping the issue. Double-talk. Obfuscating. Nothing mattered but that it worked and both were pleased by the results.

"I might have walked right into it barefaced and wound up with shit all over me," Jenkins admitted with rare gratitude.

"Never admit to anything," Sidney warned. "Even accolades can contain poison."

Sidney's first inclination had been to blame Adrienne. It hurt, more than he cared to admit, to think that she could take such a stab at his client for no apparent reason.

Adrienne vehemently denied any connection.

"We're friendly enemies, Sidney," she told him. "Let's leave dirty tricks to others."

Shortly after Sidney had called Adrienne, a call came in from Claudia.

"You'll never guess who planted that dirt on Galen," she said.

"Name the son of a bitch."

"Jason Welles."

"You sure?"

"As sure as he's gay."

"That double-crossing bastard. But why?"

"Adrienne Gale hired him to do it. He just told me."

"That bitch! I was just talking to her."

"Want me to hold on while you change your underwear?"

"Don't get cute."

"I warned you she was devious."

"She's a lying, two-faced double-crosser."

"Double-breasted, too."

"I'm glad you find it amusing. She almost ruined Galen."

"I'm sure you'll find a way to thank her."

80

Because it was a business nurtured in part by the fruit of the grapevine—that is, gossip—Sidney was privy to a plethora of real and imagined secrets not only about the rich and famous but about his competitors as well. The latest intrigue concerned the New York Skyscrapers, the pro basketball Skies, owned by Vicki Summers.

"The whole squad's higher than the Himalayas all the time," he was told by a reliable source.

That in itself was not particularly shocking to him. But when he learned that the team's owner and her public relations representative were involved in postgame drug and sex parties with the players on a regular basis, Sidney became very intrigued indeed.

"Adrienne Gale's in on them?" he double-checked his informant.

"All the way up to her forty-one-inch tits."

"Where do these bashes go on?"

"Usually at Vicki's, but sometimes right in the clubhouse after it clears."

"I've gotta crash one."

"Do what you want, but you didn't hear nothin' from me."

"I'm surprised you said that after all these years."

"Can't be too careful, Sidney. Even with you."

The prospect grew more tantalizing the more he thought about it. He envisioned raven-haired Adrienne and titian-tressed Vicki nakedly cavorting among a forest of ebony and ivory limbs. The image was vivid enough to inspire him to track down Pam and once again violate his own standing rule against sex in the offices of Sidney Bastion Associates, Ltd.

"This is an emergency," he explained to her.

"You're the boss," she replied.

It took several weeks to engineer the details and set up the scenario. Sidney found time between other missions to make it as foolproof as possible. No one would ever know he was behind it all, at least not with any certainty. He was satisfied merely to be suspected.

The raid caught everybody involved quite literally with their pants down. And their noses candied with cocaine. The headlines leaped from the sports pages to the front pages. It was a scandal of epic proportions in the world of sports entertainment. Never before had a whole team and its ownership been indicted on drug use charges.

SKY FALLS IN ON NY SKIES, the tabloid headlines screamed.

"They had more snow in the locker room than the Alps," one observer was quoted as saying.

The Federal Basketball Federation moved to suspend the entire team from future participation in the playoffs and within the league for an indefinite time in the future.

"I'm ruined," Vicki Summers moaned.

"My sympathy," Sidney wired Adrienne Gale. "Anything I can do to help, just let me know."

Revenge was sweet indeed.

81

The book came out swinging.

Aspire & Achieve: The Will & Wisdom of Galen Jenkins drew immediate attention from reviewers as well as the book-buying public. The recent controversies only increased the interest surrounding the book's release.

Sidney was jubilant as he quoted from several of the more important reviews.

" 'Full of pluck and perseverence,' " he read aloud. " 'A contemporary pioneer and American folk hero,' 'already an American legend.' Would you believe these reviews? They're fantastic!"

"They'll probably revive all the rumors," Pam Garson cautioned.

"So what? Books carry enormous weight with the American public. They're awed by them. Printing somehow lends enchantment to words. It enhances every statement made inside book covers."

"You've sure proved it in the past, Sidney."

"I believe in books as tools in this industry. You can build monuments with them."

"Then Galen's granite is half chipped already."

"He might even make Mount Rushmore."

"Another Bastion masterpiece."

"Speaking of master pieces," he said, carefully dividing the word, "that couch looks lonely and incomplete without a pair of reclining figures."

Pam reached behind herself and tugged at the zipper of her dress.

"Nudes, of course," she said as her red silk garment slid down her body and gathered in a rumpled circle around her feet. She took off her scarlet satin bra and tossed it at Sidney, who removed his shirt and tied the bra around his neck.

He never took his eyes off her as he stepped out of his shoes and dropped his pants. He wore his socks and boxer shorts with the bra-scarf around his neck over to the couch, where Pam met him wearing only her crimson garter belt and sheer black stockings.

For a brief while they both enjoyed a respite from the never-ending war of words and wit.

82

Duplicity was a big part of the game whether Sidney admitted to it or not. He wore many different hats in the course of a campaign, much as a politician running for office. There was the need to be all things to all men while yet retaining his own professional individuality. He had managed it somehow but not without sacrificing a good deal of what the world at large would call integrity.

"Integrity is an old-fashioned concept," he contended in a loose moment. "Being totally honest is a detriment to success, particularly in this business."

"May I quote you on that?" the interviewer asked.

"Of course not. I'd only deny it vehemently if you did."

He had agreed to limited, off-the-record questioning by researchers for *One Hour*, the sixty-minute television magazine show that ranked as the number-one news production on the major networks. It had been the only way he could persuade the producers to visit Vivado and talk to Raul Tampa about his plans for the island. The all-important segment was also scheduled to include a brief exchange with Paula Castle.

"This is by far the most important exposure you've ever gotten," he whispered to Paula before the taping. "Make sure you project the image you truly want for yourself."

"Why can't I go on with Raul? Why do we have to be interviewed separately?"

"They'll probably try to involve him in political issues. I don't want you cast in that light at all."

"Reese thinks the whole thing is politically risky."

"How about economically?"

"Even more so."

"How do you feel?"

"I believe in taking chances."

"Good girl. Tell them you've got the adventurous spirit of the Pilgrims. A little American flag waving would add a nice touch."

"That's the way we rehearsed it."

"Spontaneously."

"Right off the top of my head."

They laughed at their complicity. Sidney had spent all week in Vivado doing much the same thing with Raul Tampa. It was essential the interview appear extemporaneous but equally important that Tampa make no damaging faux pas.

Claudia was the first to reach him after the telecast. He had not even bothered to catch the original broadcast, leaving it to his VCR to record for later viewing.

"Sidney," she said in an ominously low voice, "how could you let them do that to you?"

"Do what?" he demanded impatiently.

"Depict you as some shadowy, sinister Rasputin lurking behind the scenes doing dirty work for a dictator."

"What the hell are you talking about? You drinking again?"

"Obviously you didn't see the show."

"I was there at the original tapings."

"I know. I saw you there. And I heard you, too. Too bad you weren't at the final editings as well."

He was flustered and confused.

"Look, Claudia, let me run it off the recorder and I'll call you back."

"Don't take any other calls before you call me."

"I was expecting congratulations."

"They double-crossed you, Sidney."

He paced the room as the opening credits flashed by. The telephone computer sparkled with lights, an indication something was wrong. Not that many people had his unlisted home numbers.

Tampa's profile filled the screen. Sidney sank into a chair and stared.

"This man of seemingly casual demeanor and easy grace," the narrator's voice intoned, "is in reality the ruthless dictator of Vivado, a tropical island as lush and beautiful as it is fraught with fear and danger . . ."

Sidney winced at the negatives in the introduction. It had been dubbed in after he had seen the earlier, unedited tape.

"Bastards," he muttered softly to himself.

The show was in four segments with similar teaser glimpses of each part in the same opening sequence. He was apprehensive now. Impatiently, he advanced the tape and then reversed it, repeating the process until he was able to pinpoint the Tampa segment.

Paula Castle came on abruptly, looking fleshy and overbearing. She was decidedly untelegenic, especially in color.

". . . a strange alliance of two seeming opposites who share a common thirst for power and prominence," the television voice related.

The unexpected shots of Sidney himself came on next. They showed him peering stealthily from a control room, his hands gesturing animatedly from time to time.

"Behind this highly questionable collaboration is the man you are seeing now, an elusive, manipulative public relations power broker whose clandestine efforts give comfort and stature to all who can afford it, even the likes of Raul Tampa . . ."

Sidney covered his face with his hands. Unbeknownst to him, the worst was yet to come.

"Integrity is an old-fashioned concept," he heard his own voice declare. "Being totally honest is a detriment to success, particularly in this business."

"May I quote you on that?"

"Of course not," he heard himself respond. "I'd only deny it vehemently if you did."

He sat there a long time after it was over before calling Claudia. The East River was especially beautiful in the late afternoon, he thought, trying to wash everything else from his mind. Its shimmer was multifaceted, a much finer effect than the sun managed on lakes and oceans. It was time he paid more attention to such things. Time he thought about anything besides how to get someone on television or radio or in newspapers and magazines.

"You're right," he said to Claudia when he finally got back to her. "They fucked me."

"It was a rotten trick."

He laughed ruefully.

"They're getting almost as good at it as me," he said.

83

Run, Sidney, run.

Hide, Sidney, hide.

He had advised others to do the same when the heat was on. There was a tendency in all men to react recklessly when confronted by a terrible surprise. It was best under such circumstances to avoid retaliation until the consequences were carefully weighed. Caution was in order when all else was in disorder.

Billy Sunshine was there—like the savior he claimed to represent—in Sidney's hour of need. He offered his retreat in the San Gabriel Mountains—the perfect haven, remote from everything and everyone.

"Nothing but food and solitude," Billy encouraged. "You can practice the three M's—meditation, mastication, and masturbation—to the maximum there. It'll be just you and my Chinese chef, Ho Chen."

"It's tempting, I have to admit."

"You've never been there alone after all the times I've invited you. Now the Lord wants you to visit Him there."

Sidney laughed reluctantly.

"You're the only guy I know with a direct line to heaven," he said.

Billy was a persuasive salesman when he chose to be. That was evidenced by his audiences and income. Before their cross-country conversation was over Sidney agreed not only to accept the Reverend's hospitality but to make a brief appearance on his Sunday telecast as well.

"My ratings are in the same league as *One Hour*, and I have something I want to say about their treatment of you last week."

"Do we work on it together?"

"Not this time, my friend. I want these to be my own thoughts expressed in my own way."

"I'm being set up again," Sidney joked.

"Only for deification."

"Oh, God!"

"Amen."

Claudia reluctantly agreed to return east to temporarily supervise overall operations during Sidney's absence. He had never before taken a vacation, much less an indefinite leave of absence. They both knew it would not last for long, but they proceeded on the assumption that it might.

She also agreed—for communications reasons only—to occupy his town house during the interlude.

"Feel free to play with any of the kittens I keep upstairs," he kidded her. "I'll be leaving tomorrow."

"I'll be arriving tomorrow."

"Never the twain shall meet."

He stayed late at the office organizing those files that required immediate attention. The transfer of power would be relatively simple, since he and Claudia had worked together so long and intimately. Still, there were personal memorandums to write, which he did in his own barely decipherable longhand.

Pam interrupted him after most of the staff had gone.

"There's a messenger here who insists on delivering a note to you personally," she said.

"Is he armed?"

"I would've let him in right away if he was," she kidded back.

"It is odd at this hour." He shrugged. "Let him in."

It was no ordinary messenger but instead a handsome, dark-haired young man elegantly dressed and mannered.

"Mr. Bastion," he greeted Sidney, "I recognize you from your television appearances. I have a message for you, sir."

He reached into the pocket of his cashmere coat and handed Sidney a small envelope. Sidney went perfunctorily for a tip.

"Oh, no sir," the young man protested. "It was my pleasure. Thank you for admitting me."

"That was a novelty," Sidney observed after he'd gone. "A young guy with manners."

Inside the envelope was a brief handwritten note on engraved vellum parchment.

"Dear Sidney," it read. "Jason lied. I did not hire him to spill the beans on Galen Jenkins. Regarding *One Hour*, it's my turn to extend sympathy. That was a cheap shot at you and the industry—which neither deserves. If there is anything I can do, consider it done. Incensedly, Adrienne."

He read it again and passed it to Pam. She digested it in a glance.

"Damned sweet of her," she said.

"Yeah."

He tore off a fresh memo sheet. Slowing himself to make his penmanship more legible, he wrote: "Dear Adrienne, you should play for the Skies when they resume because you're a champ and seven feet tall in my eyes. Gratefully, Sidney."

Pam volunteered to deliver it herself.

"We need more unity and cooperation in this business," she declared with emotion.

As usual, the Cathedral of Divine Destiny was filled to capacity. The fountains and floral displays were as ostentatious as always, the resident choirs, the Halos and Haloettes as harmonious as full-time, fully paid choruses could be.

Reverend Billy Sunshine stood before all of this grandeur in his mauve velvet robes, his hands clutching the golden pulpit, his eyes ever alert to the battery of television cameras pointed in his direction.

His voice rich and resonant, his words fervent and eloquent, he sermonized against false prophets and those "who would abuse their God-given privilege of reaching the masses through the miracle of television."

He avoided referring to *One Hour* specifically by name, but only someone who'd been asleep for the past decade could have failed to recognize the target of his spiritual tirade.

At the conclusion of his dramatic talk on this Sunday he called on Sidney Bastion to rise in the midst of the congregation to be introduced to his vast audience.

"We salute this marvelous man of the media," he chanted, "this wise counselor in communications, this saint of symbolism and sophistication who so self-lessly gives of himself in the glorification of others. May God bless our son and brother Sidney now in his pursuit of peace and a better understanding of the frailties of human nature and of the divine order that restoreth faith and replenishes the spirit. Amen."

It was even more than Sidney had bargained for. He was convinced anew there was nothing he could not survive.

Billy had his own chauffeur drive Sidney to the mountain retreat immediately after the services. The place was anything but monastic, its main residence equipped with every conceivable luxury and convenience.

"You have only to press this button," the butler explained after handing him a small remote control box, "to summon assistance any time you desire it."

He then disappeared, and Sidney reveled in an immediate sense of solitude. Tyrannies, conspiracies, and chicaneries faded from his mind as he lay back on the billowing cloud of a bed which centered but hardly dominated his huge bedroom.

How could anything be wrong in such a setting of magnificence, its spirit captured in the words engraved on a silver plaque over the bed: "Rejoice! Heaven Is An Eternal Orgasm."

Sidney Bastion, burned-out warrior with words, slipped off into his first dreamless sleep in ages, far from his field of battle.

84

There was only so much of idling and the idyllic a man like Sidney Bastion could tolerate.

He was not yet in search of nirvana, only a brief respite from the brickbats and the incessant demands on his time and ingenuity. Billy Sunshine's private retreat, with its quiet opulence and unobtrusive pampering, provided a pleasant interlude.

There was an ample stock of old and current movie tapes as well as language and exercise programs. An elaborate gym adjoined the swimming pool, and a golf driving and putting range was a step away.

He relaxed and spent nine days in peaceful solitary contemplation. Finally, though, his mind could not help but wander back to its old habits. Vicki Summers was in trouble, and the New York Skyscrapers were temporarily, if not permanently, defunct. Why not suggest to Norman Prescott that he buy the team from her and restore its credibility?

The more he turned the idea over in his mind, the more he liked it. A professional sports franchise had the potential of a humanizing effect on an overlord like Norman. Sportswriters were assigned individually to pro teams, generating a constant flow of publicity unattainable in any other department of a newspaper or TV division. The free space and time devoted to coverage of team and owner activities were unique. Nowhere else in the world of commerce was such personalized reportage guaranteed. Not even General Motors or IBM had its own covey of outside reporters filing daily stories from within.

By the time Sidney had the idea organized and finalized, his arguments pro and con formulated, he knew Prescott would go for it. Ego gratification for the media messiah! It pleased him that he was thinking so creatively so soon after the *One Hour* massacre.

Billy Sunshine had other ideas for Norman Prescott. But they did not interfere with Sidney's latest plan. He had promised not to intrude on the retreat, but the temptation was too much to resist. Having his peripatetic public relations man all to himself, a willing captive, was more than the Lord himself could be expected to deny Himself.

"Two more days and I've had it," Sidney told him as they shared cocktails on a sun-dappled patio. "Ideas are bursting like popcorn in my head, and here I am lying around like a beached whale doing nothing."

Billy was amused to find him so kinetic in such a lulling environment.

"God's blessed you with remarkable resources, Sidney," he said. "Any other man would need months to recover from your recent ordeals."

"No rest for the wicked, Billy. My mission on earth is different from yours. You're the mesmerizer, I'm the mesmerizer's messenger. But I can't blow your horn or anybody else's out here in the desert. Nobody would hear it."

"The rest hasn't hurt you, that's obvious."

"I just invented a proverb: Rest not, rust not."

"You could write a bible on ballyhoo."

"I appreciate your faith in me, Billy, and I mean that."

"Let us pray together."

They both bent their heads in a moment of silent meditation. And both had their minds on things other than appeals to the Almighty.

"I was thinking, Sidney," Billy began the moment the interlude was over, "that it would be a wonderful thing for Norman Prescott and the university if the school of journalism and communications were to be named in his honor."

Sidney smiled. "That came to you right in the middle of prayer?"

"The Lord is the ultimate communicator."

"I think there's a lot of merit in the idea."

"Then you will communicate it to Norman?"

"If the Lord doesn't beat me to it."

Sidney did not share his thoughts about the Skies with Billy. The university's own basketball team was already among the nation's most formidable, and Billy was as proud of them as he was of his new thirty-thousand-seat sports facility that had been largely financed by Norman Prescott. It wasn't the right time to plant grander sports ideas in the head of this ambitious evangelist.

"I think you've suffered enough austerity, Sidney," Billy said as he prepared to leave. "With that in mind, I brought along two of our most talented Haloettes to keep you company in your final few days."

"How thoughtful of you."

"They're used to organ music." Billy winked. "I'll leave the improvisation to you."

The girls were already in the pool, swimming naked, when he returned from saying good-bye to the Reverend. He skinned off his own clothes and joined them.

Thoreau could celebrate the wonders of being alone at Walden Pond all he wanted, but Sidney was convinced that his lovely retreat treat in Reverend Billy's pool was immeasurably more rewarding.

He blissfully frolicked with the water nymphs.

t seemed almost calculated, kicking him when he was down.

No sooner had Sidney returned to his lair in Manhattan than the morning headlines—front and back pages both—announced the sale of the New York Skyscrapers by Vicki Summers to, of all people, Mimi Aurora.

Adding insult to injury was the revelation that it had all been announced at a press conference held in the grand ballroom of the Gotham Castle!

It was a total Adrienne Gale production in Sidney's own backyard. He was stunned, angry, and disappointed all at once.

Worst of all, he had made the mistake of broaching the idea to Norman before checking the status of the franchise. The usually wary communications czar had embraced the proposal with enthusiasm and encouraged Sidney to proceed.

"Never assume," Sidney lectured his seminar students. " 'Assume' makes an 'ass' out of 'u' and 'me.' "

Oh, so trite, but oh, so true.

"I think she arranged it deliberately to embarrass me," he told Claudia.

"That's paranoid, Sidney. Nobody knew about it but you and Norman."

The all-female transaction drew heavy media play for days, making it impossible for him to ignore. The old animosity was fully revived.

"Bury her any chance you get," he instructed Pam Garson.

"But she was so sweet about the *One Hour* episode."

"Subterfuge," he retorted. "She's really just a scheming, dirty bitch."

Pam shook her head and retreated. Love and hate really were two sides of the same coin.

Norman Prescott was ominously quiet on the matter. He knew Sidney was aware it was a mark against him. Prescott did not suffer fools gladly, nor did he enjoy having them lead him to the brink of public folly.

Unbelievably, Sidney demanded an explanation from Adrienne regarding the sale of the Skies. Unsuspectingly, she agreed to meet him.

"You're making a complete ass of yourself, Sidney," Claudia said sarcastically.

"That's more than can be said for all the half-asses I have working for me."

Claudia smiled. "My bags are packed. Looks like I'm escaping New York just in time."

They had to be considered an interesting triumverate. Vicki Summers, Adrienne Gale, and Mimi Aurora. Especially as the operating heads of a professional basketball franchise.

Mimi knew nothing about basketball, football, baseball, volleyball, or Ping-Pong. Adrienne knew only slightly more, and Vicki just enough to keep the media from demanding her excommunication from all sports arenas.

Adrienne made certain all publicity regarding the transfer of ownership centered on Vicki's surrender of control to Mimi. In reality, Vicki retained a twenty-five percent interest in the team while Adrienne was awarded twelve and one-half percent in lieu of fees.

The real owner, of course, was Lars Schwinn. As Mimi's husband he had agreed to the arrangement because his diminutive bride found it exciting to be around such tall men. The media found it exciting as well. She became known by the press as "the melon-breasted midget with the megamen."

"Schwinn went to all that expense just to provide a showcase for his wife's lamentable vocalizing," Sidney was quoted by a prominent columnist who owed him a favor. "The only way anyone will put up with her singing is if they're held captive, precisely what the crowds are before a basketball game. Her rendition of 'The Star-Spangled Banner' sounds like it was written by Francis Scott Off-Key. The whole deal cries for an investigation by some patriotically minded congressional committee."

There continued to be something catalytic in both his real and his imaginary competitions with Adrienne Gale. Again he wanted to talk it out with her, again she condescended to meet with him.

"I'm working from the yacht for a change of atmosphere," he told her. "How about meeting me there."

"I can't swim."

"All the better."

"You sound like you mean it."

"Don't we in PR always mean what we say?"

She agreed to the site with some reluctance. Water made her nervous, even as a drink.

He met her at the gangplank of the ship, gleaming white against the murky Hudson.

"Lovely boat," she said.

"Ship," he corrected.

"Whatever."

"Thanks for coming."

"I had second thoughts after reading your kind words in Lyle Kenton's column."

"I thought they were rather clever."

"Why the malice, Sidney? I thought we agreed on being friendly enemies."

"Then why enlist Paula in your treachery?"

"Treachery? What an odd choice of words. Paula happens to be an old friend of Lars Schwinn, that's all. There was no chicanery involved."

"You knew I had Norm Prescott lined up to take over the Skies. That was deliberate sabotage of the plan."

"Is this thing rocking or am I just getting dizzy from the dialogue? I don't believe you! Neither Vicki, Mimi, nor I had the vaguest idea Norman Prescott had any interest at all in the Skyscrapers. Ours was a desperation deal put together to save the franchise."

"You're good, Adrienne. You think fast on your feet. Are you that good on your back?"

"You'll never know."

The heated exchange cooled after several more drinks. They had both mellowed quickly after the initial hostility. From the rear deck where they sat a good portion of the midtown and downtown skyline was visible.

"Ever get tired of Manhattan?" he asked.

"My hometown? Never."

"We're unanimous on at least one subject."

She studied him as he stared off into the distance. Subtle inroads of gray had begun tinging his dark hair, adding to his attractiveness.

"You know, we've come a long way down the same road without ever really getting to know one another."

"Whose fault is that?"

"It's the nature of the business."

"I'll be very honest with you, Sidney. Before that juvenile jab of yours in Kenton's column I was actually wondering if you ever thought of me in terms of merger."

"Murder would be more like it."

"I think you're eminently capable of it."

He laughed loudly, freed by his third glass of champagne.

Sidney appeared not to have taken her seriously, so Adrienne let the matter of a merger drop.

"Ever see the master's quarters on this tub?" he asked a short time later.

"I've never been invited before."

"Allow me to correct that oversight. Follow me."

Hand in hand he led her down a central passageway to a pair of interlocking doors. He threw them open dramatically to reveal a large cabin resplendent in blue velvet, gleaming mahogany, gold fixtures, and silvery mirrors. In the center was a magnificent bed resembling the sea with billowing waves of white-crested blue silk.

"My laboratory," he said.

"Biological experiments?"

"Advanced erotics."

She laughed, her body weaving sensually.

"You're too much of a PR animal to be into erotics."

He moved swiftly and surely now, the predator ready for the kill. It was quite unexpected in view of the circumstances, but he had been stalking her vicariously for so long he was in something of a constant state of readiness.

"You're a beautiful bitch," he whispered, his mouth pressed to her throat.

"And you're a beautiful bastard," she gasped.

They tore at one another's clothing as they fell entangled into the bed's consuming softness.

It was hours later before they emerged from this cloud of goose down, their bodies lacquered from the frenzy of their lust.

"You do think fast on your back," he said.

"Did you enjoy making a liar out of me?"

"It just proves what a consummate pro you are—emphasis on the PR."

"I'm charging you with assault and flattery."

They merged once more before parting, as though to confirm the authenticity of what had happened earlier. It was real, all right, without illusions.

Strange bedfellows were not limited to politics.

86

Coping with Johnny Gault's death, *One Hour*, the Skies, and Raul Tampa in such quick succession was a public relations nightmare for Sidney. It helped explain his perverse reaction to the shocking news that Abby Ashley had been shot and wounded by a hysterical admirer of Johnny Gault as she was leaving a New York television studio. The attack came following a particularly incisive and inflamatory interview.

"Excuse me, but hallelujah!" was how he greeted the grim news.

"Sidney!" Pam admonished him.

"She's no John Lennon. Him I cried for."

"She's also still alive. You should pray for her."

"Forgive her her trespasses? Yeah, sure."

The slight effervescent girl from West Memphis, Arkansas, bubbled on for only a few days, then the fight was over. Her "quirky quest," as she had liked to call it, had ended while the pot of gold had just begun to fill.

Abby's estranged parents followed the wish their only child had expressed in one of her diary entries. They found it to be an odd request, but then to them she had always been an odd, uncomprehensible child. She wanted to be cremated without services and her ashes strewn over the Mississippi River, "where they would flow forever past the grave of Johnny."

Not even Sidney Bastion could have devised a more moving final tribute.

They wept for her at the Gorman Group. Her refreshing combination of vitality and naïveté had endeared her to her editor and her collaborator over the many months they had labored to mold her scattered anecdotes and insights into a publishable manuscript.

If she had been a gadfly to some, she was a peppery and inspirational self-made individual to others. But it mattered not at all what anyone thought any longer.

Ironically, now both subject and author were dead, one en route to immortality, the other returning to obscurity. Only the book lived on.

In a further touch of irony, Abby's assassin turned out to be a starry-eyed small-town teenager much like herself.

"I killed the bitch and I'm glad," the girl told police detectives. "I came big when I pulled that trigger."

"Why did you do it?" they asked. "Why kill her?"

"It's not logical, it's biological," she said. "I was Johnny's twin, his soul mate. I loved him."

"Lots of people loved him."

"I don't care about anybody else. I shared my life with him and he did the same with me."

"He didn't even know you, girl. You were just one of thousands of faces out there in front of him every night."

"That's what you think, but he crawled into my bed and made love to me every single night."

Illusion and delusion. Johnny had sold it in his songs and implemented it with his erotic manner and movements. Now he was gone, his literary nemesis was gone, and a demented young girl was left to claim her stake in their aborted lives.

Hidden hearts can intertwine,
You show me yours, and I'll show y'mine . . .

They masturbated to his music and fantasized their love.

Cross my heart and hope t'die.
If I evuh tell y'one white lie . . .

It was a grim fairy tale lacking a happy ending.

*   *   *

As swift and dramatic as the assassination had been, news coverage of it faded almost as quickly from the media spotlight. There was always a new shooting or a new obituary to overwhelm the previous one. Death was a fact of life, and mourning was brief for all but those closest to the deceased. Abby had accumulated many acquaintances in her brief life but could claim few if any friends.

What mattered to her publisher was that the book had taken on a life of its own and clung to its top ranking for many weeks after her demise.

"The bitch is dead!" Sidney shouted down the corridor of his offices. "Long live the bitch!"

Obviously he was relieved by the elimination of Abby Ashley. Gone was the veiled threat she had made in several pungent interviews to go after Billy Sunshine and then Paula Castle in the near future.

Abby's parents were reunited not so much by the tragedy of their daughter's death as by the promise of the riches her legacy would bring. The girl who had left a broken home had managed from afar to mend it.

87

Doc Diamond kept right on proving the dictum that nobody had ever gone broke by underestimating the intelligence of the American public. He continued to intensify the gaudy glitz of the cheap carnival that was Gault-land.

The *Memphis Appeal* newspaper commented that it was "like a local side-show, tacky and tawdry to a T."

"A glorified flea market and shameless hustle," declared the *Press Scimitar*. "A desecration of the memory of a great and enduring artist."

Doc ignored the bad news. Glossy souvenir books, lavishly illustrated with flattering photos of Johnny and a laudatory text telling the Bastion version of the singer's life, sold in the hundreds of thousands on the premises and by mail. Videotapes of concert highlights could be viewed on giant screens about the grounds. Copies of his ceremonial funeral tape were on sale at all the souvenir stands. All the while loudspeakers boomed out his recordings day and night while powerful searchlights formed a huge illuminated cross in the sky over his tomb.

Without consulting anyone—he seldom did—Doc had commissioned a fifty-foot statue of his late partner in skintight costume clutching his guitar, his shirt pulled open to reveal his naked and medallioned chest, his leg sensuously cocked to reveal the fullest measure of his phallic glory in bas-relief. The pink plaster of Paris monument was to be the symbol of the park, perched high upon the bluffs of the majestic Mississippi, welcoming the teeming masses. A thick coat of poly-urethane made it gleam and guaranteed its longevity.

Sidney covered his face when he first saw it. "It's so beautiful," he lied to Doc, "I can't bear to look at it."

"Nothing succeeds like excess," he was forced to admit later, when cheering crowds stormed the unveiling.

Thousands of miniature replicas in various sizes were sold in the hours following the dedication. Hawkers with freezer carts lured the worshipers to buy frozen versions of the looming statue in strawberry, peppermint, or tutti-frutti flavors in various shades of pink.

"Lick a Johnny pop," they called out fervently.

Gaultland Park just grew. There was no real control or master plan. Any gimmick that looked potentially lucrative was tacked on and assimilated. Anything fit.

"Doc sure ain't no Disney," Randy Wheeler had commented with his casual but accurate insight. "He's carny at heart."

Everything about the original trappings of the park had a jerry-rig quality, like a traveling show. There were mostly ramshackle buildings and brightly colored tents with hawkers outside enticing tourists and worshipers to enter and be enchanted by some real or imaginary aspect of their idol's life.

The fans loved Johnny so completely they forgave him the disappointing cheapness. This was hallowed ground, and it did not matter to them that it was not Utopian.

The neoclassical mansion purported to have been his home and castle rose incongruously from the clutter of the park. It was outsized and ostentatious, awkward and somehow alien to the landscape.

It was pseudo Jeffersonian, with huge pillars. The double front doors were distinctively pink. They clearly represented the portals he had always sought to enter.

The mansion was, in fact, little more than a huge warren of rooms of all shapes and sizes, reflecting the bizarre changes in moods and rampant indecision of the man largely responsible for its eccentric architecture.

It was almost all facade. The image was impressive, but there were chaos and emptiness behind the impressive front.

"It's a phenomenon," was all Sidney allowed himself to be quoted as saying. "An unbelievable, only-in-America phenomenon."

It was that indeed.

eo Hatfield was adamant in his resolve to find a way out of his morass. He was beside himself with frustration over losing out—first on the career of Johnny Gault, then on the star's self-anointed biographer and the book she had spun at least partially from his woolly recollections.

Being a local success no longer satisfied his ego. When the courts threw out his claims of participatory rights to the Ashley book as marginal and frivolous, he vowed revenge with his own version of not only the life of Johnny Gault but of Abby Ashley as well.

"I know shit that would take the curl out of your pubic hair," he railed at all who would listen.

It was no sale; there were no takers. Not only did he lack meaningful publishing connections, but also his amateurish material proved repetitious and incoherent, and was further devalued by his obvious vindictiveness.

Besides, the memory of Johnny Gault, the legend, had quickly and inexorably risen above the sensationalistic disclosures of *Johnny Gault: Savage Saint.*

Gaultland was proof positive. As finally envisioned and evolved by Doc Diamond, the makeshift monstrosity could hardly handle the throngs seeking to visit it.

Cousin Leo reluctantly decided his only chance to cash in on his past associations and mishandled opportunities was to reopen the Warehouse in Memphis. The old Memphis Warehouse had been closed since Leo's big move to Nashville, but it was fairly easy to get going again. The Nashville Warehouse would continue business as usual.

At least it would put him in proximity to his past potential and provide a chance to capitalize on his legitimate claims to a place in the Gault mythology.

The new Warehouse would include its own Johnny Gault museum with artifacts and memorabilia Leo had collected ever since Johnny's popularity had begun.

It galled Doc and annoyed Sidney that this old nuisance, Leo Hatfield, had come back into their lives.

It's not literature, it's litter," Sidney kept repeating in answer to questions about the Ashley book's allegations. "Let the man rest in peace."

Peace was something Sidney longed for, but it eluded him. He had bitten deeply into the Big Apple without ever tasting its sweetness or appreciating its succulence. He seemed unable to experience pleasure.

"You take everything too seriously, Sidney," Pam told him. "Have some fun for a change."

"It's a serious world."

"You're depriving yourself."

"I love what I do. I don't know what else I could do."

She saw the quiet erosion of his features, and it saddened her. She went to him, kissed him lightly on the lips, and smiled.

"You could take time out for a quickie and then go back to your seriousness."

He kissed her back, thinking, What a good idea.

Pam always knew what to prescribe for the blues, but he could not get aroused.

"It's a great idea, sweetheart, but give me a raincheck and get me a couple of aspirins, please."

"What's wrong?"

"Just a headache, nothing serious."

"Plays hell with my sex life, though."

"I promise I'll make it up to you."

"Paula wants you to call," said Pam, switching subjects.

"She's like her buildings," Sidney said with a patient smile. "She never leaves town."

Everything had avalanched on Sidney in the past few months. The extent of the damage and drain on his psyche was exemplified by his new tolerance of, perhaps even affection for, his second most demanding client, Paula Castle.

"You've always got time for that dead singer," Paula complained. "I'm reduced to sitting around my lobbies asking people if they've ever heard of me!"

A rare smile played on his face. She was really rather amusing once the
threat of her was under control. He had done wonders for her image, and he
knew that she knew it.

"In the vast United States of America," he said soothingly, "Paula Castle is
now better known than White Castle."

"You're comparing me to a cheap hamburger?"

"Paula, you're filet mignon. You could never be hamburger."

"This is what I pay you two thousand a week to hear?"

"Twenty-five hundred," he reminded her. "I raised you after the *Vogue*
spread."

She laughed in her throaty fashion.

"Get over here," she ordered, "and earn your money."

He would never have believed at the beginning of their relationship that
her command would become mildly appealing. Being with her was an escape,
however limited.

"If anyone calls," he told Pam as he gulped down two aspirins on his way
out, "I'm busy servicing a client."

She peered at him over her mauve-tinted glasses.

"Give her my worst," she said.

89

Ever since Galen Jenkins had guided Transcontinental into the overseas market under the new TransOceanic Air logo, he had been hounded by financial investors and market analysts. They all screamed that the expansion was too rapid, with too many questionable aircraft purchases and routes of limited potential. Not the least of these was the daily service from New York to Vivado, arranged to please General Raul Tampa.

Don Samuelson again referred to Jenkins as "that bestselling, worst-managing corporate charlatan." Reports stopped just short of accusing Jenkins of stock manipulations and bribe taking. There were labor troubles as well. Travel agents soon began recommending alternative airlines to passengers in anticipation of a collapse or takeover.

Sidney brought Galen into the firm's television studio repeatedly over the next few days. Together they carefully drafted responses to the charges and posed Jenkins in the most flattering postures and softest color tones possible. It was state-of-the-art PR, and the brief, telling retorts to what was still largely media innuendo received wide pickup.

A barrage of more in-depth denials poured out over company communications lines into the newsrooms of newspapers and wire services. They hinted at libel suits and dark counterrevelations while depicting the outrage of "an honest, upright chief executive officer of a premier, patriotically motivated American airline."

It worked temporarily.

TransOceanic Air was only in its second month of offering special air-hotel-dining package tours to Vivado when a member of General Tampa's elite guard was involved in a hassle with an American visitor that resulted in the latter's death.

"Murder!" screamed the American and international press.

"Accident!" proclaimed the official Vivado news agency.

Sidney had no choice but to adopt the government stance, even though eyewitnesses claimed the tourist had been taunted and provoked by numbers of Tampa's secret police before being shot down in cold blood.

Not so, Sidney declared earnestly and vehemently to media representatives from dozens of nations.

"Tourists are safer in Vivado than in their own backyards," he insisted. "The government of General Tampa has taken extraordinary precautions to insure the safety and well-being of its guests as well as their pleasure and happiness."

The storm left the infant Vivado tourist industry in shambles. A government-sponsored seashore complex stood half completed on the Atlantic coastline. Private investors lured in by tax breaks began reneging on their commitments.

Then, an ambush of tourists by rebellious natives caused three deaths and serious injury to four others. Sidney was beside himself when the report came in.

Don Samuelson had only recently broken the story of a bribe paid Galen Jenkins by General Tampa to expedite TransOceanic's air service to Vivado. Sidney elected to appeal to the contentious commentator directly.

"Don," he said by phone, "the General is no more involved in what happened to those tourists earlier today than our own President would be in a mob killing in Little Italy. The leader doesn't live who has a harness on all his hoodlums. It's sad and unfortunate, but it could happen anywhere in these uncertain times."

"Bastion," Samuelson replied, "I have the same amount of faith in your integrity as I do in professional wrestlers. Don't waste my time and yours."

There was no further discussion. Samuelson was always brusque but never more so than when he was annoyed. The ploy had failed, so Sidney turned elsewhere immediately.

"Let's get a TV crew to Vivado on the double," he instructed his director of television. "Out of our Monaco office if we can, but out of here if necessary. I want a beach ceremony staged involving grieving Vivado citizens, women and children in particular, mourning the loss of the visitors. Bring in lots of local color emphasizing the friendliness of the people, the loveliness of the setting, the peacefulness of the environment. I'll set up all the clearances you need through the General, so pull out all the stops."

*   *   *

How trifling it seemed when Claudia called to report that Eden Langford had walked out on Gray Matthison and taken the child with her. The pettiness of show business irritated Sidney anew.

"The world won't come to an end just because their marriage does," he responded.

Claudia was annoyed.

"I wish I could quote verbatim from some of those inspiring lectures of yours—the ones about dedication to the best interests of clients."

"Their marriage has been stagnant for some time now. This'll make for some fresh copy."

"What I like best about you, Sidney, is that you're a genuine bastard, not just a pallid imitation."

"It's all grist for the gossip mill. Separations, reconciliations, marriages, divorces—what the hell's the difference?"

"People are involved, Sidney. Real, live, honest-to-goodness human beings, including one only three years old."

"You know better than to get personally involved. You have to be like a surgeon or psychiatrist and stand at the periphery—as I've told you ad nauseum over the years."

"And as I've responded ad infinitum over the same time span, that's bullshit. Ever since you've gotten yourself tangled up with these penny-ante foreign accounts, you've been neglecting your bread-and-butter accounts at home. I've run out of excuses for your lack of personal contact with people like Gray."

"I've been in touch with him."

"When you could use him, yes."

"I've had a row of rough nights with that Vivado situation." He yawned.

"Sorry I'm keeping you up. Must be time for your nap."

"Look, you're right in the middle of the Matthison mess. Believe me, it'll straighten out and we'll get some good play out of it."

"Gray's been playing around all over the place lately. Eden tells me she's sick of the whole charade. She might just open up and spill everything."

"Keep talking to her and make sure she plays her role in character. A trial separation at this stage of their marriage has a nice human quality to it."

"It won't be a trial; this is serious. You haven't even asked about the boy."

"What's he got to do with it?"

Her sigh was deep and resigned.

" 'Bye, Sidney," she said, and hung up.

She had deliberately not told him what she had only hours before reluctantly imparted to Eden. His lack of understanding would only exacerbate an already difficult, perhaps tragic, situation.

"Eden, honey," she had whispered softly over lunch, "Gray has AIDS."

Eden was stunned.

"Are you positive?"

"HIV positive," Claudia confirmed.

Eden's inner vulnerability had never been more apparent.

"I don't know whether to cheer or cry."

"You're entitled to do both, Eden."

Eden paused a long moment, her lovely face reflecting her pain.

"I think I'll cry," she said.

Gray had always contended that practicing safe sex was like "taking a shower in a raincoat."

Maybe now he knew better—now that it was too late.

Apprehensive though she was, Eden wasted no time. Two hours later she had herself and her small son tested for HIV by her trusted physician.

"Chances are you're both fine," he said reassuringly. "My office will call you the moment the lab results are in."

An anxious day later she learned that his prognosis had been mercifully accurate.

From that day forward the specter of a fatal disease was Gray's burden to carry. Alone.

90

A cademia spelled enrichment and escape to Sidney, to say nothing of ego
gratification.

Nevertheless he was disturbed that his well-attended seminars at Billy
Sunshine University had never resulted in invitations to address other college
groups, particularly such highly regarded schools of journalism as those at Columbia, Missouri, and Northwestern, among others. He had an explanation for
it, as he did for almost everything.

"They're perpetuating the prejudices against public relations by the media moguls they invite to join their faculties after their professional retirements," he declared. "That's disgraceful, narrow-minded, and dishonest because PR in essence
controls the news while media only *reports* it."

When the opportunity came to address a graduate seminar at Forsythe University in Canada, largely through the intervention of Billy, Sidney welcomed
the new opportunity to philosophize and theorize while temporarily fleeing the
relentlessness of reality. The fact that Forsythe had come under the same kinds
of credibility attacks as BSU was conveniently overlooked by Sidney in filing the
announcement of his appearance on the PR news wire. Adrienne Gale would be
certain to catch it there.

He was in an unusually open and effusive mood on the Canadian campus.
It was as though the crossing of a national boundary relieved him of the necessity
for restraint. Weeks of pressure were released in the single evening's outpouring
of observations and advice.

In a rambling, helter-skelter monologue, he delighted his student audience, if not the faculty members in attendance, with many irreverent and unorthodox opinions and perspectives.

". . . Who says you can't go around tampering with history to suit your desire or convenience? Repeat a lie often enough and eventually it supplants the truth . . ."

". . . Technology provides many new tools, but it's still human guile and ingenuity that are fundamental to success in the PR business. . . ."

". . . The way some professionals in this field employ language, they must be paying below minimum wage. . . ."

". . . To succeed you've got to become like those tinted mirrors that reflect images without flaws or blemishes. . . ."

". . . Emphasize the 'imp' in *imposter*—the aspects of mischievousness and rascality—and your client is very likely to be embraced rather than admonished by the general public . . ."

In the question-and-answer period that followed, Sidney was equally witty and trenchant. A student rose and directed his finger toward the podium.

"Have you ever been accused of being a fraud?"

"Many times," Sidney replied with a grin. "Being a fraud is not the worst sin—being a nobody is."

The assemblage of students was clearly entertained and impressed by Sidney Bastion. He, in turn, reveled in their admiration.

"The objective of it all is not to filter out just a few of your client's impurities. You should strive to dam the whole lot of them. Attila the Hun should emerge as Saint Francis of Assisi."

It was really an exercise in ego under the guise of education. Sidney always had his talks taped to make sure his off-the-cuff comments were preserved for distribution among his peers.

He kept his attaché case locked and untouched under his seat on the flight back to New York. This was a night to savor. And he did feel good. Very good indeed.

91

C laudia was just back from a fact-finding tour of Vivado. It had been her first visit and initial face-to-face meeting with Raul Tampa. Sidney listened to her impressions with a mixture of interest and impatience.

"Tampa's as charismatic as his country is beautiful," Claudia reported. "But the island is real, and he's a fake. I feel very uneasy about his true intentions."

"Since when did we become social workers? You spent too much time talking to the natives."

"As much as I could, but that wasn't much. His guards saw to that. The people are cowed, Sidney. They walk around smiling, but there's fear in their eyes. There isn't a building over there without his name on it and his picture hanging over a balcony. But when I asked the people to describe him, the response I got most often was 'He kill.' When I had the questionable pleasure of interviewing Raul himself on the subject, he said, 'A nice man like me would never kill anybody. I love the world. I love life.' "

"Can't fault him for that," Sidney said.

"Underneath it all, he hates us," she declared.

"He loves our television. I can't get him on often enough to please him."

"He's a propagandist extraordinaire."

"Remember, we represent the resorts of Vivado and not Raul Tampa or his government per se."

"You're talking to Claudia, Sidney."

"What about Paula's project?"

"It's in the Paula Castle grandiose-grotesque tradition."

"It's going to be magnificent."

" 'The Caribbean Castle on verdant Vivado,' she wrote."

"I'll enter that in the naming contest."

"First prize: two weeks there with Paula C. as your hostess. Second prize: three weeks there with Paula C."

"Which brings me to the matter of your companion on this trip."

"I figured we'd get to that sooner or later."

"Why didn't you take someone from the staff?" Sidney had heard rumors of a handsome travel mate who was not strictly business.

"I took a freelancer for a change."

"An expert on the Caribbean?"

"No, just a plain old expert."

"There's something you're not telling me, Claudia."

"There are lots of things I'm not telling you—at least for now."

"Get a full report to me."

"Right along with the expense account."

He hung up and stared absently at the skyline. There were times when he felt he could trust absolutely no one but himself. And this was one of them.

W hat do you know about a Derek Slater?" Sidney quizzed Pam that night.

"I know he's going hot and heavy with Claudia Rogers," she said. "I wondered when you'd get around to asking."

Sidney waited silently. It had been a simple matter for Raul Tampa's private police to get Slater's passport identification. Thirty-six years old, young for Claudia. Residence: Brentwood, California. Unfortunately, passports no longer listed the bearer's occupation.

The *policia* had rushed Sidney a photostat of the document, including the requisite photograph. He was not bad-looking. Not bad at all, considering the less-than flattering quality of most passport pictures.

"He's a screenwriter," Pam volunteered. "No major credits but the word is potential."

"Especially if he lands the top PR gal on the whole Pacific coast."

"There's that cynicism. I don't read him wrong. He makes his own way."

"How serious is it?"

"I've never seen her more involved."

Sidney switched subjects.

"How's the Matthison thing shaping?"

"Gray's acting like an ass."

"Eden?"

"She's a realist, a survivor."

"Will she stay quiet?"

"Let's hope so."

He bit his lip and went out of the room. Fuck it, he thought. Life was too short to let it get to him. He was up all night with the VCR, searching not for solutions but escape.

nvitations were generally easy to spot in the daily mail pile. Their off-size, embossed, and often pastel-colored envelopes gave them a special cachet amid the reams of common correspondence. Pam Garson opened all of Sidney's mail except for these special missives.

One such invitation, arriving as it did on a particularly calamitous business day, drew more than the usual attention from him. The gray vellum parchment inside the envelope announced in engraved scarlet script: "The Thomas Paine Society of the Graduate School of Journalism of Columbia University cordially invites you to attend a special lecture on Contemporary Public Relations by the distinguished public relations expert and Columbia Graduate School alumna Adrienne Gale at Town Hall on Friday, August 23rd at 8 P.M."

He pushed back from his desk, swiveled, and faced the living portrait of mid-Manhattan beyond the glass. Columbia, no less.

A sense of slippage, of retrogression, permeated him. He prided himself on having become something of a spokesman for the industry, a kind of philosopher of practical PR, and no one had really bothered to step forward to dispute him or challenge him. Not until now, at any rate.

Was she serious? he asked himself.

Is she doing it to counteract me, to surpass me, to embarrass me, to tease me?

Ridiculous, he decided finally. Why entertain any questions at all about her motives? He had already addressed the same subject comprehensively and authoritatively. She could only hope to be derivative and imitative at best.

He did attend. If he did not consciously disguise himself then he at least dressed quite differently from his norm, affecting a collegiate casualness behind tinted glasses. He carried a clipboard, ostensibly for note taking but really intended to hide his face as necessary. His chosen seat was in the last row of the half-filled auditorium.

She looked radiant on the podium. He saw her as the most sensually attractive executive one could possibly summon from any American industry to deliver a serious professional lecture.

"Larger and larger parts of our lives in this technologically advanced age have become illusory," she began earnestly. "We're living in an increasingly and disturbingly vicarious world."

She talked on astutely and often with an appealing flippancy.

"It takes about a month to become a tradition nowadays," she declared, "and just a little longer to become a legend."

Sidney found himself listening more raptly then he ever imagined he could.

". . . Almost everyone these days is time-disoriented," she continued. "Television has created a new kind of inflation. They once used to say a picture was worth a thousand words. Make that ten thousand minimum now if it's on network TV."

She was roundly applauded at the conclusion. Sidney made his escape hastily, not at all sure he liked the newfound respect she had awakened in him.

t was a relatively long time between calls from Doc Diamond.

"Sid," he said, and paused as if to honor his distinction as the only person who regularly addressed the man in this abbreviated fashion, "Johnny's first anniversary's coming up next month. I figure we should work on one helluva blast."

"Talk about time flying."

"Billy Sunshine wants in on some kinda memorial celebration. He sees it big like I do."

"Gaultland?"

"Where else?"

"Sounds good. I'll get right on it."

Sidney hung up and circled a date on his advance calendar. Johnny Gault dead a year? It hardly seemed possible.

Gaultland was outlandish, but it had the redeeming virtue of love. It was a theme park with one theme: Johnny Gault.

They came to honor him and adore him and enjoy their pilgrimage. There were picnic tables and roving vendors to service those who chose not to eat in the fast-food outlets and semigourmet restaurants surrounding the grounds.

"It's like making Bethlehem a year-round carnival celebrating Jesus, complete with barkers and sideshows," wrote one eastern critic.

Despite all the artificiality, all the crass commercialism, there was something real and lasting about Gaultland.

It was somehow in the image of Johnny himself: heroic and shabby, beautiful and cheap. Its very excesses typified his own indulgent extremes.

Another media assayer observed: "Disneyland at least admits to celebrating cartoon characters. Gaultland is dizzyland, effectively reducing a celebrated real-life idol into a caricature and his life into a cartoon strip."

Doc was as oblivious to negative criticism now as he had been throughout his life.

"If I listened t'other people," he said in a rare moment of candor, "I'd be sittin' in some cave in the mountains eatin' dented cans o'dog food."

The estate was touted by Doc as "an experience for all ages." That claim seemed to suggest some degree of discretion in exhibits and activities. None was exercised.

The Anatomia Shoppe was a prime example of Doc's callous disregard for taste. Visitors could purchase purported locks of Johnny Gault's head hair or his nail clippings, eyelashes, and pubic hair, all mounted and laminated in plastic. Also available were miniature vials of the late singer's teardrops. Prominently featured was Doc's other long-overdue inspiration, officially endorsed and authenticated replicas of Johnny's celebrated phallus.

"We have them in gold, silver, brass, bronze, and ivory, as well as the standard plastic variety," he proudly admitted to Sidney. "They're the real thing, too, taken from a living mold."

Inured as he was to client shock, Sidney was taken aback by the revelation.

"Maybe they're not illegal, Doc, but I certainly think they're ill-advised as memorial mementos."

"Wrong, Sid," Doc chuckled. "They're the hottest-moving item at Gaultland already. We cain't keep 'em on the shelves."

Sidney sighed in resignation. Catering to the lowest common denominator in public taste was a very special forte of Doc Diamond, and he had profited mightily from it.

Sidney dealt with it by contacting a doctor of anthropology at Billy Sunshine University. With encouragement, and a significant financial inducement, the professor issued a statement, printed on golden parchment paper, that would in the future accompany each copy of the mock organ.

"Part of a man's psychological life pattern is determined by the size and symmetry of his sexual organ," the statement said. "Therefore, in the interests of a better, more intimate understanding of the complexities of musical genius and in keeping with the canons of historical research, it is fitting and proper that Gaultland offers to the world this authentic limited edition phallic replica of the genitalia of the late, great Johnny Gault."

It was signed "Harrison Osgood Solters, Doctor of Anthropology, Billy Sunshine University" and came complete with a ribbon and seal verifying its integrity.

"Beautiful," Doc reacted. "Fuckin' beautiful."

The museum of erotic memorabilia was a key focus of gossip—and an enormous drawing card. Even people who had never followed Johnny in his career were curious to examine the erotic enigma of an idol.

In a Plexiglas cube was the gun he had used to masturbate movie queen Brook Forrest. Yet another showcase displayed a rifle he had allegedly rammed up the center of a member of the British royal family.

Doc had selected some of the more discreet, self-directed tapes of Johnny in sexual action, and these played off the walls of the museum to the deliberate beat of his music.

It was all in bizarre contrast to the shrine memorializing Rita Gault across the park.

There was something for everyone in the myth Johnny had become. And Doc was everywhere, making certain he was a beneficiary.

The swift and successful franchising of Gaultlands and Rita Gault gazebos not only in America but throughout the world was proving just how valid Doc's instincts were. The Japanese, the French, the Germans, the Canadians, and even the Turks had invested. The universality of Johnny's appeal was obvious.

"Johnny's more'n a legend," Doc told Sidney, "he's a piece of America."

The enterprise had become so big that Doc had finally and reluctantly brought in a management team.

"We don't have Mickey Mouse or Donald Duck," the new director declared, "but we have the magic of Johnny Gault. We can outdazzle Disney if we play our cards right."

The core focus of the franchises was to perpetuate the myth of Johnny. Shops were stocked with copyrighted souvenirs, and huge portraits of him loomed about the grounds as in some banana republic dictatorship. There were toys and games to help make Gaultland a household word among the too-young-to-know-Johnny crowd. All emphasis was on Johnny—over loudspeakers blaring his biggest hits, in the concession stands with their doll replicas of him, and in the midway rides reflecting his love of motorcycles and fast cars.

All the memorabilia was amazingly convincing. It mattered little to his fans that Johnny had clung to only one now worn and safe-deposited guitar throughout his career. In spite of this, each of the newly established Gaultlands boasted of harboring and displaying the original. Hype was hype and ripe was ripe. Doc delivered his "package of authenticity" to his franchises, and very few questioned him in their eagerness to cash in on the miracle and the myth.

Some parks included amphitheaters for celebrity concerts, others offered chapels for weddings and christenings. Almost all featured large catering facilities. The emphasis was on family, something ironically lacking in Johnny's own brief life.

At least one Rita Gault memorial gazebo was, of course, de rigueur in each location. Hardly a visitor left without a statue, brooch, or some other likeness of Rita.

"Johnny loved his momma" was an overriding theme.

Beyond adhering to a central design plan developed under Doc's direction, franchises were granted rather broad latitude to develop original extensions and variations to enhance the appeal of their parks.

Some entrepreneurs who bought into the expensive and emotionally evocative franchises were quick to experiment. Cemeteries became lucrative adjuncts to the parks. "Be buried next to Johnny," the sales pitch went. "Buy now before his special space on earth is forever filled."

The plots were among the hottest sales items in the early tabulations of overall revenue returns.

There was a sick, sad longing to it all that would be perpetuated for years to come. The parks became one of the stock market's hottest investments.

Sidney was frustrated by it all. Try as he might, he could not seem to shake off his image as being first and foremost Johnny Gault's press agent. Everything else he did continued to be regarded within and without the trade as peripheral.

"The curse is on me," he said in moments of acute consternation. "I could get God incarnate as a client and they would still identify me as the PR man for Johnny Gault."

It was a distinction most of his peers and competitors would have sold their souls to achieve.

94

H e called it "Bastion bashing."

These were the periodic sieges when the media seemed hell-bent on hobbling him. It was happening again; the journalistic pack had begun labeling Raul Tampa "the villain of Vivado" and ascribing every disruptive or terroristic act in the Western Hemisphere to the island dictator.

The latest was a Trans-Oceanic airliner crash, killing all four hundred and sixty-seven people aboard on their way to Brazil. It was almost immediately attributed to Tampa-backed terrorists.

When a mass grave was found in Haiti containing the sexually mutilated bodies of more than a hundred babies and prepubescent children, the linkage was quickly made to "the vulture of Vivado" and his alleged ambition to invade and conquer that lush but impoverished country.

"There is no way he has the resources or the will or the desire to engage in all these horrendous and deplorable actions," Sidney insisted to the media. "His interests lie in the peaceful development of his own beautiful island nation."

That pious claim was decidedly more difficult to substantiate after a dozen bodies of political prisoners, caught in an attempted palace coup, washed ashore close to the new Castle Hotel structures. They were grotesquely maimed, with their genitals stuffed into their mouths, their eyes gouged, their fingers and toes strung on wires wrapped around their throats like macabre necklaces.

"The man's a butcher," declared the Washington press. Scathing editorials denouncing Tampa filled the papers.

Sidney insisted that he represented only the resorts of the nation, which was akin to claiming that he spoke for the Vatican without having any connection with the Pope. He refused to accept that the *One Hour* exposé had forever bonded him to the power structure rather than the surf and palm trees of both nations.

And, of course, there were domestic imbroglios such as Gray Matthison's separation from Eden, rampant reports of a rift between Paula Castle and Reese Roberts, numerous campus controversies at Billy Sunshine University, and continuing exposés about Galen Jenkins.

The firm's product line had grown, and he took refuge in it when necessary. It included a national bank chain, an Italian sports car manufacturer, a French perfumer, an international chemical company, and a food conglomerate. This was the direction he had always claimed as his ultimate goal. Yet since achieving it, he had undergone a startling change of heart. When it came to the showdown, he spent as little time as possible with the corporate types and fell back to the hurly-burly show business types he had always claimed to despise. This did not escape Claudia.

"In a sense you run a factory, Sidney," she said, "and you'll always turn out more glitter than you will nuts and bolts. Gilding the lilies is your specialty."

He had heard that song before.

Fortunately there were some relative constants.

The Castle Hotels prospered in spite of Paula, or perhaps because of her, while Norman Prescott kept adding to his fortune and expanding his junk-bond-financed empire.

Reverend Billy Sunshine proved repeatedly that he could fill any amphitheater in the world by announcing his intention to be present, and even in the steamiest months of a Tennessee summer Gaultland drew its avid throngs of the fan-tourist faithful.

Gray Matthison's show remained number one in its time slot, and Gray's personal popularity continued high, despite occasional media speculation in the wake of his failed marriage to Eden.

Sidney knew the secret health problems caused by Gray's dreadful virus and kept them from the press, alluding to a degenerative arthritis problem. He couldn't help but notice, however, that the early ravages of the disease were eroding the edges of Gray's once-handsome, chiseled face.

Gray continued to survive in his Teflon way despite his deteriorating physical condition. He consumed all kinds of pills and potions, but to no avail. His fate was just a matter of time, and time was going fast.

Still, Sidney concealed the truth and sent out better stories, and the "Bastion bashing" continued, as usual.

He could only wonder at times if his full deck was stacked.

95

Adrienne Gale and Jason Welles were lunching together casually in Jason's new Third Avenue offices. Adrienne had long since forgiven Jason for exposing Galen Jenkins and then pinning responsibility for the act on her. "I would have done the same thing under the circumstances," she had reassured him.

Now, as always, their conversation turned to Sidney Bastion.

"He amazes me," Adrienne admitted. "Call him devious, double-dealing, or whatever, but he still amazes me."

"Off on another collusion course?" Jason punned.

"Nobody can coexist with Sidney. He's meant to be a loner."

"I'm not sure I agree with that. You could handle him."

"Why should I?"

"I'm not proposing it. I'm only saying you could if you wanted to."

Jason was really the only person with whom she could discuss Sidney without fear of being accused of either jealousy or intrigue. He seemed to understand all the conflicting but contributing factors in their undefined relationship.

"Which brings me to my lecture. Did you get a copy?"

"I did. I thought it was excellent."

"Thanks."

"Any reaction from the aforementioned?"

"That's the amazing part of it. He's invited me to debate him on the subject at Sunshine University."

"That's Sidney." Jason laughed.

"And," she continued, "he wants a private dialogue afterwards at some mountain retreat."

"Pretty unique proposition, don't you think?"

"Yes."

"Mr. Originality at work."

"I'm actually thinking about it. Does that surprise you?"

"Not really, Adrienne. There's always been a chemistry there."

"Highly combustible."

"Incendiary."

"I just might do it."

"Do it," he advised.

Claudia caught him off guard, just after he'd run through the network newscast tapings. She knew his nighttime routine as well as anyone, so her timing was no accident.

"Sidney," she announced softly, "I'm getting married."

He held the phone at arm's length for a moment, regarding it like a live grenade.

"That's some opening line," he said finally.

"I had to say it right away."

"You've edited me plenty in the past. What's my response?"

"Be happy. Wish me happiness."

"I'm happy. I wish you happiness."

"Thanks, Sidney."

"Do I get the name of the groom or is that privileged information?"

"Derek Slater, of course."

"Do you realize I don't even know who he is?"

"What do you think Pam and I talk about—Barbie dolls?"

"I've never met him. But my seal of approval is not required in the state of California."

"You'll love him."

He cleared his throat briefly.

"Any date yet?"

"Not definite. But soon, very soon."

"Does Billy Sunshine know?"

"No."

"He will be doing the honors, won't he?"

She hesitated before responding.

"No, Sidney," she said finally. "I wouldn't feel it was for real if Reverend Billy ran the show."

96

I t was a revelation of sorts for Sidney to see Gaultland and its satellites explode like fireworks across America and then other areas of the world. He had been reluctant to believe it possible. His good fortune lay in still being part of it despite his skepticism.

Gaultland number one, the original, had definitely become Bethlehem number two, complete with roller coasters, Ferris wheels, and tent shows. Rumors of Johnny's reincarnation regularly swept through the bars clustered on Gaultland's fringes. The *National Inquest* ran a running report of Johnny Gault spottings. There were people who swore they had not only seen him but spoken with him.

"We've got tighter security than Disney," the chief of security told Sidney. "They come here like they're meeting Jesus."

It was Gaultland *über alles* with Doc. The beautiful boy with the guitar was peripheral to the new energy generated by the park and its franchised offshoots.

"You've captured the cachet, Doc," Sidney complimented him during a tour of a new park in Louisville.

"That better be French for *cash* or *cunt*," Doc responded.

Hidden troves of Gault treasure kept being discovered. They were either merchandised immediately or squirreled away. Doc was not always forthcoming about them with Sidney, but he did recognize the importance of promotion and shared what he chose to share with his indigenous and lasting PR adviser.

Doc and Sidney both recognized the value and the importance of stressing the basic simplicity of their late but hardly dormant money machine.

"People think of Johnny as the boy next door," Sidney repeated often enough to put dents in Doc's brain. "They've forgotten about the drugs and sex. He's their hero."

Attendance at the various Gaultlands and gazebos more than bore him out.

Johnny had always been a tickler, a giggler, both baby-faced and babyish. These childlike qualities, so starkly in contrast to his satyriasis, truly endeared him to his fans. He was cuddly and warm, erotic and elusive, all at once.

"A living orgasm," one periodical had described him.

Small wonder, then, that the Johnny Gault doll became overnight the hottest item on the toy market since Barbie. Its penis rose when its guitar was plucked but remained soft and gentle to the touch at all other times. Babies slept with it; their mothers and grandmothers wept with it and made love to it. Nothing had so rapidly overwhelmed the industry since the invention of Santa Claus.

Doc could not believe the revenue it produced so quickly. The official Gaultland logo contributed immeasurably to its value. As a consequence, Doc was readily persuaded to add item after item to the Gault product line. In no time at all there were mugs and sweatshirts, perfumes and powders, even full sound systems bearing the Gaultland trademark and the handsome profile of Johnny.

"It's all trash," Sidney conceded, "but there's gold in garbage."

He called it the crow philosophy, and he was right. Crows loved glitter, and they went for it, but they never lost sight of where the food was. Neither did Doc. Or Sidney.

97

With its fondness for puns, New York's *Daily Record* might well have captioned the so-called Bastion-Gale debate "the last ruse of summer."

Billy Sunshine University was largely enjoying its vacation period with only a few thousand students in makeup courses and special programs on campus. Of these possibly two hundred showed up at Chapel Hall to hear this pair of eastern public relations luminaries scratch and scuffle. Instead, they heard them bill and coo, agreeing almost completely on the techniques and mores of their profession. It had never been Sidney's intention to participate in a knock-down, drag-out discourse with Adrienne Gale. He had simply utilized his ingenuity to lure her away from the pressures of Manhattan long enough to share more than a few hours together.

So what if the campus newspaper later declared: PR PIRANHAS PROVE PALLID PUSSYCATS? It was a loss he was willing to concede in going for the larger victory.

Reverend Billy was mercifully away on a revival tour of South America. To him such a turnout would have been embarrassing, if not downright humiliating. He would have created an audience ten times as large by declaring it a holy obligation.

Sidney had deliberately avoided that. All he'd wanted from Billy this time was the use of his campus facilities and the retreat in the San Gabriel Mountains.

Adrienne sensed she had been duped from the moment of her arrival. She had flown out in Sidney's jet and was met by him at the airport. Her debate opponent proved much too relaxed and conciliatory from the outset to be regarded as a serious challenge. It was simply not his style.

The game was nevertheless intriguing by virtue of its very novelty. Backgammon had become a bore, and she seldom had time to slip away to Atlantic City for baccarat. This little encounter was much more cat-and-mouse, spider-and-fly. Since they had never really spent any extended time together, the weekend promised to be interesting, despite the opening night debacle.

They met at poolside the morning after.

"You look out of character in swimming trunks," she observed.

"Then I'll take them off."

"Then you'll really be out of character—and out of order, too."

"On the contrary, I'm most in character and order when I'm naked." He laughed lightly.

"Strip a PR man to his true essence and you'll discover a little boy who's just lied to his mother about playing with himself."

"Is that the result of profound thought and research?"

"Practice, practice, practice." She laughed.

"We really should have gotten our act together before going onstage like we did last night. I think we made asses of ourselves."

"I'd never let it happen in New York, but out here?"

"Spoken like a true New York chauvinist."

"No matter what anyone says, the fire is there."

"But here's where you lay back and let it warm you."

He dropped onto a chaise next to her.

"Let's be serious now," he said. "Do you realize that the last time I entered the waters of this pool I was a skinny-dipper?"

"You sinned in these holy waters?" She shook her head in mock disdain, then smiled.

Inevitably he persuaded her to join him in a nude swim, followed by a session of naked sunbathing. The situation and the atmosphere were entirely too seductive for either of them to resist. He pressed the warmth of his flesh against hers and slid the measure of his manhood between her thighs.

"Pushy," she said as she pulled his head to her chest.

"It's my pleasure to inform you," he declared in labored breaths, "that you've just been selected the Most Desirable, Most Delectable Dame in the Dominion of Manhattan—"

"Sidney, stop the bullshit and start fucking."

For a change, Sidney Bastion did exactly as he was told.

98

Pierce Agee was wholly pleased by the enormous and lasting success of *The Bitch in Penthouse A*. It was still running to capacity houses on Broadway, and there were a national road company and a London production as well.

"People love to identify stage culprits with real-life figures," he said in one of his many interviews. "It creates a kind of extrasensory, spiritual bond between them."

When he was questioned about its possible effect upon a character's real-life prototype he was even more diagnostic.

"This disturbed me originally," he confessed. "I envisioned the potential destruction of an individual's integrity and self-esteem. But quite the contrary has occurred. In the case of *Bitch*, for example, it has actually synthesized the central character and made her an even more substantive and self-sufficient individual."

"You're saying that your play has actually enhanced the very life it set out to denigrate?"

"That's an unfortunate choice of words, but essentially, yes, it has probably broadened and enriched the life of the individual in question. In fact, it has without a doubt."

Paula Castle now publicly professed to love Pierce.

"He's a darling," she told interviewers. "I would dine on his entrails."

The remark was typical of her shock-speak style. She loved to say what others didn't dare to say.

"The man has a great talent and a great mind," she said at the same press conference, "but I have no idea about his cock."

"Would it make a difference?"

"If we were fucking? Of course!"

There was a ripple of laughter.

"I never judge a man by his penis, darling," she continued. "Remember, the strongest muscle in a man's body is his tongue. Now this lady's tongue will say bye-bye."

Pierce Agee took some of her remarks personally, but he refused to acknowledge any effect on his psyche.

"Loose lips are endemic to show business," he said. "Her hotels have gone to her head."

There was a good mile or two between them—mentally, physically, and psychologically—but it was clear Pierce had penetrated Paula and they both knew it. Like a surgeon, he had opened and exposed her. The wound would heal; the patient would not only survive but thrive.

99

E veryone around Johnny had been at least vaguely aware of the sex tapes. Ego and eroticism, combined with drugged abandon, had driven Johnny to record all too many of his sexual exploits.

"A stiff cock has no loyalty and no conscience," Randy Wheeler had told Abby Ashley. "Johnny'd beat his meat to take off the heat sometimes, but then he'd need to feel pussy, and we'd have to find him some."

"I'd like to fuck her face," he would tell his roadies about particular fans, groupies for the most part, who unabashedly made themselves available to him. Fellatio was one of his favorite forms of release.

It was such a graphic and pungent summation that even Abby had felt obligated to tone it down for her book. Through her literary revelations she had been the first to alert Doc to the existence of a whole lode of genuine Gault pornography. He recognized its market potential immediately.

Rock Candy, a fan sex magazine, had reported the existence of tapes and films of Johnny in erotic abandon.

"All girls to him were 'birds,' " the magazine stated, "an expression he picked up on a British tour. Those with special oral expertise he had called 'swallows.' "

It was Johnny's involvement with "swallows" that reputedly dominated the tape and film collection Doc sought to assemble and complete.

No fear of compromising Johnny's image deterred him in his search for the trove. He had uncovered bits and pieces in the past, but now the promise of a vast collection haunted him. He knew it would be worth millions on the sub-terranean porno market.

"Somebody's got the shit stashed somewhere," he insisted, frustrated by the dead ends.

He had done better with the bus tapes. They had been right there in a canister aboard the bus. One of his mysterious offshoot companies was now raking in a fortune from their surreptitious sales. Doc's righteous indignation and denunciations of them, echoed and elaborated on by Billy Sunshine, only heightened their allure. Johnny's fans were almost desperate to acquire them. The street value of good copies made legitimate album sales pale by comparison.

One by one, Doc did manage to find copies, sometimes originals, and eventually he acquired enough to establish a theater on the fringes of Gaultland featuring films of Johnny fulfilling his role as "the Jesus of Jism," *Rock Candy's* nickname for him.

His fans loved and accepted him. They expected him to be both saint and satyr.

"I come here to come," one young fan told a Gaultland guard. "Just to be near where he was turns me on."

What Sidney called "the stud stuff" had begun to appear in the "shadow press," his term for the sleazy subculture of magazines and tabloids devoted to stripping celebrities naked and revealing their passions and perversions.

There were covers and headlines magnifying the Oedipussian relationship Johnny had had with his mother. Rita the saint became Rita the seductress and child molester in these accounts.

The faithful prayed at the gazebos, denying the filth.

It was an uncomfortable dilemma for Sidney. He could cope with the sexual tapes. There were those who would argue that Johnny's sexual prowess enhanced his reputation. The largely imaginary, idyllic relationship between mother and child, however, had taken on a life of its own. Sidney had used Rita in his buildup of Johnny to such an extent that he was now stuck with her sanctified image. The popular memorial gazebos were vivid examples of how far it had gone.

Sidney shook his head, remembering a remark Doc once had made about Johnny's mom.

"Rita could suck cock better'n a bilge pump," he had said.

Johnny Gault rode the hit charts like a rodeo cowboy, the champion who would not go down. Months—years—after his death, one, two, or even three of his posthumous releases had climbed into the Top Ten.

"Summer in My Mind—Winter in My Heart" sold like sin.

"Please Don't Tease" hit number one.

"Two-Time Tilly and One-Man Milly" followed, then came another runaway hit, "Leftover Love."

All of it was money in the bank for the Doctor, who had quietly become one of the wealthiest men in America.

100

Adrienne Gale presented Sidney with copies of the Pierce Agee and Paula Castle interviews. It was their first business contact since returning from their unexpectedly intense and rewarding weekend.

"Pierce has expressed a preliminary interest in doing a play on Norman Prescott," she revealed after Sidney had finished reading the copy.

"He's no sitting duck like Paula," Sidney warned immediately. "Prescott would ruin him if he went too far."

"I agree with Pierce that it does much more good than harm, regardless."

"Norman's a very private man. The very idea of having his personal life paraded before busloads of suburban soap opera refugees would definitely be anathema to him."

"Mention it to him, at least?"

"At an opportune time."

"Soon?"

"Soon enough."

"You might point out there's a kind of guaranteed immortality in being *done* by a playwright of Pierce's stature."

"Norman's immortality is already guaranteed—thanks to his premier, protean public relations consultant."

"If bullshit were barium I'd have you X-rayed."

"You'd just love my big heart," he said.

*　　*　　*

Don Samuelson was back on Sidney's case with a TV special, "The Men Who Manufacture News."

"Why am I always singled out as the epitome of evil in this business?" Sidney wondered aloud. Samuelson had just referred to a particularly unsavory individual as being "of the Sidney Bastion ilk."

"Don't be overly sensitive, Sidney," Pam said as she joined him on the couch. "You've been ripped apart publicly before. Don't let it bother you now."

The program also took potshots at Norman Prescott, Galen Jenkins, and—of course—Raul Tampa.

At no point in the hour-long documentary on the communications industry did Samuelson have a single complimentary thing to say about Sidney Bastion or the public relations business as a whole.

"If we're such whoremongers, how come he uses our material and dates our women?" Sidney demanded.

Pam felt obligated to respond.

"He's a whore himself," she said.

"Exactly."

"We're all whores," she added.

Paula Castle's face had become inescapable lately, beaming out in its own unmistakably smug and condescending fashion from every newspaper and magazine, billboard, and bus stop, inviting one and all to be her personal guest at any of her elegant Castles.

Sidney had aligned her with an innovative and aggressive advertising agency, which kept her heavily occupied. She had been kept so busy, in fact, that she rarely bothered Sidney anymore.

Ironically, he had just cited her to Adrienne as an example of a difficult client whom he had tamed.

"The secret's in getting yourself settled into their accounting systems," he philosophized, "to the extent that any and all fees and expenses submitted are regarded as basic operating costs rather than luxury expenditures."

"You've done a helluva job on her," Adrienne assured Sidney, "for whatever it's worth."

Local polls other than Satellite agreed that Paula Castle had become the most readily identifiable, if not the most admired, woman in the New York metropolitan area.

The whole business really didn't result in any lasting art, Sidney reflected during a lull in the insanity. It was more like building sand castles or making snowmen than it was erecting monuments.

One of these days, he promised himself, he would look elsewhere for some occupation more gratifying, more enduring.

But when rumors of an impending coup in Vivado began to circulate, Paula Castle was immediately on the phone, harassing him again.

"Now my Caribbean Castles project's in jeopardy down there," she complained heatedly. "What the fuck's going on?"

"Uprisings are part of the landscape there, Paula."

"Don't bullshit me, you slick son of a bitch. My property is an island within an island lately. Caribbean Castles is surrounded by militia and cut off from native society. We're like Guantanamo."

"Tampa will cool the situation, like he's done in the past. You're going to have the number-one resort development in the Western Hemisphere, exactly as planned."

He calmed her finally with a promise to contact Raul Tampa that day and report back to her on the true rebel situation. The fact that no one else had been able to get through to anywhere on the island in days did not deter him. Promises were like confetti in his hands when he was cornered.

101

After years of beating drums and staging fanfares, Claudia Rogers wanted desperately to have a simple wedding sans all the costumes and pageantry, all the hype and hoopla.

"I want it small and intimate," she confided to Pam Garson. "No more than fifty people."

"You have that many names under Z in your personal file."

"I know it won't be easy. But that's the way it has to be."

"You could elope."

"That wouldn't do it for me. I still want church and rice and a white gown and double rings and all that."

"The sentimental sophisticate."

"I'll just have to risk alienating a lot of nice people."

"Your real friends will understand."

"They won't have to. They'll be there. It's the others I'm concerned about."

"Do it for yourself, your own way for a change."

"Thanks, Pam. I'm hoping you'll come with Sidney."

"Sidney?"

"Why not?"

"I think, unfortunately, that at this point he'd expect to take Adrienne Gale."

"Who said she was invited?"

"Problems already, Claudia."

"I don't want her at my wedding. I know her, yes, but she's no friend of mine."

"Have you talked to Sidney yet?"

"No. He's hardly the one I'd consult with on wedding plans."

"I would like to come with him."

"Then so be it. Sidney can take it or leave it."

"He might just leave it. That's how far things have moved along with them."

"It's still my wedding. This time I control the guest roster, not Sidney."

"Good for you," Pam said softly. "And for me. Good luck."

102

They were an unlikely luncheon triumverate: Adrienne, Sidney, and Pierce Agee. But past affiliations and alienations were frequently overlooked in the business, particularly when a semblance of unity could result in something good for all concerned.

Agee was ready to begin work on a play loosely based on the life of Norman Prescott.

"I think of him as a kind of William Randolph Hearst carried to the nth power," Pierce said with his customary intensity. "He's really a media Machiavelli, all the more intriguing because of his secretive methods and his almost unobtrusive rise to great power and wealth."

"Unobtrusive until Sidney," Adrienne interjected.

"Of course," Pierce agreed. "I refer to his early years."

"Why don't you just do him without looking for his blessing?" Sidney questioned. "Hell, romans à clef were around before there were Romans."

Agee smiled faintly.

"That would be a lot simpler, wouldn't it? But there's something about playwriting that eschews the easy solution and opts for the difficult. In this instance it borders on the difference between biography and autobiography. Do you understand what I mean?"

"But you wouldn't be doing his real life, would you?"

"Of course not. That would rob me of all my poetic license and thwart my own insights."

"Go on."

"I'm basically interested in the simplicity of the good and the complexity of the evil in all that I write. People are the conduits to delineate those qualities."

"It sort of baffles me, Pierce, why you want to meet your subjects to more or less confess what you are about to do to them," Sidney said.

"There's this broad assumption in America that material success guarantees happiness, power, and celebrity. It's just not so, and the reasons why it's not so are damned well fascinating. It's amazing to watch people who have ostensibly everything imaginable try to be happy in spite of their wealth."

"I guess you're right about that," said Adrienne.

"Why should Norman Prescott care anyway?" Sidney asked.

"Because he knows," said Pierce. "He knows, more than you or Adrienne or me, just how fragile the structure is despite all its seeming strength. Did you ever catch lightning bugs in a jar when you were a child? Remember how brilliantly they would glow at first, then less and less until they went out? That's essentially what I'm trying to do with this type of play, to capture the glow of a life before it goes out forever."

"Coming from you it sounds so profound, Pierce," Adrienne commented.

"It's because everything in life is so tentative, including life itself. Every moment is of profound importance."

Sidney pushed back from the table.

"You may be a little heavy for Norman, a little too abstract. I only recently restored him to ogre status, and he's happy about it."

"He won't lose any of that in my typewriter."

"Good, then maybe we can still do business."

"Congratulations," said Adrienne.

103

Sloan Bannister was shadowy and elusive without effort or intention. The nature of his life threw a cloak over everything he did.

Since the expiration of his agreement with the Bastion organization, he had moved in the quiet cadences of his craft to compile a collection of exposés culled mainly from the collaborators that had been arranged for him by Sidney Bastion.

There was a Chappaquidick in every prominent person's life, and Sloan had decided to expose some very painful secrets. His collection included many off-the-record, vehemently deniable, outrageous facts and allegations, along with out-of-context quotes and shadowy suppositions. He was a veteran author who knew the marketplace and was eager to score a blockbuster.

In the tradition of literary obscurity he had become something of a legend himself. He was the ghost behind a score of celebrity bestsellers.

"How do you compare yourself with Abby Ashley?" a talk show host questioned.

Sloan laughed nervously, then coughed, clearing his throat with a closed fist to his mouth.

"Abby Ashley? AA? Author Anonymous? Authors Androgynous? She was a literary parasite."

"In that vein, Sloan, what is your opinion of the field of public relations?"

"By comparison it turns Abby Ashley into Florence Nightingale."

"Explain, please."

"It's quite simply a socially useless abomination, a scourge on our society, a disgrace to journalism—wholly parasitic, sycophantic, and populated with leeches."

Sloan had suddenly somersaulted from obscurity into the limelight.

*I*nside Out barely survived its first encounter with Sidney. He was so enraged by some of its contents that he flung the volume repeatedly against the walls of Adrienne's bedroom. By the time he finished scanning it, the book had suffered a broken spine and considerable internal damage.

"There's a lot of suppressed violence in you," Adrienne observed. Her advance copy of the same book remained in mint condition, at least partially due to the absence of any mention of her or her clients in its pages.

"He's a fucking ingrate!" Sidney ranted. "A goddamned traitor!"

"May we quote you in our flap copy?" she teased.

"To think I trusted that bastard! He's the scum of the earth!"

"Put your money in Irving Trust next time."

"The son of a bitch took my retainer fees, let me make him rich with my clients, and then he turns rat bastard on all of us. I can't believe it. I really can't believe it."

Sidney rarely permitted himself to become so emotional. Adrienne could not refrain from being more amused than agitated.

"Imagine that ingrate calling me a bamboozler and a flimflam man! All his checks cleared, didn't they?"

Bannister's book breezily dismissed General Raul Tampa as an insignificant figure internationally while branding him "a dangerous psychopath with delusions of grandeur." Sidney railed at the style more than the substance.

"Tampa should slide down that Bannister in his combat boots and then let's see how many ribs are left. Writers are such fucking prostitutes. They use their own mothers and best friends if they have to to make a buck."

"The mass graves, the genital tortures, the sacrificial sex with pubescent girls are all bullshit then?" Adrienne questioned.

"Hearsay."

"Sinking the cruise ship off the Canary Islands?"

"No proof."

"Attempting to poison the Pope?"

"Pure guano."

"The bomb that blew Flight 303 out of the sky along with two hundred and seven people?"

"Tampa's a family person."

Adrienne shook her head.

"You really are one smooth, slick son of a bitch," she said.

"If I were Sloan, I wouldn't plan any long vacations on the sugar sands of Vivado."

"Nor should anyone else, for that matter."

"Whose side are you on anyway?"

"The country's in a virtual state of siege, Sidney."

"You sound like one of his 'well-informed' sources."

His display of umbrage was all smoke screen and Adrienne knew it. He knew very well how much the political situation had deteriorated in Vivado. The ambitious new airport project, with its incongruous superjet airstrip, was rumored to have been financed in large measure by the Vivado government. There was no way that could be construed as an effort toward promoting mutual tourism.

Sidney threw his own pitch in spite of it. General Tampa was a good and reliable friend of America; Vivado was a virgin paradise for vacationers.

"Didn't you like the part where he said you were 'all hoopla and hubris without substance or sentiment'?"

"That son of a bitch! He throws words around like he thinks he's a PR man." He paused, then focused more clearly on Adrienne.

"You're not in there, are you? No wonder you're so smug."

"Sloan Bannister gets no railing from me."

"From ingrate to smart-ass. There's no peace for Sidney Bastion."

"Try me," she said, "you tiger."

How many do we have on the Vivado account?" Sidney asked Pam Garson later that day.

"Here?"

"Overall."

"A dozen. Maybe fourteen."

"Double it."

"From where, Sidney? I'd have to pull in people from London and Monaco."

"No. Just take them off other accounts here temporarily."

"Sidney?" She paused deliberately. "What about Claudia's wedding?"

"What about it?"

"I have to know your plans to make my own."

"I have no options. I have to go."

"So do I."

"Then we'll go together."

Her sigh was deep in spite of her effort to restrain it.

"Thanks, Sidney."

Sidney denied feelings of nostalgia, but for all his protests that only the present mattered, he really did often miss the chaos and confusion of the newsrooms of his youth.

The noisy irregularity of typewriters responding to finger-activated keys had been replaced by the staccato din of printers obeying word processors. There was a certain antiseptic cleanliness and order to the computer age that had eliminated much of the clamor and color of the past. It became particularly poignant when he ventured from his executive offices into the neat sonority of his current communications center.

One of his anonymous aides—he knew only a few of his staff by given names—summoned him after an Associated Press alert regarding a forthcoming story about Vivado.

"I thought you'd like to see it firsthand, sir," the young man said.

Shades of Sidney, circa a quarter century ago.

"Thanks, I think. It can't be good news with this kind of fanfare."

They watched intently as the bulletin expanded into a detailed news story. Civilian forces were engaged in bloody fighting in the capital to unseat the incumbent government. There had been limited resistance to the surprise attacks but General Tampa was already claiming victory.

Sidney shook his head in exasperation.

"Stupid," he mumbled. "Idiotic."

Calls came in immediately from a mélange of media organizations. All were seeking background information and special insights.

"I want to reiterate the Bastion organization's position in all matters regarding the island nation of Vivado," Sidney lectured his aides assembled by now around the teleprinter. "We represent the resorts of that island and not the island itself. Therefore we cannot and will not have any comment to make concerning the internal or external affairs of its government or its leader. Period."

Back in his own sanctum, Sidney attempted without success to get through to Raul Tampa. Maybe Bannister and all the others were right after all. He had never really felt that certain of the General's sanity. It had never mattered much until now. But the United States government was certain to take a hard line after these new acts of unprovoked aggression. And a hard line could very well involve a hard look at Sidney's own involvement with the shadowy strongman of the Caribbean.

*   *   *

Word came to him indirectly, through the Vivado consulate. The ambassador himself delivered the message in private in his thickly carpeted offices near the United Nations, a few blocks from Sidney's own town house.

"General Tampa wishes to see you in Vivado," he was informed. "It is of urgent importance."

Sidney enjoyed intrigue or he would likely never have succeeded in the camouflage and subterfuge of PR. But Raul Tampa was not Johnny Gault or Billy Sunshine. The man dealt in real blood.

"Normal channels are cut off, as you must know. I'm not sure I could get clearance for such a trip at this time."

"One of the General's private aircraft will transport you."

Despite inner misgivings, Sidney agreed.

He told Pam he would be in London; he told Adrienne he would be in Monaco. Only Claudia knew his real destination.

"You're playing with fire, Sidney," she warned.

"Tampa's okay. I feel safer with him than I do with Paula Castle."

She laughed lightly.

"Remember, Sidney Bastion Associates, Limited, just wouldn't be the same without its namesake."

"It'd be asinine for him to have me assassinated."

"Who said anything about assassination?"

"You implied it. I guess I'm just jumpy."

Claudia would not be with him much longer. He already felt the loss. She had agreed to remain in charge of his West Coast operations for a limited time after her marriage. But then she was definitely going to do what she had always said she one day would: get out of the business.

"Maybe I should have limited my practice to show business after all," he said in parting.

"Too late now, Sidney."

That it was.

Sidney was met at the remote Vivado airstrip by a string of silver and white Rolls-Royces occupied by armed uniformed men. A subdued air of cordiality came only from the leader of the entourage, an imposing-looking colonel.

They traveled at a fast pace set by the lead car until they came upon a small encampment of huts.

"General Tampa is here," the colonel informed Sidney.

The limousines had halted one by one, each of them evenly spaced from the next and parallel to the lead car.

Tampa rose when Sidney entered his tent and extended his hand.

"Thank you for coming, Sidney," he said, motioning for his guest to be seated.

Sidney had never before seen Tampa so ornately dressed, in full uniform and bearing a multitude of medals. Sidney seated himself on an out-of-place canvas director's chair.

"I knew you wouldn't summon me, General, unless it were vital."

Somehow Sidney could not bring himself to address the General as Raul, as he had in the past. Nor did the General encourage it, as he had in previous encounters.

"Events have become most serious since we last talked together," the General said softly. "The time has come for swift and dramatic action to let the world know that Raul Tampa and the nation of Vivado now demand that their voices be heard and respected."

Sidney shifted uncomfortably. Despite multiple air-conditioning units droning in the background, the air was thick and humid.

"I trust you, Sidney. That is why I confide in you now. You must be prepared to answer the world's questions when my plan becomes a reality."

Sidney nodded uneasily.

"There will be bombings," Tampa continued, his voice rising. "Simultaneous explosions in different parts of the world. They will announce that Vivado is taking its rightful place among the powers of the planet, to be regarded as a glorious symbol of unity beckoning to all the imperialistically oppressed. . . ."

Tampa's dark eyes shone. Sidney's forehead jeweled with perspiration.

"I have learned well from you, Sidney," Tampa continued. "I have studied your methods for many years. I knew your name long before you ever knew mine."

Sidney grimaced. He was accustomed to being more of a behind-the-scenes man who was rarely scrutinized.

"I see how you use your clients." Tampa nodded his head knowingly and with implied approval. "One boosts the other up and is himself lifted up in the process." Tampa paused, waiting for a response.

"I guess that could describe one small aspect of my public relations approach." Sidney reluctantly agreed. His most successful projects flashed through his mind as he wondered how those successes were apparently going to backfire on him.

"I have devised a public relations scheme that will benefit us both," Tampa said. "It is so clean and simple that I wonder why one of us didn't think of it long ago."

Sidney felt the blood drain from his head.

"My soldiers will place in Gaultland a bomb that will destroy the entire property."

Sidney tried to remain expressionless, an effort just short of remaining conscious. Tampa looked pleased with himself. It occurred to Sidney that now, without question, he understood the depth of Tampa's psychosis.

"And how will this help us?" Sidney asked, hoping that Tampa did not perceive his question as an insult to his plan.

"Gaultland and Vivado will be center front page in every newspaper in America and around the world. The publicity will be unmatched in history."

Sidney nodded, surprised at his own unflappable sense of humor as he pondered the notion of a well-known but nonexistent tourist attraction. The idea was definitely flawed.

"And why are you telling me this now?" Sidney asked, his curiosity sincere.

"I like you personally. I want to be certain that you are away from Gaultland when the bomb is detonated."

"And that will be . . ." Sidney said.

"On the anniversary of my birth," Tampa announced. "Refer to your own biography of me."

If he remembered correctly, Sidney hastily figured that to be in two weeks or less.

"Thank you for your courtesy." Sidney nodded. "I will remain in my New York offices during that time."

"Ready to jump to work when the bomb explodes?" Tampa suggested.

"Exactly," Sidney agreed.

"I am destined to emerge as the towering figure of modern civilization. Serious attention will be paid to my words and deeds at last."

The General rose abruptly and extended his hand, seemingly dismissing his threat of annihilation as mere conversational fodder.

"Your pledge of secrecy is made," he said. "Honor it most diligently."

The threat was not lost on Sidney.

The colonel was silent, a machine gun on his lap, as they rode back to the airstrip. Sidney swallowed intermittently both to establish that he was still alive and to release some of the tension.

* 　 * 　 *

No sooner had Sidney returned to New York and begun breathing normally than a delegation of General Tampa's so-called students from Billy Sunshine University dropped by his offices. They announced they were on an extended field trip to study life in key American cities. Manhattan, Philadelphia, Chicago, and Washington, D.C., were paramount among them.

A hurried check with Billy Sunshine revealed that no such project had been academically authorized. Those students involved had all taken impromptu leaves of absence from the institute, leaving university officials embarrassed and uncertain about how to handle the situation.

Billy himself had ordered that the escapade be kept quiet for fear that it would reflect on the university's already questionable security and discipline.

The Reverend confided to Sidney in a call, "Tampa worries me lately. His thinking is very erratic and very paranoid."

"Get what you can from him while you can."

"That's an odd response, Sidney."

"Maybe I'm suffering from the same symptoms."

Sidney agreed with him that the student situation was best kept under wraps for the time being.

"We'll keep an eye on them while they're in New York," he promised. For Sidney, it was the understatement of the year.

The five-member delegation stayed at the Vivado consulate, not far from the Bastion offices or Sidney's home. Sidney had been surprised and disturbed at the outset by their intimate knowledge of the city's geography.

"It is a favorite subject," one of the students explained offhandedly. "To know much of the world's great cities is respected in Vivado and honored and rewarded by General Tampa."

Their continuing presence, their fascination with his firm's sophisticated communications equipment, and their seeming self-assurance beyond normal student capacities troubled Sidney and heightened the sense of urgency within him.

He longed to discuss his thoughts with someone trustworthy. But everything was too volatile and dangerous. There was the very real risk of being misunderstood—or even worse, of not being believed. He was convinced by now that might very well prove fatal.

* 　 * 　 *

Adrienne suppressed her surprise at his dinner invitation. He claimed to enjoy dining only in solitude or in large groups.

"Just the two of us," he confirmed.

She chose Lutece.

Despite his harried appearance he was in his best mood in days. He laughed readily at her pointed barbs and ordered a second bottle of wine before they were halfway through the first.

"I predict that nothing you say this evening can arouse my ire," he stated.

"You are in an unusual mood tonight."

"Maybe I've been to the mountain."

He held her hands at intervals as they talked. Their conversation was random for the most part but always reverted back to public relations.

"You really are married to the business, Sidney. But then, so am I. It has to be that way to succeed."

"If we're both married to the same partner, doesn't that make us related in some way?"

"Bigamously probably."

"I'm your husband-in-law and you're my wife-in-law."

"Can outlaws be in-laws?"

"Maybe we'd better divorce ourselves from the whole proposition."

"I'll drink to that."

They touched glasses and their eyes met.

"I'm going to need your support up ahead," he confessed.

"You've got it," she replied without hesitation.

Claudia's wedding could not have come at a more inopportune time as far as Sidney was concerned.

Not only was he ill prepared for the emotional trauma, he was increasingly haunted by the specter of time. There would be only fifteen days left after the ceremony before Tampa's threat would become a fait accompli. He could not allow that to happen, but he had still not determined how best to prevent it.

The secret had festered inside him.

Meanwhile, Pam Garson bubbled excitedly over the wedding, enchanted that Sidney had agreed to accompany her. She knew her relationship with Sidney was temporary at best, while she watched his relationship with Adrienne grow ever stronger. Pam was willing to stay in her limited role as roommate, consoling herself that her love was most true and most valuable to Sidney. She really cared for him.

Claudia proved to be a beautifully radiant bride, the happiest and most serene he had ever seen her.

"Life's begining again for me, Sidney," she whispered to him after the ceremony. "I hope we'll continue to be friends always."

"Always and forever," he whispered as he hugged her.

Her husband was softer, gentler, and more self-effacing than he had expected. Obviously, Claudia had gotten her fill of the smoothly aggressive types who formed the majority in the industry.

"I can't get over what a quiet affair this is," Pam observed a second time.

"Do I detect a note of regret in your voice?" Sidney inquired.

"She said she wanted a *real* wedding, not a media-manufactured one. I guess this is what she meant."

"No media at all as far as I can see."

"Everything's been done so exquisitely it just belongs on the cover of one of the bridal mags."

Sidney smiled.

"Claudia's getting out of the business and you're just getting hooked," he noted.

"She was too at one time, wasn't she?"

"She was," he confirmed softly.

There was neither time nor opportunity to talk to Claudia privately. Her carefully selected guest list included only those with whom she had very special, very personal relationships. Perhaps it was just as well. Nothing could be advanced by looking backward.

"You're distant today," Pam said to him later in the afternoon.

"Weddings always unnerve me."

"You mean 'there but for the grace of God,' that sort of thing?"

"Maybe."

"You were never meant to be married, Sidney."

"That has a distinctly familiar ring to it."

He took Pam to their bungalow at the Beverly Hills Hotel afterwards and made obligatory love to her. But it was empty for both of them, though neither admitted it.

"So what's your final, overall impression of Claudia's wedding?" he asked in the darkness.

"Truthfully?" She paused. "It was somehow less than I expected."

His hand moved across the bed and clasped hers.

"Everything is, Pam," he said. "Everything is."

104

E verything in his life was accelerated by the time bomb he carried within him. It was like having a fatal malady. No amount of escapism or denial could change the inevitability of disaster unless something was done.

That General Tampa was a madman was of no consequence at this stage. That Sidney had gone too far in encouraging the General's illusion of himself as a brilliant and unbeatable contemporary conquistador amounted to not only regrettable but hopeless hindsight.

All that really mattered was that a warning had to be sounded. Silently but with absolute certainty.

"I want you to emphasize my great humanitarianism," Tampa had said at their meeting.

Image, all was image, and Sidney had fallen for his own distorted depictions. Only now did he begin to realize what a dangerous game he played. It was no small or insignificant thing to manufacture and then tamper with idols and emotions.

Sidney stayed away from his offices for several days, confining himself instead to his penthouse studio atop his East River residence. There was a certain sense of security there, what with the United Nations building looming nearby. He had thought fleetingly of going there and revealing his secret to the secretary-general, thereby involving the entire world in Tampa's malicious mischief in one fell swoop. But even he knew of the UN's reputation for hesitation and indecision. The towers would fall before the issue ever reached the floor.

He longed to confide in someone but he could not. He balked at his own uncharacteristic indecision. He tried again with Adrienne but to no avail. She had not been surprised this time by his dinner invitation. His dilemma had been obvious for days, but its nature remained a mystery.

"I want to talk seriously to you about something important to both of us," he confessed over their table, "but it'll have to wait until another matter's resolved."

"That's not even double-talk, Sidney. That's triple-talk. Or maybe even mumbo jumbo."

"It's PR speak."

"You don't trust me."

"It's beyond trust."

She sighed.

"Tell me what I can do," she said.

"Soften up Samuelson for me. I need a favor from him."

"Who gets the easy assignments around here?"

He held up his hand.

"Nothing monumental. But do it later from your place, just in case."

"King, queen, and pawns all in their proper places."

"Right."

She called him later to confirm her contribution.

"He's cautious, mystified, but reasonably amenable," she said.

"Are those his words?"

"I don't talk like that."

"Thanks, Adrienne."

"I like your new mysterious image."

"I'll explain it all one day soon."

He waited until morning after a fitful night of sleep, to call Samuelson.

"Don," he began apprehensively, "I need someone to authenticate my credibility with the secretary of state. You're on personal terms with him, and I was hoping you might vouch for my validity."

He could visualize the commentator's surprised smirk.

"One doesn't normally go to one's nemeses for references, Bastion," he responded. "Or have I failed to communicate my disdain for your activities in the past?"

"This is a patriotic matter, Don. I promise you the exclusive inside story if you'll simply verify to the secretary that I'm in a position to possess information which could be of national and international importance. That's all I ask."

"You want top-level access?"

"Exactly."

A contemplative silence followed.

"If you embarrass me, Sidney, I'll run your ass right out of the country."

"You'll be on the air with the story April nineteenth and Sidney Bastion'll be your hero of the week, the month, and the year."

That afternoon his call had gone through State Department channels all the way to the secretary himself. Shortly after he was en route to Washington.

His secrets would no longer be his alone. And he never had been so glad to get rid of anything so valuable before in his life.

It was unbelievably naive of Sidney to think Tampa would not have him stalked in the aftermath of their critical meeting on the island. Or that such a murderous and mercurial personality would abide by some secret timetable as though it was sacrosanct.

No sooner was Tampa advised of Sidney's presence in Washington and his destination there than the General's master plan was immediately accelerated. All had been ready for some time, awaiting only his go-ahead signal. Typically, he had revealed to Sidney only the skeletal outline of his diabolical plot, his secret creation of devastation.

"Bastion is a fool, beneath contempt for double-crossing me!" the General raged inside his private fortress.

"Destroy the bloody infidels!" he commanded. "Let their apocalypse begin."

Even as Sidney sat tensely within the portals of real power, as opposed to his concept of PR power, a cataclysmic chain of events had begun. Highly trained terrorists loyal to Tampa set out on the evil missions they had surreptitiously rehearsed for months.

Gaultland had closed by the time the innocent-appearing delivery truck pulled into the supply area to the rear of the park. Guards paid little heed. Dozens of similar vehicles shuttled in and out nightly to feed the bodily appetites and souvenir hunger of thousands of daily visitors.

Most fortuitously, Billy Sunshine University was celebrating a special holiday for the dedication of a massive new athletic stadium on the grounds.

Few students or faculty were on campus in the critical moments after a furtive trio raced to plant their deadly missles in preordained locations. The brand-new stadium had been little more than an artist's rendering when the bombing plan was conceived. Consequently, it had luckily been left out of the sinister scheme of things.

*   *   *

Gaultland became a wasteland overnight. The majority of its shacklike structures were reduced to rubble, many of them to ashes. Fires raged and then smol-
dered for days as mournful people paid to walk and weep among the skeletal
remains. Somehow, magically, the tomb of Johnny Gault survived untouched,
and his towering pink statue still presided majestically over the debacle.

He was indeed immortal, everlasting.

"God in his heaven has surely adopted him as his son," Reverend Billy
Sunshine declared fervently to the media and to all others who would listen.

Reverend Billy had his own devastation to cope with. The campus of his
beloved university resembled a besieged battlefield. Seventy percent of the
buildings and laboratories he had so eloquently fought to finance and build
were in ruins. In spite of it all, he refused to be anything less than defiantly
optimistic.

"The forces of Lucifer can never destroy us," he declared. "Like Lazarus we
will rise again."

For Paula Castle there was a special middle finger salute from the man she had
once found so seductive. The foundations of her burgeoning hotel structures on
the island were not only demolished, they were flooded to such an extent that
the expensive property was reduced to all-but-worthless marshes.

She did not weep easily, but the news of her losses left her inconsolable for
days.

Other targets throughout the world suffered in more tragically mortal ways.
Hundreds were killed in dozens of key locations around the globe. They had
apparently been selected for their high visibility and consequent publicity value
rather than to fulfill any of Tampa's personal vendettas. Misery and agony were
incidental to the despot's quest for international recognition and absolute control
at home.

The worldwide pockets of devastation, with their terrible toll in human
suffering, did indeed focus the earth's spotlight on the relatively tiny nation of
Vivado and its cruelly tyrannical ruler. There were outcries for revenge far and
wide, but it was from within Vivado that he had the most to fear, yet feared the
least.

Sidney had finally come to comprehend the full malevolence of the ogre he
had endeavored to make a saint. He was now trying desperately to cope with his

firm's linkage, directly and indirectly, to the multiple tragedies and destruction. Not only was he forced to put the best possible spin on his association with Raul Tampa, all the while extricating himself from any current or future alliance, he also had the enormous task of handling the national media avalanche surrounding the attacks on Gaultland and Billy Sunshine University.

The stress was all at once too much for him.

Pam Garson found him trembling and sobbing on the floor of his communications center, an empty vodka bottle at his side, a loaded revolver in his lap.

"Vodka is for pretenders," he wailed.

She cradled him in her arms as a mother might harbor a distraught child, rocking and soothing him.

"I'm ruined," he cried plaintively.

"No, you're not," she responded firmly. "You're drunk, but you're far from ruined."

"My life's reduced to rubble," he insisted.

"No more than Gaultland is, and you know Doc Diamond will make it rise again."

He groaned and mumbled on, less and less coherently, for many more minutes before lapsing into a deep and fitful sleep.

Pam eased a throw pillow under his head, covered him with her coat, and let him sleep it off.

Claudia answered the summons from her old friend Pam with some reluctance but no hesitation. After all, she was out of the business and more or less still on her honeymoon according to the schedule. It was hastily revised.

She caught the next available flight and immediately took charge of the chaotic situation in New York.

The arrival of his longtime aide and confidante seemed almost magically to revitalize Sidney. In a matter of hours after her familiar whispers had aroused him from his stupor, he resumed command of his faltering empire with his trusted former lieutenant close by his side.

"It's all going to work out all right, Sidney," she assured him as they manned their old battle stations, the telephones and computers.

"I don't deserve this much loyalty, Claudia," he confessed with rare humility, "but thank you with all my heart."

"Thanks for nothing," she said, smiling. "Everybody knows you don't have a heart."

*   *   *

Doc Diamond had warehouses full of backup supplies and enough disaster insurance from Lloyds of London to all but bathe him in liquid capital. Just as he had enhanced himself in the seeming tragedy of Johnny Gault's death, he now moved swiftly again to make himself the beneficiary of another calamity.

Bulldozers quickly cleared the skeletal, burned-out structures and trash of Gaultland, allowing him to rush in mammoth tents to temporarily replace the buildings demolished by the bombings. He had only a vague notion of who Raul Tampa was. He described Tampa as "some tinhorn little dictator from coconut country," and he demanded every dollar he could strangle from his insurers.

The fact that over seventy people had been injured in the park's immolition hardly concerned him. "That's what God made insurance for," he stated. It was Gaultland above all else in his life and to hell with everything and everybody else.

Meanwhile, Billy Sunshine turned his own devastation into an immediate, worldwide fund-raising event. He was all over the newspapers and television praying and pleading for funds: "We must carry on the colossal task of rebuilding the tangibles and restoring the soul of God's chosen haven of higher learning."

There was, of course, no mention of the university's generous insurance resources. Why cause people to hesitate in dispatching sympathetic tokens of their own generosity to the glorification of God via Billy Sunshine?

Just as Pam and Claudia had predicted, Claudia was on her way back to L.A. in less than a month. She felt more than ever certain she had made the right move in leaving Manhattan originally. She was heart and soul a California girl now.

After they shared a final dinner with Sidney, Pam drove her to Kennedy Airport.

"I'm gonna miss you all over again," Pam said as they hugged and parted.

"I'll miss you, too," Claudia confessed, "but I won't miss the city. I love L.A. Take care of Sidney for me. I'll call you soon. Have fun, honey."

"Love you."

"Love you, too."

Pam smiled to herself, thinking of her friend while driving through the iridescent darkness on the way home. She wondered how much longer the allure of this life could possibly last for her as well.

*   *   *

The worldwide uproar created by the bombings had at least one redeemingly beneficial effect. It had aroused and emboldened the small but fiercely partisan rebel army hidden in the mountains of Vivado. These fearless and well-armed guerrillas had managed to elude Tampa's most elite forces for years, frustrating the volatile dictator to such a degree that those captured from their ranks were publicly hanged, upside down, as the history books showed the Italian despot, Benito Mussolini, had been strung up decades earlier.

Ironically, the true symbolism of that long-ago desecration had been lost on Raul Tampa. His ego blinded him to it. When his headquarters were infiltrated by daring rebels only days after the bombings, resulting in his triumphant capture, the invaders took no chances with a corrupt judicial system. They stabbed his body repeatedly until he bled from head to toe. Then his carcass was strung from the balcony of his palace—upside down, of course—with his penis stuffed into his mouth.

There was spontaneous rejoicing throughout the island, and the world, over the sudden death of the Devil incarnate. Remarkably few of his ostensibly loyal troops attempted to withstand the surge of joyous peasants celebrating the fall of the monster who had so cruelly dominated them.

Vivado would purge itself of its remaining vipers now that the most venomous of them had been destroyed. It was a victory for justice at long last and a testament to the ultimate triumph of good over evil. Such was the verdict of a vast majority of the international media.

A full-page headline in the *New York Daily Record* cleverly summed up the elation and relief shared by the nation. It read:

ASS

ASS-

ASS-

INATED!!!

Perhaps it was too flippant considering the terrible devastation wrought by such a ruthless tyrant. Sidney thought it was unique enough to be framed for his office wall, and he hung it next to his evidence of his proudest achievements.

105

I ronically, Sidney Bastion felt more alive now than he ever had before. There was no single or simple explanation for this unusual state of mind, but it was definitely linked with self-realization and self-esteem.

Not the least of it was associated with the grudging respect Don Samuelson paid him in his much-watched weekly summary of the news.

"Sidney Bastion has projected a most unlikely new image," he said, wrapping up his brief network acknowledgment. "That of a patriot in PR camouflage."

Samuelson also intervened on Sidney's behalf on charges that Sidney had failed to register as an agent of a foreign government. He sided with Sidney's contention that he had merely acted to promote tourism and not terrorism. Largely through Samuelson's intercession the charges were reduced considerably. Overall they resulted in a mild, middle-level reprimand and a five-year restriction on dealings with any other foreign nations.

Sidney had a full-time bodyguard now, which he found more romantic than restrictive. This had been the result of a personal threat sent out by die-hard supporters of the late dictator Tampa. It had declared ominously: "Those who defile our beloved departed leader will be hunted to the corners of the earth by the jackals of justice. They will be sacrificed to the spirit of Tampa and left to wither in the burning sun. This we swear by our lives."

It had frightened him at first, but with the closing of the Institute for Christian Unity at Billy Sunshine University and the deportation of all questionable Vivado students, he had been assured by the State Department, the Department of Immigration and Naturalization, the Central Intelligence Agency, and the

Federal Bureau of Investigation that they were aware of the movements of every lingering Tampa sympathizer in America. Sidney was no more likely to be struck down by them now than he was to be struck by lightning.

Moreover, he had become a celebrity among celebrity makers in the process. It was more than he might have imagined or could have engineered for himself.

Small wonder that he had been a main attraction at Paula Castle's Vivado Vamoose! party in the grand ballroom of the Gotham Castle, heralded even in society's jaded journals as the social event of the season.

She had taken the almost simultaneous collapse of American relations with Vivado and the assassination of its head man in the spirit of a woman who had not merely lost millions and millions of other people's investment dollars but had gained inestimable stature as a lady of courage and concern for her country above all else.

Sidney trumpeted her patriotic fervor far and wide. In the light of it all it was hardly surprising that a Satellite Surveys poll found Sidney and Paula to be among the moment's Ten Most Admired Men and Women in America.

But Sidney's real revitalization—his "rebirth," as Reverend Billy preferred to call it—was due to his more and more augmented relationship with Adrienne. She seemed able to define him as he had never been able to define himself. She motivated him and made him ricochet where he might otherwise easily become embedded. Wisely, she had stood aside during his brief reunion with Claudia.

He had always advocated flexing the truth. She somehow knew how to flex *him*. It had come after a long, involved, and sometimes eviscerating process, not without its own chicanery and malevolence on both their parts. They each possessed a unique talent for equipping others with rose-colored glasses while eschewing them for themselves. It was not reality that counted but rather what was perceived as reality.

Adrienne saw through Sidney, and he regarded her as equally transparent. What they saw in each other was similarity, and it made for a certain inexplicable affinity.

As ordered, Sidney immediately closed down his operations in London and Monaco. Ostensibly it was a temporary measure, but the truth was the Vivado fiasco had cooled his fervor for international involvement.

"Good PR is so intensely personal and dependent on the special nuances of a particular country and culture that it essentially defies any wholesale exportation," he argued.

"Save that for your next seminar," Adrienne responded.

Pam Garson was keenly aware of the slow but steady infiltration of Gale ideas and methodology into the Bastion organization. Her reaction to that was mixed. As much as she liked Adrienne, she couldn't help feeling a little jealous. After all, she still cared a lot for Sidney.

She also saw more acutely than perhaps anyone the growing depth and range of Adrienne's influence over Sidney himself. No one, not Claudia or anyone else, male or female, had ever penetrated him to such an intimate extent. It went beyond sex and similitude of interests. In the language of the streets, Adrienne had Sidney's number.

"It's sickening," Pam lamented to Claudia. "Opposites are supposed to attract. They're abominably alike."

"Then they deserve each other."

"I hate it all."

106

B
y now Adrienne had a desk abutting Sidney's. She answered the phone as
often as he did at his town house residence, a residence that incidentally
housed a complex of computers where once a dormitory of damsels had
flourished.

There had been no announcements of merger, but some things become apparent before they become reality. The staffs of both organizations had become
accustomed to working in harmony rather than competitively, a sure sign something was in the wind.

Sidney and Adrienne rarely did anything outside of business in orthodox
fashion. It was their way of defying the restrictions of a society they sought to
manipulate in the first place. Everything did not have to be synchronized no
matter what the FCC dictated. Every question did not necessarily have to have
an answer. But everything really was part hokum, part self-deception, and part
planted illusion.

Still, she belabored Sidney on one point.

"You take it all too seriously," she told him. "Do you see Billy Sunshine in
sackcloth and ashes? No, he wears custom-tailored silks. This isn't some sort of
holy calling we're in, not something directed by divine destiny, with apologies
to Billy's cathedral. There's more fraud than fidelity involved, more inconstancy
than integrity. In lots of ways it's all just one gargantuan joke."

Sidney would listen, and sometimes now he even laughed. It really was all
sort of ridiculous, sort of tilted, cockeyed. Even the wholesale destruction and
deaths had a macabre surrealism about them.

"Don't try to focus images too sharply," she cautioned. "You lose too much of the mystery in the process."

"I always hated show business clients," Sidney reflected. "Johnny Gault was a thorn in my side from the day I met him. One of the most unstable creatures you could ever hope to avoid, but now he's the most stable, reliable part of my life. I'm looking at an easy, comfortable retirement because of him."

It took Sidney time, but gradually he began to view the human panorama in much the same irreverent, kaleidoscopic fashion as did Adrienne. It was more fun her way.

She did leave it to him to make the official overture. It came early one summer evening as they sat on the open patio of his town house watching the play of lights shimmering on the river below.

"You know you're an open target out here," she reminded him.

"Surrounded by predators."

"The closer they are the more dangerous they become."

"I know. And recognizing that, I propose becoming the partner of the most proximate and dangerous member of the species. Provided, of course, she acquiesces."

Adrienne took his outstretched hand and gazed directly into his eyes.

"Unaccustomed as she is to acquiescing, which somehow sounds almost obscene, the predator in question accepts the proposition with one important proviso."

"Namely?"

"That the alliance be total."

"Mr. and Mrs.?"

"That's more like it, and Bastion-Gale Unlimited?"

"Limited to each other only."

"Kiss me, Sidney, to seal the deal."

And so it came to pass that a pair of quasi-nocturnal, avidly avaricious, and mutually adept conjurers of glowing incarnations joined forces to become one. They had once regarded one another with suspicion, hostility, and even contempt, but now they entered the hallowed Hall of Mirrors in the holy Fun House of Coney Island Amusement Park. There, in elaborate clown costumes, they were wed by a jester in the guise of an evangelist by the name of Reverend Billy Sunshine. A small gathering of friends witnessed the merry ceremony, their images distorted by the multiple mirrors into alternately serpentine, wavy, elongated, broadly squat, and superthin caricatures, all grinning like happy children throughout the brief ritual.

"It's so bizarre, it's beautiful," Paula Castle wept, dripping tears on the black crepe of her costume as the Wicked Witch of the West while smiling ecstatically.

Others were equally moved, but none more than the presiding pastor himself.

"You may kiss the bride on this, the most beautiful Halloween the world has ever seen," he declared.

Amen.